W9-AJP-513

Praise for Emma Miller and her novels

Praise for Debby Giusti and her novels

Emma Miller lives quietly in her old farmhouse in rural Delaware. Fortunate enough to have been born into a family of strong faith, she grew up on a dairy farm surrounded by loving parents, siblings, grandparents, aunts, uncles and cousins. Emma was educated in local schools and once taught in an Amish schoolhouse. When she's not caring for her large family, reading and writing are her favorite pastimes.

Debby Giusti is an award-winning Christian author who met and married her military husband at Fort Knox, Kentucky. Together they traveled the world, raised three wonderful children and have now settled in Atlanta, Georgia, where Debby spins tales of mystery and suspense that touch the heart and soul. Visit Debby online at debbygiusti.com; blog with her at seekerville.blogspot.com and craftieladiesofromance.blogspot.com; and email her at Debby@DebbyGiusti.com.

EMMA MILLER
Miriam's Heart

&

DEBBIE GIUSTI
Stranded

HARLEQUIN® LOVE INSPIRED®

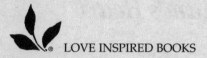

LOVE INSPIRED BOOKS

Recycling programs for this product may not exist in your area.

ISBN-13: 978-0-373-83890-5

Miriam's Heart and Stranded

Copyright © 2016 by Harlequin Books S.A.

The publisher acknowledges the copyright holders of the individual works as follows:

Miriam's Heart
Copyright © 2011 by Faulkner, Inc. and Judith E. French

Stranded
Copyright © 2015 by Deborah W. Giusti

www.Harlequin.com

Printed in U.S.A.

CONTENTS

MIRIAM'S HEART

Emma Miller

For the lost Prince of Persia
and the blessings he has brought to our family

Love comes from a pure heart
and a good conscience and a sincere faith.
—*1 Timothy* 1:5

Chapter One

❧

Kent County, Delaware—Early Autumn

"Whoa, easy, Blackie!" Miriam cried as the black horse slipped and nearly fell. The iron-wheeled wagon swayed ominously. Blackie's teammate, Molly, stood patiently until the gelding recovered his footing.

Miriam let out a sigh of relief as her racing pulse returned to normal. She'd been driving teams since she was six, but Blackie was young and had a lot to learn. Gripping the leathers firmly in her small hands, Miriam guided the horses along the muddy farm lane that ran between her family's orchard and the creek. The bank on her right was steep, the water higher than normal due to heavy rain earlier in the week.

"Not far now," she soothed. Thank the Lord for Molly. The dapple-gray mare might have been past her prime, but she could always be counted on to do her job without any fuss. The wagon was piled high with bales of hay, and Miriam didn't want to lose any off the back.

Haying was one of the few tasks the Yoder girls and their mother hadn't done on their farm since Dat's death two years ago. Instead, they traded the use of pasture land with Uncle Reuben for his extra hay. He paid an English farmer to cut and bale the timothy and clover. All Miriam had to do was haul the sweet-smelling bales home. Today, she was in a hurry. The sky suggested there was more rain coming out of the west and she had to get the hay stacked in the barn before the skies opened up. Not that she minded. In fact, she liked this kind of work: the steady clip-clop of the horses' hooves, the smell of the timothy, the feel of the reins in her hands.

If Mam and Dat had had sons instead of seven daughters, Miriam supposed she'd have been confined to working in the house and garden like most Amish girls. But she'd always been different, the girl people called a *tomboy,* and she preferred outside chores. Despite her modest dress and Amish *kapp,* Miriam loved being in the fields in any weather and had a real knack with livestock. It might have been sinful pride, but when it came to farming, she secretly considered herself a match for any young man in the county.

It had been her father who'd taught her all she knew about planting and harvesting and rotating the crops. Her earliest memory was of riding on his wide shoulders as he drove the cows into the barn for milking. Since his death, she'd tried to fill his shoes, but his absence had left a great hole in their family and in her heart.

Miriam's mother had taken over the teaching position at the Seven Poplars Amish school and all of Miriam's unmarried sisters pitched in on the farm. It wasn't easy, but they managed to keep the large homestead going, tending the animals, planting and harvesting crops and helping the less fortunate. All too soon, Miriam knew it would be harder. With Ruth marrying in November and going to live in the new house she and Eli were building on the far end of the property, there would be one less pair of hands to help.

Blackie's startled snort and laid back ears yanked Miriam from her daydreaming. "Easy, boy. What's wrong?" She quickly scanned the lane she'd been following that ran along a small creek. There wasn't anything to frighten him, nothing but a weathered black stick lying between the wagon ruts.

But the gelding didn't settle down. Instead, he stiffened, let out a shrill whinny and reared up in the traces, as the muddy branch came alive, raised its head, hissed threateningly and slithered directly toward Blackie.

Snake! Miriam shuddered as she came to her feet and fought to gain control of the terrified horses. She hated snakes. And this black snake was huge.

Blackie reared again, pawed the air and threw himself sideways, crashing into the mare and sending both animals and the hay wagon tumbling off the road and down the bank. A wagon wheel cracked and Miriam jumped free before she was caught in the tangle of thrashing horses, leather harnesses, wood and hay bales.

She landed in the road, nearly on top of the snake. Both horses were whinnying frantically, but for long seconds, Miriam lay sprawled in the mud, the wind knocked out of her. The black snake slithered across her wrist, making its escape and she squealed with disgust, and rolled away from it. Vaguely, she heard someone shouting her name, but all she could think of was her horses.

Charley Byler was halfway across the field from the Yoders' barn when he saw the black horse rear up in its traces. He dropped his lunch pail and broke into a run as the team and wagon toppled off the side of the lane into the creek.

He was a fast runner. He usually won the races at community picnics and frolics, but he wasn't fast enough to reach Miriam before she'd climbed up off the road and disappeared over the stream bank. *"Ne!"* he shouted. "Miriam, don't!"

But she didn't listen. Miriam—his dear Miriam—never listened to anything he said. Heart in his throat, Charley's feet pounded the grass until, breathless, he reached the lane and half slid, half fell into the creek beside her. "Miriam!" He caught her shoulders and pulled her back from the kicking, flailing animals.

"Let me go! I have to—"

He caught her around the waist, surprised by how strong she was, especially for such a little thing. "Listen to me," he pleaded. He knew how valuable the team was and how attached Miriam was to them, but he also knew how dangerous a frightened horse could be. His own brother had been killed by a yearling colt's hoof when the boy was only eight years old. "Miriam, you can't do it this way!"

Blackie, still kicking, had fallen on top of Molly. The mare's eyes rolled back in her head so that only the whites showed. She thrashed and neighed pitifully in the muck, blood seeping from her neck and hindquarters to tint the creek water a sickening pink.

"You have to help me," Miriam insisted. "Blackie will—"

At that instant, Charley's boot slipped on the muddy bottom and they both went down into the waist-deep water.

To Charley's surprise, Miriam—who never cried—

burst into tears. He was helping her to her feet, when he heard the frantic barking of a dog. Irwin and his terrier appeared at the edge of the road.

"You all right?" Thirteen-year-old Irwin Beachy wasn't family, but he acted like it since he'd come to live with the Yoders. He was home from school today, supposedly with a sore throat, but he was known to fib to get out of school. "What can I do?"

"I'm not hurt," Miriam answered, between sobs. "Run quick...to the chair shop. Use the phone to...to call Hartman's. Tell them...tell them it's an emergency. We need a vet right away."

Miriam started to shiver. Her purple dress and white apron were soaked through, her *kapp* gone. Charley thought Miriam would be better off out of the water, but he knew better than to suggest it. She'd not leave these animals until they were out of the creek.

"You want me to climb down there?" Irwin asked. "Maybe we could unhook the—"

"We might do more harm than good." Charley looked down at the horses; they were quieter now, wide-eyed with fear, but not struggling. "I'd rather have one of the Hartmans here before we try that."

"The phone, Irwin!" Miriam cried. "Call the Hartmans."

"Ask for Albert, if you can," Charley called after the boy as he took off with the dog on his heels. "We need someone with experience."

"Get whoever can come the fastest!" Miriam pulled loose from Charley and waded toward the horses. "Shh, shh," she murmured. "Easy, now."

The dapple-gray mare lay still, her head held at an awkward angle out of the water. Charley hoped that the old girl didn't have a broken leg. The first time he'd ever used a cultivator was behind that mare. Miriam's father had showed him how and he'd always been grateful to Jonas and to Molly for the lesson. Since Miriam seemed to be calming Blackie, Charley knelt down and supported the mare's head.

Blood continued to seep from a long scrape on the horse's neck. Charley supposed the wound would need sewing up, but it didn't look like something that was fatal. Her hind legs were what worried him. If a bone was shattered, it would be the end of the road for the mare. Miriam was a wonder with horses, with most any animal really, but she couldn't heal a broken bone in a horse's leg. Some people tried that with expensive racehorses, but like all Amish, the Yoders didn't carry insurance on their animals, or on anything else. Sending an old horse off to some fancy veterinary hospital was beyond what Miriam's mam or the church could afford. When horses in Seven Poplars broke a leg, they had to be put down.

Charley stroked the dapple-gray's head. He felt so sorry for her, but he didn't dare to try and get the horses out of the creek until he had more help. If one of them didn't have broken bones yet, the fright of getting them free might cause it.

Charley glanced at Miriam. One of her red-gold braids had come unpinned and hung over her shoulder. He swallowed hard. He knew he shouldn't be staring at her hair. That was for a husband to see in the privacy of their home. But he couldn't look away. It was so beautiful in the sunlight, and the little curling hairs at the back of her neck gleamed with drops of creek water.

A warmth curled in his stomach and seeped up to make his chest so tight that it was hard to breathe. He'd known Miriam Yoder since they were both in leading strings. They'd napped together on a blanket in a corner of his mother's garden, as babies. Then, when they'd gotten older, maybe three or four, they'd played on her porch, swinging on the bench swing and taking all the animals out of a Noah's Ark her dat had carved for her and lining them up, two by two.

He guessed that he'd loved Miriam as long as he could remember, but she'd been just Miriam, like one of his sisters, only tougher. Last spring, he'd bought her pie at the school fundraiser and they'd shared many a picnic lunch. He'd always liked Miriam and he'd never cared that she was different from most girls, never cared that she could pitch a baseball better than him or catch more fish in the pond. He'd teased her, ridden with her to group sings and played clapping games at the young people's doings.

Miriam was as familiar to him as his own mother, but standing here in the creek without her *kapp,* her dress soaked and muddy, scowling at him, he felt like he didn't know her at all. He could have told any of his pals that he loved Miriam Yoder, but he hadn't realized what that meant…until this moment. Suddenly, the thought that she could have been hurt when the wagon turned over, that she could have been tangled in the lines and pulled under, or crushed by the horses, brought tears to his eyes.

"Miriam," he said. His mouth felt dry. His tongue stuck to the roof of his mouth.

"Yes?" She turned those intense gray eyes from the horse back to him.

He suddenly felt foolish. He didn't know what he was saying. He couldn't tell her how he felt. They hadn't ridden home from a frolic together more than three or four times. They hadn't walked out together and she hadn't invited him in when they'd gotten to her house and everyone else was asleep. They'd been friends, chums; they ran around with the same gang. He couldn't just blurt out that he suddenly realized that he *loved* her. "Nothing. Never mind."

She returned her attention to Blackie. "Shh, easy, easy," she said, laying her cheek against his nose. "He's quieting down. He can't be hurt bad, don't you think? But where's all that blood coming from?" She leaned forward to touch the gelding's right shoulder, and the animal squealed and started struggling against the harness again.

"Leave it," Charley ordered, clamping a hand on her arm. "Wait for the vet. You could get hurt."

"Ne," she argued, but it wasn't a real protest. She didn't struggle against his grip. She knew he was right.

He nodded. "Just keep doing what you were." He held her arm a second longer than he needed to.

"Miriam!"

It was a woman's voice, one of her sisters', for sure. Charley released Miriam.

"Oh, Anna, come quick! Oh, it's terrible."

Charley glanced up. It was Miriam's twin, a big girl, more than a head taller and three times as wide. No one could ever accuse Anna of not being Plain. She wasn't ugly; she had nice eyes, but she couldn't hold a candle to Miriam. Still, he liked Anna well enough. She had a good heart and she baked the best biscuits in Kent County, maybe the whole state.

"Don't cry, Anna," Miriam said. "You'll set me to crying again."

"How bad are they hurt?" Miriam's older sister Ruth came to stand on the bank beside Anna. She was holding

Miriam's filthy white *kapp.* "Are you all right? Is she all right?" She glanced from Miriam to Charley.

"I'm fine," Miriam assured her. "Just muddy. It's Molly and Blackie I'm worried about."

Fat tears rolled down Anna's broad cheeks. "I'm glad Susanna's not here," she said. "I made her stay in the kitchen. She shouldn't see this."

"Did Irwin go to call the vet?" Charley asked. "We told him—"

"Ya." Anna wiped her face with her apron. "He ran fast. Took the shortcut across the fields."

"Is there anything I can do?" Ruth called down. "Should I come—?"

"Ne," Miriam answered. "Watch for the vet. And send Irwin to the school to tell Mam as soon as he gets back." The mare groaned pitifully, and Miriam glanced over at her. "She'll be all right," she said. "God willing, she will be all right."

"I'll pray for them," Anna said. "That I can do." She caught the corner of her apron and balled it in a big hand. "For the horses."

Charley heard the dinner bell ringing from the Yoder farmhouse. "Maybe that's Irwin," he said to Miriam. "A good idea. We'll need help to get the horses up." The repeated sounding of the bell would signal the neighbors. Other Amish would come from the surrounding farms. There would be many strong hands to help with the animals, once it was considered safe to move them.

"There's the Hartmans' truck," Ruth said. She waved, and Charley heard the engine. "I hope he doesn't get stuck, trying to cross the field. The lane's awfully muddy."

Miriam looked at him, her eyes wide with hope. "It will be all right, won't it, Charley?"

"God willing," he said.

"It's John," Anna exclaimed. "He's getting out of the truck with his bag."

Great, Charley thought. It would have to be John and not his uncle Albert. He sighed. He supposed that John knew his trade. He'd saved the Beachys' Jersey cow when everyone had given it up for dead. But once the Mennonite man got here, Miriam would have eyes only for John with his fancy education and his English clothes. Whenever John was around, he and Miriam put their heads together and talked like they were best friends.

"John must have been close by. Maybe it's a good sign." Miriam looked at him earnestly.

"Ya," he agreed, without much enthusiasm. He knew that it was uncharitable to put his own jealousy before the lives of her beloved horses. *"Ya,"* he repeated. "It's lucky he came so quick." *Lucky for Molly and Blackie,* he thought ruefully, *but maybe not for me.*

Chapter Two

He'd witnessed a true blessing today, Charley thought as he watched John bandaging Blackie's hind leg. Both animals had needed stitches and Molly had several deep cuts, but neither horse had suffered a broken bone. Between the sedative the young vet had administered and the help of neighbors, they'd been able to get the team back to the barn where they now stood in fresh straw in their stalls.

Charley had to admit that John knew what he was doing. He was ashamed of his earlier reluctance to have him come to the Yoder farm. With God's help, both animals would recover. Even the sight of Miriam standing so close to John, listening intently to his every word, didn't trouble Charley much. It was natural that Miriam would be worried about her horses and John was a very good vet. Reading anything more into it was his own insecurity. After all, John wasn't Amish; he didn't have a chance with Miriam. She would never choose a husband outside her faith.

Since she was a child, Miriam had had a gift for healing animals. When his Holstein calf had gotten tangled in a barbed wire fence, it had been ten-year-old Miriam who'd come every afternoon to rub salve on the calf's neck while he held it still. Later that year, she'd helped his mother deliver twin lambs in a snowstorm, and the following summer Miriam had set a broken leg on his brother's goat. More than one neighbor called on Miriam instead of the vet for trouble with their animals. Some men in the community seemed to forget she was a girl and asked her advice before they bought a cow or a driving horse.

If Miriam had been born English, Charley supposed that she might have gone to college to study veterinary medicine herself, but their people didn't believe in that much schooling. For the Old Order Amish, eighth grade was the end of formal education. He'd been glad to leave school at fourteen, but for Miriam, it had been a sacrifice. She had a hunger to know more about animal doctoring, so it was natural that she and John would find a lot to talk about.

"I think we can fix the hay wagon, but a good third of the hay is wet through."

"What?" Startled, Charley turned to see Eli standing beside him. He'd been so busy thinking about Miriam that he hadn't even heard Eli enter the barn.

"The hay wagon," Eli repeated. He glanced at John and Miriam and then cut his eyes at Charley, but he kept talking. "Front and back wheel on the one side need replacing, as well as some broken boards, but the axles are sound. We should be able to make it right in a few hours."

Eli was sharp and not just with crafting wood. Charley could tell that he hadn't missed the ease between Miriam and the Mennonite boy, or Charley's unease at their friendship.

"Right." Charley nodded. Eli was his friend and Ruth's intended. Charley had been working on the foundation for their new house today. Otherwise, he wouldn't have been at the Yoder place and close enough to reach Miriam when the accident happened. *God's mysterious ways,* he thought, and then said to Eli, "Maybe we can get together some night after chores."

"Ya," Eli agreed with a twinkle in his eye. "No problem."

"I don't know what we would have done without you," Miriam said to John as he opened the stall door for her. "When the hay wagon overturned, I was so afraid…"

Charley could hear the emotion in her voice. It made him want to walk over to her and put his arms around her. It made him want to protect her from anything bad that could ever happen to her. Instead, he stood there, feeling like a bumpkin, listening in on her and John's conversation.

"You didn't panic. That's the most important thing with horses," John said, speaking way too gently to suit Charley. "It's a good thing you didn't try to get them up without help. It could have been a lot worse if I hadn't been able to sedate them."

I'm the one who told Miriam to wait, Charley wanted to remind them. *That was my decision.* But again, he didn't say what he was thinking. He knew he was being petty and that pettiness could eat a man up inside. How did the English refer to jealousy? A green-eyed monster?

Miriam looked over toward Charley, noticed him watching them and smiled, making his heart do a little flip. Why hadn't he ever noticed how sweet her smile was?

"You were there when I needed you, too," she said. "I was so scared. One of them could have been killed."

I was terrified, but for you more than the horses. It seemed like it took an hour for me to run across the field to see if you were hurt. The words caught in his throat. He couldn't spit them out, not in front of John and Eli. Usually, he had no trouble giving his opinion, flirting with girls, cracking jokes, being good-natured Charley, everybody's friend. But not today…today he was as tongue-tied as Irwin.

He couldn't tear his eyes away from Miriam. She was wearing a modest blue dress now, a properly starched *kapp* and a clean white apron. As soon as they'd gotten the horses out of the creek and headed back toward the barn, her sisters had rushed her to the house to put on dry clothes. The blue suited her. It was almost the color of a robin's egg, without the speckles. Her red hair was freshly-combed and braided, pinned up and mostly hidden under her *kapp,* but he couldn't help remembering how it had looked in the sunlight.

This morning, he'd been a bachelor, with no more thoughts of tying himself down in marriage any time soon than trying to fly off the barn roof. He'd certainly known that he'd have to get serious in a few years, and start a family, but not yet. He had years of running around to do yet—lots of girls to tease and frolics to enjoy. Now, in the time it took that wagon to overturn, his life had changed direction. After seeing Miriam this way today, he realized that what mattered most to him was winning her hand and having the right to watch her take her *kapp* off and brush out that red-gold hair every night.

Unconsciously, he tugged his wide-brimmed straw hat lower on his forehead, hoping no one would notice his embarrassment, but Miriam didn't miss a trick. She reached up and pressed her hand to his cheek. The touch of her palm sent a jolt through him, and he jumped back, heat flashing under his skin. He was certain it made him look even more the fool.

"Charley Byler, what's wrong with you?" she demanded. "You're red as a *banty* rooster. And your clothes are still soaked. Are you taking a chill? You'd best come up to the house, and drink some hot coffee."

"Can't." He backed off as if she were contagious. He couldn't take the chance she'd touch him again. Not here. Not in front of the Mennonite. "Got to pick up Mary," he said in a rush. "Thursdays. In Dover." Every Thursday, his sister cleaned house for an English woman and his mother depended on him to bring her home. "She'll be expecting me."

"I forgot," Miriam said. "That's too bad. Mam and Anna are cooking an early supper, since we all missed our noon meal. I think they've been cooking since Mam got home from school. She wanted me to invite you and John to join us for fried chicken and dumplings. You're welcome to bring Mary, too."

"Ne." He pushed his hat back. "Guess we'll get home to evening chores."

Shadows were lengthening in the big barn, but Miriam could read the disappointment on his face. She could tell he wanted to have dinner with them, so why didn't he just come back after he picked up his sister? She didn't know what was going on with Charley, but she could tell something was bothering him. She'd known him long enough to know that look on his face.

"Another time for certain," Charley said, and fled the barn.

"Ya," she called after him. "Another time."

"Well, since Charley can't come, maybe there's room for me at the table," Eli said.

She folded her arms, turning to him. "I didn't think I had to invite you. You're family. I bet Ruth's already set a plate for you." She smiled and he smiled back. Miriam was so happy for Ruth. Eli really did love her, and despite his rocky start in the community, he was going to make a good husband to her.

"Good," Eli said, "because I've worked up such an appetite pulling those horses out of the creek, that I can eat my share and Charley's, too."

Eli lived with his uncle Roman and aunt Fannie near the chair shop where he worked as a cabinetmaker, but since he and Ruth had declared their intentions, he ate in the Yoder kitchen more evenings than not.

Miriam looked back at John expectantly. "Supper?"

"I don't want to impose on your mother." John knelt beside a bale of straw and closed up his medical case. "Uncle Albert is picking up something at the deli for—"

"You may as well give in," Miriam interrupted. She rested one hand on her hip. "Mam won't let you off the farm until she's stuffed you like a Christmas turkey. We're all grateful you came so quickly."

John picked up the chest. "Then, I suppose I should stay. I wouldn't want to upset Hannah."

She chuckled, surprised he actually accepted her invitation, but pleased. She knew that he rarely got a home-cooked meal since he'd come to work with his grandfather and uncle in their veterinary practice. None of the three bachelors could cook. When he stopped by her stand at Spence's, the auction and bazaar where they sold produce and baked goods twice a week, he always looked longingly at the lunch she brought from home.

Sometimes, she took pity on him and shared her potato salad, peach pie, or roast beef sandwiches.

Blackie thrust his head over the stall door and nudged her, hay falling from his mouth. Miriam stroked his neck. "You've had a rough day, haven't you, boy?" She took a sugar cube out of her apron pocket and fed it to him, savoring the warmth of his velvety lips against her hand. Then she walked back to check on Molly. The dapple-gray was standing, head down dejectedly, hind foot in the air, unwilling to put any weight on it. That was the hoof that she'd been treating for a stone bruise for the last week, and the thing that concerned John the most. He was afraid that the accident would now make the problem worse.

"Do you think I should stay with her tonight?" Miriam asked, fingering one of her *kapp* ribbons.

"Nothing more you can do now." John moved to her side and looked at Molly. "She needs time for that sedative to wear off and then I can get a better idea of how much pain she's in. I'll come back and check on her again before I leave and I'll stop by tomorrow. I need to see that the two of them are healing and I want to keep an eye on that hoof."

"Supper's ready!" Ruth pushed open the top of the Dutch door. "And bring your appetites. Mam and Anna have cooked enough food to feed half the church."

"Charley had to pick up his sister in Dover so he left," Miriam said, "but John and Eli have promised to eat double to make up for it."

"Charley can't eat with us?" Ruth pushed wide the bottom half of the barn door and stepped into the shadowy passageway. "That's a shame."

"Ya," Miriam agreed. "A shame." Ruth liked Charley.

So did Anna, Rebecca, Leah, Johanna, Susanna and especially Mam. The trouble was, ever since the school picnic
last spring, when Charley had bought her pie and they'd
shared a box lunch, her sisters and Mam acted like they
expected the two of them to be a couple. All the girls at
church thought the two of them were secretly courting.

"Lucky for you that Charley was nearby when the
wagon turned over," Eli said. He and Ruth exchanged
looks. "He's a good man, Charley."

Miriam glared at Ruth, who assumed an innocent expression. "It's John you should thank," Miriam
said. "Without him, we might have lost both Molly and
Blackie."

"But Charley pulled you out of the creek." Ruth followed Eli out into the barnyard. "He might have saved
your life."

Miriam could barely keep from laughing. "Charley's
the one who nearly drowned me. And the water isn't deep
enough to drown a goose." She glanced back at John.
"Pay no attention to either of them. Since they decided
to get married, they've become matchmakers."

"So, you and Charley?" John asked. "Are you—?"

"Ne!" she declared. "He's like a brother to me. We're
friends, nothing more." It was true. They *were* friends,
nothing more and no amount of nudging by her family could make her feel differently. When the right man
came along, she'd know it…*if* the right man came along.
Otherwise, she was content staying here on the farm,
doing the work she loved best and helping her mother
and younger sisters.

Ruth led the way up onto the back porch where Miriam
and the two men stopped at the outdoor sink to wash their

hands. John looked at the large pump bottle of antibacterial soap and raised one eyebrow quizzically.

Miriam chuckled. "What did you expect? Lye soap?"

"No." He grinned at her. "People just think that…"

"Amish live like George Washington," she finished. Ruth and Eli were having a tug of war with the towel, but she ignored their silly game and met John's gaze straight on. "We don't," she said. "We use all sorts of modern conveniences—indoor bathrooms, motor-driven washing machines, telephones." She smiled mischievously. "We even have young, know-it-all Mennonite veterinarians."

"Ouch." He grabbed his middle and pretended to be in pain. Then, he shrugged. "Lots of people have strange ideas about my faith, too. My sister gets mistaken for being Amish all the time."

"Because of her *kapp*," Miriam agreed. "Tell her that I had an English woman at Spence's last week ask me if I was Mennonite."

"I'll admit, I didn't know much about you until I came here. I was surprised that the practice had so many Amish clients." Eli tossed the towel to him and he offered it to her.

"Of course. We have a lot of animals." She dried her hands and took a fresh towel off the shelf for him.

She liked John. He had a nice smile. He was a nice-looking young man. Nice, dark brown hair, cropped short in a no-nonsense cut, a straight nose and a good strong chin. Maybe not as pretty in the face as Eli, who was the most handsome man she'd ever seen, but almost as tall.

John was slim, rather than compact like Charley, with the faintest shadow of a dark beard on his cheeks. His fingers were long and slender; his nails clean and trimmed short. When he walked or moved his hands or arms, as he did when he hung the damp towel on the hook, he did it gracefully. John seemed like a gentle man with a quiet air of confidence and strength. It was one of the reasons she believed that he was so good with livestock and maybe why he made her feel so at ease when they were together.

"Miriam, John, come to the table," Mam called through the screen door. "The food is hot."

It wasn't until then that Miriam noticed that Ruth and Eli had gone inside, while she and John had stood there woolgathering and staring at each other. Would he think her slow-witted, that it took her so long to wash the barn off her hands?

"*Ya,* we're coming," she answered. She pushed open the door for John, but he stopped and motioned for her to go through first. He was English in so many ways, yet not. John was an interesting person and she was glad he'd accepted Mam's invitation to eat with them.

Her sisters, Irwin and Eli were already seated. Mam waved John to the chair at the head of the table, reserved for guests, since her father's death. She took her own place between Ruth and her twin, Anna. Since John knew everyone but Anna and Susanna, she introduced them before everyone bowed their heads to say grace in silence.

Miriam hadn't thought she was hungry, but just the smell of the food made her ravenous. Besides the chicken and dumplings, Mam and Anna had made broccoli, coleslaw, green beans and yeast bread. There were pickled beets, mashed potatoes and homemade applesauce. She glanced at John and noticed that his gaze was riveted on the big crockery bowl of slippery dumplings.

Mam asked Irwin to pass the chicken to John and the big kitchen echoed with the sound of clinking forks, the clatter of dishes and easy conversation. Susanna, young-

est and most outspoken of her sisters, made Mam and
Eli laugh when she screwed up her little round face and
demanded to know where John's hat was.

"My hat?" he asked.

"When you came in, you didn't put your hat on the
coatrack. Eli and Irwin put their hats on the coatrack.
Where's yours?"

Miriam was about to signal Susanna to hush, thinking she would explain later to her that unlike the Amish,
Mennonite men didn't have to wear hats. But then Irwin
piped up. "Maybe Molly ate it."

"Or Jeremiah," Eli suggested, pointing to Irwin's little
dog, stretched out beside the woodstove.

"Or Blackie," Anna said.

"Maybe he lost it in the creek," Ruth teased.

John smiled at Susanna. "Nope," he said. "I think a
frog stole it when we were pulling the horses out."

"Oh," Susanna replied, wide-eyed.

John was teasing Susanna, but it was easy for Miriam
to see that he wasn't poking fun *at* her. He was treating
her just as he would Anna or Ruth, if he knew them better. Sometimes, because Susanna had been born with
Down syndrome, people didn't know how to act around
her. She was a little slow to grasp ideas or tackle new
tasks, but no one had a bigger heart. It made Miriam feel
good inside to see John fitting in so well at their table,
almost as if the family had known him for years.

"We won't forget what you did for the horses," Mam
said. "Even if they did eat your hat."

Everyone laughed at that and Susanna laughed the
loudest. It was the best ending to a terrible day that Miriam could ask for, and by the time John had finished his
second slice of apple pie, she was sure that he had en-

joyed his meal with them as much as they'd enjoyed his company.

Later, after she and John and Ruth and Eli had inspected the horses, John drove away in his pickup. He had one final house call before calling it a day. Eli left as well, wanting to clean the chair shop for his uncle. That left Miriam and Ruth to do the milking. Irwin drove the cows in and offered to help, but Miriam sent him off to see if Mam needed anything. Irwin was shaping up to be a good gardener, but he didn't know the first thing about milking and usually ended up getting kicked by a cow or spilling a bucket of milk.

Miriam looked forward to this time of day. She and Ruth had always been close friends and soon Ruth would be in her own home with her own cow to milk. Miriam would miss her. She loved her twin Anna dearly; she loved all her sisters, but Ruth was the kind of big sister she could talk to about anything. Of course there were some nights when Miriam might have preferred to milk alone.

"You know he's sweet on you," Ruth said. She was milking a black-and-white Holstein cow named Bossy in the next stall. Ruth had her head pushed into Bossy's sagging middle and two streams of milk hissed into her bucket in a steady rhythm.

"Who likes me?" Miriam stopped a few feet from Bossy's tail, her empty bucket in one hand and a three-legged milking stool in the other. She'd tied a scarf over her *kapp* to keep it clean and pushed back her sleeves.

"Charley. He's going to make someone a fine husband."

"I know he is. It's just not going to be me." Miriam sighed and walked to the next stall where Polly, a brown

Jersey, waited patiently, chewing her cud. "And I'm tired of you and Anna trying to make something of it that isn't."

"You like the cute vet better?"

Polly swished her tail and Miriam pushed it out of the way as she placed her stool on the cement floor and sat down. "John?"

"Was there another cute vet at supper?"

"He came because we needed him. It's his job."

"*Ya,* but you like him." Ruth's voice was muffled by the cow's belly. "Admit it."

Miriam took a soapy cloth and carefully washed Polly's bag. The cow swished her tail again. Miriam dropped the cloth into the washbasin and took hold of one teat. She squeezed and pulled gently and milk squirted into the bucket. "First Charley, then John."

"He's Mennonite," Ruth said.

"I know he's Mennonite."

"But you think he's cute."

Miriam wished her sister was standing close enough to squirt with a spray of milk. Once Ruth started, there was no stopping her. "Mam invited him to dinner, not me."

"But you like him. Better than Charley."

"Maybe I do and maybe I don't," she said. "But if you say another word about boys tonight, I'll dump this bucket of milk over your head."

It was dusk by the time John got back to the house that was both office and home for him, his grandfather and Uncle Albert. John completed his paperwork, refilled his portable medicine chest and went upstairs to shower. Once he'd changed into clean clothing, he wandered out onto the side porch where the two older men sat with their feet propped up on the rail, sipping tall glasses of lemonade. As always, the three shared the day's incidents. When his grandfather asked, John began telling them about the accident at the Yoder farm.

The third time John mentioned Miriam's name, his uncle Albert asked him if he was sweet on her. John shrugged and took a big sip of lemonade.

"She's Old Order Amish," his grandfather said.

"I know that," John replied.

"Miriam, is she one of the twins?" his uncle asked.

"I think so."

"The big one or the little one?"

"The little one."

"Pretty as a picture," Uncle Albert observed.

"Yeah," John admitted, getting up and attempting a quick escape into the house before they pressed the issue any further.

Truth be told, he *was* sweet on Miriam Yoder and he was pretty certain she liked him. And it wasn't just her looks or the physical chemistry between them that attracted him. She was easy to talk to and shared his love of animals. Although he always knew he would marry and have children someday, John hadn't seriously dated since his final year of vet school, when his girlfriend of three years had broken up with him. Alyssa, the daughter of a Baptist minister, had broken his heart and after that he had filled in what little spare time he had with family. It had been so long that he had forgotten what it felt like to be so strongly attracted to a woman. The fact that Miriam was Amish complicated the matter even further.

His grandfather chuckled. "He's sweet on her."

"Good luck with that," Uncle Albert said. "I've heard those Yoder girls can be a handful."

John paused in the doorway and looked back. "Sometimes," he said softly, "a handful is just the kind of woman a man is looking for."

Chapter Three

Miriam and Anna were just setting the table for breakfast the following morning when they heard the sound of a wagon rumbling up their lane. Miriam, who'd showered after morning chores, snatched a kerchief off the peg and covered her damp hair before going to the kitchen door. "It's Charley," she called back as she walked out onto the porch. He reined in his father's team at the hitching rail near the back steps.

"Morning." The wagon was piled high with bales of hay.

"You're up and about early," she said, tucking as much of her hair out of sight as possible. Wet strands tumbled down her back, and she gave up trying to hide them. After all, it was only Charley.

"Where are you off to?" Behind her, Jeremiah yipped and hopped up and down with excitement. "Hush, hush," she said to the dog. "Irwin! Call him. He'll frighten Charley's team."

Irwin opened the screen door and scooped up the little animal. "Morning, Charley," he said.

Charley climbed down from the wagon. "I'm coming here," he said as he tied the horses to the hitching rail. "Here."

"What?" she asked. Curious, Irwin followed her down the porch steps into the yard, the whining dog in his arms.

Charley laughed. "You wanted to know where I was going, didn't you?"

She wrinkled her nose. "I don't understand. We didn't buy any hay from your father."

"Ne." He grinned at her. "But you lost a lot of your load in the creek. My Dat and Samuel and your uncle Reuben wanted to help."

She sighed. The hay she'd lost had already been paid for. There was no extra money to buy more. "It's good of you," she said, "but our checking account—"

"This is a gift to help replace what you lost."

"All that?" Irwin asked. "That's a lot."

She looked at the wagon, mentally calculating the number of bales stacked on it. "We didn't have that much to begin with," she said, "and not all our bales were ruined."

Charley tilted his straw hat with an index finger and chuckled. "Don't be so pigheaded, Miriam. I'm putting this in your barn. You'll take it with grace, or explain to your uncle Reuben, the preacher, why you cannot accept a gift from the members of your church who love you."

Moisture stung the back of her eyelids, and a lump rose in her throat. *"Ya,"* she managed. "It is kind of you all."

Charley had always been kind. Since she'd been a child, she'd known that she could always count on him in times of trouble. When her father had died, without being asked Charley had taken over the chores and organized the young men to set up tables for supper after the funeral and carry messages to everyone in the neighbor-hood. A good man…a pleasant-looking man—even if he did usually need a haircut. *But he's just not the man I'd want for a husband,* she thought, recalling her conver-sation with Ruth last night. *Not for me, no matter what everyone else thinks.*

He walked toward her, solid, sandy-haired Charley, bits of hay clinging to his pants and shirt, and pale blue eyes dancing. *Pure joy of God's good life,* her father called that sparkle in some folks' eyes. He was such a *nice* guy, perfect for a friend. Ruth was right, he would make someone a good husband; he would be perfect for sweet Anna. But Charley was a *catch* and he'd pick a cute little bride with a bit of land and a houseful of brothers, not her dear Plain sister.

"We're family. We look out for our neighbors."

She nodded, so full of gratitude that she wanted to hug him. This is what the English never saw, how they lived with an extended family that would never see one of their own do without.

"I'm happy to make the delivery and I'd not turn down a cup of coffee," Charley said. "Or a sausage biscuit, if it was offered." He gestured toward the house. "That's Anna's homemade sausage I smell, isn't it? She seasons it better than the butcher shop."

"Ya," Irwin said. "It's Anna's sausage, fresh ground. And pancakes and eggs."

Miriam laughed. "We're just sitting down to break-fast. Would you like to join us?"

"Are Reuben's sermons long?" Charley chuckled at his own jest as he brushed hay from his pants. "I missed last night's supper. I'm not going to turn down a second chance at Anna's cooking." Then he glanced back toward the barn. "How are your horses?"

"Blackie's stiff, but his appetite is fine. Molly's no worse. I got her to eat a little grain this morning, but she's still favoring that hoof. John said he'd stop by this afternoon." She followed him up onto the porch and into the house. Irwin and the dog trailed after them.

"Miriam invited me to breakfast," Charley announced as he entered the kitchen, leaving his straw hat on a peg near the door.

Mam rose from her place. "It's good to have you."

"He brought us a load of hay," Miriam explained, grabbing a plate and extra silverware before sitting down. She set the place setting beside hers and scooted over on the bench to make room for him. "A gift from Uncle Reuben, Samuel and Charley's father."

Ruth smiled at him as she passed a plate of buckwheat pancakes to their guest. "It's good of you. Of all who thought of us."

"I mean to spread those bales that got wet," Charley explained, needing no further invitation to heap his plate high with pancakes. "If the rain holds off, it could dry out again. I wouldn't give it to the horses, but for the cows—"

"We could rake it up and pile it loose in the barn when it dries," Miriam said, thinking out loud. "That could work. It's a good idea."

"A good idea," Susanna echoed.

The clock on the mantel chimed the half hour. "Ach, I'll be late for school," Mam exclaimed. She took another swallow of coffee and got to her feet. When Charley started to rise, she waved him back. "*Ne,* you eat your fill. It's my fault I'm running late. The girls and I were chattering like wrens this morning and I didn't watch the time. Come, Irwin. There will be no excuses of illness today."

Irwin popped up, rolling his last bit of sausage into a pancake and taking it with him.

"It wouldn't do for the teacher to be late." Anna collected Mam's and Irwin's dinner buckets and handed them out. "Have a good day."

"Good day," Irwin mumbled through a mouthful of sausage and pancake as he dodged out the door. "Watch Jeremiah, Susanna!"

"I will," she called after him, obviously proud to be given such an important job every day. "He's a good dog for me," she announced to no one in particular.

"Don't forget to meet me at the school after dinner with the buggy." Mam tied her black bonnet under her chin. "Since there's only a half day today, we've plenty of time to drive to Johnson's orchard."

"I won't," Miriam answered. Their neighbor, Samuel Mast, who was sweet on Mam, had loaned them a driving horse until Blackie recovered from his injuries. They'd have apples ripe in a few weeks here on the farm, but Mam liked to get an early start on her applesauce and canned apples. The orchard down the road had several early varieties that made great applesauce.

Once their mother was out the door, they continued the hearty meal. Miriam had been up since five and she suspected that Charley had been, too. They were all hungry and it would be hours until dinner. Having him at the table was comfortable; he was like family. Everyone liked him, even Irwin, who was rarely at ease with anyone other than her Mam and her sisters.

The only sticky moments of the pleasant breakfast

were when Charley began to ask questions about John. "You say he's coming back today?"

Miriam nodded. "The stitches need to stay in for a few days, but John wants to have a look at them today."

"He thinks he has to look at 'em himself? You tell him you could do it? I know something about stitches. We both do."

"He *likes* Miriam," Susanna supplied, smiling and nodding. "He always comes and talks, talks, talks to her at the sale. And sometimes he buys her a soda—orange, the kind she likes. Ruffie says that Miriam had better watch out, because Mennonite boys are—"

"Hard workers," Ruth put in.

Susanna's eyes widened. "But that's not what you said," she insisted. "You said—"

Anna tipped over her glass, spilling water on Susanna's skirt.

Susanna squealed and jumped up. "Oops." She giggled. "You made a mess, Anna."

"I did, didn't I?" Anna hurried to get a dishtowel to mop up the water on the tablecloth.

"My apron is all wet," Susanna announced.

"It's fine," Miriam soothed. "Eat your breakfast." She rose to bring the coffeepot to the table and pour Charley another cup. "I heard your father had a tooth pulled last week," she said, changing the conversation to a safer subject.

After they had eaten, Miriam offered to help Charley unload the hay, but he suggested she finish cleaning up breakfast dishes with her sisters. A load of hay was nothing to him, he said as he went out the door, giving Susanna a wink.

"What did I tell you?" Ruth said when the girls were

alone in the kitchen. "People are beginning to talk about you and John Hartman, seeing you at the sale together every week. He's definitely sweet on you, even Charley noticed."

"I don't see him at Spence's *every week*," Miriam argued.

Ruth lifted an eyebrow.

"So he likes to stop for lunch there on Fridays," Miriam said.

"And visit with you," Ruth said. "I'm telling you, he likes you and it's plain enough that Charley saw it."

"That's just Charley. You know how he is." Miriam gestured with her hand. "He's…protective of us."

"Of you," Anna said softly.

"Of all of us," Miriam insisted. "I haven't done anything wrong and neither has John, so enough about it already." She went into the bathroom and quickly braided her hair, pinned it up and covered it with a clean *kapp*.

When she came back into the kitchen, Anna was washing dishes and Susanna was drying them. Ruth was grating cabbage for the noon meal. "I've got outside chores to do so I'm going to go on out if you don't need me in here," Miriam said.

Ruth concentrated on the growing pile of shredded cabbage.

Miriam wasn't fooled. "What? Why do you have that look on your face? You don't believe me? John is a friend, nothing more. Can't I have a friend?"

"Of course you can," Ruth replied. "Just don't do anything to worry Mam. She has enough on her mind. Johanna—" She stopped, as if having second thoughts about what she was going to say.

"What about Johanna?" Miriam didn't think her sister Johanna had been herself lately. Johanna lived down the road with her husband and two small children, but sometimes they didn't see her for a week at a time and that concerned Miriam. When she was first married, Johanna had been up to the house almost every day. Miriam knew her sister had more responsibilities since the babies had come along, but she sometimes got the impression Johanna was hiding something. "Are Jonah and the baby well?"

"Everyone is fine," Anna said.

"Later," Ruth promised, glancing meaningfully at Susanna. "I'll tell you all I know, later."

"I'll hold you to it," Miriam said. She thought about Johanna while she fed and watered the laying hens and the pigs. If no one was sick, what could the problem be? And why hadn't Mam said anything to her about it? Once she'd finished up with the animals, she went to the barn to give Charley a hand.

Dat had rigged a tackle to a crossbeam and they used the system of ropes and pulleys to hoist the heavy hay bales up into the loft. It was hard work, but with two of them, it went quick enough. They talked about all sorts of things, nothing important, just what was going on in their lives: Ruth and Eli's wedding, harvesting crops, the next youth gathering.

After sending the last bale up, Miriam walked to the foot of the loft ladder. Charley stood above her, hat off, wiping the sweat off his forehead with a handkerchief. "I'm coming up," she said.

He moved back and offered his hand when she reached the top rung. She took it, climbed up into the shadowy loft and looked around at the neat stacks of hay. It smelled heavenly. It was quiet here, the only sounds the cooing of pigeons and Charley's breathing. Charley squeezed her fingers in his and she suddenly realized he was still holding her hand, or she was holding his; she wasn't quite sure which it was.

She quickly tucked her hand behind her back and averted her gaze, as a small thrill of excitement passed through her.

"Miriam," he began.

She backed toward the ladder. "I just wanted to see the hay," she stammered, feeling all off-kilter. She didn't know why but she felt like she needed to get away from Charley, like she needed to catch her breath. "I've got things to do."

"What you two doin' up there?" Susanna called up the ladder. "Can I come up?"

"*Ne!* I'm coming down," Miriam answered, descending the ladder so fast that her hands barely touched the rungs.

Charley followed her. He jumped off the ladder when he was three feet off the ground and landed beside her with a solid *thunk*.

"I came to see how Molly is." Susanna looked at Miriam and then at Charley. "Something wrong?"

Miriam felt her cheeks grow warm. *"Ne."* She brushed hay from her apron, feeling completely flustered and not knowing why. She'd held Charley's hand plenty of times before. What made this time different? She could still feel the strength of his grip and wondered if this feeling of bubbly warmth that reached from her belly to the tips of her toes was temptation. No wonder handholding by unmarried couples was frowned upon by the elders.

"Ne," Charley repeated. "Nothing wrong." But he was looking at Miriam strangely.

Something had changed between them in those few seconds up in the hayloft and Miriam wasn't sure what. She could hear it in Charley's voice. She could feel it in her chest, the way her heart was beating a little faster than it should be.

Susanna was still watching her carefully. "Anna said to tell you to cut greens if you go in the garden and not to forget to meet Mam."

The three stood there, looking at each other.

"Guess I should be going," Charley finally said, awkwardly looking down at his feet.

"Thanks again for bringing the hay, Charley. I can always count on you." Miriam dared a quick look into his eyes. "You're like the brother I never had."

"That's me. Good old Charley." He sounded upset with her and she had no idea why.

"Don't be silly." She tapped his shoulder playfully. "You're a lifesaver. You kept me from drowning in the creek, didn't you?"

"In the creek? Right, like *you* needed saving." He laughed, and she laughed with him, easing the tension of the moment.

They walked out of the barn, side by side with Susanna trailing after them, and crossed the yard to the well. Charley drew up a bucket of water, and all three drank deeply from the dipper. Then he went back to the barn to guide the team and wagon down the passageway and out the far doors. By the time he'd turned his horses around and driven out of the yard, Miriam had almost stopped feeling as though she'd somehow let him down. Almost...

Later, in the buggy on the way to the orchard with her mother, Miriam had wanted to tell her about the strange moment in the hayloft with Charley. In a large family, even a loving one, time alone with parents was special. Miriam was a grown woman, but Mam had a way of listening without judging and giving sound advice without seeming to. Miriam valued her mother's opinion more than anyone's, even more than Ruth's and the two of them were the closest among the sisters. But this afternoon, she didn't want sisterly advice; she didn't need any more of Ruth's teasing about her friendship with John Hartman. Today, she needed her mother.

But before she could bring up Charley, she needed to find out what Ruth and Anna had been hinting about after breakfast, concerning Johanna. If Johanna had trouble, it certainly took priority over a silly little touch of a boy's hand. She was just about to ask about her older sister when Mam gestured for her to pull over into the Amish graveyard and rein in the horse.

Sometimes, Mam came here to visit Dat's grave, even though it wasn't something that their faith encouraged. The graves were all neat and well cared for; that went without saying, but no one believed their loved ones were here. Those that had died in God's grace abided with Him in heaven. Instead of mourning those who had lived out their earthly time, those left behind should be happy for them. But Mam—who'd been born and raised Mennonite—had her quirks and one of them was that she came here sometimes to talk to their father.

When Mam came to Dat's grave, she usually came alone. This was different and Miriam gave her mother her full attention.

"You know we had a letter from Leah on Monday," Mam said.

Miriam nodded. Her two younger sisters, Leah and

Rebecca, had been in Ohio for over six months caring for their father's mother and her sister, Aunt Jezebel. *Grossmama* had broken a hip falling down her cellar stairs a year ago, and although the bone had healed, her general health seemed to be getting worse. Aunt Ida, Dat's sister, and her husband lived on the farm next to *Grossmama,* but her own constitution wasn't the best, and she'd asked Mam for the loan of one of her girls. Mam had sent two, because neither *Grossmama* nor Aunt Jezebel, at their ages, could be expected to act as a proper chaperone for a young, unbaptized woman. No one, least of all Miriam, had expected the sisters to be away so long.

"What I didn't tell you," Mam continued, "was that this arrived on Tuesday from Rebecca." She removed an envelope from her apron pocket. "You'd best read it yourself."

Miriam slipped three lined sheets of paper out of the envelope and unfolded them. Rebecca's handwriting was neat and bold. Her sister had wanted to follow their mother's example and teach school. She'd gotten special permission from the bishop to continue her education by mail, but in spite of her sterling grades, no teaching positions in Amish schools had opened in Kent County.

Miriam skimmed over the opening and inquiries over Mam's health to see what Mam was talking about. It wasn't like her to keep secrets, and the fact that she hadn't said anything about what was in the letter was out of the ordinary and disturbing.

As she read through the pages, Miriam quickly saw how serious the problem was. According to Rebecca, their grandmother had moved beyond forgetfulness and both sisters were concerned for her safety. *Grossmama* had never been an easy person to please, and Leah and

Rebecca had been chosen to go because they were the best-suited to the job.

Dat had been their grandmother's only son and she'd never approved of his choice of a bride. She'd made it clear from the beginning that she didn't like Mam. Even as the years passed, she never missed an opportunity to find fault with her and her daughters. Miriam had always tried to remember her duty to her grandmother and to remain charitable when discussing her with her sisters, but the truth was, the prospect of *Grossmama*'s extended visit for Ruth's marriage was something Miriam wasn't looking forward to.

According to Rebecca's letter, *Grossmama* had accidentally started fires in the kitchen twice. She'd taken to rising from her bed in the wee hours and wandering outside in her nightclothes, and was having unexplained bouts of temper, throwing objects at Leah and Rebecca and even at Aunt Jezebel. *Grossmama* had also begun to tell untruths about them to the neighbors. She refused to take her prescriptions because she was convinced that Aunt Jezebel was trying to poison her.

Miriam finished the letter and dropped it into her lap. "This is terrible," she said. "What can we do?"

Mam's eyes glistened with unshed tears. "I've been praying for an answer."

Miriam closed her hand over her mother's. "But why didn't you tell us?"

"I've talked to your aunt Martha."

"Aunt Martha?" If anyone could make a situation worse, it would be Dat's sister. "And…"

"She is *Grossmama*'s daughter. I'm only a daughter-in-law," Mam reminded her. "Anyway, Martha thinks that Rebecca may be exaggerating. She thinks we should go on as we are until they come here for the wedding."

"While *Grossmama* burns down the house around my sisters?"

Mam laughed. "I hope it's not that bad. As Rebecca says, she and Leah take turns keeping watch over her and they turn off the gas to the stove at night."

"But why isn't Aunt Martha or Aunt Ida or one of the other aunts doing something? She's *their* mother!"

"And she was Jonas's mother, my mother-in-law. God has blessed us, child. We're better off financially than either of your aunts. Martha's house is small and she's already caring for Uncle Reuben's cousin Roy. If your father was alive, he'd feel it was his duty to care for his mother. We can't neglect that responsibility because he isn't here, can we?"

"You mean *Grossmama* is coming to live with us?" Miriam couldn't imagine such a thing. Her grandmother would destroy their peaceful home. She was demanding and so strict, she didn't even want to see children playing on church Sundays. She objected to youth singings and frolics, and most of all, she couldn't abide animals in the house. She would forbid Irwin to let Jeremiah through the kitchen door.

"Nothing is decided," Mam said. "I spoke to Johanna on Tuesday evening. I meant to discuss it with the rest of you, but then you had the accident with the hay wagon and the time wasn't right. I just wanted time alone to tell you about this."

"Ruth doesn't know?"

"We'll share the letter with her when the time is right. She's so excited about her wedding plans and the new house, I don't want to spoil this special time for her. And Anna, well, you know how Anna is."

"She'd look for the best in it," Miriam conceded. "And she'd probably want to take a van out to Ohio tomorrow and make everything right for everyone."

Her mother nodded. "You're sensible, Miriam. And you have a good heart."

"What do you need me to do, Mam?"

"For now? Pray. Think on this and look into your heart. If what Rebecca says is true, we may have to open our home to your grandmother. If we do, it must be all of us, with no hanging back. We have to do this together."

"All right," Miriam promised. Thoughts of Charley and the uncomfortable moment with him faded to the back of her mind. Her family—her mother—needed her. "But what shall we do right now?" she asked.

"Drive the horse to the orchard," Mam said with a smile. "We'll need those apples all the more with the wedding coming. We've got a lot of applesauce to make."

"*Grossmama* hates cinnamon in her applesauce."

"Does she?" Mam's eyes twinkled with mischief. "And I was just thinking we should stop at Byler's store to buy extra."

Chapter Four

Early Saturday morning, two days after Miriam's accident with the hay wagon, preparations began for Sunday church at Samuel Mast's home. Anna, Ruth, Mam and Susanna joined Miriam and most of the other women of their congregation to make Samuel's house ready for services and the communal meal that followed.

Since Samuel, the Yoders' closest neighbor, was a widower, he had no wife to supervise the food preparation and cleaning. Neighbors and members of the community always came to assist the host before a church day and Samuel was never at a lack for help. It seemed to Miriam as if every eligible Amish woman in the county, or a woman with a daughter or sister of marrying age, turned out to bake, cook, scrub and sweep until Samuel's rambling Victorian farmhouse shone like a new penny.

Miriam carried a bowl of potato salad in her right hand and one of coleslaw in her left as she crossed Samuel's spacious kitchen to a stone-lined pantry beyond. Although the September day was warm, huge blocks of ice in soapstone sinks kept the windowless room cool enough to keep food fresh for the weekend. A large kerosene-driven refrigerator along one wall held a sliced turkey and two sliced hams, as well as a large tray of barbecued chicken legs. Pies and cakes, pickles, chow-chows and jars of home-canned peaches weighed down shelves. The widower might not have been a great cook, but he never lacked for delicious food when it came to hosting church.

As Miriam exited the pantry, closing the heavy door carefully behind her, she nearly tripped over Anna, who was down on her hands and knees scrubbing the kitchen linoleum. At the sink, Ruth washed dishes and Johanna dried and put them away while Mam arranged a bouquet of autumn flowers on the oak table. "What can I do to help?" Miriam asked.

Anna dug another rag out of the scrub bucket, wrung it out and tossed it to her. Miriam caught the wet rag, frowning with exaggeration at her sister.

"You asked." Anna grinned. She knew very well that Miriam's strong point wasn't housework, but she also knew that when it came down to it, her sister was a hard worker, no matter what the task.

Chuckling, Miriam got down to assist Anna in fin-ishing the floor. Johanna, who had a good voice, began a hymn in High German, and Miriam, Anna and Ruth joined in. Miriam's spirits lifted. Work always went faster with many hands and a light heart, and the words to the old song seemed to strike a chord deep inside her. It was strange how scrubbing dirty linoleum could make a per-son feel a part of God's great plan.

Aunt Martha had taken over the downstairs living room and adjoining parlor, loudly directing her daughter Dorcas and several other young women in washing win-dows, polishing the wood floors and arranging chairs.

But it didn't take long for Johanna's singing to spread through the house. Soon, Dorcas's off-key soprano and Aunt Martha's raspy tenor blended with the Yoder girls to make the walls ring with the joyful song of praise.

Samuel's sister, Louise Stutzman, came down the steep kitchen staircase, leading Samuel's daughter Mae, just as Johanna finished the chorus of their third hymn. The four-year-old was cranky, but Susanna, who'd come in the back door to find cookies, held out her arms and offered to take the little girl outside to play with the other small children.

"Gladly," Louise said, ushering Mae in Susanna's direction.

Susanna's round face beamed beneath her white *kapp.* "Don't worry. I'll take good care of her."

"I know you will, Susanna. All the children love you."

Susanna nodded. "You can bring baby Mae to our li-bary. Mam says I am the best li-barian there is."

"Librarian," Mam corrected gently.

Susanna took a breath, grinned and repeated the word correctly. "Li-brarian!"

"Mam had our old milk house made into a lending library for the neighborhood," Anna explained. "Susanna helps people find books to take home. And she goes with Miriam to buy new ones that the children will like."

Louise smiled at Susanna. "That sounds like an important job."

"It is!" Susanna proclaimed. "You come and see. I'll find you a good book." Anna held the door open and Susanna carried a now-giggling Mae outside.

"Susanna has such a sweet spirit," Louise said. "You've been blessed, Hannah."

"I know," Mam agreed. "She's very special to us."

Miriam liked Samuel's older sister. She was a jolly person with a big smile and a good heart. She was always patient and kind to Susanna, never assuming that because of her Down syndrome, Susanna was less than safe to be trusted with Mae.

Louise had come from Ohio on Friday and brought Mae along for a visit with her father. When Samuel's wife died after a long illness, baby Mae was only a few months old. None of Samuel's family thought that he could manage an infant, since he already had the twins, Peter and Rudy, Naomi and Lori Ann to care for. Reluctantly, Samuel had agreed to let his sisters keep the baby temporarily, with the understanding that when he remarried, Mae would rejoin the family. Louise had offered to take Lori Ann as well, but Samuel wouldn't part with her.

Everyone thought that Samuel would marry after his year of mourning was up. And considering that he was the father of five, no one would have objected if he'd taken a new wife sooner. But it had been four years since Frieda had passed on, and Samuel seemed no closer to bringing a new bride home than he'd been on the day he'd ridden in the funeral procession to the graveyard.

Samuel made visits to his family in Ohio to see little Mae, and his mother and sisters brought the child to Delaware whenever it was his turn to host church services. The shared time was never very satisfactory for father or daughter. Mae was a difficult child, and Samuel and her sisters and brothers were strangers to her. The neighborhood agreed that the sooner Samuel took a wife and brought his family back together, the better for all.

The problem, as Miriam saw it, was that Samuel hadn't shown any real interest in any of the marriageable young women in the county or those his sisters paraded before him in Ohio. Samuel Mast was a catch. He was a devout member of the church, had a prosperous farm and a pleasant disposition. And, he was a nice-looking man, strong and healthy and full of fun. No one could understand why he'd waited so long to remarry.

Miriam and the Yoder girls thought they knew why, though.

Despite the difference in their ages—Samuel was eight years younger than Mam—it looked to Miriam and her sisters as if Samuel liked their mother. She and Ruth had discussed the issue many times, usually late at night, when they were in bed. They both thought Samuel was a wonderful neighbor and a good man, but not the right husband for Mam.

Hannah had been widowed two years and, by custom, she should have remarried. The trouble was, she wasn't ready, and neither were her daughters. Dat had been special and Miriam couldn't see another man, not even Samuel, sitting at the head of the table and taking charge of their lives. Not yet at least.

Among the Plain people, a wife was supposed to render obedience to her husband. Not that she didn't have a strong role in the family or in the household; she did. But a woman had to be subservient first to God, and then, to her husband. Miriam couldn't imagine Mam being subservient to anyone.

Growing up, Miriam had never heard her parents argue. It seemed that Mam had always agreed with every decision Dat ever made, but as Miriam grew older she realized that, in reality, it was often Dat who'd listened to Mam's advice, especially where their children were concerned. In that way, Mam was different.

Mam had been born a Mennonite and had been baptized into the Amish church before they were married. Miriam sometimes wondered if that was what made her mother so strong-willed and independent. Would another man, even a man as good-natured and as sweet as Samuel, be able to accept Mam's free spirit? Certainly, he'd ask her to give up teaching school. Married women didn't work outside the home.

If they married, would Samuel expect Mam to move into his house? What would happen to Dat's farm? To the Yoder girls, including herself? And what about Irwin? His closest relatives were Norman and Lydia Beachy; he'd lived with them when he first came to Seven Poplars, but that hadn't worked out well. That was why Irwin now lived with Miriam's family. If Mam and Samuel were to marry, would Samuel want to send Irwin back to the Beachy farm?

Mam and Miriam and her sisters had made out fine in the two years since Dat's death. It hadn't been easy, but they managed. There were a lot of ways a stepfather could disrupt the Yoder household, and thinking about it made Miriam uneasy. Ruth leaving to marry Eli was enough change for one year. Wasn't it?

"Whoa," Anna said. "That section of the floor is already done."

Miriam looked up. As usual, she'd been so deep in her thoughts that she'd forgotten to pay attention to what she was doing. "Oops."

Anna laughed. "Go on. You've been inside too long. Find something outside to do."

"You certain you don't mind?" Miriam asked.

"Scrub the back porch, if you want," Louise suggested. "It doesn't look as though Samuel has thought of that in a while." She pointed to the screen door. "There's another bucket by the pump."

"Go. Go," Anna urged. "Any more women in here and we'll be tripping over each other."

Miriam went out, found a broom and proceeded to sweep the sand off the porch. She hadn't been at it more than two minutes when Charley shouted to her from the barnyard.

"Morning, Miriam."

"Morning, Charley."

He was raking the barnyard clean of horse droppings, and she assumed that he'd come with the other men to make the farmyard and barn ready for Sunday's gathering. If there was work to be done, you could always count on Charley to be there.

He'd leaned his rake against the barn and started toward the porch, when Miriam heard the sound of a truck engine. As she watched, John pulled up in his truck, with *Hartman Veterinary Services* printed on the side.

"Who's that?" Anna asked as she pushed open the screen door.

"John." Miriam's heart beat faster and she felt a little thrill of excitement. What was he doing here?

Anna snickered. "He was at our house before eight this morning. Is he going to follow you everywhere?"

John blew the horn and waved.

Miriam felt her cheeks grow hot, but she waved back.

"Who is it?" Louise stepped out on the porch behind Anna. "Oh, the vet. Samuel told me that he'd asked him to come. One of his best milkers has a swollen bag. He didn't want it to get worse." She glanced at Anna. "You say he was at your house this morning?"

"He's sweet on Miriam," Anna explained.

Miriam could hear her sister's smile, even if she couldn't see it. "He is not," Miriam protested, sweeping harder. "He came to check on one of our horses. She's developing a hoof infection. John's watching it."

Anna giggled. "More like he's watching you."

"The English vet?" Louise frowned. "Not good." She waggled a finger. "You shouldn't encourage him."

"I'm *not* encouraging him," Miriam said. "We're friends, nothing more."

"He's not English," Anna supplied. "He's Mennonite."

"Ach." Louise shook her head. "Worse, even. You know what they say about those Mennonite boys. Wild, they are."

"Miriam," Mam called from inside the house. "Can you give me a hand with this?"

As she turned to make her escape into the kitchen, Miriam saw Charley walk toward John's truck and lean in the open window. She would have given her best pair of muck boots to hear what those two were saying to each other.

Miriam's eyelids grew heavy. When they drifted shut, Anna poked her hard in the ribs. Miriam gasped, straightened and sat upright. Then she glanced around to see if anyone else had caught her dozing off. Luckily, no one seemed to be watching her.

She was seated on a long backless bench with the other single girls on the women's side of Samuel's parlor. Wide pocket doors allowed a good view of the living room with its chairs for the older members, the bishop and preachers, and guests.

Uncle Reuben was still speaking. The hands on the tall case clock against the staircase read 12:45 p.m. The

Sunday service should have been over half an hour ago, and there was still a prayer, the benediction and a final hymn to go. The wooden bench under Miriam was getting harder and harder, and she wiggled to find a more comfortable spot.

Despite the open windows and the breeze, it was warm in the room. She could see Susanna, sitting next to their mother, with her head on Mam's shoulder. Her little sister's face was perspiring and Mam was fanning her. Miriam was warm, too, but not uncomfortably so. It was something else that made her uneasy. The hairs on the back of her neck prickled. She felt as though someone was watching her, but again, when she scanned the two rooms, she saw no one staring in her direction.

Miriam tried to concentrate on her uncle's sermon. He'd been talking about Noah and the hardships of spending so many weeks on the ark during the constant rainfall, but he'd moved on to Jonah and the similarities between the faiths of the two men. Uncle Reuben was known for his long rambling sermons, especially when there were important visitors. She didn't think it was *hochmut* or pride on his part that made him go on so, as much as wanting to put the church in a good light.

She wished he'd get back to Noah's story. Hearing Uncle Reuben tell about Noah gathering the animals had brought back the excitement of the movie Eli had taken her to at the Dover Mall a few months back. She could see the bears and the giraffes and the monkeys, in her mind's eye, climbing the ramp to the ark, two by two, obedient to God's word.

Miriam tried to listen to what her uncle was saying about Jonah, but she still had that feeling that— Charley! Her gazed suddenly settled on him.

He was standing between the main room and the kitchen with a group of his chums, young men who'd come in too late from the barn to be seated, and he was grinning at her. From across two rooms, Miriam could tell that he had been staring at her and that he had seen her falling asleep during Uncle Reuben's sermon. When they made eye contact, he shook his head ever so slightly, obviously admonishing her, that silly grin still on his face. Worse, the other boys had apparently caught her as well. She could tell by the looks on their faces. They were all struggling not to laugh out loud and cause a scene.

Miriam was beside herself. Who knew when they'd come in? Standing in the kitchen doorway, they could slip outside, have a glass of iced tea, grab a slice of pie and then pop back into the sermon without the elders being any the wiser. She'd made a mistake by falling asleep, but mocking her for it was wrong. When she got hold of Charley, she'd tell him so in no uncertain terms.

"Miriam." Anna nudged her again.

Everyone was standing for the benediction and she'd been paying so much attention to Charley and his friends that she'd lost track of where they were in the service. Following the prayer, the deacon announced the date and place of the next service and church ended with a hymn. Miriam and Anna filed out with the unmarried girls and went directly to the kitchen to find an apron and help get the midday meal served.

Since the day was so nice, the young men had assembled the tables outside. Once everyone had left their seats, the boys carried out the benches used in the house for service. Earlier, the girls had set the tables. Now it was a matter of getting the hot food to the tables. The guests, ministers and bishop took their places, followed by the older men and lastly the younger men. The boys and girls would eat at the second seating, so they gathered in groups to talk or ran errands for the women working in the kitchen.

Soon, all the men were eating. Miriam and Anna were assigned the job of carrying pitchers of iced tea, water and milk to the diners. To Miriam's dismay, she found Charley on her side of the table.

"Enjoy your nap?" he whispered.

She poured his glass full of milk. Charley didn't like milk, so it seemed like an act of revenge, even if it was small.

He didn't seem to notice. "Hey, I've got to talk to you later," he continued under his breath. "I've got great news. If you can stay awake until then."

"We saw you," Charley's friend Thomas whispered as he held out his mug for milk. "Sleeping during church, weren't you?"

"I was not," Miriam protested.

"Don't tell lies on Sunday," Charley teased. Then he met her gaze and lowered his voice. "You know I'm just teasing. We've all done it. Meet me later. Wait until you hear."

Miriam passed on to the next man at the table, annoyed with herself for dozing off during the sermon. She'd be hearing about it for weeks from the boys, and sooner or later, it would get to her cousin Dorcas and then to Aunt Martha. Anna should have pinched her to keep her awake.

It wasn't like her to fall asleep during church, although in summer, a lot of the men did. She'd been up since five, and they'd been busy all day yesterday as well. She supposed it was a small sin, but it had been mean of Charley to make more of it than it was. Of course, what could she expect? He always was a tease, making fun of everyone and everything, including himself. Good-time Charley.

It was three hours later when Charley found her and by then, Miriam had almost forgotten her earlier annoyance with him. She was sitting on the side porch with Johanna's three-year-old on her lap. Jonah had gotten his finger slammed in the screen door by an older child and Miriam was soothing him and applying ice to the boo-boo.

"Here you are." Charley stepped up onto the porch from the lawn. "I've been looking everywhere for you."

"Busy day," she replied, trying to shush Jonah.

Her nephew was still crying on and off and trying to tell her how the accident had happened and how his father had said he was a baby for crying. "*Not* a baby," he protested. "Hurts."

"No, you are not a baby," Miriam agreed. "Katie is the baby and you are the big brother."

"So, what I've been wanting to tell you," Charley started in. "Larry Jones stopped by yesterday. He wants me to work for him full time. Larry's got a contract to work on the hospital addition. I'll have steady masonry work from now on. Isn't that great?"

"Uh-huh," Miriam agreed above the din of the next wave of sobs. "That's wonderful." She stood up with Jonah in her arms. "He mashed his finger in the door. It's a bad pinch, but I don't think anything is broken."

"Hurts," Jonah wailed.

"All right, we'll find your Momma and see what she thinks."

Charley was still looking at her, his face all alight. "Do you know what this means?" he asked. "The steady job?"

"I guess a regular paycheck. That's great." She looked down at her nephew in her arms. "I think I'd best find Johanna. If Jonah gets too upset, he'll throw up his dinner. And he ate a lot of chicken and dumplings, didn't you?" She looked into the little boy's teary eyes as she walked away. "It will be all right. I promise."

"But, Miriam…" Charley said. "I wanted to talk to you…"

"Later," she promised and hurried off with Jonah to find her sister. To her surprise, Charley trailed after her. As she reached the kitchen door, her mother was just coming out with Susanna.

"Jonah got his finger pinched in the door," Miriam explained. "I was looking for Johanna."

"Poor dumpling," Hannah exclaimed, taking him from Miriam. "We'll have to see what we can do about that."

Susanna's eyes widened and her face paled. Miriam knew that her little sister was especially tenderhearted and hated the thought of anyone being in pain.

"Jonah will be fine," Miriam assured Susanna, patting her arm.

Susanna blinked as tears filled her eyes. "Poor Jonah," she said.

Charley cleared his throat. "I have important news, Hannah."

Her mother looked up at him. "*Ya?* Good news, I hope."

"*Ya.* It is." He straightened his shoulders. "Larry Jones wants me to work with him on the new wing for the hospital. I'll have steady work."

"Excellent," Mam said, shifting the little boy to her hip. "You're a good mason. They couldn't have anyone more dependable."

"Oh, there's Johanna," Miriam said as she caught sight

of her sister coming into the kitchen from the pantry. "Johanna. Jonah needs you."

Mam carried Jonah inside where he was immediately surrounded by sympathetic mothers, aunts and grandmothers. By the time Miriam glanced back over her shoulder to speak to Charley again, he had retreated to male territory in the barnyard.

It was after six when Mam, Miriam, Susanna and Anna walked across the pasture toward home. It had been a busy day, but a satisfying one. There were still cows to be milked, eggs to be gathered, chickens and pigs to feed and water, but Miriam actually looked forward to it. This was a good time, chatting with Mam and Anna, remembering the laughter and shared worship of another peaceful Sunday.

"It's good that Charley got steady work," Mam said.

"Uh-huh," Miriam agreed. "He certainly was excited about it."

Anna rolled her eyes. "I wonder why."

"Well, he would be pleased," Miriam said. "He didn't have much work last winter. People weren't doing much building around Dover."

"He made a special point of telling Mam about the job," Anna reminded her.

"So?" Miriam frowned. This teasing about Charley and her was getting a little annoying.

"Hey, Miriam!" Irwin called. He'd gone on ahead to get a start on the chores. Now, he climbed up a fence and waved. "Your boyfriend's here!"

Anna glanced at Mam. "I wonder which one?"

"That's not funny," Miriam said, but she quickened her step, wondering who Irwin was talking about.

As if he'd read her mind, Irwin shouted, "It's John. He wants to see Miriam in the barn."

"I'm coming," Miriam called, then turned back to her mother. "He must have stopped to see Molly on his way home."

"Two times he comes on a Sunday?" Mam didn't sound particularly pleased. "Susanna, go with your sister."

Miriam glanced at her mother, not certain she'd heard her mother correctly. "It's just John," she said. "I told you Molly's leg was warm this morning and we're concerned about an infection. Why do I need Susanna—?"

"Two times to come on his day off," Mam repeated, setting her mouth the way she did when there would be no changing her mind. "You do as I say, Miriam. Take your sister with you. See to the horse and nothing more. I am lenient with you girls because I trust you, but we'll give the neighbors no cause for scandal."

Chapter Five

"Wait," Susanna cried. "Wait for me. Mam said I have to come with you." Her short legs pumped as she tried to catch up. "Wait, Miriam."

Miriam stopped and tried to compose herself. When Susanna reached her, she took her little sister's hand and smiled at her. "You're getting faster," she said.

Susanna grinned. "Mam said that I'm s'posed to—"

"*Ya,*" Miriam agreed. She let go of Susanna's hand and straightened her sister's *kapp*. "You like John, don't you?"

Susanna nodded, and Miriam caught her hand again. Together they walked toward the barn. Miriam could feel Mam's gaze boring into her back, but she didn't look back.

Maybe Anna is right, Miriam thought. *Maybe he is coming to see me.* A delicious shiver passed through her. She had to admit that thinking of John as more than a friend was exciting. But it was scary at the same time. She'd never considered that an English boy might be attracted to her. Of course, being a Mennonite, John really wasn't an Englisher, but he wasn't Amish, either. The church would frown on anything beyond the friendship she and John had right now, even if she wanted it to be more. It would be wrong, wouldn't it?

But then, God did work in mysterious ways. Ruth and Eli were proof of that. Who would ever have thought the bad boy Eli Lapp would have been the right boy for her sister, and yet with every passing day, Miriam was more sure he was. What if God had a plan for Miriam that was just as unexpected? What if it was God's plan for her that she not live her life in the old way?

The idea intrigued her. There were so many things about the outside world that called to her. The possibility of more education was the first that came to mind. If she got a high school diploma, could she work in an animal hospital? Could she become an animal technician?

She pushed open the barn door and held it for Susanna. Inside, it was cooler. "Hello, John," she called. "Here we are."

He stood up, removed his baseball cap, ran his hand through his hair, and put the hat back on. "I thought you'd be home from church earlier."

"We stayed to help clean up and to visit."

"Ya," Susanna chimed in. "We had chocolate cake and ginger cookies."

They walked through the barn to join John in Molly's stall. The mare was contentedly chewing a mouthful of new hay. "How is she doing?" Miriam asked, stroking the horse's neck.

John patted Molly's rump. "Good girl," he murmured.

His gaze met Miriam's, and she knew instinctively, that whatever concern he had for the horse, he'd come to see her as well. She waited.

Outside, in the pound, the cows mooed. It was past

time for milking. They'd stayed too long at Samuel's. Any minute, Irwin and Anna would be here to help with evening chores. "Is Molly worse?"

"Her hoof doesn't seem any worse than this morning," he answered, "but it really isn't any better, either."

"I'm applying the medicine exactly as you told me," Miriam assured him. She couldn't help thinking how cute he was, and how not-Amish he looked in his jeans and long-sleeve T-shirt and green ball cap that read *John Deere*.

"Ya," Susanna said. "Miriam's making Molly better. I love Molly."

John looked at Susanna and then back at Miriam, and she realized that he wanted to tell her something without her sister hearing.

Miriam glanced at Susanna. "I think Molly needs a new mineral block." She picked up the remains of the one in her feed box. "There's a new one in the feed room. Could you get it, Susanna?"

Her sister nodded and hurried away, eager to help, as always.

Miriam felt a small twinge of guilt to have deceived Susanna to get her out of the way, but she trusted John. If it was bad news, Miriam would want to pick the time and the place to tell Susanna. She crumpled a corner of her apron into a ball and glanced at him expectantly. "Molly isn't worse, is she?"

"It feels like the hoof is heating up. Here." He crouched down beside the mare and laid his hand gently on Molly's leg just above the hoof.

Miriam crouched beside him and then he surprised her by grabbing her hand. She didn't know what to do. It was warm and big and—

"Right here." He pressed her hand to the same spot he'd just touched. "Feel it?"

He was so close, she could smell fabric softener. Even though his jeans were dirty from being in barns, his shirt was clean. He'd put on a clean shirt before coming.

Miriam tried to block out John and just feel what he was trying to get her to feel. Molly's leg was definitely warm. "*Ya.* I feel it."

He stood up, reached into his pocket and pulled out a small red cell phone. "I was thinking. In case she spikes a fever, or if you needed to ask me—anything…about her treatment. If you had questions." He passed her the phone. "I want you to have this."

She stared at the cell phone in her hand. It was a lot smaller than a deck of cards and so bright that it almost glowed. "A phone?"

Some of the boys who considered themselves *rum-springa*—in their running around years—had phones but Miriam didn't know any girls who did—at least not in Kent County. Telephones weren't allowed by the *Ordnung,* the church rules.

"I don't know," she hedged. She wanted the phone badly. She'd always been fascinated by them. It was so tempting to take it. John was right. If there was a problem in the night with Molly, she could reach him right away, instead of walking to the chair shop and using the phone there.

"It's okay, right? For something like this? I don't want to get you in trouble." His brow furrowed and she saw how concerned he was for her. "This is the power button. You push that and then hit #1. I programmed in my number. To send, you hit this button."

"I know how they work," she assured him. "I see the

English customers using them all the time at Spence's and in the stores." She hesitated, feeling the weight of the phone in her hand.

"I thought…since you haven't officially joined the church yet, it would be okay. You having the phone." He sounded nervous. But in a good way.

"*Ya,* that's true," she said. Having a cell phone or using it to call the vet wasn't really against the *Ordnung*. Since she hadn't joined the church, she wasn't bound by the same restrictions that baptized members were.

When the accident happened, no one thought it was wrong to use the phone at the chair shop to call the vet. In fact, the objection to telephones was the phone wires that connected them to the English world, not the actual phone. A cell phone didn't have a wire.

Miriam stared at the phone in her hand. She knew she didn't have much time. Susanna would be back, and if she saw the phone, she'd tell everyone about it. That was the bad thing about her little sister. Whatever Susanna knew, she repeated it to anyone she spoke to. And nothing Miriam could say would make her understand that her having a phone wasn't a sin—or that she didn't have to tell Mam about it.

"So this would just be for calling you if Molly got worse?" Her heart was pounding so hard that she was afraid that John could hear it. *Say no,* she told herself. She looked at him.

He took her hand with both of his, cradling hers, cradling the cell phone. His hand felt warmer than the phone and Miriam felt a thrill run to the tips of her toes. This close to him again, she felt almost dizzy.

"I'd be lying if I said it was just for the mare," John admitted. "I like you a lot. And I want you to call me whenever you want." He squeezed her hand and then released it. "We're friends." He hesitated. "But I think it's more than friends, Miriam. I think we're past that."

"You're Mennonite," she said, so softly that it was barely a whisper.

"I know."

"And I'm Amish."

"Yes."

"There would be problems."

"You're right."

"It wouldn't be easy, if we…"

He shook his head. "No, it wouldn't, but we should see, don't you think? We should find out if…if it *is* more than friendship."

"I've got the block." Susanna held it high as she skipped toward them from the feed room.

A stray chicken squawked and scurried out of Susanna's way.

"Close the door so the rats can't get in," Miriam shouted to her sister. Dat had lined the whole feed room in sheets of tin to keep out vermin. Even the door was mouseproof.

"You have to tell me if you want to keep it, Miriam. I know you want to," John pressed quietly. "Will you take it?"

She looked up into his eyes and a bubble of mischief rose in her chest. She'd always been a little rebellious. She'd ridden horses when girls weren't supposed to. She'd played ball with the boys and walked the ridgepole on the barn when everyone else was afraid to.

"Dare you," John challenged.

She slipped the red cell phone into her apron pocket. "If Mam finds out, I'll be in big trouble."

"Me, too." He chuckled, and she laughed with him.

It would be their secret, Miriam thought. She couldn't wait to try out the phone, to talk to him in the night. Just the thought of calling him on the little red phone made her face feel warm. *This is temptation,* she thought. But will it lead to something more? Only time would tell.

"Here you go." Susanna walked into the stall, carrying the mineral block.

"Good work." John looked at Miriam and then back at Susanna, again. "You're a big help, Susanna, the best." He patted Molly's withers. "I guess I'd best be getting on home," he said. "I have an early call in Felton."

"Ya," Miriam agreed. "I have to get to the milking. It's late."

"I leave the house at about seven," he said. "And it takes me about twenty minutes to get there." He was telling her to call him. *Tomorrow.*

"Seven," she repeated, already planning how she could get away—maybe into the old milk house that served as a library. The walls were thick there. She could make her call from there and no one would hear.

"Mam says get on with the milking," Irwin called, banging open the barn door.

Miriam looked up, noting that Irwin hadn't said Hannah but Mam. It was the first time she'd heard him refer to her mother as Mam.

"Before they burst," Irwin continued. He stopped and scowled at John. "Out late, aren't you?"

"I was on my way home from another call. Just thought I'd check on Molly." If John thought he was being rude, he didn't act like it.

"Never saw so much fuss over a hoof," Irwin grumbled. "I'll let the cows in, Miriam."

"'Night," John said, walking away. "Talk to you soon, Miriam."

She nodded. "Soon." The phone in her apron pocket pressed hot against her thigh. "Thanks for stopping by." She knew that her mother would not approve of her taking it, but she also knew she'd make that call to John tomorrow morning.

"Hello, is this John?" Miriam asked loudly. It was 7:15 a.m. on Monday, and she'd ducked into the old milk house. She was so nervous that her hands were shaking.

He laughed. "You punched in my number. Who else would it be?"

The radio music in the background ended abruptly and Miriam guessed that John had turned it off.

"Are you still there?" he asked.

"*Ya,* I'm here." She held the cell phone tightly. All night she'd kept thinking of things that they'd talk about, and now that she'd actually reached him, her mind had gone blank. It felt so strange, using a phone just to talk. She had plenty of experience using phones; she called to make appointments for people all the time. But this was different.

"How's Molly?"

"Good. Same as last night." She peered out the window, hoping that Irwin or Anna wouldn't discover her here. If they did, what reason could she give for being in the library so early? What she was doing wasn't hurting anyone, but it was private. And if there was one thing difficult to find growing up in a house with six sisters and an observant mother, it was privacy.

"Hoof infections are tricky. She's not out of the woods yet," John said.

She could picture him at the wheel of the truck, a bottle of root beer in one hand. John liked his soda. He always bought one for himself and one for her when they shared lunch at Spence's. She began to relax a little. "What is your call this morning? You said you were going to Felton."

"Oh, just routine immunizations. It's a horse farm. Trotters. They want me to certify a two-year-old for sale. He's going to Tennessee."

Once the talk turned to horses, it was easy to fall into a comfortable conversation with John. She liked the way that he treated her as an equal, as if she understood everything. Most of it, she did.

"I was wondering," he said.

"*Ya,* of what?"

"Wednesday I have to drive to Easton to pick up something for my grandfather. There's a nice little restaurant over there. Maybe you could go with me, just for the ride."

Like a date, she thought. Was she ready for that? First the cell phone and then sneaking off for the day with him. Mam would never give her permission, not unless she took one of her sisters with her, and probably not then. But was it wrong to want to go with John? They'd had lunch together lots of times at Spence's. What would make that all right and going with him to Easton the wrong choice?

"I can't," she said. "We're making applesauce with Johanna on Wednesday." That wasn't really a lie. Mam had mentioned that they might do that one day this week. Maybe she wasn't ready to take such a big step, or maybe the thought of sneaking behind Mam's back made her feel small and mean.

"Maybe another time, then."

"Maybe," she agreed. She could imagine him pulling off his ball cap and running his hand through his short hair, the way he did when he didn't know what to say. A lump rose in her throat. She didn't want to do anything to hurt her friendship with John, but she didn't want to betray her mother's trust, either. "I think I had better go. They'll wonder where I am."

"All right. It was nice talking to you. Can you call me again tonight?"

"What time?" She lowered her voice.

She could hear Irwin calling to Jeremiah. Irwin always played with the little terrier in the morning before chores. Irwin would throw a stick and Jeremiah would run after it, then Irwin would try to get the dog to bring the stick back. But the ragtag little terrier had ideas of his own and he'd tease Irwin by running circles around him. It was a fun game, but Irwin and the dog could spend a half hour fooling around when there were chores to be done.

"Ten?" John suggested.

Miriam shook her head. "Too late. I share a bedroom with my sister, and I'd have to sneak out. How about nine?"

"Ok, nine it is. Wait, will you be at Spence's tomorrow?"

"*Ya.* At least this week. We have eggs and jams to sell."

"I'll see you there, then."

"I have to go, John. 'Bye." She hit the Off button.

Now, what to do with the phone? She didn't want to carry it around all day with her. What if it fell out of her pocket? What if Anna or Ruth noticed the bulge and asked what it was?

She climbed on Susanna's chair and pushed the red

phone back on the top shelf, then slid a book on Pennsylvania Dutch Recipes in front of it. The book was old and tattered and had once been sold to tourists. Mam said the recipes weren't very good, but Aunt Martha had donated the book, so it had to go in the library.

She got down off the chair and looked at the book. No one had borrowed it since the library opened, and if they did, Susanna would knock the book down with the broom handle Irwin had found for her. No one would ever see the red cell phone and no one would know that she was secretly calling John Hartman.

Miriam crossed her fingers and said a prayer that they wouldn't.

As she and Anna began setting up their sale table at Spence's Bazaar the following morning, Miriam glanced around anxiously for John. She'd told him that she'd call last night, but she hadn't been able to think of an excuse to get away. They'd had a family emergency.

What would she say to him? She couldn't share family problems with John, but neither did she want him to think that she'd promise to call and just not do it. She wondered if he would act differently if he did show up. Would Anna suspect that something more than their usual friendship was going on? Would she be able to talk to John as easily as they had in the past? Her stomach knotted. She'd not been able to eat this morning. Instead of her normal hearty breakfast, she'd had a slice of toast and a cup of coffee. If this was what romance was, she wasn't certain that it was as much fun as everyone insinuated.

And, besides worrying about John, she couldn't get Johanna out of her mind. Johanna and the children had showed up at the back door just as they were finishing supper last night. Johanna's eyes were red and Miriam suspected that she'd been crying, but her oldest sister would never admit such a thing. Johanna had asked her and the others to watch the children. She said she needed to talk to Mam. Naturally, they all wanted to know what was wrong, but Johanna was the stubborn one. Whatever her problem was, no one would know until she was ready to reveal it.

Mam and Johanna had spent the better part of two hours together in Mam's bedroom. Miriam had wanted to find some excuse to creep down the hall and listen at the door, but she'd never do such a thing. She had to respect Johanna's privacy, but it wasn't easy. She, Ruth and Anna were all worried. Only Susanna was her normal happy self, rocking baby Katie in the big rocker Dat's father had handcrafted until the baby had drifted off to sleep.

It had been after nine when Mam had asked Miriam to hitch Blackie to the courting buggy and drive Johanna and the baby home. Mam had tucked Jonah into her bed and promised that someone would drop him off in the morning. Miriam had tried to find out what was wrong, but Johanna remained tight-lipped. When they'd gotten down from the carriage at Johanna's house, everything was dark.

"Pray for our family," Johanna had said as she'd carried a sleeping Katie up her back steps.

"But, are you all right? Are you sick?" Miriam had called after her in a hushed voice. "Is something—?"

"Just pray for me, sister. God has a plan for us. I know He does."

Miriam and Anna had discussed Johanna on the buggy ride to Dover this morning, but Anna didn't seem to know much more than she did. "It's a problem with Wilmer,"

Anna said. "Not sickness, at least not of the body. He's strong as a plow horse. But I don't think it is a happy marriage."

None of them had really liked Wilmer Detweiler when he'd started coming around the house. He had a steady job in construction and he was a faithful member of the church, but he was moody. Miriam, especially, couldn't see why fun-loving Johanna would be attracted to him. Everyone had thought that Johanna and Charley's older brother Roland had been courting for two years, but they'd apparently argued and then broken up. As usual, no one had been able to pry anything out of Johanna.

But if Johanna and Wilmer's marriage was in trouble, that was serious. They had two children together, and among the Plain people, marriage was a sacred bond made before God. The couple became one when they took their vows and there was no breaking that union. Marriage was for life.

"Miriam!"

Two jars of strawberry jam toppled out of the basketful that she was carrying from the back of the buggy to the table. Anna caught them both before they hit the ground.

"Whoa, easy," Anna said. "Pay attention to what you're doing, twin. We spent too many hours making that jam to waste it."

"Ya," Miriam agreed. Lucky that Anna, despite her size, was so quick. "I was thinking about Johanna and Wilmer."

Anna nodded and her cinnamon-brown eyes watered up. "On my knees, last night, I prayed for them."

Across the drive, Aunt Martha and Dorcas had a display of fall flowers for sale along with the wooden toys Uncle Reuben made in his spare time. There was a Noah's ark and an array of animals, a simple sailboat with a long string so that a child could sail it and a girl's market basket with wooden eggs, vegetables and cups and saucers, all painted to look real.

Aunt Martha and Uncle Reuben's farm wasn't as productive as many others in the community; they'd always had to struggle, but they worked hard every day. Miriam hoped Uncle Reuben would find customers for his toys. Most English children, it seemed, wanted electronic toys that blinked and squealed and flashed, rather than simple handmade items.

Miriam was putting a quart of grapes on the table when suddenly someone came up behind her and put their hands over her eyes.

"Stop it." Embarrassed, she pulled at the hands. It was a man, not a woman. "Let me go," she said. She could imagine everyone staring at her.

"You have to guess first," Anna said with a giggle from beside her.

"John."

"Wrong." Charley took his hands down and stepped back.

Miriam whipped around and looked from him to Anna. She could feel her face growing hot. She wanted to run away and hide.

"Just me," Charley said with a frown of obvious disappointment. "Just good old Charley."

Miriam could hear Dorcas laughing behind her. "Charley, I didn't—"

"If you were looking for John, you didn't miss by much," he said. He wasn't smiling now. Hurt showed in his eyes, and his voice was tight. "Here comes your Mennonite boy now."

Chapter Six

"Hey, Charley, here comes trouble," shouted Harvey Borntrager. He and two other Amish boys were leaning against the wall of the poultry shed. Harvey laughed and gestured toward John Hartman, walking toward the Yoder stall carrying a cardboard tray of hot drinks.

Charley pushed his straw hat back on his head with an index finger and glared at Harvey. "That's enough," he warned. He'd taken the morning off from working on Eli's house, hoping to get a chance to talk to Miriam alone, and now, here came John again. It wasn't fair, but no matter how out-of-sorts he was with Miriam, he wouldn't stand by and let Harvey and his gang poke fun at him.

"Just looking out for your interest," Harvey said.

"Mind your own business, or you'll have me to deal with later," Charley warned. He glanced back at Miriam. "So, I guess I'm the third wheel here, right?"

Miriam shoved the quart basket of grapes across the table and hurriedly pushed another after it. She turned abruptly to face him. "What are you talking about?"

"Him. People think you like John, maybe more than you should."

"That's not fair."

"Maybe it is and maybe it isn't."

"Don't make a fuss, Charley. Everybody's looking at us."

"I guess they are. Maybe with good reason." He could feel her aunt Martha's eyes boring into his back. He glanced over his shoulder and Dorcas waved.

"Morning, Charley," Dorcas called.

"Morning," he said, before turning back to Miriam. He raised his gaze to meet hers directly. She looked as if she were about to burst into tears. Suddenly, his anger drained away. The thought of making Miriam cry was worse than attempting to explain how confused he felt about her friendship with John. "I guess I'll see you later."

She nodded.

He turned, straightened his back and walked directly toward John.

"Morning, Charley." John grinned and held up the tray. "Coffee? I've got extra."

"Ne."

He wanted to have it out with John right here, to tell him to stay away from his girl, but it wasn't the Amish way. The Bible taught that a man should be kind to his neighbors, that he shouldn't harbor bad thoughts in his heart. That went for everyone, including Mennonites and Englishers. It was probably nothing but jealousy and John hadn't done anything wrong. He had to keep reminding himself that Miriam was Amish. She'd never look at someone from another faith. Nothing John could do or say could steal her away from the Plain people.

"Got to do something," Charley muttered as he hurried past John. He couldn't stand here and watch Miriam laughing and talking with him. He'd find her before she left the auction and they'd have that talk. He'd make her see how he felt.

Charley's abrupt behavior puzzled John. It was clear that something had upset him. He wondered if he and Miriam had argued. Did the Amish argue? He supposed they must, like anyone else, but he'd never seen anything but gentle speech between them. Oh, men could be rowdy, even tell off-color jokes, but as a rule they seemed to possess an inner calm. He wished he could say that about himself.

"Good morning," Anna called. "Is that coffee I smell?" She giggled. "I told Miriam you were bringing us hot coffee."

"Indeed, I am," John said. "And some raisin buns."

Anna reached for one. "Sticky buns, yum. My favorite."

"Coffee, Miriam?" He held up a paper cup. "Milk and one sugar. Is that right?"

"Ya." She nodded. Her hand trembled as she took the coffee. "Thank you."

Anna giggled again. "Thank you, Dr. John. I missed my second cup at breakfast."

An egg customer approached and John stood aside as Miriam waited on her. "I'd like to buy some of your blueberry jam for Uncle Albert," he said when the English woman had moved on to look at the next table. "He loves it."

"We've got plenty," Anna said. "Eight dollars for a pint, five for the half-pint. And we've got strawberry, as well. Miriam made the strawberry."

He smiled at Miriam. "In that case, I'd better have three large jars of each."

"That's a lot of jam," Miriam said, beginning to put jars into a plastic bag. "You don't need to buy so much."

"But I do," he assured her. He wanted to ask her why she hadn't called him last night, to tell her that he'd waited to hear from her, but he didn't want to say anything about the cell phone in front of Anna. "We need something to make breakfast edible," he finished. "Something tasty."

"Then I'll put in a jar of honey, no charge," Miriam said. "Because you're such a good customer."

"I'd better get some more jam out of the buggy." Anna went to the carriage, opened the small door in the back and began to rummage in the cardboard boxes.

"I waited for you to call," John whispered, when Anna was too far away to hear. "What happened?"

"I can't talk now." Miriam glanced across at her aunt Martha's stand. "I'll be in trouble."

"Can you have lunch with me?"

"If Anna comes, too."

"All right. Meet me inside at one."

"Not inside," Miriam said. "Too many people."

Her cheeks were flushed as pink as her lips, and a few curls had escaped from her *kapp*. John was struck again by just how pretty she was. She didn't wear a dab of makeup and her simple green dress had a high neck and long sleeves. But he found her fresh and adorable from the toes of her sensible black athletic shoes to the crown of her bonneted head. "Where, then? The picnic tables under the trees?"

"All right," she agreed. "Now take your jam and go before Aunt Martha comes over and chases you away."

He chuckled. "She would, too, wouldn't she?"

"I'm afraid so."

* * *

As John was leaving, an older couple trailed by a little girl stopped to ask Miriam about eggs. The woman was dressed in pink sweats with shiny pink and white sneakers, and the man had a mustache and a big belly that hung over his Bermuda shorts. He was carrying a tiny white poodle with a blue bow and blue toenails. The child, wearing a pink tutu, a rhinestone-studded top that read *Hot Chick* and silver flip-flops, waved a blue, half-eaten lollypop nearly as large as her head.

"Are these eggs organic?" the woman demanded in a loud voice. "I only buy eggs from free-range chickens." By her accent, Miriam thought she might be from Jersey City or New York.

"I want ice cream," the child whined. "You said I could have ice cream." She threw her lollypop into the dirt, kicked it under the table and then began to yank on the woman's sleeve.

"Stop that, Melody. Be nice."

The dog snapped at the child.

"Ice cream after lunch," the man said. "Are...your eggs...white...or brown?"

He had the same accent as the woman, but he spoke in an artificially choppy manner to Miriam, as if he were trying to make himself understood in a foreign country without speaking the language.

"Why is she wearing that funny hat?" the little girl demanded.

"She's a Quaker," the woman explained. "They have to dress like that."

"White or brown?" the man repeated loudly.

Miriam gestured at the open carton of large brown eggs on display and wondered if he was color-blind. She knew that she should answer his question, but she was afraid that if she opened her mouth, she might burst into laughter.

"Ice cream!"

The dog began to yip.

"She's not a Quaker. She's Aim-ish," the man corrected. "Merle said this was an Aim-ish market."

"Chocolate!"

"You prefer white eggs." The woman ignored the now-screaming child. "I'm not sure you'd like brown. What do they eat?"

Miriam gritted her teeth. Did the woman want to know what the chickens ate or the eggs ate? She was still thinking about Charley and John and what Aunt Martha would just have to report to Mam, but she couldn't afford to offend customers, even rude ones who thought she was deaf.

"They only speak Pennsylvania Dutch, Mildred," the man said. "Don't you?" He raised his voice and the dog barked louder. "You speak Dutch?"

"Ice cream!" the child demanded and began to kick the woman's ankle.

"Can I help you?" Anna bustled up to the table wearing her widest smile. "I speak English."

Gratefully, Miriam let her sister deal with the tourists while she hurried back to the horse and smothered her laughter in Blackie's neck. Most of the people she dealt with at the sale were pleasant, but some were so ignorant they were just silly.

Sales for the next two hours were good. They sold all the eggs and jam and even took an order for one of Johanna's custom-made quilts. As it neared one o'clock, Miriam and Anna packed up the few items that hadn't sold, watered Blackie and strolled over to find an empty picnic table in the shade. As usual, Anna had packed a big lunch. There would be more than enough fried chicken, potato salad, deviled eggs and brownies to share with John.

He was already seated at the weathered table when they arrived. Miriam smiled when she saw that he'd brought sodas and a pizza and spread newspapers out to make a clean place to eat. "We've got enough for you to take home for dinner," she teased. "Then you won't have to eat Uncle Albert's cooking tonight."

"Amen to that," John said.

Anna laughed. "Maybe you should learn to cook, John."

"No, I'll leave that to you girls. It's all I can do to boil an egg."

"You don't boil eggs," Anna retorted with a twitter. "You just bring them to a simmer, turn them off and put the lid on. You let them cook in hot water, not boil them. Makes green streaks if you boil them."

Miriam took a seat across the table from John and he passed her a root beer. "How was your morning?" she asked.

He began to tell her about the calf he'd gone to tend as Anna dug in to the pizza. Miriam nibbled on a chicken leg. It was nice here, sitting in the shade, laughing and talking. She felt comfortable with John, as though she belonged here in the outside world. Her family and community might consider him an outsider, but he didn't seem like that to her. There were other people around them at tables, a few Amish but mostly English. No one seemed to be paying any attention to the three of them, as though it was perfectly normal for friends of different faiths to share lunch and laughter.

Nearby, a truck radio blared country music and John

tapped the table in time to the rhythm. Miriam was having a wonderful time, eating pizza and drinking her soda pop, until Charley and two of his buddies walked up.

"Something looks good," Titus said. "Is that your chicken, Anna?"

Anna looked at Titus, averted her eyes and blushed. "Help yourself," she offered, waving to the feast spread out on the newspapers. "There's extra paper plates and plastic forks."

His brother Menno reached for a drumstick and took a seat at the table next to Anna.

"And there's plenty of pizza," John offered. "Charley?"

Charley shook his head. "Not hungry."

"No, sit down and join us," Miriam said, suddenly uncomfortable. "We're having lunch."

Charley hooked a thumb in the waistband of his jeans. "I can see that."

Miriam's embarrassment changed to annoyance. Charley was being deliberately difficult. She didn't want to hurt Charley's feelings, but he had no right to act this way. He was making a big thing of her friendship with John, almost as if he were jealous and doing it in front of Menno and Titus.

But then she remembered that he'd told her he wanted to talk to her. He'd tried to talk to her after church and again later on Sunday. She couldn't imagine what he had to tell her, since he'd already shared his news about the new job, but she didn't want to be unkind. "Charley was hired to work on the new construction at the hospital," she said.

John smiled. "Glad to hear it."

"Steady work," Titus said. "I've got a job there, too."

"You're both masons, aren't you?" John asked.

"Ya." Titus pushed a forkful of potato salad into his mouth. "Charley's uncle taught us both the trade. It pays good."

Anna glanced up at Titus, saw him grinning at her and blushed until her cheeks looked like she'd stained them with beet juice. Miriam knew that her sister liked Titus, but he was a good-looking boy, popular with all the girls. And Charley's sister, Mary, had said that Titus was walking out with a girl from one of the neighboring Amish churches.

Miriam didn't know if Menno had a girlfriend, but she doubted that he'd be interested in Anna, either. As much as she loved her twin sister, she was afraid that Anna was too Plain for the boys their age. Most young men, like the English boys, went for cute girls.

John passed a slice of pizza to Titus. Soon everyone was talking and sharing the lunch, all but Charley. He just stood at the end of the table watching Miriam as if he expected her to say something. The trouble was, she didn't know what she was supposed to say.

"I guess we'd better get home," Anna said when they'd finished most of the food. "I don't think we left enough for your family for supper, John."

"That's all right. I'll pick up some sandwiches."

Charley pushed his hat back. "Are you coming to Ruth and Eli's house-raising Saturday?"

He glanced at Miriam, then back at Charley. "Am I invited?"

Charley shrugged his broad shoulders. "Anybody's welcome. At least anybody who knows one end of a hammer from the other. But I guess they don't teach that in college, do they?"

It was John's turn to stiffen and flush to the roots of

his hair. "Not at vet school, at least," he answered as he rose to his feet. "But I can probably muddle through. All right if I come, Miriam?"

"We would be pleased to have you," Anna said quickly.

Miriam scowled at Charley. "We start early. Seven. And don't bring lunch. We'll have plenty at noon."

"Ya." Anna glanced up at Titus through her lashes and smiled. "Plenty of food."

"I have to warn you." Charley shook his head. "It's hard work, raising a house. You may get blisters on those soft hands."

Menno chuckled.

"Don't worry about me, Charley." John seemed to throw back his narrower shoulders. "I'll be there on time and I'll outwork you."

Titus groaned. "These Mennonite boys can be touchy."

For long seconds the air across the picnic table seemed charged with energy and then Charley grinned. "We'll see about that, college boy," he said. "Bring a hammer if you have one." He walked away. "Come on, fellows. I think the cow auction is starting. We wouldn't want to miss anything."

Miriam glared at him. "No, I guess you wouldn't."

John watched as the three walked away across the parking lot. "I want to come to the house-raising, Miriam, but I don't want to make trouble for your family."

"There won't be any trouble," she answered softly. "I don't know what's gotten into Charley. He's not usually like that."

"He's jealous of you and Miriam," Anna told John.

"It was just lunch," Miriam protested. But she knew that wasn't quite true. There was more between her and John than friendship, and Charley had seen it.

Later, on the ride home in the buggy, Anna brought up Charley's rude behavior. "He's jealous, I tell you," she said. "And I'd say Charley has good reason."

"That's silly," Miriam argued, fingering the leather reins in her hands.

"What's silly is my sister has two beaus and I can't get one. How fair is that, I ask you?"

"Stop it. I don't have two beaus."

"You like John." Anna gazed at her earnestly. "Can you deny it?"

"What if I did?"

"It will cause trouble, twin. Mam's Amish now, she thinks Amish. She won't let you run off with a Mennonite. You can count on that. Best you take Charley and be happy with him."

"But I don't love Charley," Miriam said, slapping the lines over Blackie's back so that the gelding broke into a fast trot and the buggy swayed back and forth. "If you like him so well, you take him."

"Gladly," Anna replied sadly. "But we both know that he'd not have me. When I get a husband, *if* I get a husband, he'll be seventy years old with a beard down to his waist and an Adam's apple the size of your *kapp*."

Miriam softened and reached out to pat her sister's hand. "That's not true, Anna." She hesitated. "But what's wrong with John? He's sweet."

"Sweet he may be and easy on the eyes, but he's not Plain. I can't see you going against the family and the church to marry a Mennonite." Anna leaned back on the buggy seat, folding her arms over her ample bosom. "You're playing with fire, if you ask me."

"Maybe I am," Miriam conceded. "But I don't want

to settle. I want what Mam and Dat had…what Ruth and Eli have. I want a love that will last forever."

"And can a Mennonite boy give you that?"

"Not a *Mennonite boy*. John. John Hartman. He's a good man, Anna."

"Do you love him?"

"I don't know." Miriam pressed her lips tightly together. "I guess I just want a chance to find out."

Chapter Seven

After Miriam and Ruth finished milking that evening, Miriam ducked back into the milk house to recover the cell phone. When she turned it on, she saw that it indicated three missed calls—all from John. She didn't want to try and reach him now because she was expected in the kitchen to help put supper on the table. Neither did she feel at ease leaving the phone here. She knew it wasn't logical, but all day, she'd kept worrying that Susanna would find some reason to collect a book off the top shelf and somehow discover the phone.

In some ways, Susanna was a child, but in others, she was smart. She'd recognize the cell phone for what it was and take it straight to Mam. In fact, she wouldn't even wait until Mam got home; she'd probably march it straight to the schoolhouse and tell Mam right in front of all the children, and then everyone in the community would know. Cell phones were not strictly forbidden by the *Ordnung,* because there were no wires or lines connecting the phone to the English world. Some of the men, especially those who had businesses, carried cell phones, but she didn't know of a single woman in Kent County who had one.

She didn't need another thing to worry about. All day she'd been going over what had happened at lunchtime with Charley. The look on his face had really upset her. It bothered her that she had obviously hurt his feelings, but what right did Charley have to be jealous of John? Charley wasn't her boyfriend. Why was he being so difficult? It had been both unlike him and unkind to tease John about his carpentry skills. Yes, John had an education. What was wrong with that? How could he be a veterinarian if he hadn't gone to school for so long? It was unfair to give John a hard time about choices he'd made in his life, especially when their whole community depended on John and his uncle and grandfather.

Her friendship with John meant a lot. And if it was more than friendship, if it was the beginning of something more, she had the right to pursue it, didn't she? Mam would be the first one to urge her to follow her heart, wouldn't she? Hadn't she given up her own faith to become Amish for Dat? And hadn't she found peace and love in the Amish community? What if God had the same intentions for Miriam?

She wanted to ask her mother for advice, but Mam already had so much else on her mind with the wedding and Johanna and the troubles with *Grossmama*. And at some point, Miriam felt as if she had to begin making some of her own decisions. If she was old enough to be thinking about becoming a wife, and God willing a mother, wasn't she old enough to begin making her own decisions?

"Miriam?" Anna called from the back porch.

Miriam glanced back at the top shelf, wondering if

she should return the phone to its hiding place, then decided against it.

"Miriam! Supper!"

That was Mam. And it didn't pay to be late to the table; Mam didn't tolerate tardiness without a good explanation.

Miriam dropped the cell into the deep pocket of her apron, hurried out of the milk house and up to the house.

"What kept you?" Ruth asked when she walked into the kitchen. She was studying her with an expression that said she knew Miriam was up to something.

Miriam put a finger to her lips and silently formed the word, *"Later."*

Ruth scowled, but let it drop.

The household wouldn't be the same once her big sister moved into her own home with Eli. Even though Ruth would only be across the field, Miriam would miss her terribly. She wondered if she should confide in Ruth about the phone, but thought better of it. Ruth already had too much on her mind, too, with the coming wedding and the house construction. This should be a happy time, not one in which she need worry about Miriam's silly little problems.

The delicious odor of potato soup filled the big kitchen. After she'd gotten home from school, Mam had fired up her much beloved black and nickel wood-burning cookstove, made the soup using last night's leftover potatoes and baked a pan of biscuits and three apple pies. Keeping the oven temperature just right on the cookstove was tricky, and Miriam and Ruth much preferred the modern gas range that ran on propane. Fortunately, their kitchen was large enough for both stoves and having two came in handy when there was a lot of baking to do.

Irwin was already at the table, hair slicked straight

back and smelling of hair tonic. Miriam noticed that his straw-colored hair needed cutting again. Irwin was still small for his age, but his hair and ears seemed to grow faster than anyone else Miriam knew. She had to admit that, despite his skinny frame, he was a much more attractive boy than he'd been when he'd first come to live in Delaware.

Mam never did things halfway. Strictly speaking, Irwin was a hired hand, but Mam had taken him under her wing and treated him like a son. She'd bought him sturdy work boots, sewn him new shirts and pants and bought him a Delaware-style Amish straw hat. And when she realized how bad his eyesight was, she'd removed money from the crock in the root cellar and taken him to an optometrist. Now, Irwin sported new wire-frame glasses, was doing much better in his schoolwork and didn't peer down his nose like a weasel at everyone.

Miriam washed her hands, got a pitcher of water and another of milk from the refrigerator and brought them to the table. Eli was there, as usual, seated across from Ruth and staring at her as though she were the prettiest thing he'd ever seen in his life. Susanna took her seat, followed by Mam, Anna and Ruth. Miriam hastily poured drinks for everyone and sat beside Anna. Everyone bowed their heads for silent grace and then they began to eat. Miriam loved Mam's potato soup. She made it with lots of onions and celery. They'd grown a lot of celery in the garden this year and Mam always found ways to use the extra.

"Silas stopped by the school this afternoon," Mam said. "His oldest son is coming from Oregon to take over the farm. Silas and Susan plan to move into the *Grossdaadi* house."

"Eli's been hired to do some renovations to the place,"

Ruth explained. "Silas wants to close in the porch to make a room to fix clocks."

Anna nodded. "Silas's son and daughter-in-law have a big family."

"They do," Mam agreed. "Four younger ones will be coming to school, and I believe there are four older unmarried boys and a grown daughter."

"Four?" Susanna giggled as she buttered a biscuit. "That's good. Maybe one of them will want to marry Anna. Or me!"

"Hush, Susanna." Anna's face flushed. "What a thing to say."

"But you don't have a boyfriend." Susanna waved a dripping spoon. "Roofie has Eli. Miriam has Charley, and—"

"Charley is *not* my boyfriend," Miriam corrected.

Susanna bounced up and down in her chair. "But Anna said so! Anna said he was courting you." She turned to her sister. "Didn't you, Anna?"

"Shh, daughter." Mam passed the honey to Susanna. "Put some of this on your biscuit."

Susanna's round face screwed up. "But Anna did say Charley—"

At that instant, Miriam's pocket began to play a ringtone. Horrified, she snatched the phone out of her apron and fumbled with the buttons in an attempt to shut off the loud country tune. The cell phone slipped through her fingers, hit the floor and slid across the smooth linoleum, coming to rest under the table.

"What was that?" Susanna cried. "Is it a radio?" She peered under the table.

Eli tried to keep a straight face, failed miserably and began to choke into his napkin.

Miriam got down on her hands and knees and scrambled for the phone.

"It is!" Susanna declared, popping her head up over the edge of the table. "It's a radio!"

Miriam reached for the phone just as Irwin gave it a little kick, sending it spinning away to lodge under Anna's chair.

"Irwin!" Miriam squealed.

Irwin snickered. "Sorry." By now, Eli was roaring with laughter and Irwin's terrier was barking loudly and racing around the table.

Anna scooped up the phone, which had begun another round of music, and tossed it to Miriam who turned it off.

Miriam slowly climbed out from under the table, tucked the offending phone back into her apron pocket and took her seat. Anna clamped her hand over her mouth and made muffled noises of amusement. Ruth's lips were pressed tightly together, but she was trying so hard not to laugh out loud that tears were rolling down her cheeks. Eli gave up and fled to the porch, still laughing.

Mam, seemingly deaf and oblivious to the chaos in her kitchen, rose from her chair, went to the stove and filled her soup bowl a second time. "Would anyone like more soup?"

Miriam stared at her. It wasn't possible that Mam hadn't heard the phone ring. "Mam," she began softly. "I—"

"Miriam has a radio," Susanna said. "I want one, too. Can I have a radio, too?" When Susanna said it, it came out more *way-de-o* than *radio,* but everyone understood her perfectly.

"Eli," Mam called. "Would you like to come in off the porch and have more soup?"

He opened the kitchen door and came back in, still red-faced.

Irwin looked from Miriam to Mam and back to Miriam. "She has something in her pocket," he said.

Miriam glared at him.

"I would rather you don't bring your cell phone to family meals," Mam said, returning to the table with another bowl of the steaming soup. "It's not fair to interrupt the rest of us."

Miriam felt as though she was about to burst into tears, and they wouldn't be tears of laughter. "You're right. I'm sorry." She removed the phone from her pocket and held it out to her mother.

"I assume that John lent it to you so that you could... call him if Molly took a turn for the worse." The expression in Mam's gaze was loving and admonishing at the same time. She didn't take the phone. "It may be that there is some problem. Perhaps you should go outside and call him back."

She nodded, feeling like she did the day she'd pulled all the tail feathers out of Aunt Martha's peacock. She'd been ten years old then, but she could still remember this same look from her mother. "I didn't mean for it to disturb supper."

"I'm sure you didn't." Mam glanced around the table. "Who wants apple pie with vanilla ice cream for dessert?"

Miriam carried the cell phone back to the milk house, went inside and closed the door behind her. Her hands were shaking as she punched the button that dialed John.

He answered on the second ring. "Miriam?"

"*Ya.* It's me."

"I was wondering if you'd found a way to go with me

tomorrow to Easton to pick up those supplies for the practice. I don't want to get you in trouble, but...but I really want you to come."

"I promised Mam I'd go to Johanna's tomorrow. To help her with the applesauce. I don't know how to get out of it." She wouldn't tell him about getting caught with the phone, at least not now she wouldn't. The fault was hers. How could she have been so foolish as to leave it turned on in her pocket? Now everyone in the family had had a laugh at her expense, Susanna would spread the news at church and there would be a price to pay later with Mam.

"I'm not leaving until eleven. I have to make two calls first in the morning. If you change your mind, you can reach me. How's Molly?"

"There's still a discharge from the hoof, but I'm cleaning it exactly like you showed me." Now that they were talking about the mare, Miriam felt more comfortable. She knew that she should hang up and return to the house to clean up the supper dishes, but it was nice sitting here in the semi-darkness chatting with John. She loved hearing the sound of his voice, and when he spoke, she could picture him as he'd been at lunch.

Would it be so terrible if she went with him in the truck tomorrow? She wasn't a child. She was a woman grown. Surely, she could ride in a friend's vehicle and have lunch at a restaurant without causing a scandal, couldn't she?

The following morning, Miriam sat across from Johanna at her kitchen table, explaining last night's disaster with the cell phone. Her sister had cut a generous slice of Mam's pie for each of them and had made a pot of herbal tea. Little Jonah was playing on the floor with a wooden top and the baby was asleep upstairs.

"I tell you, Mam didn't blink an eye," Miriam said.

"I wish I could have been there." Johanna chuckled. "I would have loved to see Susanna and that silly Eli."

"But I feel so bad."

"For what? Being young?" Johanna cut off a forkful of pie, bent and popped it into Jonah's mouth.

"More!" he cried.

"No more until after your lunch." Johanna wiped the corner of his mouth with her thumb. "Who didn't eat his cereal this morning?"

"I like pie."

"I'm sure you do. Now, be a good boy and run upstairs and see if Katie is still sleeping."

Obediently, Jonah scampered away to do as she'd asked. When he was safely out of hearing range, Johanna clasped Miriam's hand. "You're doing nothing wrong, sister," she said. "You're *rumspringa*."

"You know our church doesn't recognize *rumspringa*."

"Not *officially,* because they're concerned for our safety." Johanna gave her a sly smile. "But they recognize the *spirit* of it. Within limits. The point is that you're young and not yet baptized. You're supposed to jump the fence now and then."

"But with a Mennonite boy?" Miriam had already told Johanna about John, about how she felt about him and about the invitation to ride to Easton with him. The only thing she hadn't shared was what had happened with Charley and his friends at Spence's.

Johanna squeezed her hand. "The man you pick will be your husband for the rest of your life. Don't choose too hastily and don't close any doors."

"But if…" It was hard to talk about this, even with Johanna, because she didn't know herself what she wanted. "What if I don't know what I want? Who I want? Everyone's trying to pair me up with Charley, but my heart tells me that John…" She let her sentence go unfinished; she didn't know quite what she was trying to say.

Johanna made a small sound of impatience. "You have to be careful with that. Your heart can play tricks on you. You've known Charley all your life. He's a good man, steady and he obviously cares for you. You can't ignore that."

"So you go along with Anna and Ruth? You think that—"

Johanna clapped her hands together once. "Hush. Listen to what I'm saying. No one can tell you who to love. How do you know what path God has chosen for you? Mam was born Mennonite. Is she a bad person?"

"No, but—"

"So. Mam is a good person and John is a good person. But you don't know if you're really attracted to *him* or to the fact that he's different than what you know. John's exciting. He makes your heart race and sends chills down your backbone."

A lump formed in Miriam's throat. "You're teasing me."

"No, I'm not. I'm telling you, don't be afraid to find out what you want. Go with John to Easton. So long as you don't lie to Mam if she asks you where you were today, you haven't done anything terrible."

"But she'll say 'no' if I ask."

"Would she?"

"Maybe I should have asked her."

"What do you want to do, Miriam?"

She looked up shyly at her sister. "I want to go—more than anything."

"Then go. Call him on your fancy red cell phone and tell him you've changed your mind. Go and have a good time." She leaned forward, her elbows on the table. "So long as you don't do anything that would shame Mam or yourself, you have nothing to worry about."

Miriam felt the phone in her pocket. "He may have changed his mind. He may not want me to go now."

Johanna rose and went to a row of pegs on the wall and took down a blue scarf. "Of course, he does. Take this. If you wear my scarf, instead of your *kapp,* the English won't stare at you as they pass by in their vehicles."

"Take off my *kapp?*" Miriam's eyes widened. "What will John think?"

"He'll think you are a pretty girl that he likes having along for the ride. If he is the man you think he is, he will think nothing bad. But if he has other thoughts about one of Hannah Yoder's daughters, improper thoughts, best you learn that right away."

Chapter Eight

John took his eyes off the road long enough to glance at Miriam, sitting beside him in the cab of the truck. "You're not sorry you changed your mind and came along, are you?" he asked her.

She looked up from the radio dial she'd been adjusting, and the expression in her cinnamon-brown eyes answered his question. *"Ne."* She shook her head. "I'm not. Are you sorry you asked me?"

"No way, this has been fun. Really. I'm so glad that you took me up on it."

He couldn't get over how different she looked without her *kapp*. The blue checked headscarf covered only the crown of her head and the bun at the nape of her neck. He hadn't realized how pretty her auburn curls were in the sunlight or how easily she'd been able to slip into his world. He'd expected Miriam to be uncharacteristically quiet—even shy, out of her element—but she wasn't. She'd taken the restaurant in stride, just as she had the unexpected stop to assist an injured cat they found in the road.

They'd come upon the Siamese cat, lying in the other

lane, soon after they'd crossed the Delaware-Maryland line on the way to Easton. Miriam had been out of the truck before he'd even turned off the engine. The animal was bleeding from the mouth and he assumed that a vehicle had hit it. Ignoring his warning to be careful, she'd snatched up a towel from the back of the truck, dashed out into the road and scooped up the cat before an approaching tractor trailer could finish it off.

His method would have been more cautious. He wouldn't have moved the animal until he'd assessed the damages it had suffered and made sure it wouldn't bite him, but Miriam hadn't hesitated. "He's not seriously hurt," she had pronounced, murmuring soothing sounds to the cat as she approached his truck. "He just had the wits knocked out of him. I think he's lost a tooth."

A little water applied to the scrapes and a few moments' time proved Miriam's diagnosis to be top-notch. Within minutes, a woman had come out of a nearby house, claimed the cat and she'd promised to take it to her own vet for a thorough checkup. But since the cat was squalling so indignantly and squirming so strongly, John had to agree with Miriam. The cat may have used up one of its proverbial nine lives, but it seemed fine.

"How did you know that it wasn't hurt badly?" he'd asked Miriam at lunch, over a crab cake sandwich, coleslaw and French fries.

She'd shrugged. "I just knew. Don't you feel it when animals are sick or dying? When you look into their eyes, you can tell."

"Not very scientific."

"*Ne.*" She'd grinned at him. "But there's more to caring for animals than the science of it, isn't there?"

"Are you ever wrong?" he'd asked.

"Only our Lord was perfect. I make mistakes every day." She'd wrinkled her nose mischievously. "I just try not to make the same ones over and over."

Her mention of God had made him a little uneasy. He'd been raised in a Mennonite home, and his mother and sister were active in the church. As a boy, he'd attended the youth functions and never missed services, but he didn't consider himself particularly religious.

"I think you have a gift," he'd said. "Uncle Albert has it. I've seen him treat animals that I've thought would be fine. He believed that they'd die and they did. And I've watched him deliver a seemingly dead calf and bring it back to life."

"Not him," she'd corrected softly. "He may have helped, but it is the Almighty that gives life and takes it away."

"Maybe. Or maybe the God you have such faith in touches some people, giving them knowledge they wouldn't otherwise have."

She'd shrugged again. "We all do our best, John. But we can't save them all. Some animals have a will to live and get better and some give up. I believe Molly's hoof will heal. Don't you?"

He'd been reluctant to answer. The mare's infection was proving difficult and he'd already decided that he'd ask Uncle Albert to come with him when he made his next visit to the Yoder farm. He hoped his uncle would have some idea as to what to do next, because he knew how much the horse meant to Miriam and her family.

"What would your mother say if she knew you were seeing an Amish girl?" she'd asked, changing the subject and surprising him with her candidness.

He'd chuckled. "Am I *seeing* an Amish girl? Is this

what this is? Or is it two colleagues spending an afternoon together?"

"I'll have to think about that," she'd replied as she stole one of his fries, dipped it in ketchup and ate it.

"What about you? Will you be in trouble? If you're seeing an Englisher?"

"You're not English, you're Mennonite."

"Okay. Will you be in trouble if you're dating a Mennonite?"

Miriam had nodded solemnly and then smiled. "Absolutely. But this is my *rumspringa* time. I've got an excuse."

"*Rumspringa,* hmm?"

"*Ya.* Don't you watch television? Some Amish throw off their *kapp*s and run wild."

He'd laughed. "So I've heard." And then he'd leaned closer. "Seriously, you should think about what I said. You have a gift for healing. Have you ever thought of going to veterinary school yourself?"

"Thought of it, but it's impossible," she'd replied. "So long as I remain in the community, my education is finished. My church doesn't believe in an English education. We are Plain people."

He'd wanted to take her hand, but sensed that if he did, she'd retreat from him. Instead, he met her gaze. "But you're different than the others, Miriam. You don't seem to be the kind of person to live your life behind walls."

"Walls to some, maybe," she'd agreed. "Loving arms to others."

"I'd like you to meet my sister sometime. I think you'd like her."

"Is she at home with your mother?"

"No. She's away at school. She's a college sophomore and she's studying to be an elementary teacher."

Miriam had nodded. "I thought about taking the teaching job at Seven Poplars School, when Mam remarries. I think I'd like it, being with the children every day."

"Hannah's getting married?"

She'd shrugged. "It's been two years since Dat died. She'll be expected to take a new husband soon. It's our way."

"And the lucky man?"

She'd then smiled mischievously. "I think it will be Samuel Mast. He's younger than Mam, but he spends a lot of time with his feet under our table. He has five children who need a mother, but he's well set up. His farm is one of the finest in the county. As Anna would say, Samuel is a catch."

"What makes you think it's your mother who attracts him? It might be you he likes."

"Me?" She'd chuckled at the idea. "*Ne.* Not me. Samuel likes women who are more…*meadle.*" She'd used her fingers to tug the corners of her mouth into the caricature of a smile. "A girly-girl. Not so tomboy as me. Samuel would be ashamed to see his wife behind a plow or mending a fence."

"Don't sell yourself short, Miriam," he'd said. "You're special. And if Samuel Mast or any other man can't see that, then he doesn't deserve you."

"And what makes you think I'd want Samuel? Or *any* husband for that matter?"

He'd thrown up his hands in surrender. "I stand corrected." And they'd both laughed easily together.

A few moments later, he'd ordered them each a refill of their sodas to go, and reluctantly, he'd turned toward Kent County and home. She'd remained in the truck, listening to the radio, when he stopped at an Easton veterinary practice and picked up several nineteenth-century veterinary surgical tools that Dr. Bierhorst, who was retiring, was giving to his grandfather. They'd then laughed and talked easily the rest of the way to Seven Poplars.

"Where do you want to get out?" he asked her as he approached the Amish schoolhouse. It was after four, the children had all left and her mother would probably be home at the farmhouse. "Should I take you back to your sister's?"

"Ne." She lifted her chin.

Sunlight, coming through the window, tinted the freckles on her nose the color of gold dust, and he felt a rush of protectiveness. "Where, then?" He didn't want her in trouble for going with him. The truth was, there would be consequences for them both once others found out. *If* others found out.

Neither mother, he suspected, would be happy. His mother would probably be the more upset of the two. His mother held certain beliefs about the Old Order Amish; she thought they were backward and uneducated. He had to agree with her that they were uneducated, he supposed, but many were every bit as intelligent as students that he'd worked with in college. And, as farmers or craftsmen, few could surpass them. He'd always admired the strong work ethic among the Plain people—he'd just never thought that he would be so attracted to a young woman whose background and faith were so different from his own.

"Take me home," Miriam said.

He blinked. "Home?"

"Ya, John."

He liked the way she said his name, the same as everyone else, but different—solid. He smiled at her. "You're brave."

She laughed. "In for a penny, in for a pound." And then her gaze grew pensive. "I went with you and I had a good time. I won't ruin that by lying to my mother."

"Sure, I'll take you home, if that's what you want. But if she doesn't ask where you were—"

She leaned close and brushed his lips with the tips of two fingers. She smelled of green apple shampoo and something elusive, something fresh and sweet, something that brought a constriction to his throat.

"Hush, don't say it. Don't tempt me, John. Believe me, with Mam, it's better to come clean and face whatever storm comes."

Her fingers were warm and her touch was almost a caress. "If your mother is angry with you, Miriam, I should go in with you."

Miriam shook her head. "Tomorrow will be soon enough for that. I know her better than you. Today, she will not want to deal with you. She'll tell me what she thinks and she'll pray tonight. I have no doubt that she'll have plenty of fuss left over for you in the morning…. If you happened to come by to check on Molly."

"If you think that's best. But I feel like a coward."

Miriam chuckled. "Sometimes even the most courageous of men must be diplomatic. If Mam loses her temper with me, we'll hug and make up, but if she loses it with you and says things she later regrets, she will be shamed. You're not one of us, John, and you don't understand our ways. For Mam's sake, wait. I promise you, she may yet burn your ears tomorrow."

Mam was standing on the back porch, arms folded over her chest, watching as John stopped the truck. Miriam could feel her mother's gaze on her as she got out. "See you tomorrow," she called.

"First thing in the morning." John waved at her mother and pulled away. "Hannah."

"So, he drove you home from Johanna's," Mam said as Miriam approached the steps.

Miriam steeled herself. "No. He asked me to ride to Easton and have lunch with him and I did."

"You told me you were going to your sister's."

"*Ya,* Mam. I did, but then I went with John."

Her mother stepped in front of her, blocking her path. "John Hartman is not Amish."

"I know that, Mam."

"Hmm."

A flicker of something that might have been respect flickered in her mother's eyes. Miriam took a deep breath. "I rode in John's truck and ate lunch in a restaurant in the middle of the day. I did nothing to be ashamed of. You have my word."

"So, my daughter comes and goes as she pleases without a word to me?"

Miriam touched her arm. "I have to see for myself, to know which path God wants me to take."

Mam nodded. "So I told your uncle. Reuben saw you in John's truck and came here after school to tell me. He asked me if I knew what you were doing."

Miriam swallowed. "What did you tell him?"

Hannah folded her arms over her chest. "I said that he should take care of his daughter and leave you to me and your sisters."

Miriam's eyes widened. "You didn't!"

"*Ya,* she did." Anna pushed open the screen door and

stepped onto the porch. "You should have seen the look on Uncle Reuben's face."

"He wasn't happy," Ruth called over Anna's shoulder. "A fine mess you've made, Miriam. Today, of all days."

Miriam glanced back at her mother. "Why? What's wrong? Is someone sick?"

"We are all well, except for Rebecca," Mam said. "I had a phone call at the chair shop today from Rebecca. Eli had to fetch me from the school. *Grossmama* has had a bad week. She tried to push Ida down the stairs and she gave Rebecca a black eye."

"*Grossmama* hit her? Poor Rebecca!" Miriam said.

"Ida thinks her mother and Jezebel and your sisters should come here now, instead of waiting for Ruth's wedding," Mam said, going back up the steps to the porch. "I agree. Your grandmother is too much for Leah and Rebecca right now. I told them to arrange for a driver and I would pay the cost."

"I'm so glad," Miriam cried, following her. "I've missed Leah and Rebecca so much."

"We've been cleaning," Anna said. "Getting the bedrooms ready for *Grossmama* and Great Aunt Jezebel."

"When are they coming?" Miriam asked.

"As soon as Leah can hire a van," Mam said. "I should have insisted they come home before this. It was too much on your sisters."

Miriam took her mother's hand and they followed Anna and Ruth into the kitchen. "Will they be here before the house-raising on Saturday?"

Mam shrugged. "Who can say? But we have more than enough to keep us busy. Your *Grossmama* was never easy, and she will be even more difficult, now that she's not herself."

"And she hates us," Susanna piped up from where she stood near the stove. She'd obviously been baking because there were sugar cookies cooling on the table, and she had flour all over her apron and on her nose.

"Not hate," Mam corrected. "That is not a word we use, Susanna. We hate no one."

"Bad people?" Susanna suggested.

"*Ne.* We hate no one," Mam repeated firmly. "I'm sorry to say that I'm not her favorite person, but I don't believe that *Grossmama* hates me."

"So why can't Aunt Martha take her?" Miriam asked. "*She's* her daughter."

"Because *Grossmama* dislikes Aunt Martha even more than she does Mam," Ruth said, a smile tugging at the corners of her mouth.

Mam put an arm around Miriam's shoulder. "Enough of such talk, girls. Your Aunt Martha has her own burdens to bear. Imagine what living in this house would be like if we could not have peace in our own kitchen? If a mother and daughter were constantly at odds? You should find charity in your hearts for your aunt, not criticize her."

"Aunt Martha is too much like *Grossmama*," Anna mused.

"That may be," Mam said, "for people sometimes suggest that my daughters are as wayward as I was."

"You, wayward? Never." Miriam pinched a broken piece of cookie from the table and popped it in her mouth.

"In any case, your grandmother, her sister Jezebel, and Leah and Rebecca will be here in a matter of days," Mam said, "and we must be ready to welcome them."

"On top of the house-raising," Ruth reminded.

"So…" Mam's eyes narrowed. "Miriam. Where is your

kapp? Don't tell me you went among the English with your head covered only by a scarf?"

"I thought it would cause less talk."

"A scarf is a head covering," Anna put in hopefully. She was a good sister, always there to defend Miriam.

"But not Plain enough when among the English. Next time, you will wear your *kapp* or not go into a restaurant at all." Mam arched an eyebrow. "Unless you're ashamed of us."

"Ne," Miriam said. "I'm not ashamed of my faith."

"Praise God for that, at least." Her mother turned away. "Go on, now, and help your sisters with the upstairs floors. I'll cook supper."

"But the chickens need—"

"Irwin is tending the animals. You need not concern yourself until milking time. And one more thing." Her mother turned back, both hands resting on her hips.

"Ya?"

"You had a visitor this afternoon. Just before Uncle Reuben arrived."

"Who?" Miriam asked.

"Charley. He wanted to talk to you. He says he's been trying all week."

Miriam's heart sank. "Charley Byler?"

Anna snickered. "And what other Charley has been mooning around our back door like a lovesick calf?"

"He tells me he has promise of steady work," Mam said. "And he asked my permission to court you."

Chapter Nine

By eight on Saturday morning, the sound of hammers and saws echoed across the Yoder farm. The day was bright, the grass still damp with dew and the air redolent with the first hint of autumn. Next to Hannah's house, women and girls set up tables in the yard, while boys took charge of arriving horses and buggies. At the construction site across the field, six men were already raising the frame of the first wall on Ruth's new home. Friends and neighbors were coming from every direction, on foot, in wagons piled high with lumber and on push-scooters.

At the site of the new house, Miriam, Ruth and Anna walked among the newcomers, offering mugs of steaming coffee, paper cups of apple cider and apple donuts dusted with sugar that Anna had just pulled from the oven. Ruth's cheeks glowed pink with excitement as she tossed a hot donut to Eli.

"Who made this?" he asked with a grin. "You or Anna?"

"Eat it and guess," Ruth replied.

He propped his hammer against the foundation, took a bite of the cake and teasingly held it out to her. "Good. Really good. Must be Anna's."

Giggling, Ruth snatched the donut and ran off to finish it, while Eli mimed his loss to his laughing companions.

As a wedding gift, Mam had given Ruth thirty acres of land with fine road frontage, across from the chair shop where Eli worked. Unsaid, but understood, was that if he worked hard, Eli would someday become a partner with Roman in the business that Dat had started years ago.

No wonder Ruth was so happy; she had a good man who loved her and her friends and neighbors were building them a new house and barn. And perhaps, best of all, she'd never have to be far away from Mam and Susanna and Johanna. She'd always have the blessings of church and family close around her.

Anna, on the other hand, seemed a little wistful to Miriam this morning. Anna would never envy a spoonful of joy of her sisters', but it had to hurt that at twenty-one, no one had ever asked to drive her home from a singing or chose her picnic basket at a school auction. No boy had ever come courting Anna and none had tried to steal a kiss behind the schoolhouse. What Anna had said was true. It wasn't fair that Miriam had two fellows wanting to walk out with her while Anna had none.

Please, God, Miriam prayed silently. *Can't You send someone who doesn't care that my sister is so Plain? Someone who can see past her big hands and broad shoulders to the beauty inside?*

"Anna!" a male voice called.

Miriam turned hopefully to see who was calling her sister's name, but her heart sank when she saw that it was only Samuel, wanting coffee and a donut. Why couldn't it have been Roland or Titus seeking her out, or even one of the boys from the other Amish churches?

"Good donuts," Samuel said, reaching for a second. "You make the best apple donuts, Anna."

Peter and Rudy ran up, and each waited for a donut. If Samuel wasn't there, they would have begged Anna and she would have given them one, no matter how many they'd already had, but they had a healthy respect for their father. The two were mischievous, but they usually pulled their pranks out of Samuel's sight.

Anna took pity on them and handed each one a donut. "Are you boys helping with the building?"

"Ne," Samuel said, removing his hat and wiping the sweat off his forehead. "These rascals would be more in the way than they're worth. Back to Hannah's with the two of you," he ordered. "Tend to the horses and do whatever the women ask."

"Daa-t," Rudy whined. "Can't we—"

"Off with you."

Peter looked at Anna, hoping for support, but she shrugged and the two dashed off toward the big house.

"Good coffee, too," Samuel told Anna, holding up his mug. "Strong, like I like it."

"Samuel!" Roman called. "We need you on this beam."

Samuel lingered for a moment. "Well, duty calls." He nodded to Miriam and Anna and strode back toward the spot where the men waited to raise another wall.

Anna watched him walk away, a big man, tall and broad, nearing forty, and in the prime of his strength. "He'll make a good stepfather," she said. "He'll provide well for Mam and Susanna."

Miriam nodded. The thought of her mother remarrying was beginning to become more acceptable. No one would ever take the place of Dat. No one could. But Samuel would be kind to Susanna and Mam would have the

little boys she'd always wanted. Peter and Rudy needed
a mother, as did their younger sisters. It would be a sensible match, with the two farms running side by side.

"I'll have some of that cider."

Anna poked Miriam. "You awake?"

Miriam realized that someone had been speaking to
her. She'd been so lost in her thoughts that she hadn't
noticed. She turned and nearly bumped into Charley.

"I thought I'd best get some of those donuts before
Samuel and his twins ate them all," he said.

"Help yourself," she said, giving him her full attention.

He took a mug of cider from her tray. "Good day for
a house-raising."

She nodded. It was a good day and she was grateful
to God for the kind weather. A hard rain would have
delayed the construction, but this day was perfect, not
too hot, with a light breeze. "The house will be perfect
for them. You did a fine job on the foundation, Charley.
I know Ruth and Eli are grateful for your hard work."

A slow smile spread across his face. He *was* a nice-
looking boy, with an honest chin and warm eyes. "I try
my best," he said.

She nodded. "I mean it. Everyone knows how solid
your work is. You deserve the new position helping build
the new wing at the hospital."

Anna moved away, leaving them in what would be
the barnyard of the new place. The grass here was nearly
knee-high in places, and the last of the Queen Anne's
lace and black-eyed Susans lingered, adding their white
and gold and brown to the green carpet that spread out
around them. Usually, the cows pastured here, but Mam
had kept them out of the field for the last two months,

due to the construction. Eli would probably get a good hay crop off his acres before winter.

"Oops." Charley laughed as a honeybee landed on the rim of his cup. "Wouldn't want to swallow that."

"Your cider would have a kick," she agreed, with a chuckle.

"Ya." He nodded and took a sip of cider. "Heard your grandmother isn't coming, after all. That's too bad. I know Leah and Rebecca would have liked to have been here for this."

"All the arrangements were made, then *Grossmama* fell again. The same hip. The doctor says she can't travel for now." She met Charley's gaze, knowing he would understand how her heart went out to her sisters. "Poor Leah and Rebecca, they're having a time. But both refused to come home when Mam offered to try to make other arrangements."

"Your sisters are nice girls. Of course, I think all the Yoder girls are." He cut his eyes at her.

Miriam smiled at him. She just couldn't help herself. Charley always made her feel good about herself. "You should go back to work."

"I should. But listen, I need you to do something for me. I want you to send Irwin with the refreshments," Charley said. "Later, when all the men get here. The talk might get a little rough." He grimaced. "Not for your ears."

"I'll keep that in mind." She didn't know that she agreed with him necessarily, but she appreciated his thoughtfulness.

"Men tell jokes. Sometimes they are not...what you would hear at church." He glanced at his feet. "No harm is meant, but..."

She touched his sleeve. "It's okay. I understand."

"Good." He looked up. "You and Anna, any of you, shouldn't hear such things."

"And women talk about matters men certainly don't want to hear," she told him. "So we're even."

"We're even." He nodded with a smile.

"Now, I'll ask something of you, Charley," Miriam said. "Be pleasant to John, if he comes."

"What? You think he might not show?"

"I don't know if he will or not. He might be called out on a case. But if you're mean to him, I'll be very unhappy. It wouldn't be fair. Most of the people here are Amish. He might feel like an outsider."

"He *is* an outsider, Miriam. That's the thing. He's a nice guy. I like John, but he isn't one of us." He looked right into her eyes. "And he isn't for you."

She stiffened. "That's for *me* to say, not you."

"Miriam! I'm going back to the house for more coffee and donuts," Anna called. "That second batch should be out by now."

She shoved the tray of cider into Charley's hands. "Wait! I'll come with you!"

"Dangi," Charley called after her. "For the cider."

"Just remember what I said about John. Don't be rude to him."

"Wouldn't think of it."

As Miriam and Anna walked away, Anna leaned close and whispered, "You're too hard on him."

Miriam sighed. "You're probably right. It's just that I don't know what to do about him. For years, he was content to be the boy I'd play in the mud with. Now, he wants more of me, and I… I don't know if I can give that."

"Well, just be sure that's really how you feel," Anna

said. "Some other girl will snatch him up and you may be sorry." She took Miriam's hand. "Like what happened to Johanna's Roland."

"Johanna's Roland?" Miriam stared at her in surprise. "I know they used to walk out together, but that was before she met Wilmer. She's a married woman. You shouldn't say such things about our sister. That's all in the past."

"Mmm," Anna replied. "*Ya,* it is in the past, but it's still what happened. If Johanna and Roland hadn't argued, he might be our brother-in-law instead of Wilmer. And I think Johanna would be a lot happier." She whispered the last sentence in Miriam's ear.

Miriam stopped and looked into Anna's eyes. "Do you know something I don't? Has Johanna complained about her husband?" she asked, in shock.

Anna shook her head. "*Ne.* Johanna would never complain, but I watch her. I see her look at Roland sometimes, when she thinks no one is watching. Her heart is heavy, twin."

Miriam thought about what Anna was saying. "I've never really liked Wilmer, but he's a devoted church member and he provides well for his family. What do you think is wrong? What have I missed?"

"Sometimes I don't think you notice what's in front of your nose."

"What haven't I noticed?" Miriam asked, feeling badly that she hasn't been more aware of what was going on in her dear sister's life.

Anna bent and picked a black-eyed Susan. For a few seconds, she twirled it between her big, plump fingers and then began to pluck the petals, one at a time. "It is wrong to bear false witness and wrong to gossip, but my heart aches for Johanna, so to you, I will confide what I suspect."

Miriam waited, her breath caught in her throat.

"Do you see Wilmer playing with Jonah?"

"*Ne.* I never have, but I thought that maybe when he was older…" She trailed off. "Not all men are like Samuel or our Dat. Many don't have an easy way with young ones."

"Wilmer is dark—dark beard, dark bushy eyebrows, swarthy skin. Roland is fair, as is little Jonah."

"What of it? Johanna is a redhead like the rest of us. It's only natural that Jonah be fair-skinned with light hair. He takes after our family."

"And the baby, Katie? She is dark-haired like Wilmer, *ne?*"

Miriam took a step back. "Stop it, Anna. That's evil. You're not suggesting that Wilmer isn't Jonah's father, are you?"

Anna's eyes grew hard as winter wheat. "I would never suggest such a terrible thing. You know our Johanna. Pure she was on her wedding night. Mam and I washed her sheets. I saw the proof with my own eyes."

"Then why would you think such a thing?" Miriam shook her head. She'd never expected to hear such words out of Anna's mouth—not Anna. She thought well of everyone.

"I'm afraid Wilmer thinks otherwise," Anna confessed. "When Jonah was born, he took one look at him and walked out of the house. He didn't speak to Johanna until the following day, and I heard her tell Mam that Wilmer asked whose child he was."

"Such wickedness. He's a stupid man. Too foolish to

realize what a good wife he has. But that was more than three years ago, nearly four. Surely, he can't..."

Anna shrugged. "All I know is that last year, when things seemed really bad between them, I saw Johanna with a bruise on her face. She said that she'd bumped into a pantry door, but there were also bruises that looked like fingerprints on her wrist. Mam went to Bishop Atlee. I don't think Wilmer has struck her again, but something is wrong in that house."

"And you never told me?"

"It was a great weight on my heart." She plucked the last petal from the black-eyed Susan and tossed the broken flower away. "Why should I burden you when I could pray for them myself? And I do, every night."

"Then why tell me now?"

Anna was thoughtful for a moment. "Because I think Johanna chose the wrong man. And I want to make sure that you, my dear twin, don't make the same mistake. You and I are almost the same person, despite our outward differences. Better for you to be an old maid like me than to make a bad marriage and live to regret it."

Miriam's knees went weak. How could this all have happened without her knowledge? And how could Anna have borne this trouble alone? "You think I mean to choose John? And leave the faith?"

"I believe John is a good person. I can't say what life God intends for you. Just be certain it's not the world that calls to you, rather than the man. You are wise in so many ways, much smarter than I am. But when it comes to simple truths, you sometimes rush past without seeing what is in front of you."

Miriam looked away. "You mean Charley. You think I'm discounting him?"

"I mean you must think about what is best for you. Not for the family. Not even for the church. Ask the Lord for guidance. Whatever you choose, this man or that, or none, I will always love you, Miriam. And I will always be there for you."

"Don't be so quick to judge yourself, Anna, or to say that you aren't smart. That's not true."

Anna sighed. "Which of us sat through third grade classes for two years, and which twin skipped the fifth grade?" Tears welled in her dark brown eyes. "It doesn't matter that I'm not a person for books. I bake the best apple donuts in the county, don't I?"

"In the country. No one in Ohio or Pennsylvania can touch you."

Her sister's eyes lit up with a smile. "Don't say such things. Would you have me guilty of *hochmut?*"

Miriam chuckled and they started to walk again. "A little of my own *hochmut* wouldn't hurt you. I have more than enough to share."

Anna's expression grew serious. "I do worry about my pride in my cooking. The Bible tells us that it is a bad thing."

"But honesty is right and good. And didn't Jesus tell us that we must love ourselves? You're a treasure. We all know it and you should, too."

"If only some young man would see it."

"Someone will," Miriam promised, grabbing her hand and squeezing it.

"That's what Mam says, but…" She sighed.

"No buts, twin. Who knows what could happen? You may marry before me. I think I like *rumspringa.* I may decide to stay single for years."

"Not too many, I hope. Your children will be as dear

to my heart as the ones I will never mother. Unless some widower with eleven children takes pity on me." Anna giggled. "Not that I would mind stepchildren, but I look at Johanna's baby and I long for one of my own."

"All in His time." The beep of a horn behind her caught Miriam's attention and she turned and looked over her shoulder. John had just pulled into the yard beside the foundation of the new house. Behind his truck was a trailer piled high with a bathtub, sink and toilet. "Look!" Miriam pointed, turning back toward the new house. "John did come. What's all that stuff?"

"I don't know," Anna said. "But I'd guess it's a bathroom for Ruth and Eli. Let's go back and see."

"Charley won't like it," Miriam said. "Didn't he tell us to stay away from the work site?"

"Ya," Anna agreed. "But you had no intention of doing so, did you?"

Miriam laughed. *"Ne."*

"Nor me," Anna said, giggling. "Anybody who's been anywhere near Irwin when he's cleaning the pigpen would have heard those bad words already."

They strolled back across the field toward John's truck. He saw them coming and waved. Miriam stopped a few yards away, folded her arms over her chest and motioned to the trailer with her chin. "What's all that?"

John beamed. "For the house. One of Uncle Albert's clients is remodeling his house. They were going to throw everything in the dump. It's hardly been used at all. The tub and sink were from a guest bathroom. I hope they won't mind blue. For free?"

"Surely they should pay something," Miriam said. "They couldn't mean to give them away."

John shook his head. "Mr. O'Malley said Eli would be

doing him a big favor if he took them off his hands. He'd have to pay to dispose of them and you pay by weight." The other men had stopped work and were walking toward the trailer. "Eli!" John called. "Take a look at this and see what you think."

Anna glanced at Miriam. "A whole bathroom! Lucky for Ruth and Eli."

"Ya," Miriam agreed.

"These friends of John's are good people to share what they didn't need and John was good to think of it." Anna grimaced. "But what will Aunt Martha say if Ruth gets a *blue* toilet?"

Miriam laughed, putting her arm around her sister's waist. "The Lord *does* provide. And who are we to show *hochmut* and be too proud to use an Englishman's john?"

Chapter Ten

Charley knew he was in trouble when he saw John pull a tool belt from the bed of his pickup. He'd expected that John would bring a new hammer with the price tag still on it and little else. Instead, the wide leather belt that the Mennonite strapped around his waist was obviously well-used and of professional quality. Either John had borrowed an experienced carpenter's tools, or he had more experience than hammering just a few nails.

The day just seemed to get worse from there.

It wasn't long before John proved his worth in the construction, and Charley felt himself hard put to keep up with him. John not only knew the trade, but he was a hard worker who didn't mind taking orders from their gang boss. Charley's only saving grace was that while John might have been even more skilled with a hammer, Charley was definitely stronger, and was called upon several times when there was a heavy job to be done. Charley was ashamed that he'd misjudged the vet so quickly when he obviously hadn't known anything about him.

Charley didn't usually draw conclusions about people without careful consideration, but he felt a natural competition with John from the first day they'd met, when Miriam had been all smiles introducing them. The thing was, he genuinely liked John. It was just that he felt threatened by John's obvious interest in Miriam.

An hour after John arrived, his uncle Albert and three other Mennonite boys showed up, ready to pitch in. "Sorry to come late," Albert said after he'd introduced his team. "I had an emergency at the office this morning."

"Glad to have you," Eli said. "The more hands, the quicker the work goes." Eli glanced at John. "He's no stranger to hard work."

Albert smiled and nodded. "He put himself through college working construction." Albert walked to the rear of his truck and fired up a gas-powered generator. In the bed of the truck were several different kinds of electric saws that could be run off the generator. "I thought we could set up a saw table."

"Sounds good to me," Eli shouted, above the roar of the motor. "Power saws will make the construction go even faster."

"Let's get this section up!" Samuel gave the signal, and the six men on his team, including John, began the strenuous task of raising the west wall of the house.

Charley threw his weight into the frame. The six of them lifted the heavy wooden structure into place, and Samuel and Eli began to attach braces. Charley pulled a handful of nails out of the bag on his belt and began hammering them in, securing the bottom wall plate to the floor joist. Beside him, John was doing the same thing. John's hammer struck with a steady rhythm and Charley quickened his pace to keep up.

Beside the house, Albert Hartman switched on a circular saw he'd plugged into his generator. Other men,

Amish and Mennonite, carried lengths of marked lumber to be cut to size. From the other sides of the house, Charley could hear framing going up. Nearly thirty men had gathered to help with the house-raising, while another ten, under Johanna's husband's supervision, were working on Eli's new barn.

The more experienced men were detailed to the house site, while the boys and less-skilled carpenters built the stable and assembled a windmill. The barn had to be solid and waterproof, but the county inspector wouldn't be nearly as particular about that structure as he would the house. Neither would be wired for electricity; that went without saying.

By the time the dinner bell rang for the midday meal, Charley's shirt and hair were damp with sweat. His arms ached and his fingers had cramped from driving nails steadily for hours. John seemed equally ready for a break, but Charley watched to see that they laid down their hammers at the same time.

Unhooking their tool belts, they left them lying on the house's plywood subfloor and walked across the field toward Hannah's house and the waiting food. Neither Charley nor John spoke directly to each other, although there was plenty of easy talk and joking as the group of men prepared to fill their empty bellies and quench their thirsts.

When they reached the farmyard, men ahead of them had already lined up by the pitcher pump to wash their hands and faces. Charley motioned to John. "Over here," he said, leading the way to another faucet at the base of the Yoder's windmill. One of the girls had left a cake of soap and fresh towels.

John pulled off his ball cap, bent and stuck his head

under the running water. His brown hair was cut short and he didn't seem to mind when his blue T-shirt took a fair share of wetting. Charley handed him a towel, and then began washing up.

Miriam came up behind them. "Food's on," she said. "Take a seat wherever you like at the tables."

Charley ran a hand through his wet hair, slicking it back off his face before putting his straw hat back on. Just looking at Miriam made his heart feel too big for his chest. He knew that a man wasn't supposed to dwell on outer appearances, that what was inside a person mattered more. But Miriam was so beautiful, like a butterfly in her lavender dress and starched white *kapp*.

He wanted to pull her into his arms and inhale the clean, sweet scent that was hers alone, but he knew better. If he tried to take advantage of their friendship, who could guess what she'd do? She'd certainly be angry. She'd push him away, maybe even shove him backward into the mud puddle and make a fool of him in front of John.

Charley knew he had no right to claim Miriam as his own; she'd given him no indication that she felt the same way about him. But every drop of blood in his body told him that this was the only woman for him. He might find someone else, marry her, make a family and live a Plain life, but he'd never feel the joy that burst inside him like Fourth of July firecrackers every time Miriam smiled at him.

He'd heard that she'd gone off with John in his truck without a chaperone. Everyone in the neighborhood had heard. Word was that Reuben had gone to the house to scold Hannah for letting Miriam run around with a Mennonite boy, but no more had come of it.

Most likely, Hannah had told her brother-in-law to mind his own business. Hannah was no shrinking violet. She'd always stood up for her girls with all the pluck of a banty hen with a flock of chicks.

Miriam was like her mother Hannah in a lot of ways. She was strong. She'd make a good wife and a good mother. If he couldn't have her—if he lost her to John— he'd have to seriously consider leaving Kent County. He'd never be happy here, seeing her with another man, knowing they could never be together.

"Thanks for coming," Miriam was saying to John. "And tell your uncle and the others from your church how much we appreciate it."

John grinned.

Girls would think the Mennonite was decent-looking, Charley supposed. Not too old to marry for the first time, maybe twenty-nine or thirty. John's features were even and pleasant. He had good white teeth and eyes that met yours straight on when he spoke.

Charley didn't doubt that most girls would think John was a lot more handsome than he himself was. Charley didn't waste much time looking in a mirror, except to shave and he didn't grow a lot of beard to begin with. But he wasn't pie-faced or cross-eyed, at least, and he had a chin, not like his friend Menno whose jaw kind of melted into his neck.

Charley's eyes were a clear blue and his sandy hair was thick and a little unruly. He might not be as tall as John, but he had strong shoulders and good arms. He doubted that John could lift a three-month-old calf over his head without breathing hard...or guide a horse-drawn plow from sunup to sundown.

No, he was no Eli, who had a face that could sell toothpaste. He was just ordinary Charley. But his love for Miriam Yoder wasn't ordinary and he meant to marry her before the church and cherish her all the days of his life. He'd not give her up without a fight and he'd be boiled for an egg if he'd let a Mennonite in a blue truck come between them.

All Charley had to do was convince *Miriam* that he was the man for her…

Somehow, Charley and John ended up sitting at the table, side by side. They had a place halfway down, right in their age group, between the young men, old enough to do a full day's work, and the married men. The older fellows, the preachers, Bishop Atlee, the deacons and John's uncle Albert were at a second table under the shade trees. The younger table was definitely the livelier of the two, with lots of laughter and joking. Charley always enjoyed this kind of fellowship with the men in his community, both married and unmarried. Days like this had a way of building bonds that would last a lifetime.

"More tea?"

Charley turned to see Miriam standing beside him, a brimming pitcher of iced tea in her hands. *"Dangi,"* he said. He offered his empty glass and Miriam filled it to overflowing. When a little spilled over, he set it down and licked his fingers.

"John? Would you like some?"

Charley was surprised when John said that he did. He'd hardly sipped his tea, and he hadn't eaten more than a little girl. He wondered if maybe Amish food didn't suit John. There was plenty to be had: every kind of meat, from baked ham to fried chicken, fried rabbit, hamburgers, hot dogs, turkey legs and platters of cold cuts.

Bowls of macaroni salad, potato salad, three bean salad, Dutch slaw and cabbage-filled peppers were crowded beside tureens of hash browns and potato dumplings. Platters of deviled eggs, cheese, bread, celery and fried eggplant were surrounded by pickles, chowchow and vegetables of all kinds. There'd be more desserts than a sensible man could eat, but Charley didn't want to ruin his appetite until he'd finished the main courses. With all the work to be done this afternoon, he needed to keep up his strength.

"I can't believe how fast the house is going together," John said to Miriam.

"That's the idea. It's why so many people come together to help," she answered.

Charley didn't like the tone of her voice: soft, flirtatious. He could just see her out of the corner of his eye. Thinking fast, he drank his tea in three long gulps and held up his glass. "Miriam. I'd appreciate—"

"Maybe I should bring you a pitcher of your own," she teased, but she came back around him, away from John, and refilled the glass.

But John was sneaky. He tipped over his glass as pretty as could be, spilling tea on the tablecloth and on himself and Charley. "Oops. Miriam. I think I need a refill, too."

Charley wiped at his pant leg as the other guys at the table, knowing full well it hadn't been an accident, began to laugh. "Miriam, you'd better bring a barrel of tea for those two," Titus called.

"A wagon load," Menno chimed in.

Charley put his hand on the pitcher to keep her from returning to John. "What would you suggest for sweets?" he asked.

"Her!"

Whoever that wiseacre is will pay, Charley thought. "Mind your mouth," he snapped, throwing a warning glance in the direction of the guys seated across the table from him and John. "Miriam? Pie or cake? What looks best?"

"No dessert for you until you finish your dinner," she said. "John's plate is clean." She had an innocent expression on her face, but mischief twinkled in her eyes.

Charley knew that she was on to him when she pried his fingers off the iced tea pitcher.

She made a point of turning her attention to John. "John, would you like me to get you a clean glass?"

"I can get it, if you'll just show me the way." He was off the bench before she could answer and the other boys at the table hooted and stamped their feet. Before Charley could come up with anything equally clever to do, Miriam and John walked away, leaving Charley staring at a full glass of iced tea, two chicken legs and a mound of potato salad.

Anna, having witnessed the whole thing from the end of the table, walked over and leaned over Charley's shoulder. "Would you like to try some apple cider? Might have better luck."

He looked up to see her smiling at him and wiped at his wet pant leg that was now sticky. "I think I'm already all wet."

"Not to worry," she soothed, quietly, her words meant only for him. "Miriam's coming to the young people's singing tonight, and it's Amish only. John won't be invited. You'll have her all to yourself."

He nodded and reached for the piece of chicken on his plate. Maybe Miriam would let him drive her home from the gathering. When he got her alone, he could ask if he could court her. Now that he'd spoken with Hannah, he was free to do so. He doubted John had gotten *that* far, otherwise he'd have surely heard. Things might be dark, but he hadn't lost yet. He still had a chance to win her heart, and the singing would be the perfect place to begin.

"I think you spilled the tea on purpose," Miriam said, when she handed John a new glass. "That wasn't very kind."

"No," he agreed. "It wasn't, was it?" He grinned. "I don't think Charley likes me very much."

"That's not it." She hesitated, trying to figure out how to explain her situation with Charley to John. Then she just came out with it. "Charley wants to court me. He hasn't asked me yet, but only because he hasn't been able to catch me alone. He already spoke to Mam."

John's gaze grew serious. "What are you going to say?"

She shrugged. "I don't know. That's the problem." She pressed her lips together.

He nodded. "It's a big decision. You should keep in mind that you have, you know, other options."

She looked up at him. "Do I?"

"Miriam!" Ruth called from across the yard. "We need more tea at the bishop's table."

"Guess I'm keeping you from your work. I'll get their table."

John picked up a second pitcher and she was filled with a pleasant surprise. Dat had been a great man, but never, in her life, had she seen him tend to such a menial task. "That's women's work."

"With Gramps and Uncle Albert, I'm the serving boy.

I'm good at this. Watch me." John winked at her and strode toward the seniors' table. Some of the older men rolled their eyes, but either John didn't notice, or didn't care. He started refilling glasses and taking orders like he'd been doing it all his life.

Maybe he had, she thought. What did she know about how Mennonites did things? Or the English? Maybe men outside the Amish community washed dishes at their wife's side and swept front porches after supper. She knew so little about the outer world, and she had to admit, she was curious.

Uncle Reuben said something to John and waved him to an empty seat beside him. John glanced up at her, nodded to Reuben and sat down, placing the now-empty pitcher on the table.

Johanna came up beside Miriam, watching her, watching John. "People are talking about you and John," she whispered. "Better be careful."

"They wouldn't be talking if Charley wasn't so silly. He made a scene and called attention to us."

"Right." Johanna chuckled. "Speaking of making a scene, have you seen our mother?" She gestured toward the back porch where Mam seemed deep in conversation with a man in a blue checked shirt. "John's Uncle Albert. Albert Hartman."

"He's our guest. She has to be nice to him."

"Nice or *nice?*" Johanna put a finger to her lips and snickered.

"What do you mean?"

"While you're busy flirting with Charley and John, Mam's not above a little flirting of her own."

"I was not flirting!" Miriam's mouth gaped. "And how can you say such a thing about Mam?"

Johanna chuckled. "Use your eyes." She motioned toward their mother and Albert Hartman. "You know, they were sweet on each other when they were young."

"She'd never consider a Mennonite. She might have grown up Mennonite, but she's Amish now." She turned to her sister. "She would never—would she?"

"Maybe the two of you aren't as different as you think," Johanna said with a shrug. "Maybe Mam is using Albert to push Samuel into popping the question. After all, Samuel's been putting his feet under her table for more than a year without ever coming right out and asking her to marry him."

"Maybe," Miriam agreed. "Or maybe God's will is more mysterious than we can understand. Maybe He wants women to follow their hearts, not their heads, even if it means taking a road less traveled."

"Some of the boys want cider," Dorcas said, approaching the drink table and filling her pitcher. She glanced at Johanna. "Did you tell her?"

"Ya." Johanna folded her arms. "Like I told you, it's nothing. Charley was making a joke, is all. Just being Charley."

Dorcas drew herself up to her full height and dried her hands on a towel. "You poke fun at him and it's wrong," she said. "He's worth two of that Mennonite boy."

Miriam prayed for patience. Dorcas was Anna's best friend. "I haven't done anything wrong."

"Flirting, leading a good man on. You call that right?" Dorcas sniffed. "My mother saw you, and she'll go to Hannah. You don't set a good example for the younger girls—how to act. Maybe you should think more about the hereafter and joining church, than riding in pickup trucks and making a scandal."

"And maybe you should think more for yourself, Dorcas, and not parrot everything your Mam says." Johanna dumped a scoopful of ice into her cousin's tea pitcher. "You might get a boyfriend or two of your own if you laughed more and criticized less."

Two bright pink patches glowed on Dorcas's cheeks as she snatched up the pitcher and hurried away.

"That was harsh," Miriam murmured to her sister.

Johanna shrugged. "Harsh but true. She needs somebody to set her straight or she'll never find a husband. She acts like she's forty."

"She's right, though. Aunt Martha will blame Mam for what I did. She always does."

"Don't worry about Mam. She can handle Aunt Martha."

"You girls serving or gossiping?"

Miriam whirled around, surprised to find Charley standing so close behind her. She felt her face grow hot and hoped he hadn't overheard what she and Johanna had been saying to each other.

"What do you want now?" she demanded.

"More tea." He held out an empty glass.

Her eyes widened, and Johanna giggled.

Charley laughed and lowered his glass. "*Ne.* I'm teasing you. I've had more than enough." He looked down at his damp trousers. "I'm not sure whether I'm wearing more iced tea than I drank or not. I came over because I wanted to ask you to ride home from the singing with me tonight."

"I think I'd best find something to do…somewhere else," Johanna said, walking away.

"*Ne.*" Miriam grabbed her sister's arm.

"So, will you, Miriam? Will you ride home with me tonight?" Charley pressed.

"Say *ya, Miriam!*" yelled Menno and Titus and Roland and a half dozen more young men at the table, all together.

"You know you want to," Menno added.

"Charley Byler, you are the most, most—"

"Persistent," Johanna supplied, giggling.

"That isn't what I was going to say," Miriam answered. She could feel her temper rising. All the men were staring at her, even those at the bishop's table. In another minute, she was going to dump a bucket of ice over Charley's head.

Johanna saw the look on Miriam's face, sighed, then turned to Charley. "Go back to the table and have your pie," she told him. "She'll ride with you."

Miriam clasped her hands to her sides, curling her fingers into tight fists. She didn't like being put on the spot by Charley in front of people this way. And Johanna wasn't helping matters. "I won't," she protested.

"She will," Johanna corrected, giving Charley a friendly nudge and waving toward his table. "Go on, now, before you embarrass her even more."

Charley grinned. "Later, then. I've got lots to talk to you about, Miriam."

"And I've got lots to say to you, too," she promised, her tone not nearly as kindly as his. "I can't wait."

Chapter Eleven

It was after eleven that evening when the young people's social at Norman and Lydia's farm finally broke up. It had been a long day, but Miriam was not in the least tired. The youth gathering, with the usual singing and party games, had been more fun than she'd expected, and even though Johanna had trapped her into riding home in Charley's buggy, she wasn't dreading it like she thought she would.

The get-together had been larger than normal, as teens and young adults from the neighboring districts who'd come to help raise the house and barn had been invited. Ruth and Charley, both with good voices, had acted as song leaders, while Eli had directed the circle dances, cornhusking contest and apple dunking. Miriam's all-girl team was defeated in the cornhusking by the boys, amid a thunder of stamping feet and raucous cheers. However, Susanna upheld the family honor by plunging her head completely underwater and coming up with the first apple in her teeth. Her prize was a basket of pears and she was so excited she could hardly talk.

The young people's dancing-games weren't the same

as English dances, but were more like old-fashioned folk dances. The participants held hands and skipped in a large circle, while others clapped and sang along. The fun came when the couple in the center locked arms and moved in the opposite direction until one of them returned to the circle and chose another to take his or her place. Girls sometimes danced with other girls, but boys never did.

When the person leaving the circle picked a new victim, they usually sought out someone who would cause the most laughter from the group or the one they suspected their old partner was sweet on. It was the game leader's job to see that the teasing never became mean and that everyone was eventually chosen, so that no one was left out.

Adult chaperones kept their distance, and if some boys held hands with their partners a little longer than was necessary, or if they were more than enthusiastic when it came to swinging a girl, the behavior was usually overlooked, so long as the participants remained in full view of the group and no kissing or inappropriate touching occurred. Any infraction and the guilty party would find themselves banned from future events and their parents visited by district elders.

All the same, it was at these frolics that romances often blossomed, and a girl who'd never looked at a certain boy twice might decide that there might be more to him than she'd supposed. It was all very confusing to Miriam. She liked John, perhaps even wanted him to walk out with her, but watching Charley tonight made her less sure. He wasn't exciting and he didn't make her heart race…or did he?

Things had begun to look differently to Miriam when

she'd accidentally overheard a conversation between Charley and John just after the men had finished the day's work on the new house. She'd finished the evening milking and had been about to leave the barn when she'd heard Charley, on the other side of the door, call John's name. When John murmured a response, she'd stopped short, hoping that Charley wouldn't cause trouble again.

"You did a good day's work for a college boy," Charley had said heartily.

She'd crept forward and peeked around the corner of the barn. John and Charley were standing in a group of men that included Roland and Samuel. Charley was grinning.

"And not just a good day's work for a Mennonite, either. A good day's work for an Amish," Charley had said as he extended his hand. "Sorry if I was a jerk before. Thanks for pitching in."

John had grasped the offered hand and shook it. "No problem. I was glad to be a part of it." He smiled. "I mean that. It was something, building a house that fast."

"We couldn't have finished as much as we did today without your help," Charley said. "You're all right for a Mennonite." The other men had laughed and John and Charley had both joined in.

Miriam had then retraced her steps to the cows, waited a few moments and then left the barn. By that time, the others had scattered. Neither John nor Charley were anywhere to be seen.

But Miriam hadn't been able to forget the conversation she'd overheard. Charley was obviously jealous of John, but he'd been man enough to admit when he was wrong and offer the hand of friendship. And he'd done it in front of his friends and neighbors. That took courage and reinforced what she already knew about her old friend. Charley had a good heart and he could laugh at his own mistakes. Realizing how important that was, somehow made her feel differently about him tonight. She hadn't been able to stop thinking about him. And when it had been Charley's turn to swing her around in *Skip to My Lou,* she'd found that his strong arm and the gleam in his eyes had sent goose bumps down her spine.

"Miriam?" Susanna's voice broke into Miriam's thoughts. "Help me." Panting, Susanna staggered out of the shadows, a heaping basket of pears in her arms. "They're falling everywhere."

The pears were piled high, and every time Susanna took two steps, one would roll off the top and fall to the ground. Then, her little sister would place the basket on the ground, put the errant pear back on, and pick up the container. It was far too heavy for Susanna to begin with, and there was no way she could maintain her balance long enough to reach the buggy without having the same thing happen over and over.

"Wait." Miriam scooped up another pear rolling through the grass.

Susanna trudged forward, mouth set, small rounded shoulders straining. "Did you see? Did you see me? I won! I dunked bester than anybody."

"You did dunk better than anyone else." Miriam took the basket from her sister's hands. "You were the best apple dunker of all. Wait until Mam hears."

"Can I have a pear?" Charley came out of the shadows and lifted the basket out of Miriam's grasp.

Susanna giggled. "*Ne.* Silly. They're green. Pears gotta wi-pen."

"Ripen," Miriam corrected softly. "And you're right, Susanna. They do have to ripen before we eat them."

Charley smelled good. Miriam caught the distinct scent of Old Spice aftershave as she leaned down to grab another pear Susanna had lost. She passed it to her sister. "Would you like to ride home with me in Charley's buggy?" she asked.

"Sorry, no room tonight." Charley placed Susanna's basket in the back of the Yoder buggy. Then he caught Miriam's hand. "Susanna will have to ride with Anna. I borrowed Roland's two-seater."

"Miriam," Anna said, already seated on the buggy bench. "Maybe you'd better not. Mam will say you should have a chaperone."

But Miriam let Charley lead her away by the hand and together they climbed into the courting buggy. Before she could think twice, Charley had gathered the lines and snapped them over the back of his pinto gelding. They rolled out of the farmyard with the horse at a fast trot.

"Miriam!" Anna called after them.

"See you at home!" she shouted back.

When they reached the end of the Beachy's lane, Charley turned the pinto's head in the opposite direction of the Yoder farm.

"Where do you think you're going?" Miriam demanded, grasping the side of the seat as he made the turn.

"Taking you home."

"This way?" She tried to sound stern, but it came out in a burst of amusement.

He had a silly smile on his face, like he was so proud of himself and of his clever bending of the rules. "I didn't say how long it would take me to get you home, did I?"

"You cheat," she protested. He'd let go of her hand

when he was guiding the horse out of the barnyard and onto the blacktop, but now he grasped it again. She tried to pull away, but he held on tight. "Charley." Small sparks of pleasure ran up her arm. "Let me go."

"I don't want to," he answered. "You're too hard to catch."

She looked at him. "Maybe I don't want to be caught."

"Miriam, please. You've been running away from me for days." His tone turned serious. "Let me say what I have to say, before I lose my nerve."

The worn leather of the seat felt soft under her fingertips. "I can't remember you ever having trouble before talking to me."

"That's because you usually understand me so well. Sometimes you know what I'm thinking or how I'm feeling without me even having to say anything. So I *thought* when I told you about my new job that you'd understand."

"Understand what?"

"What I was trying to tell you." He groaned uncomfortably. "Miriam, I was trying to tell you that I want to court you."

For long seconds and then minutes, there was no sound but the creak of the buggy wheels, the rustle of the harness and the steady rhythm of the gelding's hooves on the roadway. Her mouth felt dry. Because Mam had warned her, she'd thought about what she was going to say when he asked her. She'd rehearsed how she was going to explain to Charley why she didn't want to walk out with him, but now that the time had come, she wasn't sure what to say. She didn't *know* what to say because she didn't know how she felt about the idea.

"Miriam," he said, finally breaking the awkward silence. "You're supposed to say something."

He was still holding her hand, his grasp warm and so...*nice.* "I... I'm thinking."

"So tell me what you're thinking."

"I'm thinking that I like you, Charley. We've always been such good friends," she hedged. "But I never thought of us like that—courting."

"I understand that, but maybe you should. Friendship is a place to start. It wouldn't be much sense to court if we hated each other. Do you hate me?"

She shook her head. "You know better than that. It's just that courting, marriage, they're big steps." She felt emotion welling up in her throat. She felt so awful for saying this, for hurting Charley, because she knew she was, but she had to be truthful with him, didn't she? "The truth is," she blurted, "I don't know what I want... or *who* I want."

He threaded the lines through his fingers and slowed the horse to a walk. His voice remained calm, not squeaky like hers had become. "You've been walking out with John."

"No, I haven't," she protested. "I rode to Easton with him. We had lunch in a restaurant. That was all."

"And you had a good time?"

She took a deep breath. This was so hard, being completely honest. With herself and with Charley. "Yes," she admitted, "I did."

"Did he kiss you?"

She stiffened, glancing at him. "That's none of your business."

"Well, just in case." He knotted the lines around the dash rail, slid over and took her in his arms.

Before she could muster a protest, Charley leaned close and kissed her. His mouth was warm, his breath clean. Without realizing she was going to do it, she leaned forward and kissed him back. Their lips fit together perfectly, and sweet tingly sensations made her giddy.

Breathless, she pushed him away. "Do you make a habit of kissing the girls you drive home from singings?"

"I suppose I do." He chuckled in the darkness as he took the reins again. The horse had never broken stride.

"Charley Byler!"

"I'm kidding. You're the first, Miriam, the first girl I ever kissed. Just now." He grinned.

She folded her arms over her chest, trying to convince herself that she didn't like it…that she didn't want him to kiss her again. "That's not true," she accused. "What about Ada Peachy? I saw you kiss her behind the schoolhouse at the seventh grade picnic."

"Doesn't count," he argued firmly. "She kissed me. Missed my mouth and kissed my nose. I ran away." He took hold of her hand again and gently squeezed it.

She pulled her hand away from his, but only after she savored the feel of it for a second. "Why did you kiss me? Because we have no chaperone? Because you think I'm wild enough to do anything?"

He chuckled. "Because I've wanted to kiss you for a long time. A very long time. And because I want to marry you."

"Take me home, Charley."

"Will you?"

"Marry you?" she asked, incredulously.

"Well, yes. But that's not my question, for now. My question, for tonight, is will you think about letting me court you?"

She knotted her fingers together, still able to feel the heat of his hand on hers and the taste of his mouth. Her heart was beating faster than the horse's hooves were striking the road.

She wanted to refuse. She'd been practically forced to ride home with him, and he'd taken advantage of that by kissing her. Wasn't that reason enough to say no?

She brushed her lower lip with a fingertip. But maybe, just maybe, there was more to this man beside her than she'd imagined, and maybe she'd be a fool not to give him the chance to prove it. Making up her mind, she raised a finger to him. "No more kisses," she warned.

He nodded. "No more kisses until we're pledged."

"No one said anything about pledging *or* courting. I'm promising nothing tonight but an open mind. You can come around, sometimes, but you can't tell people that we're courting, because we're not. Now, turn the buggy around and take me home."

"*Ya,* Miriam, whatever you say." He chuckled, lifting the reins. "But you must admit, it was a *very* nice kiss."

The following day was Sunday, not the worship Sabbath but the day for relaxation and visiting with family and friends. After breakfast, Miriam took the buggy and picked up Johanna and the children, which was their usual routine on off Sundays. Johanna loved nothing more than spending time with her mother and sisters, and Wilmer seemed equally satisfied with the arrangement.

"Wilmer likes to spend the Lord's Day in peace and quiet, not listening to babies wail," Johanna explained on the way home. "He studies German, reads his Bible studies and writes to his family in Kentucky."

"Mmm," Miriam agreed. "They do get noisy." Jonah was standing between her knees, his small hands on the leathers, pretending to drive Blackie.

"Sometimes," Johanna agreed.

She was wearing a maroon dress, white apron and *kapp,* all clean and starched, but worn. Her shoes, Miriam noticed, were the same navy sneakers she wore every day, and they had seen better days, as well. Wilmer made a good living on his construction job, but he was frugal with his money when it came to his wife and children. It annoyed Miriam that Wilmer was a spiffy dresser for an Amish man, but the only new clothes her sister ever got were the ones Mam made for her. She'd have to mention Johanna's shoes to their mother.

"Get up!" Jonah shouted and shook the leathers. The gelding broke into a trot and the boy laughed.

"Easy," Miriam soothed. "You must be gentle. Never jerk on the reins. It hurts the animal's mouth." She took a firm hand on the lines as a pickup passed the carriage.

"Ya," Jonah agreed. "Okay."

Katie, seated on her mother's lap, laughed, kicked her feet and waved her arms. She was a happy, chubby-cheeked baby with bright eyes and an adorable laugh.

"How did it go last night? With Charley?" Johanna bounced Katie on her knee. "I've been waiting to hear."

"It went all right." She glanced at her sister. "But that was rotten of you, to tell him that I'd ride home with him from the singing without my say-so."

Johanna shrugged. "Just doing my job as your big sister. You shouldn't be too quick to pick a husband."

"Who says I am?"

Katie yanked her *kapp* off and threw it in the air. Johanna caught it and plopped it back on the baby's head. *"Ne.* You must wear your head covering, sweetie."

Miriam looked at Johanna. "What makes you think I've picked a husband?"

"Mary. Charley's sister. She said John and you were walking out. That he was courting you." Johanna's expression turned serious. "You need to make certain it's what you want. You shouldn't decide against Charley without putting some serious thought into it."

Becoming frustrated, Miriam gripped the reins tighter. "Who was it who told me to go with John to Easton? You! Now you're trying to force Charley on me?" She stared at the road straight ahead. "Which one do you want me to go with? John or Charley?"

"Both. Neither." Johanna placed a firm hand on Jonah's shoulder. "Do not jump up and down. If you can't behave, you'll have to sit in the back of the buggy."

"I'm good," Jonah protested, and immediately stopped hopping.

"*Ya,* you are a good boy. *Most* of the time. But you have to be careful in the buggy. Do you want to fall and have the wheels run over your noodle?"

Jonah giggled.

"I've got him." Miriam wrapped an arm around the child's waist.

Johanna returned her attention to her sister. "So what do you think about Charley?"

"I don't know what I think."

Johanna shifted Katie to her shoulder. "And John?"

"I don't know that, either."

"Good," Johanna pronounced. "So, it's best that you see both of them. Go places, do things, have fun, with both of them. Be certain in your heart before you choose."

"But how will I know? I like them both," Miriam admitted. "John's exciting, and Charley's…" She leaned close to her sister's ear. "He kissed me on the way home last night."

Johanna's eyes narrowed and she glanced at her son. "How was it?" she whispered.

"Nice."

"All right, then. Now, the thing to do is to kiss John and see how they match up."

"Johanna!" Miriam glanced at her sister, then at the road again. "What would Mam say? What kind of advice is that for a big sister to give her younger one? Would you have people say I'm fast?"

"Better fast than foolish."

Chapter Twelve

The following day, Charley stopped by his brother Roland's house after supper. He'd intended on visiting Miriam, but as he was walking down the road, halfway to her house, John had passed him in his truck. John backed up and asked if Charley wanted a ride, explaining that he was going by the Yoders' to check on Molly.

Not wanting to share Miriam with John, Charley had changed his original plans. "Thanks just the same," he'd said. "But I'm on my way to Roland's." John had offered to give him a lift to Roland's driveway, but he'd refused that, too, saying that he needed to stretch his legs.

It wasn't exactly the whole truth, but close enough. And now that he was here in his brother's kitchen, bouncing his nephew, Jared, on his knee, Charley was glad he'd come. Pauline, Roland's wife, was expecting twins and wasn't well. She was lying down and Roland was cleaning up the supper dishes.

"Ride a horse, ride a horse," Charley said to little Jared, and then swung him high in the air. "And don't let him throw you!"

Jared squealed with laughter. "More! More!" he demanded in the German dialect the English called *Pennsylvania Dutch*. Jared was too young to speak or understand English. Most Amish children learned it in the first grade when they went to school, although Charley and Roland's mother had taught them both English and German from babyhood on.

"Enough, enough," Roland protested. "It's his bedtime."

Charley noticed that the boy was already bathed and in a clean nightshirt and diaper. "You have this routine down good," he said, handing the giggling child over to his father.

Roland lifted Jared onto his shoulders. "A family's needs must be met, brother. Give me a few minutes to tuck him in. Pour yourself some coffee. I'll be down as quick as I can."

While Roland went upstairs, Charley picked up a dish towel, dried the knives and forks on the counter and put them away. He found a broom and swept the kitchen before helping himself to the coffee on the back of the stove. When Roland returned, Charley saw that his brother's face looked troubled.

"We were all praying that the new endocrinologist would help Pauline," Charley said. "I hear Bishop Atlee goes to him."

Roland nodded. "I feel bad, brother. Her condition. It would have been better for her if she hadn't gotten pregnant again, but…" He shrugged. "The doctor seems good, but carrying two babies is hard on her, what with her diabetes. The midwife tells us that they may come too soon."

"It's a terrible disease."

Charley knew that Pauline had needed to take insulin daily since she was a teenager, but she'd seemed so much better in the first year of her marriage. Now, she'd gotten worse—a lot worse—and Roland's medical bills were mounting. The Amish carried no health insurance as the English did. Instead, the community pitched in when there was a need.

"*Ya.* My wife is a good wife and mother. She wanted more babies so badly." Roland looked around the kitchen. "You swept? No need for that. I was going to do it."

"It's not easy for you, either, Roland. When Mam hears—"

"*Ne.* Don't worry her. Pauline's sisters have been a help with Jared. We're making out. It's good you stopped by. We don't get enough time to talk. Remember when we were kids? It seemed like we were never apart."

Charley laughed. "I remember. You were always getting me out of one scrape or another. And you were always giving me advice to keep me out of trouble."

"Which you *never* listened to. Always the jokes and teasing for Charley." Roland lit an oil lamp. It cast a yellow circle of light across the table and began to smoke until he turned down the wick. "It can't go on, you know." Roland peered over the top of his glasses and fiddled with the wick again. "Time you settle down, get baptized and start courting that pretty Yoder girl."

"Which one?" They both laughed. Roland knew which Yoder girl Charley fancied. But then, *everyone* knew.

"Seriously, little brother. You've got that steady job you were wanting. If you're not careful, someone else will snatch her away. Maybe even that John Hartman."

Charley slid his cup away and met his brother's steady gaze. Behind Roland's thick glasses were big blue eyes, full of wisdom and compassion. "I asked her if I could court her," Charley admitted. "I even kissed her. Just once. When I drove her home from the singing last night."

Roland tugged at his short beard. "Not something I'd mention to Preacher Reuben if I were you. She let you?"

Charley shrugged. "I think she liked it as much as I did, even though she acted mad afterward." He was quiet for a second. "But that's not the thing. You know, I've always expected that we'd marry, someday. Everybody knows it. Didn't I buy Miriam's pie last spring at the school fundraising picnic so I could eat with her? Right in front of everyone?"

"That you did. So, what's your problem?"

Charley brought his palms together as if in prayer, before lightly tapping his chin with his index fingers. "Now that I've finally gotten around to asking her if I can walk out with her, she doesn't seem all that interested. I think that Mennonite has stolen my thunder."

"More like, your girl." Roland got up, went to the refrigerator and brought back a blueberry pie and two forks. "Help me eat this," he said. "Mam keeps sending pies over. Pauline can't eat them and they're making me fat."

Charley looked at the pie. "So you want to make *me* fat?"

"Blueberries. They give you brain power."

"Which I'm lacking, compared to the *veterinarian*," Charley took one of the forks and cut off a mouthful of pie.

"*Ne.* That's not true. You were always the smart one in the family. Who won the eighth grade spelling bee?"

Charley grimaced. "Miriam."

"Okay, bad example. But you always got a hundred percent on your fractions and long division. And that doesn't really matter, not when it comes to being a good husband. You just need to figure out how to show Miriam that *you'll* make a better husband than John will."

"Not easy." Charley forked pie into his mouth and chewed. "Competition's stiff. He's got that truck and he makes more money than I do. They're both interested in healing animals. I don't even have a house to take her to, if she *would* marry me."

Roland tossed him a paper napkin. "Blueberry. There on your chin."

Charley laughed, wiping his chin. "Flaky. Mam makes good pies."

"You ever think maybe you don't need a house? Who does all the cooking at the Yoder place?"

"Mostly Anna, I guess. Sometimes Hannah. The other girls pitch in."

"And who does most of the outside chores? Putting in the crops? Milking the cows?"

"Miriam. She's always liked farming better than housework. And she's good at it. Did you see her corn crop last year?"

"My point. And how well do you get along with her mother?"

"Hannah? Fine. Who doesn't like—" Charley broke off and stared at Roland. "You mean…live there? At the Yoder place?"

"Why not? If it suits Miriam, why not? So long as Hannah is all right with it. They could certainly use another man for the heavy work, and it's a big house."

"It is. Miriam said they don't even use the rooms over the kitchen. And there's the *Grossdaadi haus*. We might—"

"*Ne.*" Roland shook his head. "Mam said that Alma said that her mother and aunt might be coming to live with Hannah, once her mother-in-law can travel. I got the idea that there were some problems the Yoder girls in Ohio were dealing with, but Mam didn't say what."

"Hannah's going to take her in? A daughter-in-law? Why don't Alma or Martha take her? *They're* her daughters."

"Alma told Mam that Lovina can't stand her, and she never did get along with Martha."

"I've seen enough of Lovina to know she can be a handful, plus there's her sister, Jezebel. A lot for Hannah and the girls."

Roland smiled. "All the more reason it would make sense for you to help out by staying on the farm. What with you having a steady job now, it makes more sense than you taking Miriam home to Mam and Dat's. Can you see our father letting Miriam plow his fields?"

"Hardly." Charley grinned at the thought. "It does seem sensible. But how does that help my immediate problem of getting Miriam to agree to let me court her? How can I compete with John? She likes him a lot, and they've got taking care of animals in common. Plus, he's such a good guy. He helped out with the house-raising and he even brought Eli and Ruth that bathroom stuff."

"John is worldly, and a good man, that's true enough. But it would be a big step for Miriam to leave the Amish faith. Don't be so quick to give up, brother. Put your trust in God to do the right thing for all of you. If He means for Miriam to be your wife, no one can come between you."

"But *John* is coming between us, Roland. Chances are, he's standing there in the Yoder barn with her, *right this minute.*"

"So why are you here?" Roland stood up. "Get on over there, boy. Let her see that you care about her. And don't try to be someone you're not. She can depend on you, Charley. You're steady. Make certain she remembers that." He went back to the refrigerator, took out another blueberry pie and handed it to him. "Here, take this. It will give you an excuse for coming over so late."

Charley clutched the pie. "You think I should?"

Roland opened the kitchen door. "Get going, before she starts kissing John."

And for once, Charley did as Roland advised.

Late Tuesday afternoon, Miriam was cleaning Molly's stall when her mother came into the barn, a kerchief tied over her head and picked up a pitchfork.

"Mam, I can do this. There's no need for you to—"

"You think I don't know how to muck a stall?" Her mother smiled. "Sometimes hard work is what we need." She scooped up a heap of dirty straw and dumped it into the wheelbarrow. "So how is the mare? Will the infection heal?"

Miriam nodded. "It looks like it will. She's much better. John expects her to make a full recovery in a few weeks."

"He comes a lot, John."

"He cares about Molly."

Her mother leaned on her pitchfork. "He comes to see more than the mare, I think."

Miriam didn't answer. They continued working, side by side.

"Aunt Martha told me that the neighbors wonder why the vet comes here so much for a sore hoof. You know how people like to talk, to gossip."

Miriam pushed the gate open and pulled the wheelbarrow out into the passageway. "That should do it. I'll go up into the loft for fresh straw."

Her mother stepped in front of her, blocking her way. "We have to talk about this, child."

"I'm not a child." Miriam rested one hand on her hip. She was taller than her mother, but only by an inch. "I'm twenty-one. I know what I'm doing."

"So, all grown up, you are? No longer need a mother's advice?"

"It's because John's Mennonite, isn't it?" She looked into her mother's face. "You were once Mennonite. Were you ungodly? Is he a bad man because he wasn't born Amish?"

"No one said anything about ungodly. Come." Hannah took her hand and led her to a hay bale. "Sit," she said.

Miriam sat. "Mam, you don't understand. John is—"

"Listen to me," her mother interrupted. "Do you love him with all your heart? Are you ready to leave your family, your church, everything you know for *his* world?"

"I don't know. I *like* him a lot. I feel all giddy when I see him. He makes me laugh, and…"

"He's new and exciting."

Miriam nodded. "So many things he takes for granted, things I would like to do and see. But how can I be sure?"

Hannah grasped her hand and squeezed it. "When I met your father, Jonas, it was the same way for me. This world…" She glanced around the barn. "This quiet, peaceful world, it was different than what I'd grown up with."

"But your life revolved around God, too." Miriam stared at the dirt floor. "How did you know that Dat was the one man for you?"

"Like you, there was another boy that favored me. His

family and mine were close. They'd served on a mission with us to Canada. My mother wanted me to marry him."

"You went to Canada? You never told us that." Miriam's eyes widened. "Why didn't I know that? Where in Canada? How old were you?"

"It was long ago. Our work was with the Indian people in the north. I don't remember a lot, just the games I played with the tribal children and the cold winters. Two years, we were there. We came back when I was eight." She grew thoughtful. "It isn't just John that the community is talking about. Charley was here last night, too, wasn't he?"

Miriam nodded. "He came just after John left. He brought us one of his mother's blueberry pies."

"If you are thinking seriously of John, is it fair to encourage Charley?"

"The problem is that I can't say I don't want to encourage Charley, too."

"It isn't the custom to walk out with two boys at the same time. Some consider that fast, for a girl. Not Plain."

Miriam scuffed her shoe in the straw. "I haven't joined the church. I don't have to follow the rules yet."

"The Amish way is not an easy one. It's not for everybody. It may not be your way. It's the reason I haven't pressed for you to be baptized yet. I wanted you to embrace our faith with your whole heart, to realize that the rules are not walls but wings that will someday lift you to heaven."

She looked at her mother. "Have you ever been sorry that you left the Mennonites to become Amish?" It was something that she'd always wanted to ask, but had been afraid to.

Hannah shook her head. "Never. Not even when I lost

my dear partner, not even when some of my family closed their doors to me and my children. It was the right thing for me. I had dreamed of being a missionary to faraway lands, and instead I found joy here, in this tranquil place."

"If I choose John, will you close your door to me, Mam?"

"Never." She grabbed Miriam's hand, squeezed it and let it go. "And neither will your sisters. But do not join the church and then leave. So long as you are not baptized in our faith, the leaders cannot shun you. You will always be welcome at home."

"What do you think of Charley?"

"As a man or as your husband?" Mam asked. She went on before Miriam could answer. "He has a good heart. And he's a hard worker. You will never go hungry if you marry Charley. He's also generous, with his feelings and material things. You'll never wear old shoes while he wears new."

Mam's words were the closest Miriam had ever heard her speak against Johanna's husband. But Miriam was sure she was not mistaken. Mam was referring to Wilmer.

"But the problem is, I like them both," Miriam explained. "How do I know which one is best for me?"

"It would mean two very different ways of life."

Miriam sighed. "I realize that, Mam. But I can't decide which one I'd be happier with." She swallowed, trying to dissolve the constriction in her throat. "How do I know what God wants me to do?"

"It's not easy. He has given us free will, and with that comes the possibility of choosing wrong and having to live with the consequences."

"You want me to pick Charley, don't you?"

Mam chuckled. "I want you to pick the man who will

make you the happiest. I want you to marry the man who will help you become the woman God intends you to be."

"But I don't know who that is. John hasn't even asked to court me. I think he wants to—I know he does. But he hasn't said it in so many words."

"And Charley did?"

"Yes, but he asked you first. He's asked everyone. I'd be surprised if he hasn't asked Uncle Reuben's permission." She pushed back hair that had escaped from her kerchief. "How can I know what's right when everyone is pushing me into Charley's arms?"

Her mother got to her feet. "I would tell you to pray, but I know you have prayed and will continue to do so. Know that I pray for you, and your sisters do, too. But no one can make this decision but you."

Miriam nodded thoughtfully. "So maybe I have to make my own rules. Decide my own way."

"Take your time. And whatever decision you make, I will always love you as much as I love you at this moment."

"I guess I need to find out John's intentions, don't I?" She was speaking as much to herself, as to her mother.

Mam smiled. "That would seem to be a good place to start." She leaned close and kissed Miriam's cheek. "I have faith in you, daughter. You have a good head on your shoulders. You'll figure this out."

"I hope so," Miriam said.

Her mind was already racing. What *was* wrong with having two boys court her at once? She didn't give a rotten apple for what Aunt Martha and the other gossips thought. What she needed to do was find out exactly how John felt about her. And if he wasn't truly interested in a serious relationship that might lead to marriage, then her question would be answered—at least as far as John was concerned.

As for Charley, he remained an equally big question, but for different reasons. Was he really just a friend, as she had insisted to everyone, including herself? Or was he more? *That* she'd have to think about.

Chapter Thirteen

Miriam waited until her mother and sisters had retired to bed before retreating to Johanna's old bedroom over the kitchen. The only way to reach this portion of the house was through the kitchen and up the back staircase. Although the rooms were furnished, this area was rarely used since Johanna had married and Leah and Rebecca remained with *Grossmama*. It was the only place in the house that was private enough for the phone call Miriam wanted to make to John.

Deciding to ask him his intentions was frightening. Actually doing it was more so. Her fingers trembled as she waited for him to answer.

"Miriam?"

"*Ya*, John. It is me." He'd been there earlier in the evening tending to Molly. Obviously, he hadn't expected her to call. "Am I bothering you?"

"No, of course not. Wait. I'll walk outside," he said. Miriam heard footsteps and the creak of a door, then the sound of his boots on the wooden porch. "All right." John chuckled. "I didn't want my grandfather listening in. And he would."

She took a deep breath. Why was this so awkward? Earlier, in the barn, they'd laughed and talked easily. She'd leaned on the stall door as John had brushed Molly's hide until she shone. "I have a question to ask you," she said.

"Okay." He sounded curious, but amused, too.

"Do you like me? But not just *like*…" She caught her lower lip between her teeth. "John, is it more than *like?*" She took a deep breath and just said it. "Do you want to court me?"

There was a moment of silence long enough to make her wish she could shrink down to the size of a mouse and crawl away.

Then he chuckled. "Isn't this conversation a little backward? I thought *I* was the one who was supposed to ask you about how you felt about *me*."

"This is not easy." Her knees felt weak, her palms sweaty. She sank down in the center of the braided rug. "I have to know, John. It's important. And…and if I was wrong to think that you—"

"You aren't wrong. I think…" It sounded as if he took a deep breath. "Miriam, I think I may be in love with you."

How sweet those words sounded. But she had to be sure what he meant. "Love is one thing," she said hesitantly. "Courting and marriage are another. I have to know if you're serious."

"I'm serious." He spoke firmer now. "I would like to court you, Miriam Yoder—walk out with you. Whatever you call it. I like you better than any girl I've ever met. Seeing you is the highlight of my day. That said, I have a question for you. Have you thought about how difficult this would be? Our families…"

"It's *all* I think about. But I want to know you better—to be alone with you, see more of your world. I don't know if it's love I feel. I think it is, John, but I want to be sure."

"So do I."

She felt warm all over now. Still a little nervous, but a good nervous. "You're not angry, that I asked you this?"

"Nothing you do or say could make me angry, Miriam."

"Don't be so fast to say that." She hesitated. "Because you should know that Charley has already asked to court me."

More silence. And when John finally spoke, his voice had lost the easy, teasing tone. She could almost see his shoulders tightening, his lips thinning. "And what did you tell him? Did you say yes?"

She lay back on the rug. "It would be easy if I liked Charley best. My family would like that. My church. They expect me to marry Charley or someone like him. Me, I don't know what I want. I like Charley, but I don't know that he makes me feel the way you do," she dared.

"So?"

She exhaled. "So I need to find out."

"You want to date both of us?" John sounded out of sorts now, almost cross.

"I think it would be best," she said. "Maybe I am in love with you…or maybe it is your world I love. And maybe, with Charley…maybe with Charley, I haven't given him a real chance, because I already know his world. Our world."

"What we're talking about is some sort of competition, here. I thought the Amish didn't go for competition—that it wasn't Plain."

A wave of sadness brought tears to sting the back of her eyelids. "You're angry with me." She could see him in her mind's eye, his broad forehead, the curve of his bottom lip. Her heart plunged. What if she'd ruined everything by being too forward?

"Just surprised. This is a lot to take in."

"Too much, maybe. It could be that this would never work for either of us. For me to walk in your world…for you to fit in mine."

"Yes," he agreed. "I see that." Emotion made his voice deepen. "But I'll do whatever I have to. I'll prove to you that I'd be the best husband for you. I'm not going to give you up without a fight."

"We do not fight. And I don't believe it is the Mennonite way, either. And this isn't a *competition*. It's important that we both go into this with our eyes open. For me, marriage is forever, John. If I choose you, I will never walk away from you. I will honor and cherish you all the days of my life."

"Me, too. What other people think doesn't matter. It's you and me, what we want. It's our life."

"*Ne,* John. Our life includes our families, our church. Most importantly, I must be certain that I choose the path that God intends for me."

"I respect that. But do you think you could become Mennonite? I can't see you remaining Amish if we're together. It would be too difficult for our children."

"I've thought of that," she assured him. "It's a real consideration."

"I don't attend services as regularly as I should. It's only fair that you know that being part of the church isn't as important to me as it is to you."

"I don't know if I could leave the Amish faith, but if

I change to a more liberal church, it wouldn't mean forgetting God's part in my life."

"I wouldn't ask you to."

Her stomach was still queasy, but she was beginning to feel hopeful again. "I told my mother that I care for you. She advised me to be certain. You know she was raised Mennonite and converted for my father."

"Uncle Albert told me that."

"So, she knows what it's like to make such a difficult decision. If we...if we *date,* we will come to know each other better, to see if what you feel...if what *I* feel is the love that makes a marriage."

"Wow. Heavy stuff."

She laughed softly. "But this will be Amish dating. Not English."

"Mennonite?"

"Maybe. We will see. But I cannot shame my family. We must do nothing that will disgrace them—or us. We have to be chaperoned."

"Chaperoned?" He laughed. "We weren't chaperoned when we went to Easton."

"That was different. It wasn't a *date.* And it was during the day."

"I don't really understand the difference. We were still alone."

She nibbled on her lower lip. "It's complicated, John. A lot of it has to do with appearances."

"What have I got myself into?"

She dared a little smile. "That's what I intend to find out."

"So, next weekend. Will you go out with me?" he asked. "On a date?"

"Sunday is church. Saturday, I will be free."

"Saturday it is then. Would you like to go to the beach? The amusement rides are still open on the weekends. Ferris wheel? Carousel? Are you game?"

"*Ya,* John. I will go with you. It sounds like fun. I've never been on a Ferris wheel. Can we eat hot dogs and salt water taffy and candy cotton?"

"All the candy cotton you want." He chuckled. "But one thing I insist on."

"And that is?"

"Charley Byler cannot go with us to the beach."

She giggled. "I agree. No Charley."

It was Thursday morning before Charley made it back to the Yoder farm to finish the back steps on Eli and Ruth's new house. Miriam waited until Mam and Irwin had gone to school and Susanna, Ruth and Anna were busy with the washing before walking across the field toward the little house. She carried a cup of coffee as an excuse, in case she lost her nerve. "Morning, Charley," she said, coming around the corner of the house. "I brought you coffee."

He looked up at her and grinned. "And I was just sitting here thinking how much I'd like to have a second cup. I only had time for one this morning before I left."

Miriam smiled back. She'd been annoyed with Charley for so long that she'd forgotten how sweet his smile was. She felt a rush of affection and realized that no matter how much she'd denied it, she did care for Charley. But how could she like Charley if she was in love with John? Suddenly, her plan, which had seemed so sensible, seemed to leave her more confused than ever. Did she like either of them enough to marry, or was she so fickle that she'd become infatuated with any good-looking boy who glanced her way? Maybe Aunt Martha was right, and she was *fast*.

Charley stood and wiped his broad hands on his canvas apron. He'd been laying bricks and bits of cement clung to his trousers and shirt. "Appreciate this," he said. "The coffee...and a chance to talk to you alone."

She looked at the steps. How could she make him understand what she was about to say? "Good job." She pointed to his masonry. "Solid. I can see Ruth running up and down them."

"It's a good house." He took a sip of the coffee and looked at her.

She felt herself blush. "I didn't come just to bring you coffee," she said.

He grinned again, removed his straw hat and wiped his forehead with the back of his hand. "It's going to be hot today."

"Don't you want to know why I came?"

Charley chuckled. "I figured you'd tell me in your own good time."

She sat down on the grass and picked a cloverleaf. "Were you serious when you asked if you could court me?"

His blue eyes narrowed. "What do you think?"

She met his gaze. "I've decided you can, if you want to."

"What?"

"You can court me—walk out with me."

"Hmm." He regarded her thoughtfully. "What convinced you? My fancy way with brick steps or the kiss in the buggy?"

"Charley Byler! How can you bring up such a thing?"

"How can you forget it?"

She felt her cheeks grow as warm as the grass she

sat in. "It isn't proper to talk about such things." She put her hand on her hip. "So now I suppose you think I'm wild? So you won't want to court me anymore?" She was teasing him, of course. Giving him a taste of his own medicine.

He reached forward to catch her hand, but she was too quick for him. She twisted away, but before she could scoot back, he caught hold of one bare foot. "*Ya,* Miriam. I do. I want you more than anything; I want you to be my wife."

"Let go of me, Charley Byler! My foot's dirty." She struggled to break free.

"*Ne, ne,* just stay and talk to me."

"Let me go first." He did as she asked and she scrambled to her feet and backed away. "Are you crazy?"

"I'd never do anything to hurt you. You know that. You know how I feel about you."

"Then keep your hands off me." Now she planted both hands on her hips. "What's come over you?"

"You have, Miriam. You make me crazy…thinking about you all the time…wondering if I have a chance with you."

"If I agree to walk out with you, there's something you should know."

"I get another kiss?"

It was all she could do to not laugh. Where did he get the nerve? "You *do not,*" she said, with more feeling than she felt. "That was a mistake."

He sighed dramatically. "I can hold your hand?"

She shook her head. "And not my foot, either." She took a step toward him, looked up, then down at the ground. "There is something else, though. About John."

His brow furrowed. "What about John?"

"I might be in love with him."

"You might love John, yet you want me to court you?" He looked at her as if she were the one acting crazy.

She nodded. "It's the only way. I want to walk out with you both. And then I can choose. Once I know which one is right for me."

Hurt flashed in his eyes and he turned back to his work. Without another word, he picked up the trowel, scooped up cement and tapped it onto the top of a brick.

"You don't have to, if you don't want to," she said, drawing closer.

"You want to court both of us?"

"Mam knows."

"It will cause talk."

"Some people always gossip."

"They will say you are wild and I am a fool." He slammed the brick into place.

"No one who knows you will say you're a fool, Charley. And we will be properly chaperoned."

"Just you and me, or you and the Mennonite?"

"Both. I don't want to cause a scandal. I just want to be certain."

"And if I refuse to be a part of this nonsense?"

"I will be sorry, but I'll still walk out with John."

"And he's agreed to this?"

"John? *Ya.* He has."

"Then he is a fool."

"Charley! What a thing to say."

"What a thing to do." He looked back at her. "You are not like every other Amish girl."

"Maybe not," she said. Then she dared a little smile. "But that's what you like about me."

Chapter Fourteen

Susanna squealed with joy as the Ferris wheel turned, lifting them in the air before pausing, suspending them high over the amusement park. It was twilight and everywhere below, lights were blinking on. Miriam could still make out the ocean to the east and the narrow white ribbon of sand along the water's edge.

The basket swayed and Susanna clutched Miriam's hand. "Falling!"

"No," John assured her. "We won't fall. Look, you can see the merry-go-round. Hear the music?"

"Music," Susanna agreed. "I like the *merry-go-around.* I want to go down."

Miriam slipped an arm around her sister's shoulders. "We won't fall," she assured her. "It's all right, Susanna."

"I want to go down," Susanna said. "My tummy hurts."

Miriam looked at John. "I warned you not to buy her more cotton candy."

John smiled. "She'll be fine, won't you, Susanna? You're just like a bird, flying in the air, round and round."

John's hand covered Miriam's and Susanna's, and Miriam felt a little thrill at his touch. She'd deliberately put her sister between them. It was too easy to be intimate on these rides and she didn't want to be tempted. In spite of Susanna's fears, they were both having a wonderful time.

The day had been one marvel after another. Susanna had laughed at herself in the silly curved mirrors. They'd thrown balls at silly red and yellow wooden clowns, and she'd beaten John. She'd knocked every one down and won the prize—a stuffed bear that she gave to a little Hispanic girl in a red dress who'd been cheering her on. John had treated them to pizza, the sweet that she'd learned was called cotton candy—not candy cotton—and a frozen chocolate banana on a stick. They'd ridden the merry-go-round and played miniature golf on the roof of a building, with the ocean as a backdrop. She'd beaten John at the golf game as well, and he'd teased her about it. Best of all, they'd taken off their shoes and walked down to wade in the waves that washed against the beach.

The Ferris wheel began to rotate again. Susanna screamed as the rocking basket descended toward the ground and then rose again, even faster. Salt air blew against Miriam's face, threatening to tear away her *kapp* and send it flying through the night sky. With her free hand, she grabbed the knot under her chin and held tight. The earth rose to meet them at a frightening speed. When the Ferris wheel finally came to a stop, she was dizzy and her first steps were unsteady.

John caught her arm. "Easy. We can't have you taking a tumble," he said.

Now that they were back on firm ground, Susanna's fears appeared to have dissolved. "Let's go again!" she urged, clapping her hands and doing a little dance from side to side. "Let's go again."

"That's enough for one night." Miriam straightened her sister's *kapp* and tied it firmly to keep it from blowing away in the stiff breeze.

A sunburned couple in shorts and sweatshirts gawked and pointed at Susanna, but whether they were staring at her Amish clothing or because she had Down syndrome, Miriam didn't know. When the woman fished a camera out of her purse and aimed it in Susanna's direction, John stepped in front of Susanna, blocking the shot. The man said something rude, and Miriam could see John quickly losing his temper.

Miriam took hold of Susanna's hand and tucked her free arm through the inside of his elbow. "Let's go. We have to get up early in the morning for church."

"I'm sorry about those people," John said, hustling them away from the Englishers.

"It's not your fault," Miriam said. "It happens all the time." She would have let go of John's arm, but he held her firmly. A small flush of excitement made her giddy, and she hoped he wouldn't think she was too forward.

Susanna's short legs pumped as she hurried to keep up. "We're gonna ride in the blue truck!"

"Yes," John agreed. "In the blue truck."

"Can I blow the horn?" Susanna begged. "Can I?"

"Ne," Miriam said. "The horn is for emergencies. We could frighten another driver."

"Or a horse," Susanna said.

"Or a horse," John agreed.

Miriam glanced at him. "It was a lovely day. Thank you for taking us." They walked out of the noisy building with its flashing lights and loud music, back to the truck parked on the street.

"Can we come again tomorrow?" Susanna asked. "I

like the merry-go-around. I want to ride the white horse with the bell."

Soon they were driving down Rehoboth Avenue in light traffic. Susanna's nose was pressed against the truck window, staring at the tourists that crowded the sidewalks and flowed onto the street. "That girl is in her underpants!" Susanna declared. "Where's her dress?"

"Shh, don't look. She's English," Miriam explained, clapping a hand over her sister's eyes. "That's her swimming suit."

Susanna wiggled aside so that she could see. "But I can see her— She's bad."

"Not bad," John corrected. "Just not Plain. They're different."

"She's silly," Susanna said. "Fast."

"Susanna," Miriam admonished. "We don't talk about people."

"But—"

"Shh."

John chuckled. "She's right. The girl is silly. She'd be prettier with more clothes on."

"Do you really think so?" Miriam asked.

"I do. I think you're beautiful, just as you are."

They rode in silence for a little while, and soon Susanna was asleep, her head on Miriam's shoulder.

"Did you have fun?" John asked, quietly.

Miriam nodded. "I've been to the ocean before, but never Fun Land. I had a wonderful time."

"Have you ever been swimming?"

"*Ya*. Sometimes we go to a little beach on the bay. Not with swimming suits, but in our clothes. My sisters and I play in the water."

"My mother has a swimming pool in her yard. I could take you there. I know she has extra suits for my sisters."

Miriam chuckled. "Not for me. The Old Order Amish are more…more conservative than the more liberal Mennonite churches, I think. I don't judge girls who wish to wear revealing clothing, but we are taught to dress modestly."

"No swimming."

"No swimming in bathing costumes," she corrected him.

"Got it." He smiled at her in the darkness. "There's a charity spaghetti dinner at Uncle Albert's church next Friday night. Would you like to come?"

"The Mennonite church?"

"Yes. But there won't be a regular church service. I think a missionary's going to give a PowerPoint presentation and a talk afterward."

"What's that? A PowerPoint presentation?"

He glanced at her, but didn't look as if he thought she was dumb for asking. "It's sort of like a slide show, only it's done on a personal computer and then shown on a movie screen. But we wouldn't have to stay for that, if you didn't want to," he said quickly. "Would you be allowed to come, do you think?"

"If I bring one of my sisters. There aren't rules against going to other church benefits, John. The Old Order Amish Church isn't as strict as you seem to think."

"I'd like you to meet some of the members. If you…if we decide to go to the Mennonite church, they'll be part of our community."

"I've been thinking a lot about that." Miriam spoke softly, not wanting to wake Susanna. "I can't even imagine becoming part of a new church. It's such a big decision."

"You don't need to make it yet." He smiled at her. "Unless you don't like spaghetti."

"Love it," she confided. "And it's the one thing Mam never learned to cook. Hers is all tomatoey. But don't you dare tell her that I said so."

"Wouldn't think of it," he said, reaching down and taking her hand in his. "I'm so glad you came today. I had fun, too, a lot of fun."

Her breath caught in her throat. She and John were holding hands, and it made her feel warm and safe. "Even with Susanna along?"

He laughed. "Especially with Susanna."

"And we went up high! High!" Susanna exclaimed. It was Sunday morning and Mam, Irwin and Miriam's sisters were just leaving the house for church. Susanna was telling her mother for the fourth time about her ride on the Ferris wheel and the blue cotton candy John had bought her the night before.

Services were at Charley's parents' house today, and Miriam had hitched Blackie to the family buggy. Since Mam was bringing food to share at the noon meal, they had loaded the bowls and covered trays into the back of the carriage, along with the jars of lemonade and iced tea.

Miriam guided Blackie close to the back steps. "Everyone ready?" She yawned, covering her mouth with the back of her hand. It had been late when she'd gotten home from her date with John, and she'd lain awake for a long time thinking of all she'd seen and done...and thinking of John and what it would be like to be part of his world.

"Charley!" Susanna pointed. "Morning!"

"Morning, sunshine!"

Miriam turned to see him strolling around the corner of the barn, hands in his pockets. She glanced at Ruth, who shrugged and climbed up into the buggy. Miriam got down and walked across the yard. "Isn't church at your house?" she asked.

"*Ya.* I thought I could walk you there." He lifted one eyebrow. "Unless you're too tired after your Saturday night date."

"I'll be happy to walk with you. It will give me a chance to stretch my legs before services. Let me tell Mam."

"Maybe you need one of your sisters to walk with us, so that it doesn't worry your uncle Reuben?" Charley suggested.

"We'll be fine," she assured him.

If they cut across the fields, it was less than two miles to Charley's father's place, and the day was perfect—sunny, but not too hot, with just a hint of autumn in the air. The way led through the back pasture, over a stile that Dat had built, through Samuel's woods and past the school. Neither of them spoke. But surprisingly, she wanted to talk to Charley. She wanted to point out the warbler flitting through the bushes and the last of the summer's clover, bursting with white blossoms. And she wanted to tell Charley about the rude woman who'd wanted to take Susanna's picture at the amusement park.

Once they reached the road that ran in front of the school, they walked along it for a few hundred yards before taking a farm lane that crossed an English farmer's property. Miriam couldn't stand the silence between them any longer, she said, "Not so long ago and you were taking this lane every day to the schoolhouse."

"*Ya.* I was."

She waited. When he added nothing more, she had to force down her irritation. This walk had started out pleasantly, but she could tell now that Charley had a bee in his hat over something. She could see it in his face—in the way he held his mouth. "We waded in the waves yesterday. At the ocean. The water was warm."

"September. Should be."

She looked at him. "And you would know so much about the Atlantic Ocean?"

"As much as you."

"Don't be mean, Charley."

"Am I being mean? I came to walk you to church, didn't I?" He stooped and picked a dandelion blossom and then another. When he had three, he braided the stems together, and then handed them to her. "See, like an Englishman, I give you flowers."

She laughed. "Some bouquet."

That broke the ice. Soon they were teasing and chatting as they had before Charley had ruined everything by asking if he could court her. She liked Charley like this: familiar, sweet, funny.

"Fish are biting good in Dat's pond," he said. "Maybe tomorrow, after supper, we could try and catch a few bass."

"Mam likes fish. It would be good if I could catch enough for breakfast."

"Bring Irwin. We'll make him clean the fish."

"He'll love that."

"Can you clean fish?" He stopped, pushed the brim of his hat up with a forefinger and looked at her.

"Sure. Dat taught me when I was little."

"And I can clean fish. So it's only fair we give Irwin

the chance to learn how to do it, isn't it? And it will give him something to complain about, so he'll be happy."

Miriam chuckled. "He does whine a lot. I think he does it to get attention."

"Exactly." Charley tugged her bonnet string. "So we're building his character. Something even your uncle Reuben would approve of."

She tried to look serious. "This is Sunday. We're on our way to church. It's not a time to poke fun at a preacher."

Charley shook his head. "I wouldn't think of it. Preacher Reuben is a wise man. He'd be happy that we're taking an interest in Irwin—taking him fishing, having him along as a chaperone *and* showing him the value of work."

She brushed a piece of straw off her Sunday apron. "It sounds right when you say it like that, but I don't trust you. You're always up to something."

"Ne." Charley started walking again, matching his longer strides to her shorter ones. "I'll come for you both in Dat's buggy if you want."

"No need. We can roller-skate as far as your lane. Ruth bought Irwin a good pair of used skates last week at the auction. I know he's dying to use them. We'll meet you at the pond."

"I'll take you fishing on the ocean, if you want. There are charter boats going out of Lewes. I could hire a driver and—"

"I don't want to fish in the ocean, silly," she interrupted, touched that he would offer. "I'm happy just fishing for bass in your Dat's pond. You don't have to impress me."

"Not like John?"

"What I do with John on a date is one thing. What I do with you is another. Just be yourself, Charley. Don't act jealous and don't try to make me feel bad that I'm having fun with John. Just be my friend like you've always been...someone I can trust and tell my secrets to."

He kicked at a tuft of grass. He was wearing black leather high-tops and they looked new. In fact, his coat and blue shirt were new, as well. Charley looked especially fine on this Sunday morning. He'd shaved, and someone—probably his mother—had trimmed his hair.

"Do you have secrets, Miriam?" he asked.

"Not really. You know what I mean. I can tell you what I'm thinking. But if I did have secrets, I'd like to think that I could tell you."

"You can tell me anything. You ought to know that by now. I'd never judge you or think less of you, no matter what you say or do."

"Thank you. That means a lot to me."

They walked on, closer now, but not touching. Alone like this, it was more important than ever that they do nothing that would be considered improper. The trees were close on either side of the farm lane and the branches grew together overhead, forming an archway of light and shadow.

Birds fluttered overhead through the canopy of green leaves, calling to one another and singing cheerfully. From time to time, Miriam could catch a flash of scarlet or blue feathers as a cardinal or blue jay flew up at their approach. Miriam had walked this way dozens of times to Charley's house, but she'd never seen the woods so beautiful.

"Would you come early enough to share supper with us?" Charley asked after a few minutes. "Tomorrow, before we go fishing—you and Irwin. Mam will have plenty. She always does. Usually, on Monday, she makes a pot of vegetable soup to go with whatever is leftover from dinner."

Miriam hesitated. "Not yet, I think. If Irwin and I come to eat, everyone will think that you and I…that we've come to an agreement."

"Oh." He sounded disappointed.

"But I could pack a picnic and the three of us could eat at the pond." She smiled at him. "Before we start catching all those fish."

Charley nodded. "You're right. Mam would think it was settled and she'd start dropping hints about wedding dates. The picnic is a better idea."

"A lot simpler for both of us."

"It's what I am, what I'll always be," he said. "*Simple.* I work with my hands and try to follow God's laws as instructed by our faith and the *Ordnung.*" He looked into her eyes. "But I'd promise to love you and care for you more than anybody else could. I want us to be together, to make a good Amish home, and God willing, I want us to have children together. Is that wrong, Miriam?"

She shook her head. "Not wrong, but it would be wrong if I didn't feel the same way about you. If we weren't right for each other."

"You know, I think I've always loved you."

"Charley, don't. Please. Let's keep it not so serious."

"But we're walking out together. This is when I'm supposed to tell you what I feel in my heart. Isn't it?"

"We're walking out to see if we're…" She stopped and then started again. "I know how I feel, but I don't know how to explain it."

"I think you love me, too, but you're just too stubborn to admit it."

"Charley, I—"

"What is this?" a deep voice demanded.

Miriam looked up to see Uncle Reuben standing in the path ahead of them. "We're not late for services, are we, Uncle?"

"Ne!" His expression was stern, his posture rigid. "You should not be here together without someone," he said. "It looks bad for young people to walk together without a chaperone. You know better."

"It's my fault," Charley said. "I walked over to the Yoders' this morning and asked Miriam to—"

"You and I will talk later." Uncle Reuben pointed toward Charley's house just visible through the trees. "Go and join the men. It is Miriam I wish to speak to."

Appearing uncertain, Charley glanced at her, then back at Uncle Reuben. "If she's in trouble, it's not her fault," he defended. "I'm not leaving her."

"Charley Byler. Are you questioning my authority?"

Charley shook his head. "No, Preacher Reuben. But we did nothing wrong and I wouldn't want you to think otherwise. I was just walking Miriam to service."

Her uncle frowned. "What I have to say to Miriam is private."

"Go on, Charley," Miriam urged. Her knees felt weak, but she knew she was innocent of any wrongdoing. "Please, Charley," she murmured. "It'll be all right. I've done nothing to be ashamed of."

Uncle Reuben motioned to Charley. "Go on now, before you make things worse."

Charley met her gaze, saw that she meant what she

said and reluctantly walked away. When he was out of hearing range, her uncle took her hand in his.

"There is talk, Miriam, talk that worries me."

She blinked back tears. "Is this my uncle speaking to me, or my preacher?"

"Today," he said, "I speak to you as one of the shepherds of our faith. I have come, child, to deliver your first official warning from the bishop."

Chapter Fifteen

Miriam's stomach knotted as she stared at her uncle. He appeared so solemn in his good black coat and black felt hat. Usually, he looked like the other men in the community, but a bit Plainer. He wore his battered straw hat way into the fall, his old suspenders that had come apart and been knotted on the left side and worn blue trousers with patches on the knees. Not today. This morning, he looked the stern Amish preacher that the English liked to picture on their postcards.

Uncle Reuben was a serious man who rarely smiled, but his faded blue eyes were usually kind and his voice soft. Today, his tone was grating and she saw no kindness in his expression, nothing but disapproval and disappointment.

She was in trouble, *real* trouble. Among the Old Order Amish, the rule of the bishop and his two ministers was law. Their decisions on behavior in the community were absolute. If they decided that her behavior was loose, she could be placed under *meidung*. If she was shunned, she would be forbidden to enter the worship service…unable to sit at the same table with her family and friends. Those she loved most might be forced to close their doors to her.

"What are you warning me about?" she managed, when she found her voice.

"You know what. Your behavior with the veterinarian."

"I don't know what behavior with John you're talking about," she protested.

"Bishop Atlee, Deacon Samuel and Preacher Perry have all mentioned your name to me this week. And what they said wasn't praiseworthy. It's my duty to tell you that you are treading on thin ice." He let go of her hand. "A witness told me that John Hartman dropped you off at your house last night, very late. And you were alone. This was not a trip in the middle of the day, as was the day you went to Easton which, as you know, was concern enough. But this is too much. Miriam Yoder does not ride in a car seated next to a man in the dark, unchaperoned."

"I *was* with John last night, but I *wasn't* alone. My sister was with me. He took us to Rehoboth Beach."

Her uncle studied her face. "I was told differently."

"By whom?"

"That's not important. What matters is your reputation and that of our community."

Miriam summoned all her courage. She had known there would be consequences to her decision to court two men at once and it was up to her to defend that decision. "Uncle Reuben, I have a right to know who is bearing false witness against me."

"Is it false?"

"Absolutely. Susanna was with us. You can ask my mother and sisters. Mam gave me permission to go to the boardwalk with John, but we had Susanna with us the whole time."

"Then why didn't your brother-in-law see Susanna in the cab of John's truck? Wilmer told me that he saw only the two of you, and you were sitting in the middle, beside John."

Miriam felt a flare of anger. Wilmer was spying on her? What other reason would he have had for being there that time of night? But she made herself remain calm. She nodded. "That's true, I *was* sitting beside him in his truck. But Susanna was there, too. She fell asleep. I had my arm around her and her head was in my lap. When we arrived home, Ruth and Anna met us at his truck. Susanna was so sleepy that they had to help her up the stairs to bed." She felt a quick surge of anger. "I can't believe Wilmer went to you with this. With…with falsehoods!"

"It was out of concern for your welfare and for that of your family. He means you only good, Miriam. With your father dead and your mother with no adult sons, your sister's husband might be considered the head of your family."

"Wilmer Detweiler?" She set her hands on her hips, her face flushing with anger that she fought again to keep out of her tone. "How can he take my father's place? He hardly ever walks through our door and he never speaks to any of us. Wilmer is a moody, mean-spirited man and if he went to you, it was to get me in trouble."

"Hush such talk," her uncle said. "Wilmer is a member of our church, husband to your own sister. Where is the charity in your heart?"

"Where's the charity in his?" She caught herself before she said more. It would be wrong to accuse Johanna's husband of being a bad father to his own children, or of Wilmer having an unkind reason for going to Reuben with this tale. She would be no better than he if she made such accusations.

He raised his hands, palm out. "Miriam."

"You're right," she said, lowering her gaze respectfully. "Perhaps my brother-in-law did mean the best for us. But he was mistaken. I wasn't alone with John last night. Not for a minute."

"I believe you," her uncle said after a moment. "But I must ask you, what is John to you? Have you thought what you may be risking, to associate so freely with a Mennonite?"

"Yes, Uncle, I have thought of it. And the truth is, I don't know how I feel about John. I'm trying to find out."

"So you *are* walking out with John?"

"I like him very much, Uncle Reuben. He's my friend." She tried to think before she spoke. "And…and if what I feel is more…"

"Then why are you allowing Charley to court you?"

She sighed. "It's complicated."

"It's wrong. It puts Charley in a bad light. You must decide if you want to be baptized and live according to the *Ordnung* or leave us and go out among the English. And know that if you do go, you will break your mother's heart, not to say that of your sisters and all those in Seven Poplars who love you."

"But I haven't yet been baptized." She gazed into his craggy face. "Shouldn't I see something of the world before I make the decision?"

Her uncle sighed. "The outside world is not as exciting as you might think." He glanced toward Charley's house. "Enough. We will be late. I will tell the bishop and the other elders that Wilmer was mistaken."

"So I'm not in danger of being punished?" Emotion caught in her throat. "Of being shunned?"

"Oh, child, where is your understanding? No one said anything of being shunned. Do you think that *meidung* is an act of punishment? One we would place on you lightly or without sufficient cause? Shunning is an act of love, Miriam, used only in the most extreme cases to save one of our own."

"And there are two warnings before shunning," she said. She looked up at him. "Is this still the first?"

"I think you should be more concerned about your attitude and not the legalities of your situation, but I see no reason to give you an official warning if Wilmer was mistaken. But as your uncle, I warn you to be more careful." He gestured toward the Byler house. "Go now and take your place among the women. It would not do to interrupt services on the Sabbath."

"Go without me, Uncle. I need a few minutes alone."

"You give me your word that you will come?"

She nodded. "I will. I need the peace of church right now more than ever."

Uncle Reuben hurried away and Miriam just stood there on the wooded lane, trying not to cry. How had she caused so much trouble for her family when all she wanted to do was to make the right choice for her future? She felt so confused, so…not in control.

"Miriam?" Charley stepped out from behind a wild rosebush not twenty feet away. "Are you all right?"

She blinked. "I thought you went—"

"I'm sorry, Miriam." He came to her and took her hands. "I started to do what he told me, but I couldn't leave you. I doubled back and hid in the trees. You don't need to worry. I didn't hear what Preacher Reuben said to you, but—"

She pulled her hands out of his. "No, I want to tell you." She caught one bonnet string between her fingers and twisted it nervously. "Wilmer went to my uncle and accused me of going out with John alone, last night. It's not true." Quickly she explained that Susanna had been with her all evening. "And Uncle Reuben says that I'm being unfair to you because I've gone places with John and that people are talking."

Charley bristled, then pulled her close and hugged her. "They'd better not say it to me."

She laid her head on his shoulder for a long minute, feeling small and frightened in his arms.

He released her, stepped back and gazed into her eyes. "You're doing nothing wrong, Miriam. Take all the time you need. You know I love you and want you for my wife, but I want you to be certain that it's me you want. I don't want to be second-best, the man you were forced to marry to make everyone else happy."

"I'd never do that to you," she promised, rubbing her eyes. A few tears escaped down her cheeks and Charley handed her a new handkerchief from his pocket.

"Do you feel like going to church?" he asked. "If you don't want to, I'll stay with you. I could walk you home or—"

"I want to go to services. No matter how bad I feel, the hymns and listening to God's word always lift my spirits." She sniffed. "And if I didn't go, it would look like I'm ashamed—that I *have* something to hide."

He offered his hand again. "Then, let's go together."

She smiled, but tucked her hands behind her back. "Gladly, but there's no need to shock anyone. It *is* the

Sabbath. And we'd better hurry, or we'll be late and we'll both be in hot water."

Side by side, they walked across the field to Charley's mother's house, where the sounds of the first hymns were already sounding. "You go in through the kitchen," he suggested. "Your mother will think you've been helping out with the babies. I'll come from the front. Some of the younger guys are always sneaking in during the first hymn. No one will notice."

She laughed. "Wishful thinking. You and me both late? Everyone will notice."

He grinned at her. "It won't be the first time we've been in trouble, though, will it?"

"Hardly," she agreed. They were approaching the back of the farmyard. Rows of black buggies were lined up, but the horses had been turned into the pound or tied in the barn and sheds. Nothing was stirring but one gray tomcat and a bantam rooster.

"Before you go, I wanted to ask you something," Charley said as they reached the farmyard. "After church, this evening, could you take a ride with me—with one of your sisters, or *all of them?* Reuben can come, too, if he wants." He grinned and she grinned back. "I've got something I want you to look at."

"What is it?" she asked.

"You'll see. It's a surprise."

It was after seven o'clock that night when Hannah, Susanna, Charley and Miriam arrived at a home near Felton. Charley had hired a driver so that they wouldn't be out on the roads late in his father's buggy. It was evident to Miriam that the owners must be English, because the prefab house had a large satellite dish on the side lawn and an SUV and a pickup in the driveway.

"Tony works with me," Charley explained. "He knows that we use horses and he thought I might know someone who could help."

Puzzled, Miriam followed her mother and sister out of the van. The driver remained inside, listening to the radio, as Charley led the way to a white lean-to shed in the backyard. It had a Pennsylvania Dutch hex sign painted on the door and a fake weather vane on top. They were met by a man and a boy about six years old that Charley introduced as Tony and T.J. The little boy stared at them, but Miriam didn't mind. She knew that their Amish clothing must look as odd to T.J. as his red and yellow cartoon T-shirt and his short-cropped hair with the little rattail at the back appeared to Susanna.

"A fellow from the Air Force base boarded the pony here at my sister's for a few weeks," Tony explained as he opened the door to the shed. "Sherry loves animals and she can never pass up a sob story. The guy told her he rescued it from some trailer park and that it was temporary, her keepin' it, but then he must have been transferred or something because his phone was disconnected when she tried to call him when she didn't hear from him."

"Tony told me that the horse needed medical care," Charley explained to Miriam and her family.

"It's gentle enough to let kids crawl all over it." Tony walked in and switched on a ceiling light. "Sherry doesn't have the money to pay for a vet or to buy horse chow. This week she got a postcard from California. The guy who left the animal said sell it for what he owed her in board." He shook his head. "Sherry doesn't want to sell it. She feels sorry for it. She just wants to find the horse a good home."

Miriam wasn't listening anymore. Her attention was fixed on the ragged pony tied to a ring on the far wall. It was a brown and white pinto, standing about fourteen hands, with a dark mane and tail. Sadly, the animal appeared to be in terrible condition, ungroomed, hooves grown out, mane and tail tangled and so thin that her ribs showed.

"Poor *maedchen*," she crooned, going to the pony and stroking her neck. An empty bucket lay overturned on the concrete floor amid a few handfuls of what appeared to be corncobs and lawn clippings.

"Like I said." Tony sounded apologetic. "He needs a vet, but Sherry's a single mother with three kids and an ex that doesn't pay regular child support. She can't afford to take care of another stray."

Charley came to Miriam's side. "What do you think? Tony said Sherry told him the pony's trained to a carriage. With a little fattening up, she might make a good addition to your farm."

"It's a girl?" Tony bent and peered at the pony's underside. He was a big man with a bigger belly, bald, with the complexion of someone who'd spent a lifetime working outdoors. "Sherry thought it was a boy horse."

"It's a mare," Charley said, trying not to laugh.

Miriam checked the pony's teeth and then scratched behind her ears. She could see that the animal was young, no more than five or six years old, but her hooves were in terrible shape. Miriam couldn't tell if they'd ever been trimmed. They were cracked and so long that they curled up in the front. The pony was watching with huge brown eyes, eyes that seemed to be begging, *Help me. Please, get me out of here.*

Miriam picked up one of the pony's hooves, and then another. She ran her hands over the pinto's legs and felt the belly. Through it all, the animal stood patiently. Even the little mare's long coat was a disgrace. Tufts of hair were coming out and there was a bare spot on one hip. As Miriam inspected the raw skin closely, she saw tell-tale evidence of lice. She shuddered with distaste and quickly snatched her hand away.

Angry thoughts of what she would like to do to anyone who left a pony in this condition filled her, and when she turned to look at her mother, she could hardly speak. "Mam?"

Hannah nodded.

"You say your sister will let us have the pony for nothing?" Miriam turned to Tony. "Could we take her tonight?"

"Tonight?" The Englishman's eyes widened in surprise. "Sure, you can have her tonight, but we don't have a horse trailer."

She felt for the red cell phone in her pocket. "Lucky for us, we have a friend who does have a trailer."

"Ya," Charley agreed. "A friend of the family who happens to be a vet. So the pony will get good care."

"And a good home," Miriam said. "It's obvious that she needs it." She glanced at Charley. "Thank you," she murmured. "You're the best friend of all."

As September slipped into October and the trees turned from green to red and gold, Miriam's days and nights were filled to overflowing. With Molly and the new pony to care for, crops to get in and the usual farm chores, she was too exhausted to worry too much about her future or the possibility that she could still be banned for her *loose behavior*. Instead of worrying, she tried to take each day as it came, accepting God's simple pleasures around the farm.

The pony, named *Taffy* by Susanna, was already looking much better. Charley's brother Roland, a skilled farrier, had trimmed her hooves. John had given her a thorough medical examination and prescribed vitamins, a special horse feed, lots of grooming and medication for her infestation with lice. Because of Taffy's sweet disposition, Miriam guessed that the pony had suffered from the owner's ignorance and lack of care, rather than abuse. In any case, the entire family seemed delighted with her. Once Taffy regained her health, Miriam was certain that the little mare would make a dependable driving pony.

With Hannah's approval, Miriam continued seeing both John and Charley over the next three weeks. Always properly chaperoned, she walked to church with Charley, fished in his father's pond, went to husking bees and picked grapes and apples with him. Some evenings, Charley came by the Yoder farm and they played catch with a softball in the yard or a quiet game of cards with the family.

Dates with John were more exciting: the spaghetti supper at his uncle's church, lunch at a Mexican restaurant, a trip to the library, an afternoon movie at the mall and routine visits to care for ill or injured animals. Miriam took care never to do anything that her mother would consider inappropriate or that might bring censure from the church elders. If Miriam wasn't accompanied by one of her sisters, she took Irwin along.

On a Saturday in mid-October, Miriam and John were

picking pumpkins at Samuel's farm when the two finally found a few minutes alone. Irwin had been helping, but he and Samuel's twins had gone off to join a softball game at the field beside the school. Technically, she and John were unchaperoned, but they were in a field in plain view for anyone who drove by to see, and therefore couldn't be accused of sneaking behind anyone's back to be alone.

Molly, recovered from her hoof infection and now pronounced by John as sound enough for light work, was hitched to the small cart. Eli had suggested that they sell decorated pumpkins for Halloween at his shop. Samuel had a bumper crop this year and was willing to let the Yoder girls have them for fifty cents each. It seemed a good idea that might bring in a little extra cash, so the whole family was helping out. John had come by to visit and was pressed into the pumpkin project. Miriam was in charge of the picking and Ruth, Susanna and Anna would do the painting.

Miriam was barefoot, her hair decently covered by a lavender scarf, as John lifted the pumpkins out of the muddy field and handed them up to her where she stood next to the cart. They already had more than a dozen in the vehicle when Miriam reached to take a particularly fat pumpkin with a long twisted stem. As she grabbed the pumpkin, her hand brushed John's and she blushed as she felt a jolt of excitement.

The pumpkin slipped out of her fingers, bounced off the low side of the cart and smashed on the ground. John grabbed her by the waist, lifted her into the air and set her down in front of him on the tailgate of the cart. Then, he leaned closer and kissed her.

"John!"

"What?" His eyes were sparkling.

"You...*we* can't do this." She pushed at his shoulders, putting a little distance between them.

"Why not?"

"Because...because you cannot be so familiar with me. We've talked about this. There can be no kissing."

"How about if I ask you to marry me?" He gazed into her eyes, a smile on his lips. "*Then* do I have a right to a kiss?"

Chapter Sixteen

"Marry?" Miriam's eyes widened. "You're asking me to marry you?"

He laughed. "That was the point of my courting you, right?"

She hadn't expected this. Not yet. Certainly not today. "And…and you're asking me now?"

"Why wouldn't I? You're special, Miriam. You're smart and funny and full of life. We'd be happy together—I know it. And…" He looked down at the ground, then up at her again. "And I think it's time we decided. We've seen enough of each other to know if this is what we want. I know it's what I want. And you'd have so much more freedom as a Mennonite."

She nodded, suddenly frightened and excited, at the same time. "It's a big decision," she heard herself say.

What was wrong with her? This was what she wanted, wasn't it? John was such a wonderful man, everything any woman would want in a husband: patient, gentle, hardworking. She could love him, if she didn't already. She could see herself having his children. But…*but what?* she wondered.

"Miriam?" His brow creased. "You're not saying anything. A man asks you to marry him, you're supposed to…say something."

She let her hands fall to her lap. "I care for you so much," she said, "but the truth is, I don't know if I could abandon my faith…my family."

"You wouldn't be abandoning your family. You said yourself that if you become Mennonite, you'd still be welcome at your mother's table."

"But not church." She felt a sudden tightness in her chest. "If we were Mennonite, our children would not be welcome in the Amish church, either."

"We can figure it out. I'll do anything you want. I mean it." He pulled off his ball cap. "I'll become Amish, if that's what you want. How would I look in a straw hat?"

At first, she thought John was being silly, but she realized that beneath the joking, he was serious. "You would do that for me?" she murmured, gazing into his eyes. "You'd give up being a Mennonite? You'd become *Plain,* for me?"

"I would." He tossed his hat into the wagon. "As long as your bishop would give me some kind of exemption— so that I could continue my veterinary practice. I have to drive to care for my patients and I couldn't work in the clinic without electricity. But, maybe they could make an exception. I could be Amish at home and Mennonite in the world. I must not be the first man to do that."

"But your own faith, John, your family? How would they feel if you turned Amish?"

He shrugged, his handsome face growing serious. "What they want doesn't matter. I only care about us. I think you'd fit in well in the Mennonite life, but I mean it. I'll do whatever it takes to make you happy." He captured a loose lock of her hair that had escaped her scarf and wound it around his finger. "So will you marry me, Miriam Yoder? Will you be my wife?" He hesitated. "You're still not saying anything."

"I need time, John." She looked into his handsome, honest face. "I'm sorry, but I can't tell you this second. Can I have a few days?"

"Take all the time you need."

"All right," she promised, getting to her feet in the cart. She was trembling. He'd done it, asked her to marry him. She'd been so sure that if he did, when he did, that she'd say *yes*. He'd even offered to become Amish so she wouldn't have to leave her family or her church. So why hadn't the words come out of her mouth? Why hadn't she told him she would marry him? What was wrong with her? "I'll give you an answer soon."

"Tell me that you haven't made up your mind yet," he urged. "Tell me I still have a chance."

"You do," she said, smiling at him as she tossed his cap back and moved to the front of the cart. She unwound the leathers from the peg where she'd wrapped them and flicked the lines over Molly's back. "Walk on," she said.

She looked back, her heart full of love. John was still standing there with his hat in his hands, watching her. Her mouth still tingled from his kiss and her heart was racing. She could still feel the warmth of his touch.

Above, the sky was a brilliant blue, the clouds white drifting puffs of meringue. The air was rich with the scents of ripening pumpkins and fertile soil. *Please, God,* she prayed silently. *Help me to make the right decision. Help me find Your plan for me.*

It was Susanna who found Miriam later, sitting on the swing in the front yard, deep in thought. Susanna had smudges of white and green paint on her chin and nose, and a big streak down her skirt. Both chubby hands were covered in the poster paint that she'd used to decorate the pumpkins.

"Miriam!" Her little sister ran toward her, *kapp* strings flying. "Did you see Kitty-Cat? I want to show her my pun-kin."

Miriam wiped her eyes and smiled at her little sister. She didn't want Susanna to see that she'd been crying. Susanna's heart was so big that she could never bear to see anyone unhappy. She possessed a child's innocence, and a compassion that embraced every living thing. But Miriam couldn't explain her dilemma to Susanna. How could she expect Susanna to understand what she herself couldn't?

Miriam didn't know what to do. Two good men loved her and she couldn't decide between them. Worse, she'd let both of them kiss her and she'd liked it. What kind of Amish woman was she? Why couldn't she be as certain of her place in God's plan as Anna was? Why couldn't she make up her mind about something that should have been so simple? She didn't even have to choose between her faith and John's if she didn't want to. So, did she love John or did she love Charley?

Susanna came to stand in front of her. "What's wrong, Miriam?" She touched her cheek. "You sad?"

Miriam sniffed and nodded. She wished she had Charley's handkerchief. She knew she needed to blow her nose. She was afraid to speak. If she did, she was afraid she'd start crying all over again.

"Why?" A calico cat strolled out from under a lilac bush, elegant tail curved over her sleek back. "Kitty!" Susanna dove for her pet and returned with the purring cat in her arms. "I painted a pun-kin," she told the animal. "Want to see?"

"I think you painted Susanna," Miriam said, forcing a smile as she looked at her sister's paint-smudged face. Love for her little sister enveloped her like a hug. Susanna might be different from most people, but she brought joy to everyone around her.

"You want to see my pun-kin, Miriam?"

Miriam nodded. "In a little bit."

"You're sad," Susanna repeated. "Why are you sad?"

"I have a big decision to make, and it's hard."

"Mam says ask God. He knows."

"I have asked Him, Susanna," Miriam admitted. "Over and over, but I can't hear His answer."

"You have to listen. Mam says, 'Listen, Susanna. Open your ears.'"

The cat had curled up contentedly in Susanna's arms. "Do you pray?" Miriam asked.

Her sister nodded.

Miriam stroked the cat's head, and Kitty purred louder. "Why don't you go show Kitty the pumpkin you painted?"

Susanna tilted her head and patted Miriam's shoulder. "God loves you. Don't be sad."

Another tear trickled down Miriam's nose. "But I don't know what to do. I keep thinking and thinking, and I still don't know what's best."

Susanna's lips pursed and her brow furrowed in thought. Miriam could almost see the wheels turning, and she waited to see what would come out of Susanna's mouth.

"I think you should ask Charley."

"Ask Charley?" Miriam stared at her sister in confusion. She hadn't told her sister what decision she was trying to make.

"Ask Charley. He's smart. Not like me. He tells me things all the time when I don't know the answer."

It seemed to Miriam as if suddenly the clouds parted and the front lawn was bathed in warm, glowing sunlight. *Ask Charley? Ask Charley! Of course. That was the answer. Ask Charley.* She jumped up, threw her arms around Susanna and hugged her. "Don't ever think you're not smart! You are, Susanna. Thank you!"

"What?" Susanna demanded, but Miriam was already running toward the backyard.

Irwin's blue push-scooter was leaning against the porch. Miriam grabbed it and began to roll it toward the driveway. "Hey!" Irwin called. "Where you going with my scooter?"

"Just borrowing it!" Miriam shouted over her shoulder.

"Miriam!" Anna called from the front porch. "Where are you going?"

Susanna dashed around the house. "Charley's," she explained. "Miriam's going to ask Charley."

To Miriam's dismay, Charley wasn't home. His sister told her that Charley was at Roland's, laying block for a new chicken house. "Is something wrong?" Mary asked. "Do you need me to hitch up the buggy and drive you over?"

Miriam shook her head. "*Ne.* I'll be fine."

She turned and pushed the scooter back down the Bylers' lane and along the road past the schoolhouse. Cars and trucks whizzed past, and once an Amish horse and wagon rolled by and Lydia Beachy and two of her daughters waved.

"Hey, Miriam," Lydia called as she bounced a baby on her knee. "Would you like a ride?"

Miriam waved back, but shook her head. She didn't want to explain to Lydia or her girls why she was chasing Charley around the neighborhood. "I'm good," she said.

The Beachy buggy clattered past, little Elsie hanging half out the back door. Miriam was about to shout a warning, but then Verna yanked her back in and secured the door.

Miriam kept pushing the scooter and Susanna's words kept sounding in her head. *"Ask Charley. Charley's smart."* Maybe that was the answer. All she knew was that the despair that had smothered her for days had suddenly dissolved. Instead of sadness, she felt hope. One way or another, she had the feeling that everything would be settled once she found Charley. He knew her better than anyone. He'd tell her what to do.

By the time she got to Roland's lane, Miriam's leg ached from pushing the scooter, and she was hot and sticky. She stopped at the pitcher pump in the yard and pumped up a cup of cool water and then splashed her face to clean off the road dust. She left the scooter leaning against the pump and walked to the site of the new chicken house behind the barn.

Charley and Roland were both there, and Roland's two-year-old was with them. Someone had given Jared a big spoon and some plastic cups. The little boy was eagerly digging in a pile of sand, giggling and tossing sand in the air. An older neighbor, Shupp Troyer, was leaning on a stack of concrete blocks and giving advice on how the structure should be built.

"Charley, I need to talk to you," Miriam said, as soon as she greeted everyone. "Alone."

Charley exchanged glances with his brother, shrugged and finished tapping in the block he'd been laying. "Best see what she needs," he said to the two men. "Might be important."

As Charley walked away from the foundation, little Jared threw up his arms and squealed. "You want to come?" Charley swung the wiggling toddler up onto his shoulders. Jared giggled and grabbed hold of Charley's ears. "Easy on the ears," Charley protested. "I've only got two."

"You sure you want that trouble?" Roland called after them.

"*Ya.* He'll be fine," Charley assured him.

Charley was good with children. It seemed that they all loved him and he had immense patience with them. *He'll make a great father,* Miriam thought.

Nervously, she led the way back around the barn, past the calf pen, to a small pond beside a maple tree, with leaves already turning a brilliant red. The banks of the pond were thick with clover and Roland had built a high-backed bench on a small stretch of sand overlooking the water.

Heart in her throat, Miriam took a seat on the bench. Charley wrestled Jared off his shoulders, retrieved his straw hat and Jared's, and sat the little boy between them.

"What is it?" he asked.

Jared slid down off the bench and began to use his hat as a sand bucket.

"Jared, don't," Miriam said.

"*Ne,* let him be," Charley said. "It will keep him happy." He pointed to the water. "Stay here," he warned. "Don't get near the water or you'll have to go in the house with your mother."

Jared nodded and began digging a hole.

Charley looked at Miriam again and waited.

She folded her hands in her lap and stared at them. Her

mouth was dry and her chest felt tight. She'd come this far; she couldn't let her nerve fail her now. "I need you to let me say what I have to say," she managed. "Don't say anything. Just hear me out first."

"All right," he agreed. The muscles in his face were taut, the expression in his eyes curious, but guarded.

"You know I've been thinking about you and John and which one I'm meant to be with. I've also been struggling with the decision to join the Amish church."

Charley nodded. "I do."

She swallowed. This was so difficult. She had to know the answer to her question, but she didn't want Charley to give the wrong answer. "I don't know too much about the Mennonite faith, but what I've learned seems good. What I wanted to ask you is if you've ever thought about not being baptized in *our* church?"

"Not join the Amish church?" Charley looked startled.

Jared began crawling toward the water, Charley snatched him up and put him back closer to the bench. "I mean it, Jared. Stay here, or back to the house and nap time."

Jared shook his head. "Na, na, na."

Miriam tried again. "What I meant was…would you be willing to turn Mennonite to marry me? If I wanted to become Mennonite?"

"You don't want to be Amish?" His mouth firmed.

She lifted a finger. "Please. Just listen."

Charley frowned, but he didn't say anything more.

"If we married and joined the Mennonite church, we could still live in Seven Poplars. You could keep your job, and we could see our families regularly. We could buy a truck and learn to drive it. We could go places. See things."

"This is what you want?" He glanced down at Jared and then back at her. He stared full into her eyes. "You want me to abandon the Amish church for a truck and a faster way of life?"

Jared began piling sand on Charley's high-top work shoe.

Miriam reached for Charley's hand. "I didn't *say* I wanted you to leave the church. Not that, exactly. I wanted to know if *you'd* stop being Amish if that was the only way I would agree to marry you."

Charley gripped her hand. When he spoke again, his voice was rough. "I love you, Miriam. I love you more than I love Roland or my sister or my mother, more than my own life. I want to make you my wife. I want us to have children together, but I want to raise them in our faith."

She held his gaze. "But what if leaving the Amish church is the only way I'd marry you?"

"If I had to stop being Amish to marry you…"

She waited, holding her breath for his answer.

He broke off, his voice ragged with emotion. "I can't do that, Miriam, not even for you." He shook his head. "I'm the same as I've always been. I'm a Plain man, like my father and grandfather, all the way back to the old country."

A maple leaf floated down, sailing past the bench to land on Jared's outstretched knee. "La-la-la," he squealed, grabbing the leaf with both hands.

Tears clouded Charley's blue eyes. "Ask me anything else, Miriam. Anything else I would do for you, but this is where I fit in God's world. I'm just good old Charley. I'm not the kind of man who can change my faith, not even for you."

"You're certain?"

"From the bottom of my heart." He took a breath. "So if you want to be Mennonite, I wish you happiness with John."

Chapter Seventeen

Miriam smiled at him. "You mean that, don't you? You really mean you want me to be happy—even if it's with John?"

He nodded. "Of course. I love you. Why wouldn't I want you to be happy?"

The hurt in Charley's eyes was a raw wound. Miriam could feel her heart constricting. It had never occurred to her that both men might fall in love with her. And now, no matter which man she chose, she would have to refuse the other. How had she been so foolish as to let this go so far? Tears filled her eyes. "You say you love me, but do you trust me?"

His answer came all in a rush. "With my life."

She had to see John. *Now.* She had to tell him her decision. "Could you come with me to talk to John? I know it's a lot to ask, but I can only say this one time—and I need both of you to be there."

Charley picked up Jared, dusted off his clothing and adjusted the little boy's small hat. His gaze was on his nephew, not Miriam, as he said, "You're going to marry John and leave the faith?"

A rush of joy filled her, making her want to spin and shout, to throw up her arms to the sky and laugh. "I didn't say that. I just said trust me, Charley. Now, come with me." Her tears were already fading. "Please."

"Do you know where John is? Is he at the office? We just can't go tearing around Dover chasing him in the buggy."

"*Ne*. I don't know, but I can find out."

Charley frowned as she pulled the red cell phone out of her apron pocket and pushed the button that would *speed dial* John's cell. Jared giggled and reached for the red phone with both chubby hands.

"Hello, John? It's Miriam." She took a breath and explained what she needed.

In seconds, she hung up and turned back to Charley and Jared. "He's at Hershberger's farm. Perry has a calf with a barbed wire cut. John offered to come here when he's finished tending the heifer, but I asked him to meet us at the schoolhouse. Halfway in between." She glanced around. "School's out for the day, and we can talk there in private."

Charley nodded. "I can drive you there." He shifted Jared to his shoulder. "But we'll have to bring this bundle of mischief with us. Roland needs to take Pauline to the doctor and I promised him I'd keep the boy until they got back."

"We can take him. No problem. And it will please Uncle Reuben that we have a chaperone." She chuckled. "Even if a small one."

Charley grinned at her. "*Ya*. You must set a good example for your sisters."

The tension seemed to ease between them as they walked back to where Charley had left his open buggy. There, Miriam lifted Jared into the seat while Charley went to tell his brother where they were taking the boy. In just a few minutes, Charley returned to hitch his horse to the buggy. "Just as well Jared's going with us," he said. "Shupp wanted to know where we were off to and did your mother know."

Miriam chuckled. "Shupp is as bad as Aunt Martha. Such a gossip, he is."

Jared picked that moment to pull off his hat and sent it flying.

Charley retrieved the boy's straw hat, climbed up into the seat and gathered the leathers in one callused hand. "You sure you know what you're doing?" he asked Miriam as he passed Jared's hat to her. "You won't regret what you've decided?"

She smiled at him over Jared's head. "Never." She smoothed back the toddler's hair and placed the hat on his head.

"Keep your hat on," Charley ordered as he drove out of the barnyard. "Just like Dat does."

As they passed the house, Pauline waved from an open upstairs window. "Look." Miriam pointed. "There's your Mam."

Jared giggled, bounced up and down and waved with both hands.

Neither Miriam nor Charley spoke as he guided the horse out of the lane and onto the blacktop road. A tractor trailer and a line of cars passed, but Charley paid them no mind. He kept the gelding at a fast trot and didn't pull off onto the shoulder until a convertible ran up on them and blew the horn.

Jared's face paled and his lower lip came out. It appeared that he was about to burst into tears until Charley took him onto his lap and let him hold the ends of the reins. "Shh, shh," Charley soothed. "This is a good horse. He's not scared of the cars and you shouldn't be, either."

Jared sniffed and clung tight to the leathers.

"What a big boy you are," Miriam encouraged. "Your Dat will be proud of you."

As they passed the chair shop, they saw Eli and Ruth standing outside the front door and waved. "Eli's making her a walnut table as a wedding gift," Miriam said. "Roman's giving them two chairs to match it, but it's a surprise."

Charley nodded. "It will be a happy day, their wedding. I hope your sisters can come home to share in Ruth's joy."

"*Ya.* They will. Aunt Martha and Dorcas have promised to go out and stay with *Grossmama* for the week so Leah and Rebecca can be here."

Charley looked dubious. "That doesn't sound like Martha."

Miriam smiled. "She's a good woman, Charley. Sometimes, it's hard for her to show it. But she knows how important it is to Mam to have us all here for Ruth's wedding." She grasped the railing as Charley reined the horse across the intersection and turned onto the road that led to the schoolhouse.

"It goes to show, you shouldn't make hasty judgments," Miriam said. "Even when it comes to Aunt Martha."

"*Ya,*" Charley agreed. "I suppose it does." He hesitated. "I've been taking instruction from Preacher Perry, for my baptism. I didn't say anything to you before, but…"

"So you are definitely going to join the church?" she asked. "There's no chance you would change your mind?"

He shook his head. "Not even for you."

She took a deep breath and stared out at the fields of corn on either side of the road. These were English farms.

Soon a giant combine would roar down the rows and harvest the corn...while at the Byler place and many others, it would be Amish men cutting the corn stalks with machetes and stacking them in shocks. It was as though the Amish were caught in a previous time, she thought. Everything we do is the old way, following tradition, even if it means more work. But, she had to admit, the rows of corn shocks stretching across the fields made for a beautiful sight.

John's truck was parked beside the schoolhouse. Charley guided the horse into the drive and up to the hitching rail. Miriam climbed down and reached up for Jared.

"Swing!" he cried, pointing. "Swing!"

"I'll take him," Charley offered as he tied the gelding to the post.

"Later," Miriam said. Holding Jared by the hand, she walked over to where John waited by the pickup.

"Who have you got here?" John asked.

While Miriam made the introductions, John opened the glove box and took out a package of pretzel sticks. "Okay?" he asked, before offering the little boy a pretzel. Miriam nodded, and Jared plopped down on the grass with a pretzel in both hands and a smile on his face.

John looked from Miriam to Charley. "I guess this is serious," he said.

Miriam's courage wavered. This was so hard. How could she say what had to be said? How could she make them understand how she felt without hurting either John or Charley?

"I think she's made up her mind," Charley said, coming to stand beside Miriam. He crossed his arms over his chest. "I want to wish you both—"

"Charley Byler, will you hush and let me say my piece," Miriam blurted.

Then John started to speak and she held up a hand. "That goes for you, too, John Hartman." She felt a little light-headed and wished she was at home milking the cows, or even peeling potatoes, anywhere but here.

Miriam took a deep breath. "I want you to know, I love you both," she said softly. She looked at one man and then the other. "John, you have opened new windows to the world for me. And, Charley... Charley, you've always been my best friend."

Charley and John looked at each other and then back at her. They both looked nervous.

Heat flushed under Miriam's skin; she was shaking inside. What if she messed this up? What if she lost both of them in the telling?

It didn't matter. She had to be honest, to them and to herself. "If I have hurt either of you, I'm sorry from the bottom of my heart. I mean that. I never meant to hurt anyone."

"I just want you to be happy," Charley said. He picked up Jared and cradled the boy against his chest. "That's what's important, Miriam. I'll always be your friend, if you'll let me."

She smiled at him. "I hope you will. I hope we'll always be best friends." Then she turned and reached for John's hand, and his face lit with an inner flame.

"Miriam..." John murmured.

She placed the red cell phone in his palm and closed his fingers around it. "This belongs to *your* world," she murmured. "It was kind of you to lend it to me, but I don't need it anymore." She moved to stand beside Charley and Jared. "I love you, John, but as a dear, dear friend, not as a husband."

John nodded. "You're going to marry Charley, after all."

"I love him, and he and I are meant to be husband and wife," she answered. "I realized that when Charley told me that he couldn't change his faith, not even for me. You're a good man, John, but my husband must be a man of strong faith. His love for God must be stronger than his love for me."

"I think I understand." John hung his head as he slipped the red cell back into his pocket, but then he looked up again. "But I still want to be your friend…and Charley's, if he'll let me."

But she wasn't listening. She was gazing up into Charley's eyes. "If he'll have me after I've been so foolish."

"Me?" Charley croaked. "You want *me?*"

John cleared his throat and reached for Jared. "Let me take this little guy," he said hoarsely. "Give you two a minute alone." He turned his attention to Jared. "Would you like to blow the truck horn?" he asked the toddler, tickling his belly.

"Beep! Beep!" Jared shouted with a giggle.

Charley stood staring at her as John walked away. "Me?" he repeated.

"*Ya,* you." She was crying, tears flowing, her lower lip quivering. "Will you marry me, Charley?"

He didn't move a muscle. She wasn't sure that he was breathing. "When?" he asked.

She let out a great sigh of relief, smiling through her tears. "Um… I don't know." His question took her by surprise. "We've got to join the church first. Be…be baptized."

"When?" he repeated.

She threw her arms around him. "Weddings are in November, you great ox. Will you marry me in November?"

His arms closed around her in a hug so tight that it took her breath away. *"Ya,"* he agreed. "In the Amish faith I will make you my wife, as soon as the bishop will allow. And all my life I will love you, Miriam Yoder... every day. And every day, I will thank God for you."

On the second Thursday of November, the Yoder house overflowed with guests—not only Bishop Atlee and the ministers and deacon of their church but two visiting bishops and three additional ministers from Pennsylvania. Hannah was everywhere, bustling about, directing the setup of chairs for the church service and the last-minute preparations and storage of food in the kitchen. Assisting her were her daughters: Anna, Susanna, Johanna, Leah and Rebecca and her best friend Lydia. Already, men and women were taking their places for the ceremony and the first stanzas of the opening hymns were spilling through the windows and doors into the yard. Upstairs, the two couples had spent the last hour and a half in council with the bishops and ministers.

At ten minutes past nine, by the tall case clock on the stair landing, Samuel came down the steps. Immediately, those who were still milling around took that as a signal to be seated. "Hannah, it's time," Samuel called from the bottom of the steps. "You don't want to be late to your own daughters' wedding, do you?"

Cheeks flushed, Hannah brushed back a stray strand of hair, smoothed her apron and hurried to take her place in the rows of chairs. Samuel winked at her as he crossed the aisle. "It will be fine," he mouthed silently, and took up the hymn with the others once he'd reached the men's section.

Hannah was too nervous to utter a sound. She fumbled with her hymn book, found the page and then lost it. Rebecca, with Susanna in tow, took a chair to Hannah's right, took the book and found the correct page for her mother. Anna, Leah and Johanna moved quietly into seats behind them as the bishops and ministers came down the stairs and entered the ministers' row.

"Here they come," Rebecca whispered.

Heads turned and waves of whispers flowed under the words of the hymn as Ruth and Eli came down the stairs hand in hand. Ruth's dress and cape were the blue of Susanna's eyes, and the depth of her smile brought a tear to Hannah's eye. Behind them, equally as solemn and equally as beautiful came Charley and Miriam. Her younger daughter had chosen a deeper shade of blue, more summer sky than her sister's clothing. Both wore crisp white *kapps,* the symbol of their reverence before God.

Rebecca squeezed Hannah's hand. "They look happy," she whispered.

"*Ya.* Happy." Hannah found her voice and took up the words of the old song of praise for God's blessings.

The two couples took their places in the front row. Miriam clasped Ruth's hand and leaned close. "Scared?"

"*Ya.* You?"

Miriam glanced up at Charley. How handsome he looked in his black coat and vest, how solid. She shook her head. "Not with Charley," she murmured.

Charley looked down at Miriam and smiled. "I love you," he murmured as Bishop Atlee cleared his throat to begin his sermon.

"I love you, too," Miriam breathed. "From the bottom of my heart. Forever."

Epilogue

Winter...

Charley opened the inner stairway door and stepped into the spacious finished attic that ran the length of Ruth and Eli's new house. Both hands were full and Miriam hurried to take the mugs of hot cocoa before he spilled them.

"How's the geometry going?" he asked as he placed the plate containing two slices of apple pie on the table that divided the bedroom area of their apartment from the living area.

"Almost done." Miriam pointed to her desk. "Two problems to go." She eyed the pie. "I suppose I could take a break."

"*Ya,*" he agreed. "So the cocoa doesn't get cold." He glanced around the single room. "The curtains look nice. You must have put them up today while I was at work."

Miriam sighed. "Ruth did. Anna finished sewing them while I was cleaning the stalls." The curtains did look nice. They were simple white cotton, identical to those in her mother's house and exactly the same as the ones on Ruth's windows on the floor below, but they set off the paneled pine walls and the blue denim covering Mam had sewn for her couch and Charley's easy chair.

She loved their new home, not under Mam's roof as Charley had suggested, but under Ruth and Eli's. They had the big finished attic that would someday, God willing, offer bedrooms for a large family of children. For now, it was perfect for her and Charley. She could remain on the home farm, continue caring for the animals and putting in crops, and she and Charley could have the privacy that any newly married couple wanted. To make the arrangement even better, Eli, Charley, Irwin and Roland had spent two Saturdays adding an outside staircase so Miriam and Charley didn't have to walk through Ruth's kitchen to get in and out.

Charley had plans to add a small kitchen in the front of the open room, but she didn't care when. Cooking had never been one of her better skills. As it was, they ate breakfast with Ruth and dinner and supper at Mam's. To balance out the living arrangement, Charley paid rent and Miriam cared for Taffy, a wedding gift to Eli and Ruth.

Charley settled into his comfortable chair, set his cocoa on a table and motioned to her. "Come sit here, with me."

Miriam smiled. This had become a habit with them at the end of the day. She'd cuddle up in his lap and they'd talk, tease or just enjoy being close and warm. She liked being married and she especially liked being married to Charley. So many exciting things had happened in the months since they'd taken their vows together.

A delay in the hospital construction had given them three weeks to travel west to visit friends and distant relatives. Together, they had ridden a steam train to an old mining camp in Colorado, stared in awe at the Grand

Canyon in Arizona and waded in the Gulf of Mexico in Texas. So many new sights and sounds, so many memories to cherish… And best of all, when they'd returned to Delaware, Charley had surprised her with the best wedding gift she could imagine.

He'd gotten permission from Bishop Atlee, Uncle Reuben and Preacher Perry for her to continue her education by mail. She could get her high school diploma and some college from a Christian school so that she would be fully qualified to teach at the Seven Poplars' School if her mother chose to retire the post. It was the most wonderful gift anyone could have given her.

Charley held out his arms and Miriam went into them. As always, she felt safe and happy. Charley was everything any Amish girl could want in a husband and he'd promised her that they would make decisions together in their new family.

She curled up and laid her head on his chest. He smelled good, better even than the cocoa with marshmallows on top that he'd brought upstairs. "Have I told you how much I love you, Charley Byler?" she teased.

"Not in the last hour."

"I do."

"Do what?"

She giggled as she stroked his bristly chin. As a married man, Charley was expected to grow a beard. His was somewhat reluctant to grow anything resembling Samuel's neatly trimmed and lush beard and all the men teased him about it. "I love you, husband." She waited.

Charley didn't say anything.

"Well?" she demanded.

"Well what?"

"Do you have something to say to me?"

"It's snowing out. Big flakes. We should be able to build a snowman tomorrow."

"Snowing?"

"*Ya.* Cold, white, frozen water. You know, *snow.*"

When she listened, she could hear the howl of the winter wind and imagine the snow falling. It made their home seem all the more a perfect nest, high in the trees, safe from the world. "Are you sorry you chose me, Charley?"

"Are you sorry you didn't pick that fancy Mennonite boy with the ball cap and the pickup truck?" He tickled her until she squealed with laughter. "Tell the truth," he said.

"Ne. Ne." She wrapped her arms around his neck and kissed him tenderly. "Only you, Charley. You are the only man for me...the only husband. I was just too blind to see it."

"Not as blind as me or I would have made my move long before that city boy caught sight of you." He kissed her again. "I love you, Miriam. And I thank God every day for giving you to me."

"It's like Susanna said," Miriam said. "We have to listen if we want to know God's plan for us. Not just pray for an answer, but listen."

"Have I told you that I love you?" he teased.

"Not in the last thirty seconds."

"I could tell you every thirty seconds for the rest of our lives."

She giggled. "Our cocoa would get cold."

"Then we'll have to drink it cold, I suppose," he said. "With the pie."

"Oh, I forgot the pie."

"Pie later, kissing first."

"Whatever you say, Charley." He kissed her again and

sweet sensations danced from the tip of her nose to the soles of her feet.

"Just remember that," he murmured. *"Whatever you say, Charley.* You keep saying that, and we'll never have a disagreement."

"Yes, husband," she said meekly, then tugged at his chin whiskers.

"Ouch."

"Just so you remember your promise. We decide together."

"To kiss or eat pie?"

"Maybe both."

"Ya," he agreed. "Both is good. But each in its own time." And he leaned over and blew out the lamp.

* * * * *

STRANDED

Debbie Giusti

This book is dedicated to Frank Forth, a member of the Greatest Generation who fought in the Battle of the Bulge. Thank you, Frank, for your service, your love and your support.

Greater love hath no man than this,
that a man lay down his life for his friends.
—*John* 15:13

Chapter One

Gripping the steering wheel with one hand, Colleen Brennan shoved a wayward lock of red hair behind her ear with the other and glanced, yet again, at the rearview mirror to ensure she hadn't been followed. She had left Atlanta two hours ago and had been looking over her shoulder ever since.

Her stomach knotted as she turned her focus to the storm clouds overhead. The rapidly deteriorating weather was a threat she hadn't expected.

"Doppler radar...storms that caused damage in Montgomery earlier today...moving into Georgia."

Adjusting the volume on her car radio, she leaned closer to the dashboard, hoping to hear the weather report over the squawk of static.

"Hail...gusting winds. Conditions ideal for tornadoes. Everyone in the listening area is cautioned to be watchful."

The darkening sky and gusting winds added concern to her heavily burdened heart. She didn't like driving on remote Georgia roads with an encroaching storm, but she had an appointment to keep with Vivian Davis. The army wife had promised to provide evidence that would convince the authorities Trey Howard was involved in an illegal drug operation.

Hot tears burned Colleen's eyes. She was still raw from her sister's overdose and death on drugs Trey had trafficked. If only Colleen had been less focused on her flight-attendant career and more tuned in to her sister's needs, she might have responded to Briana's call for help.

Colleen had vowed to stop Trey lest he entice other young women to follow in her sister's footsteps. If the Atlanta police continued to turn a blind eye to his South American operation, Colleen would find someone at the federal level who would respond to what she knew to be true.

Needing evidence to substantiate her claims, she had photographed documents in Trey's office and had taken a memory card that had come from one of the digital cameras he used in his photography business, a business that provided a legitimate cover for his illegal operation.

She sighed with frustration. How could the Atlanta PD ignore evidence that proved Trey's involvement? Yet, they had done just that, and when she'd phoned to follow up on the information she'd submitted, they'd made it sound as if she was the drug smuggler instead of Trey.

Despite her protests, the cop with whom she'd dealt had mentioned a photograph mailed to the narcotics unit anonymously. The picture indicated Colleen's participation in the trafficking operation she was trying to pin on Trey.

Foolishly, she had allowed him to photograph her with a couple of his friends. A seemingly innocent pose, except those so-called friends must have been part of the drug racket. From what she'd learned about Trey over the past few months, he'd probably altered the photo of her to include evidence of possession and then mailed it to the police.

Too often he'd boasted of being well connected with law enforcement. Evidently, he'd been telling the truth. In hindsight, she realized the cop had probably been on the take.

She wouldn't make the same mistake twice. No matter how much she wanted Trey behind bars, she couldn't trust anyone involved in law enforcement at the local level. For all she knew, they were all receiving kickbacks.

Later tonight, after returning to the motel in Atlanta where Colleen had been holed up and hiding out, she would overnight copies of everything she had secreted from Trey's office, along with whatever evidence Vivian could provide, to the Drug Enforcement Administration's Atlanta office. Surely Trey didn't have influence with the federal DEA agents, although after the pointed questions she'd fielded following her sister's death, Colleen didn't have a warm spot in her heart for cops at any level.

Glancing at her GPS, she anticipated the upcoming turn into a roadside picnic park. Vivian had insisted they meet in the country, far from where the army wife lived at Fort Rickman and the neighboring town of Freemont, Georgia.

Colleen glanced again at her rearview mirror, relieved that hers was the only vehicle on the road. Vivian was right. Meeting away from Freemont and Fort Rickman had been a good decision. Except for the storm that threatened to add an unexpected complication to an already dangerous situation.

Turning into the picnic park, Colleen spotted a car. A woman sat at the wheel. Braking to a stop next to the sedan, Colleen grabbed her purse off the seat and threw it in the rear. Then stretching across the console, she opened the passenger door, all the while keeping the motor running.

Clutching a leather shoulder bag in one hand and a cell phone in the other, Vivian stepped from her car and slipped into the front seat. She was as tall as Colleen's five feet seven inches, but with a pixie haircut that framed her alabaster skin and full mouth, which made her appear even more slender in person than in the photographs Colleen had seen on Facebook.

Fear flashed from eyes that flicked around the car and the surrounding roadside park.

"Were you followed?" Vivian nervously fingered her purse and then dropped it at her feet.

"I doubled back a few times and didn't see anyone." Colleen pointed to the thick woods surrounding the off-road setting. "No one will find us here, Vivian. You're safe."

Rain started to ping against the roof of the car. Colleen turned on the wipers.

"I don't feel safe." Vivian bit her chipped nails and slumped lower in the seat. "And I'm not even sure I should trust you."

"I told you we'll work together."

"What if my husband finds out?"

Colleen understood the woman's concern. "He was deployed. You were depressed, not yourself. If you're honest with him, he'll understand."

"He won't understand why his wife accepted an all-expense-paid trip to a Colombian resort while he was deployed to a war zone. He also won't understand how I got involved with Trey Howard."

Colleen's sister had been as naive as Vivian. Briana had been used and abused by the drug dealer, which made Colleen realize how easily Vivian could have been taken in by Trey.

"My sister made the same mistake. Two other women did, as well. That's why I contacted you. You still have a chance to escape."

Vivian glanced out the window. "My husband has orders for Fort Hood. We're moving in three weeks." She raked her hand through her short hair. "I'll be okay, unless the cops find out I smuggled drugs into the country."

"I'll mail whatever evidence you brought today to the DEA without mentioning your name or mine. They won't be able to trace anything back to either of us." Colleen rubbed her hand reassuringly over the young woman's shoulder. "Besides, you didn't know what was in the package Trey had you bring into the US for him."

"I knew enough not to ask questions, which means I could end up in jail." Vivian shrugged away from Colleen and reached for the door handle. "I made a mistake meeting you."

"Vivian, please." Colleen grabbed the young woman's arm before she stepped from the car.

A shot rang out.

Vivian clutched her side and fell onto the seat.

Colleen's heart stopped. She glanced into the woods, seeing movement. A man stood partially hidden in the underbrush, a raised rifle in his hands.

Trey.

A car was parked nearby. She couldn't make out the make or model.

"Stay down," Colleen warned. Leaning across the console and around Vivian, she pulled the passenger door closed.

Another shot. A rear window shattered.

Vivian screamed.

Fear clawed at Colleen's throat. She threw the car into gear and floored the accelerator. The wheels squealed in protest as they left the roadside park.

A weight settled on Colleen's chest. Struggling to catch her breath, she gripped the steering wheel white-knuckled and focused on the two-lane country road that stretched before them.

"He tried to kill me," Vivian gasped. Tears filled her eyes.

Colleen glanced at the hole in the window and the spray of glass that covered the rear seat. "He tried to kill both of us."

She should have known Trey would follow her. He loved fast cars, and no matter what he was driving today, her Honda Civic couldn't outrun his vehicle of choice.

Hot tears burned her eyes. "Our only chance is to find a place to hide and hope Trey thinks we continued north toward the interstate."

He'd eventually realize his mistake and double back to search for them. By then, they would have left the area by another route.

"I'm scared," Vivian groaned.

Refusing to give voice to her own fear, Colleen focused on their most immediate problem. "What's near here that could offer shelter? We need to stow the car out of sight."

"An Amish community." Vivian pointed to the up-coming intersection. "Turn left. Then take the next right.

There's a small shop. An old barn sits in the rear. It's usually empty when I drive by."

Colleen followed the younger woman's directions, all the while checking the rearview mirror.

Vivian glanced over her shoulder. "If he catches us, he'll kill us."

"Not if we hole up in the barn. He won't look for us there."

The army wife pointed to the upcoming intersection. "Turn right. Then crest the hill. The Amish store is on the other side of the rise."

Colleen's stomach tightened with determination. She turned at the intersection and kept the accelerator floored until the car bounded over the hill.

The rain intensified. Squinting through the downpour, she spied the Amish store. One-story, wooden frame, large wraparound porch. Just as Vivian had said, a barn stood at the side of the shop.

Colleen took the turn too sharply. The tires squealed in protest. A gravel path led to the barn. The car bounced over the rough terrain.

She glanced at the road they had just traveled. Trey's car hadn't crested the hill. Relieved, Colleen drove into the barn. Before the engine died, she leaped from the car and pulled the doors closed, casting them in semi-darkness.

Outside, wind howled. Rain pounded against the wooden structure.

"Help me." Vivian's voice.

Colleen raced around the car and opened the passenger door. The woman's face was pale as death. Blood soaked her clothing. For the first time, Colleen saw the gaping hole in Vivian's side.

Removing her own coat, Colleen rolled it into a ball and pressed it onto the wound to stem the flow of blood. Holding it tight with her left hand, she reached for her cell and tapped in 9-1-1.

Before the call could go through, a ferocious roar, both powerful and insistent, gathered momentum, like a freight train on a collision course with the barn. Even without seeing the funnel cloud, Colleen knew a tornado was headed straight for them.

The barn shook. Hay fell from the overhead loft. The noise grew louder. Colleen's ears popped.

Swirling wind enveloped them. Clods of Georgia clay and shards of splintered wood sprayed through the air like shrapnel.

She threw herself over Vivian, protecting her. *God help us*, Colleen prayed as the tornado hit, and the barn crashed down around them.

"Frank," Evelyn screamed from the kitchen. "There's a tornado."

Startled by the tremor in his sister's voice, Frank Gallagher pulled back the living room curtain. His heart slammed against his chest at what he saw. A huge, swirling funnel cloud was headed straight for her house.

"Get to the basement, Evie."

Her sluggish footsteps sounded from the kitchen as she threw open the cellar door and cautiously descended into the darkness below. Injured in a car accident some years earlier, Evelyn's gait was slow and labored, like a person older than her 42 years.

"Duke?" Frank called. The German shepherd, a retired military working dog, appeared at his side.

"Heel." Together, they followed Evelyn down the steep steps.

An antique oak desk sat in the corner and offered additional protection. Frank hurried her forward.

"Get under the desk, Evie."

A deafening roar enveloped them. Frank glanced through the small basement window. His gut tightened.

Debris sailed through the air ahead of the mass of swirling wind bearing down on them.

His heart stalled, and for one long moment, he was back in Afghanistan. The explosion. The flying debris. The building shattering around him.

Trapped under the rubble, he had gasped for air. The smell of death returned to fill his nostrils. Only he had lived.

Duke whined.

"Frank," Evelyn screamed over the incessant roar. She grabbed his arm and jerked him down next to her.

Frank motioned for Duke to lie beside them. The thunderous wail drowned out his sister's frantic prayers. All he heard was the howling wind, like a madman gone berserk, as chilling as incoming mortar rounds.

He tensed, anticipating the hit, and choked on the acrid bile that clogged his throat. Tightening his grip on his sister's outstretched hand, Frank opened his heart, ever so slightly, to the Lord.

Save Evie. The prayer came from deep inside, from a place he'd sealed off since the IED explosion had changed his life forever. Just that quickly the raging wind died, and the roar subsided.

Frank expelled the breath he'd been holding.

Evelyn moaned with relief. "Thank you, God."

Crawling from under the desk, he helped his sister to

her feet and then glanced through the window. Mounds of tree limbs, twisted like matchsticks, littered the yard. At least the house had been spared.

He pulled his mobile phone from his pocket. No bars. No coverage.

Evelyn reached for the older landline phone on the desk. "I've got a dial tone."

"Call 911. Let them know the area along Amish Road was hit and to send everything available. Then phone the Criminal Investigation Division on post. Talk to Colby Voss. Tell him the Amish need help."

"Colby would tell you to stay put, Frank. You're still on convalescent leave."

Ignoring her concern for his well-being, Frank patted his leg for Duke to follow him upstairs.

Another close call. Was God trying to get his attention? A verse from scripture floated through his mind, *Come back to me.*

In the kitchen, Frank yanked his CID jacket from the closet and grabbed leather work gloves he kept nearby. Pushing through the back door, he stopped short and pulled in a sharp breath at what he saw—a different kind of war zone from what he'd experienced in Afghanistan, but equally as devastating.

The tornado had left a trail of destruction that had narrowly missed his sister's house. He searched for the Amish farmhouses that stretched along the horizon. Few had been spared. Most were broken piles of rubble, as if a giant had crushed them underfoot.

A sickening dread spread over him. The noise earlier had been deafening. Now an eerie quiet filled the late Georgia afternoon. No time to lament. People could be trapped in the wreckage.

"Come on, boy." Frank quickly picked his way among the broken branches and headed for the path that led through the woods. He ignored the ache in his hip, a reminder of the IED explosion and the building that had collapsed on top of him. Thankfully, a team of orthopedic surgeons had gotten him back on his feet. A fractured pelvis, broken ribs and a cracked femur had been insignificant compared with those who hadn't made it out alive.

Still weak from the infection that had been a life-threatening complication following surgery, Frank pushed forward, knowing others needed help. Skirting areas where the tornado had twisted giant trees like pickup sticks, he checked his cell en route and shook his head with regret at the lack of coverage.

At the foot of the hill, he donned his leather work gloves and raced toward the Amish Craft Shoppe. A brother and sister in their teens usually manned the store.

"Call out if you can hear me," he shouted as he threw aside boards scattered across the walkway leading to the front porch. "Where are you?" he demanded. "Answer me."

Duke sniffed at his side.

"Can you hear me?" he called again and again. The lack of response made him fear the worst and drove him to dig through the fallen timbers even more frantically.

An Amish man and woman tumbled from a farmhouse across the street. Their home had lost its roof and a supporting side wall.

The bearded man wore a blue shirt and dark trousers, held up with suspenders. Dirt smudged his face and his cheek was scraped.

"The store was closed today," he shouted, waving his

hands to get Frank's attention. "The youth are at a neighboring farm."

"You're sure?" Frank was unwilling to give up the search if anyone was still inside.

The man glanced at the woman wearing a typical Amish dress and apron.

"*Jah*, that is right," she said, nodding in agreement.

"What about your family?" Frank called. "Was anyone hurt?"

"Thanks to God, we are unharmed, but our neighbors are in need." The man pointed to the next farmhouse and the gaping hole where the wall and roof had been. He and his wife ran to offer aid.

Before Frank could follow, he glanced at the nearby barn. The corner of one wall remained standing, precariously poised over a pile of rubble. At that moment, the cloud cover broke, and the sun's reflection bounced off a piece of metal buried in the wreckage.

Something chrome, like the bumper of a car. The Amish didn't drive automobiles, but a traveler passing by could have been seeking shelter from the storm.

He raced to the barn and dug through the debris. "Shout if you can hear me."

A woman moaned.

"Where are you?" Frank strained to hear more.

All too well, he knew the terror of being buried. His heart lodged in his throat as the memories of Afghanistan played through his mind.

Duke pawed at a pile of timber, his nose sniffing the broken beams and fractured wood.

He barked.

"Help."

Working like a madman, Frank tossed aside boards

piled one upon the other until he uncovered a portion of the car. The passenger door hung open. Shoving fallen beams aside, he leaned into the vehicle's interior.

A woman stared up at him.

"Are you hurt?"

She didn't respond.

Hematoma on her left temple. Cuts and abrasions. She was probably in shock.

"Can you move your hands and feet?"

She nodded.

"Stay put, ma'am, until the EMTs arrive. You could have internal injuries."

She reached for his hand and struggled to untangle herself from the wreckage.

"You shouldn't move, ma'am."

"I need help." She was determined to crawl from the car.

"Take it slow." Frank had no choice but to assist her to her feet. She was tall and slender with untamed hair the color of autumn leaves. She teetered for a moment and then stepped into his arms.

He clutched her close and warmed to her embrace. "You're okay," he whispered. "I've got you. You're safe."

"But—"

She glanced over her shoulder. He followed her gaze, his eyes focusing on a second woman.

Black hair. Ashen face. A bloodstained jacket lay wadded in a ball at her waist.

Pulling back the covering, Frank groaned. Her injury hadn't been caused by the storm.

She'd taken a bullet to the gut.

Chapter Two

Where were the emergency response teams?

Police, fire, EMTs?

Frank removed his belt and wove it under the victim's slender waist. Determined to keep her alive, he cinched the makeshift tourniquet around the rolled-up jacket to maintain pressure and hopefully stop the flow of precious blood she was losing much too fast.

He glanced at the redhead hovering nearby. She looked as concerned as he felt. They both knew that without immediate medical help, the injured woman wouldn't survive.

"If you've got a cell, call 9ll."

She pulled a phone from her pocket and shook her head. "There…there's no coverage."

The gunshot victim needed an ambulance and needed it fast. Frustration bubbled up within him. After ten years with the US Army's Criminal Investigation Division, Frank didn't like the only conclusion he could make with the information at hand.

"Why'd you shoot her, ma'am?"

Red shook her head, her eyes wide. "I did no such thing."

He pointed to the demolished car. "This is your Honda?"

She nodded.

"How'd she end up in your car?"

"I… I stopped at the picnic park about a mile from here. She needed help. I opened the passenger door, and a shot rang out."

"Did you see the shooter?"

Red rubbed the swollen lump on her forehead. "I… I don't remember."

"Don't remember or don't want to remember?" Even he heard the annoyance in his voice.

The woman stared at him, her face blank. Maybe she was telling the truth.

"What's your name, ma'am?"

"Colleen… Colleen Brennan."

"You're from around here?"

"Atlanta."

Which didn't make sense. "But you just happened to pull into a nearby picnic park?"

Her green eyes flashed with fear.

Trauma played havoc with emotions and memory. Frank wanted to believe her, but he knew too well that the pretty woman with the tangled hair could be making up a story to throw him off track.

Duke sniffed at her leg. She reached down and patted his head.

A raspy pull of air forced Frank's attention back to the gunshot victim. She moaned.

Sirens sounded in the distance.

He leaned into the car. "Stay with us, ma'am. Help's on the way." Hopefully it would arrive in time.

Her glassy eyes focused on Colleen. Frank turned to stare at her.

The redhead blanched. The lump on her temple cried for ice, and the scrapes to her cheek and hands needed debridement.

"After your friend's treated, we'll have the EMTs take a look at you."

"I'm fine." Colleen's voice was lifeless.

Slipping past her, he waved his arms in the air at the approaching first responders. Two ambulances and a fire truck from one of the rural fire stations.

The emergency crew pulled in front of the Craft Shoppe. Frank motioned them closer to the barn, where they parked and jumped from their vehicles.

"Two women are injured." Frank pointed to the collapsed structure. "One with a bullet wound to her gut. She's lost blood. The other woman has a knot the size of a lemon on her forehead and could be in shock."

Hauling medical bags and a backboard, a pair of EMTs waded through the collapsed wreckage around the car. A second set of paramedics set up an emergency triage area near the second ambulance.

"We'll need you to step away from the car, ma'am," one of the EMTs told Colleen.

Her brow furrowed. She peered around them at Frank.

Seeing the confusion in her gaze, his anger softened. "It's okay," he assured her. "They're here to help."

Despite the niggling worry that Colleen Brennan may have been involved in the shooting, he reached for her. "Come toward me, and we'll get out of their way."

She offered him her hand. Her skin was soft, but clammy, which wasn't good.

"Let's see if someone can check your forehead."

She shook her head. "Vivian's the one who needs help."

"You know her name?" Although surprised by the revelation, Frank kept his voice low and calm. "What's her last name?"

"I... I don't remember." Colleen pulled her hand from his grasp. "We were trying to get away—"

She hesitated.

"Away from—" he prompted.

"A man. He was in the woods. Tall. Dark jacket. Hood over his head. He had a rifle."

"Did you see a car?"

She shook her head. "Not that I remember."

Selective memory or a partial amnesia brought on by trauma?

"Come with me." Frank ushered Colleen to the triage site. Duke followed close behind.

A pair of EMTs helped her onto a gurney pushed against the side of the ambulance. One man cleaned her hands and face and treated the scratches on her arms while the other took her vitals, checked her pupils and then applied an ice pack to the lump on her forehead.

"You've got a slight concussion, but you don't need hospitalization," he said. "Is there anyone who can check on you through the night?"

She shook her head. "I... I live alone."

"In Atlanta," Frank volunteered.

An Amish man stumbled toward the ambulance. Blood darkened his beard. The EMTs hurried to help him.

"You'll spend the night here in the Freemont area,"

Frank told Colleen. Before she could object, he pointed to the one-story brick ranch visible in the distance. "My sister, Evelyn, owns the house on top of the knoll. There's an extra room. You can stay with her."

"I... I need to get back to Atlanta."

"From the looks of your car, travel anytime soon seems unlikely. Downed trees are blocking some of the roadways and won't be cleared until morning."

"Is there a bus station?"

"In town, but you need to talk to law enforcement first."

The downward slope of her mouth and the dark shadows under her eyes gave him concern. She looked fragile and ready to break.

"I... I don't know your name," she stammered.

"It's Frank Gallagher, and the dog's Duke."

Her face softened for a moment as Duke licked her hand, then she glanced back at Frank.

"You're a farmer?"

He shook his head. "I'm an army guy. CID."

Seeing her confusion, he explained, "Criminal Investigation Division. We handle felony crimes for the military."

Her eyes narrowed. "You're a cop?"

He shrugged. "More like a detective. What about you?"

"Flight attendant."

"Hartsfield?"

She nodded, indicating the Atlanta airport.

One of the EMTs returned and pulled a bottle of water from a cooler. "I want you to sit up, ma'am, and drink some water. I'll check on you again in a few minutes."

Frank pointed to the nearby fire truck. "You relax while Duke and I talk to the guys from the fire department."

Rounding the ambulance, Frank glanced at the road. A line of first responders and Good Samaritan townspeople had arrived to help in the rescue effort. The scene farther south was probably the same, with people flocking to the area in hopes of aiding those in need.

Glancing back at Colleen, he was relieved to see she had closed her eyes and was resting her head against the side of the ambulance.

Static played over the fire truck's emergency radio. A tall, slender guy in his midtwenties stood nearby. He wore a navy blue shirt with the Freemont Fire Department logo and a name tag that read Daugherty.

His face brightened when he saw Duke.

"Nice dog."

"Daugherty, can you can patch me through to the local police?"

"No problem, sir."

Once Frank got through to the dispatcher, he explained about the gunshot victim. "Colleen Brennan was the driver of the vehicle. She'll be staying overnight at Evelyn Gallagher's house." He provided the address.

"Everyone's tied up with the rescue operation," the dispatcher explained. "I'll pass on the information, but be patient."

After disconnecting, he requested a second call to Fort Rickman.

"Did you want to contact the military police?" Daugherty asked.

"That works."

He connected Frank to the provost marshal's office. After providing his name, Frank requested all available military help be sent to the Amish area.

"Roger that, sir. I believe we've already received a request for aid, but I'll notify the Emergency Operations Center, just in case. They'll pass the information on to General Cameron."

"Any damage on post?"

"A twister touched down. Some of the barracks in the training area were in the storm's path. No loss of life reported thus far. The chaplain said God was watching out for us."

Frank wasn't sure he'd give God the credit. If the Lord protected some, why were others in the storm's path? "What about Freemont?"

"We've got some spotty reports. A trailer park on the outskirts of town was hit with some injuries. A few shops downtown and a number of the old three-story brick buildings on the waterfront."

"The abandoned warehouses?"

"That's correct. We're awaiting more details from the local authorities. The information I received is that Allen Quincy is heading the civilian relief effort."

"The mayor?"

"Yes, sir. He's asked for our help. We've called in all personnel. I'll pass on the information about the Amish area."

"Let the Red Cross and medical personnel know, as well."

"I'm on it, sir."

"Do you have landline access?" Frank asked.

"To main post only."

"See if you can contact CID Headquarters. Ask for Special Agent Colby Voss. Tell him Special Agent Frank Gallagher is at the Craft Shoppe, located at the northern end of Amish Road. We're going to need him."

"Roger that, sir."

Colby's wife, Becca, had been raised Amish. She knew the area and the local Amish bishop, but Becca was on temporary duty out of the state so Colby was the next best choice.

He and Frank had joined the CID years earlier and had served together before. Frank could attest to Colby's ability both as an investigator and diplomat.

The Amish were a tight community and preferred to take care of their own. After the tornado, they needed help. Colby might be able to bridge the gap between the Amish and their *English* neighbors.

Frank thanked Daugherty for the use of his radio. He and Duke returned to the ambulance in time to hear the EMT reassure Colleen.

"Looks like dehydration was the problem, ma'am," he told her. "Your vitals are better so you're good to go."

"What about that lump on her forehead?" Frank asked.

"She should be okay, especially if someone checks on her through the night."

"It's nothing to worry about," Colleen insisted as she hopped down from the gurney.

Frank reached out a hand to steady her. She held on to him for a long moment and then nodded her thanks. "I'm okay."

"Ma'am, you need to take it easy for the next day or two," the EMT cautioned.

"And the gunshot victim?" Frank asked, his gaze flicking to the other ambulance.

"They're preparing to transport her to the hospital at Fort Rickman, sir."

"Not the civilian facility in Freemont?"

"She was conscious long enough to give her last name. Her husband is a sergeant on post. Sergeant Drew Davis."

Frank didn't recognize the name, but if Vivian was an army spouse, the CID would be involved in the investigation. With the Freemont police working hard on the storm-relief effort, the military might take the lead on the case.

Tonight, everyone would focus on search and rescue. By morning both the Freemont cops and the military law enforcement would have more time to question Colleen. Until then, Frank would keep her under watch.

Too many things didn't add up. In spite of being on convalescent leave, Frank needed to learn the truth about how a military wife with a gunshot wound had ended up in Colleen's car.

Colleen tried to ignore the pointed stare of the CID agent who had dug her from the rubble. His deep-set eyes and gaunt face were troubling and cut her to the core. In fact, the only redeeming quality about the guy was his dog.

She rubbed her temple, hoping to drive away the pounding headache that had come with the storm. Her memory was fuzzy at best, and she had difficulty recalling some of the most basic information, especially pertaining to Vivian. Without thinking, she'd left her purse in her car along with the memory card.

A pickup truck pulled to a stop in the triage area. The driver, a middle-aged farmer wearing bib overalls and a baseball cap, rolled down his window and nodded to the EMT.

"We found a guy hunkered down in a ditch just over that ridge." The farmer pointed to the rise in the roadway. "His sports car was destroyed, but he survived, although he's scraped up a bit. Face could have been in worse shape if he hadn't been wearing a sweatshirt. Looks like the hood protected him. A guy with an SUV is bringing him your way."

Hooded sweatshirt. Colleen's heart jammed in her throat. Trey had a sporty BMW, although she hadn't seen which of his many cars he was driving today.

If he was the injured man, Colleen had to get out of sight. She'd come back later for the things she'd left behind.

A gold SUV headed down the hill.

Her stomach fluttered. She turned and started to walk away.

"Where are you going?" Frank called after her.

To hide.

What could she tell him? *Think. Think.*

Her stalled brain refused to work. Searching for an answer, she glanced at the house on the knoll.

"I'm taking you up on that invitation to stay with your sister." Even she heard the tremble in her voice.

Frank raised his brow. Surely he wouldn't rescind the offer?

Her pulse throbbed and sweat dampened her back.

The SUV drew closer.

Colleen waved Frank off. "Stay here and help with the rescue operation. I can find my way up the hill."

She lowered her head, wrapped her arms around her waist and started along the path with determined steps. Keeping her back to the approaching car, she was grateful for the descending twilight and the shadows cast from the tall pines. The path wound along the roadway for a short distance and then burrowed deeper into the woods.

If only she could reach the denser underbrush before the SUV got too close. She couldn't let Trey see her.

Flicking a quick glance over her shoulder, she recognized the firm set of Trey's jaw and the bulk of his shoulders as the car pulled to a stop.

No mistaking the man riding shotgun.

At that moment, he glanced up.

Ice froze her veins. Her heart slammed against her chest. If Trey recognized her, he would track her down. Not only did Colleen have incriminating photos, but she had also witnessed him shoot Vivian in cold blood.

She increased her pace and darted along the path.

"Wait, Colleen."

The military CID agent ran after her, along with his dog.

Stay away from me, she wanted to scream, but reason won out. She needed Frank. She was stranded without a car with a killer on the loose. She needed the security of his sister's house and his protection throughout the night.

Later, she'd return to the wreckage and retrieve her purse and the memory card. Tomorrow, she'd catch the bus to Atlanta. From there, she'd hop a flight for the West Coast and disappear from sight. She'd leave Trey behind along with the special agent who didn't understand what she was trying to hide.

Frank wondered at Colleen's rush to get away, but then, he wasn't the best at reading women. Case in point Audrey, who said she'd wait for him. The memory still burned like fire.

"Wait up, Colleen."

Frank ran after her. His hip ached, and his breathing was tighter than he'd like.

Before the IED, he'd never questioned his strength.

Now he had to weigh everything in light of his physical stamina.

Drawing closer, he grabbed her arm.

She turned troubled eyes filled with accusation. "Let me go."

Releasing his hold, he held up both hands, palm out. "Sorry. I didn't mean to upset you."

She glanced through the bramble to the triage area, where a cluster of rescue workers gathered. "I'm still shaky."

An understatement for sure. "You've been through a lot today. The temperature's dropped since the storm. You must be cold."

"A little."

He shrugged out of his windbreaker and wrapped it around her shoulders. "This should help."

"What about you?"

"Not a problem." He pointed to the path. "Let's keep going while there's still some light."

"Are you sure your sister won't mind taking in a stray?"

He almost smiled. "She welcomed me a few weeks back with open arms. If I had to guess, I'd say she'd enjoy having another woman in the house. She claims I get a bit snarky at times."

"I'm sure she loves your company."

"She loves Duke."

Colleen almost smiled. "Who wouldn't?" She patted his head, and he wagged his tail, enjoying the attention.

"You've got brothers?" Frank asked, hoping to learn more about the reclusive flight attendant.

She faltered. Her face darkened. "One sister. She passed away four months ago."

"I'm sorry."

"So am I."

"Watch your step." Frank pointed to an area littered with rocks. Taking her arm, he supported her up the steep incline.

"Thanks," she said when they reached the top.

Stopping to catch her breath, she glanced over her shoulder. Frank followed her gaze. Darkness had settled over the small valley, but headlights from the response vehicles and flashing lights from law enforcement cut through the night.

A number of Amish buggies were on the street. Lights from additional rescue vehicles appeared in the distance. Frank needed to get Colleen settled and then return to the triage area and wait for personnel from post to arrive.

If anything good came from the tornado, it was the wake-up call that Frank had been lingering too long, nursing his wounds. He didn't want to appear weak. Not to the military or the other CID agents. Most especially not to himself.

Colleen turned back to Evelyn's house and paused for a long moment. Perhaps she was as unsettled about moving forward as he was. Frank could relate.

But that wouldn't change the problem at hand. He needed to learn more about Colleen Brennan and the gunshot victim. Why were they on the run, and who was after them?

Chapter Three

Some of Colleen's nervous anxiety eased when Frank opened the door to his sister's home, and she stepped inside. The dog followed.

A brick fireplace, painted white, drew her eye along with a beige couch and two side chairs, nestled around a low coffee table. An oil seascape hung over the mantel flanked by built-in shelves filled with books. She neared and glanced at the titles, seeing some of her favorites.

Frank came up behind her. "Did I tell you Evelyn is a librarian?"

"I'm in here," a voice called from the kitchen.

He motioned for Colleen to follow as he headed toward a small hallway that led to a keeping area and open kitchen.

A slender woman, early forties, with chestnut hair and big blue eyes, stood behind a granite-topped island and greeted Frank with a warm smile. She was fair and petite and contrasted with her brother's rugged frame and broad shoulders.

Colleen and her sister had shared similar facial structures, although Briana had been golden-haired like their mother, while Colleen inherited her flaming-red locks from her dad. Seeing the warmth of Evelyn's welcome made Colleen long for her own sister.

"I'm baking a ham and making potato salad for the rescue effort." She stirred mayonnaise into the bowl of boiled potatoes and sliced hard-boiled eggs.

As Colleen moved closer, Evelyn glanced up. The look on her face revealed her surprise at finding a visitor. She wiped her hand on a dish towel.

With a pronounced limp, she moved around the island and opened her arms to greet Colleen with a hug. "Welcome. Looks like you were caught in the storm."

The sincerity of Evelyn's voice touched a raw edge in the depths of Colleen's self-control. Her eyes burned and a lump formed in her throat in response to the genuine concern she heard in the older woman's voice.

Frank quickly made the introductions, his tone suddenly curt and businesslike and so opposite his sister's soothing welcome. As if unsure of where to stand or what to do next, he headed for the coffeepot.

"Care for a cup?" he asked Colleen before glancing at his sister. "Decaf, right?"

"Always at this time or I'd never sleep."

"A glass of water might be better," Colleen said. "But I don't want to trouble you."

Duke nuzzled her leg. He held a tennis ball in his mouth and wanted to play. Before she could take the ball, Frank motioned him to the corner, where he dropped the toy and obediently lay down.

"Good dog."

Frank turned to his sister. "Colleen's car was damaged by the tornado. She lives in Atlanta and hopes to return home in a few days."

"Preferably tomorrow," she quickly added.

"You need a place to spend the night." Evelyn's eyes were filled with understanding. "We have a spare room. Of course you'll stay here."

Turning to Frank, she added, "Did you bring her luggage?"

"I've got a carry-on bag in the trunk of my car, but I didn't think about it until now," Colleen admitted.

"I'll get it when I head back to the triage area," Frank volunteered.

Colleen held up her hand. "No need. I'll get it in the morning."

"Is there anyone in Atlanta you want to call who might be worried about you?" Evelyn asked.

"That's kind of you, but I have a cell phone." Colleen patted her pocket, reassured by the weight of her mobile device.

"You might not have coverage," Evelyn said. "Some of the cell towers were hit by the storm. Thankfully our landline is still working."

"I take it you got through to the rural fire department," Frank said to his sister.

She nodded. "Which was a blessing. They passed on the information to emergency personnel in town. The local radio station quoted the mayor as saying search-and-rescue operations would continue into the night and throughout the next few days."

"At a minimum." Frank glanced at his watch. "I need to hurry back."

"You need to eat something," Evelyn insisted.

He shook his head.

"Then I'll make a sandwich to take with you."

"More of your attempts to fatten me up?" His tone held a hint of levity that surprised Colleen.

Evelyn opened the refrigerator and pulled out lunch meat, cheese and mustard. As she layered the meat and cheese on two slices of bread, Frank grabbed a glass from one of the overhead cabinets. He filled it with ice and added water from the dispenser on the door of the refrigerator.

"You'll need your coat," Evelyn said, cutting the sandwich in half and wrapping it in foil.

Colleen accepted the water from Frank. From all appearances, his sister was the nurturing type, and despite the macho persona he tried to impart, the CID special agent seemed to readily accept her advice.

"I'm changing into my uniform. Fort Rickman's getting involved, and I want to help them set up."

"You're still on convalescent leave, Frank."

"Only for another week."

He glanced at Colleen and then headed into the hallway that led to the front of the house. "Back in a minute."

While Frank changed, Evelyn showed her to a guest room located behind the kitchen. "This doubles as my office and sewing room. I hope you won't mind the clutter."

A computer sat on a small desk, and colorful baskets filled with fabric and threads were neatly tucked in the shelving that covered the far wall. A double bed, nightstand and small dresser took up the rest of the space.

"If the weather warms tomorrow, you can use the screened-in porch." Colleen pointed to the French doors leading to the private sitting area. "It's usually nice this time of year, although tonight the temperature's a bit chilly."

"It's a lovely room, Evelyn, but I fear I'm putting you out."

"Nonsense. I'm glad Frank found you."

Which he had. He and Duke had found her in the rubble. If they hadn't, no telling how long she and Vivian would have been trapped.

"You're fortunate the storm spared your house," Colleen said as she glanced outside at the downed branches littering the yard.

"God answered our prayers."

Colleen nodded. "I'm sure the Amish folks prayed, as well."

"Of course. Their faith is strong. In fact, they are a resilient community and a forgiving people. They'll rebuild."

"I hate to see dreams destroyed."

Evelyn nodded knowingly. "If only we knew what the future would hold."

The melancholy in her voice gave Colleen pause. Perhaps Evelyn had her own story to tell.

"Frank said there's a bus station in Freemont."

Evelyn raised her brow. "You're in a hurry to get back to Atlanta?"

The question caught Colleen off guard. "As…as soon as possible."

Mentally weighing her options, she realized none of them were good. She couldn't fly without her driver's license and airline identification. Both were in her purse, buried in her car.

She had planned on a fast trip to Freemont to gather the last bit of evidence she needed to send Trey to jail. Now Vivian was in the hospital, and Colleen was stranded in an area devastated by a tornado. To add to her situation, she was holed up with a law enforcement officer who made her uneasy.

A tap sounded at the entrance to her room. She turned to find Frank standing in the doorway. He was clean-shaven and dressed in his army combat uniform. Maybe it was the boots he wore or the digital print of the camouflage that made him seem bigger than life.

She needed to breathe, but the air got trapped in her lungs.

"I'll be back later. Don't wait up, sis."

"The sandwich is on the counter."

"You're spoiling me." Raising his hand, he waved to Colleen and then hurried toward the kitchen.

"The sandwich," Evelyn reminded him.

"Got it," he called before the front door slammed closed behind him.

"Why don't you wash up and come back to the kitchen for something to eat." Evelyn motioned toward the hall-way.

"Thanks, but I'm not hungry."

"A bowl of soup might be good."

The woman didn't give up.

As if on cue, Colleen's stomach growled, causing her to smile. "A cup of soup sounds good."

Once Evelyn returned to the kitchen, Colleen pulled back the curtain in the bedroom and watched Frank lower the back hatch on his pickup truck. Duke hopped into the truck bed and barked as if eager to get under way.

Frank climbed behind the wheel. The sound of the engine filled the night. He turned on the headlights that flashed against the house and into the window, catching her in their glare.

She stepped away, hoping he hadn't seen her. Much as

she appreciated Evelyn's hospitality and grateful though she was of having a place to stay, Colleen worried about Frank's questions and the way he stared at her when he thought she wasn't looking.

After her sister's death and her own struggle with the Atlanta police, Colleen wanted nothing more to do with law enforcement. Now she was seeking shelter in the very home of a man she should fear.

Only she didn't fear Frank. Something else stirred within her when he was near. Unease, yes, but also a feeling she couldn't identify that had her at odds with her present predicament. She needed to leave Freemont as soon as possible, but until she retrieved her purse and the photo card, she had no other choice but to stay with Frank and his sister.

Hopefully she wasn't making another mistake she would live to regret.

A desire to protect her stirred deep within Frank when he saw Colleen standing at the window as he pulled his truck out of the drive. She had a haunting beauty with her big eyes and high cheekbones and the shock of red curls that seemed unwilling to be controlled.

Did her rebellious hair provide a glimpse into who Colleen really was? She tried to maintain a quiet reserve, yet perhaps a part of her longed to be free like the strands of hair that fell in disarray around her oval face. That disparity between who Colleen tried to be and whom he had caught a glimpse of when she wasn't looking gave him pause.

Driving down the hill from his sister's house, Frank thought of his own past, and the picture he had painted for his life, all with broad brushstrokes. At one time, he'd had it all and thought the future would provide only more positive moments to share with Audrey. He found out too late that she lived life on the surface and wasn't willing to go beneath the false facade she had created.

Frank had thought she understood about sacrifice for a greater good. He'd realized his mistake when she left him, unwilling to be tied down to a wounded warrior who had to face a long, difficult recovery.

At this point, Frank didn't know who he was. Too many things had changed that clouded the picture. He certainly wasn't the same man as the cocky, sure-of-himself CID agent patrolling an area of Afghanistan where terrorists had been seen. Perhaps he had been too confident, too caught up in his own ability to recognize the danger.

Not that he could go back or undo what had happened. He had to move forward. Donning his uniform tonight was a positive step. The stiff fabric felt good when he'd slipped into his army combat uniform.

At least he looked like a soldier, even if he wasn't sure about the future. Would he continue on with the military or put in his papers for discharge?

A decision he needed to make.

Headlights from a stream of military vehicles appeared in the distance when Frank parked at the barn. Two more ambulances from Freemont had arrived to transport the injured, and radio communication was up and running among the various search-and-rescue operations.

A fireman with wide shoulders and an equally wide neck approached Frank. "Thanks for helping with the relief effort."

"How's it look so far?"

"At least twelve Amish homes and barns have been destroyed. Close to twenty people have been identified as injured. No loss of life, but we're still looking."

"I heard Freemont had damage. A trailer park and some of the warehouses by the river."

"Might be time to clean out that entire waterfront," the fireman said, "but the mayor and town council will make that decision."

Noting the approach of the convoy, Frank pointed to a grassy area between the Amish Craft Shoppe and the collapsed barn. "Can you get someone to direct the military personnel to that level area where they can set up their operations center?"

"Will do." The fireman called two other men who used flares to direct the military vehicles into the clearing.

Frank saluted the captain who crawled from his Hummer.

"Thanks for getting here in a timely manner, sir." Frank introduced himself. "I'm CID, currently on convalescent leave, but I reside in the area and wanted to offer my assistance."

"Appreciate the help." The captain shook Frank's hand and then smiled at Duke. "Nice dog."

"He's a retired military working dog. Duke lost his sense of smell in an IED explosion, but that doesn't stop him from helping out when he can."

Frank passed on the information the fireman had shared about the damage and the injured.

"I've got engineers who will check the structural integrity of the homes still standing once we're assured all the victims have been accounted for." The captain pointed to a group of soldiers raising a tent. "We're setting up a field medical unit to help with the injured. That way the ambulances can transport those needing more extensive medical care to the hospital."

"The local fire and EMTs have a triage area you might want to check out, sir."

"Thanks for the info. I'll coordinate with them."

The captain headed for the civilian ambulances just as Special Agent Colby Voss pulled to a stop in his own private vehicle, a green Chevy.

He climbed from his car and offered Frank a warm smile along with a solid handshake. Instead of a uniform, Colby wore slacks and a CID windbreaker. "I thought you were still on convalescent leave."

"Another week, but I'm ready to get back to work."

"Wilson will like hearing that. We're short staffed as usual, and he'd welcome another special agent."

Frank appreciated Colby's optimism. "Did anyone notify you about Vivian Davis, a gunshot victim who got caught in the storm? She's a military spouse. EMTs took her to the hospital on post."

"The call could have come in while I was away from my desk. Do you have any details?"

"Only that she flagged down a driver at a picnic park farther south, saying she needed help. A shot rang out, the woman was hit. She and the driver escaped."

"Did you question the victim?" Colby asked.

"Negative. She was slipping in and out of consciousness. EMTs needed to keep her alive."

"I'll notify CID Headquarters. What about the driver?"

"Colleen Brennan. She's a flight attendant from Atlanta. Her vehicle is buried under rubble." Frank pointed to the spot where the barn had once stood. "She won't be driving home anytime soon. My sister has a spare bedroom. I invited her to stay the night. The local police don't have time for anything except search and rescue, and I know Fort Rickman is probably equally as busy. I thought keeping an eye on her here might be a good idea, at least until we get through the next twenty-four hours or so."

"Was she injured?"

"A slight concussion and some cuts and scrapes. Nothing too serious, although she was pretty shook up and not too sure about some details. I'm hoping she'll be less confused and more willing to talk in the morning." Frank pointed to the barn. "I'm planning to check out her car if you're looking for something to do."

"Sounds good, but I've got to call Becca. She left a message on my cell after seeing video footage about the storm on the nightly news. Give me a few minutes, and I'll catch up to you."

"The last remaining portion of the barn looks like it could easily collapse, so be careful. If you've got crime scene tape, I'll cordon off the area."

"Good idea. We don't need any more injuries." Colby opened his trunk and handed the yellow roll of tape to Frank.

He grabbed a Maglite from his truck and patted his leg for Duke. "Come on, boy."

The two of them made their way to what remained of the barn. Frank heaved aside a number of boards and cleared space around the rear of Colleen's vehicle before he opened the trunk.

Aiming the Maglite, Frank saw a carry-on bag with a plastic badge identifying Colleen's airline.

"Let's check up front," he told Duke, after he had retrieved the bag and placed it on the ground.

The dog whined.

"What is it, boy?"

Duke climbed over the fallen boards and stopped at the passenger seat, where Vivian had lain earlier. Blood stained the upholstery.

"You're upset the woman was injured." Frank patted the dog's flank. "I am, too. We need to find out who shot her and why."

Bending, he felt under the seat. His fingers touched something leather. He pulled it free.

A woman's purse.

He placed it on the seat and opened the clasp. Shining the light into the side pocket, he spied Vivian's government ID card and driver's license. Tissues, face powder and high-end sunglasses lay at the bottom.

Leaning down, he again groped his hand along the floorboard. This time, his fingers curled around a smartphone. He stood and studied the mobile device.

An iPhone with all the bells and whistles.

He hit the home button. A circle with an arrow in the middle of the screen indicated a video was primed to play.

Colleen claimed to have happened upon the distressed woman, but if the two had arranged to meet, the video might have been meant for Colleen to view.

Frank hit the arrow, and the footage rolled. A man sat at a booth with Vivian sitting across from him. From the angle, the camera appeared to have been upright on the table, perhaps in a front pocket of her purse with the camera lens facing out.

The guy didn't seem to know he was being recorded. The audio was sketchy. Frank turned up the volume.

"You brought the package?" The man's voice.

"Relax, Trey. I don't go back on my word."

Trey?

She slipped a rectangular object across the table. The man nervously glanced over his shoulder.

Frank stopped the video. His gut tightened. He'd been in law enforcement long enough to know what the small package, shrink-wrapped and vacuum sealed in plastic, probably contained.

Snow, Flake, Big C.

Also known as cocaine.

Chapter Four

While Evelyn busied herself in the kitchen, Colleen hurriedly ate a bowl of homemade soup and a slice of homemade bread slathered with butter.

"A friend is stopping by shortly." Evelyn wiped the counter and then rinsed the sponge in the sink. "He's a retired teacher and works with the hospitality committee at church. Ron's organizing a meal for the displaced folks and the rescue workers."

A timer dinged. She opened the oven and pulled out two green bean casseroles and a baked ham.

"The Amish want to take care of their own, but with so many homes destroyed they'll need help. Thankfully, I had a ham and fresh vegetables in the fridge, many grown by my Amish neighbors. They also baked the bread you're eating."

"It's delicious."

Finishing the last of the soup, Colleen scooted back from the table and headed to the sink. "I was hungrier than I thought. I'm sure the homeless will appreciate the food." She rinsed her dishes and silverware and loaded them in the dishwasher.

"I'd invite you to join us, but you look worn-out," Evelyn said. "Better to get a good night's sleep. There will be plenty of ways to get involved in the days ahead."

"I'm going back to Atlanta."

Evelyn nodded. "That's right. I didn't mean to change your plans, but if you decide to stay longer, you know you're welcome."

A knock sounded. She hurried to open the front door and invited a man inside. Returning to the kitchen, she introduced Ron Malone. He was of medium build and height but had expressive eyes and a warm smile, especially when he looked at Evelyn.

For an instant, Colleen had a sense of déjà vu.

Shaking it off, she tried to focus on what Evelyn was saying. Something about organizing the food.

"Colleen was driving through the area when the tornado hit," Evelyn explained. "Her car was damaged. She hopes to get back to Atlanta in a day or two."

Tomorrow.

"I'm amazed at the immediate response from so many who want to help." Colleen shook Ron's outstretched hand. "I doubt the same would happen in Atlanta."

"I think you'd be surprised about the number of caring people even in the city."

Colleen didn't share his opinion, but Evelyn's friend had an engaging manner, and from the way Evelyn was smiling, she must think so, as well.

"If you don't mind, I'll say good-night and head to my room."

Evelyn gave her a quick hug. "Hope you sleep well."

Colleen didn't plan to sleep. She planned to do something else, something she didn't want Evelyn to know about.

Timing would be important. She needed to be back at the house before Frank came home. He was the last person she wanted to see tonight.

Once the front door closed and Ron had backed out of the driveway, Colleen left the house through the French doors and scurried across the yard to the path in the woods. Gingerly, she picked her way down the hill.

A large military tent had been erected since she'd left the triage area. It was located close to the Amish Craft Shoppe and well away from the barn.

Staying in the shadows, she inched forward, grateful that her eyes had adjusted to the darkness. All along Amish Road, flashing lights illuminated the ongoing rescue effort.

Glancing back, she saw the glow in Evelyn's kitchen window like a beacon of hope in the midst of the destruction. The sincere welcome and concern she had read in her hostess's gaze had brought comfort.

If only she could sense a bit of welcome from Frank. He revealed little except a mix of fatigue and frustration. The only time she'd seen his expression brighten was when he'd talked to his sister. Other than that, he'd seemed closed, as if holding himself in check.

Judging by his appearance, he must have either been sick or sustained an injury. Her heart softened for an instant before she caught herself and reeled in her emotions. She didn't want to delve into his past or any pain he carried. She had enough of her own.

Her eyes burned as she thought of her sister. Too often, Briana had called begging for money to buy more drugs. Colleen had adopted a tough-love attitude that had backfired. She had hoped going after Trey would ease the burden of guilt that weighed her down. Now Vivian was injured, and the evidence she had planned to give Colleen was buried in the rubble.

Squinting into the night, Colleen saw the outline of her Honda, partially covered with debris. The passenger door was still open. Using her cell phone for light, she approached the car and leaned inside.

Working her hand across the floorboard, she searched for two purses, one of which contained the evidence Vivian had promised. The other—her own handbag—held the tiny memory card filled with digital photos.

Trying to recall the series of events when she pulled into the roadside park, Colleen bent lower. Vivian had dropped her purse at her feet as soon as she'd climbed into the car. Colleen extended her arm under the seat and then stretched down even farther.

A hand touched her shoulder.

She jerked. Her head knocked against the console, hitting near the spot injured earlier in the storm. The pain made her gasp for air. Rubbing the initial knot that was still noticeable, she turned to stare into Frank's dark eyes.

"Looking for something?" His voice was laced with accusation.

"My...my carry-on bag," she stammered.

He gripped her upper arm and pulled her from the car.

"What are you doing?" Her voice cracked, making her sound like a petulant child when she wanted to be forceful and self-assured.

"Let go of my arm," she demanded, more satisfied with the intensity of her command.

"Promise me you won't run."

She straightened her back. As if she could outrun Frank.

"I was searching for *my own* luggage in *my own* car. That doesn't warrant being manhandled."

His head tilted. He released his hold on her.

She rubbed her arm. He hadn't hurt her, but he had been aggressive.

Dark shadows played over his steely gaze. "What were you really looking for, Colleen?"

Refusing to be intimidated, she held her ground. "I just told you. My carry-on."

"Which I found in the trunk of your car." He held up the shoulder bag Vivian had carried. "Was this what you wanted?"

"That's Vivian's purse. She dropped it on the floor when she slipped into the car."

"Then maybe you were looking for her cell." He held up the iPhone.

"Should I have been?"

He leaned closer. "You tell me."

"Look, Frank, we're not getting anywhere fast. I'm sure Vivian would like her purse and phone back. As for me, I'm not interested in either item."

"Did Vivian tell you about the video? The near-field communication function was turned on. Had she planned to send a copy of the video to your phone?"

"I don't know anything about a video."

Vivian had evidence she'd wanted to share. A chill ran down Colleen's spine. Frank had found what Vivian had promised to provide.

He tapped Vivian's phone. A picture appeared on the screen of a rectangular object wrapped in plastic.

Colleen leaned in to view the screen. "What's in the shrink wrap?"

"Don't play dumb. You know exactly what the package contains."

She pulled back, frustrated by the hostility in his voice.

When she didn't respond, he took a step closer, too close.

"Coke. Crack. Crystal." He glared down at her. "You get the message?"

His eyes narrowed even more. "Were you and Vivian working for the guy in the video, only maybe Vivian was dealing on the side? Maybe she wanted to rip him off? He got angry and followed her."

Frank hesitated for half a heartbeat. "Or was he following you? Did you and Vivian plan to blackmail him? Maybe you wanted payment for the video. Did you ask for cash, or did you want the payoff in drugs?"

Anger swelled within her. Frank was just like the cops in Atlanta.

"Do you always jump to the wrong conclusion?" she threw back at him. "Must not bode well for your law enforcement career."

Fire flashed from his eyes. She had struck a sore spot. He took a step back and pursed his lips.

"We need to talk." He glanced up the hill. "At Evelyn's house."

"You mean you're not going to haul me off to jail?"

"Tell me the truth, Colleen. That's all I want. Why did you meet Vivian at the roadside park? Who's the guy in the video? Was he the shooter? If so, why'd he come after you? If you'll answer those questions, then I'll listen. If you're unwilling, I'll transport you to CID Headquarters tonight."

She raised her chin with determination and stood her

ground. "I'm not military. You don't have jurisdiction over me."

A muscle in his neck twitched. "Then I'll contact the local authorities."

"They're busy, tied up with the aftermath of the storm. I doubt they'd be interested."

"You're wrong. A woman was shot. She was in a video and appears to have been dealing drugs. The local authorities may be busy, but they're not that busy."

Colleen breathed out a deep sigh of resignation. She didn't have a choice. "You're right, Frank. We need to talk."

"I've got my truck." He pointed to where it was parked on the far side of the Amish store.

If only she had noticed the vehicle earlier. She would have turned around and returned to Evelyn's house and not attempted to search her car while Frank was in the area.

Hindsight wouldn't help her now.

She walked purposefully toward the pickup with Frank following close behind.

Duke stared at her from inside the cab. Frank reached around her and opened the passenger door. "Down, boy."

The dog jumped onto the gravel driveway. Colleen slipped into the passenger seat.

Once Duke was secured in the back of the pickup, Frank returned to the barn and stretched crime scene tape around her car. Her heart skittered in her chest. The yellow tape made everything that had happened today even more real. She raked fingers through her thick curls. What had she been thinking, trying to cover up information from the authorities?

Her eyes burned. She clenched her fists, blinking back

the tears. She needed to be strong. If she broke down, Frank would think she had something to hide.

Walking back to his truck, he raised his cell phone to his ear. Was he answering a call or making one? To local law enforcement perhaps?

Would the police be waiting for her at Evelyn's house? She bit her lip and looked into the darkness. How had she gotten into this predicament when all she wanted was to talk sense into Vivian and gather more evidence against Trey?

Frank rounded the car and slid into the driver's seat. His long, lean body hardly fit in the confined space. She tried to imagine him bulked up. Perhaps he wouldn't seem as menacing then. Somehow his pensive expression and hollowed cheeks gave him a frosty appearance that was less than approachable.

He turned the key in the ignition. Colleen was glad for the rumble of the engine and the sound of the wheels on the gravel drive as he backed away from the Amish store.

She didn't want to talk to Frank, yet that's what would happen shortly. Colleen wouldn't lie, but she couldn't tell him everything. He'd be like the other law enforcement officers she had approached.

They hadn't believed her.

Frank wouldn't believe her either.

Instead of driving up the mountain, Frank headed to where the rescue crews were working farther south along Amish Road.

Colleen didn't question the change of direction. Instead she gazed out the passenger window as if distancing herself from Frank.

Through the rearview mirror, he saw Duke balanced

in the truck bed, his nose sniffing the wind. The dog had an innate ability to read people. Duke had taken to Colleen from the onset, yet Frank wouldn't make a judgment about Colleen based on his canine's desire for attention.

Nearing the rescue activity, he pulled to the side of the road and cut the engine. "I'll just be a minute."

She nodded but didn't question the stop.

Duke whined to get down.

"Stay and guard the truck." *Guard Colleen, as well.*

Huge generators operated the emergency lights and rumbled in the night. Frank's eyes adjusted to the brightness, and he quickly searched for a familiar face in the wash of rescue personnel.

Spying Colby near one of the medical vehicles, Frank hurried forward. The other agent held up both hands and shrugged with regret.

"Frank, I'm sorry. I got caught up in a problem with the Amish and never made it to the barn. Did you find what you were looking for?"

"I found Colleen." Frank glanced back at the truck. She held her head high and stared straight ahead. If only he could tap into that defensive shell she wore as protection.

He turned back to Colby. "Any chance you can spare an hour or two?"

"We're in good shape here. What do you need?"

"Colleen was rummaging through her car. Supposedly she was searching for her carry-on bag. Earlier I had found Vivian's phone with a video showing what appeared to be a drug exchange."

"You know we're not allowed to search a suspect's cell phone without a warrant."

Frank nodded. "I was checking to see if it still had

power. The video came up on the screen. I didn't have to search for anything, and I didn't access her call log, much as I would have liked that information, as well."

"You think both women were dealing?"

"I'm not sure what to think, but Colleen's ready to answer questions, and I want you there since I'm not officially on duty."

"You could take her into post."

Frank nodded. "That's an option, but Fort Rickman's digging out from the storm. I doubt anyone wants to stop that effort to question a witness when we can handle it here."

"Good point. I'd be glad to serve as another set of eyes and ears. Give me a minute to let the captain know that I'll be away from the area for a bit. I'll meet you at Evelyn's house."

Frank appreciated having another CID agent present when he questioned Colleen. She seemed legit, but even pretty young things with red hair popped pills and dealt drugs. Better to be cautious instead of making another mistake. Frank hadn't seen Audrey for who she really was. He needed to be right about Colleen.

Was she a deceptive drug dealer or an innocent woman caught in the wrong place at the wrong time?

Chapter Five

Knowing Frank would be thorough with his questioning, Colleen climbed from his truck as soon as they got back to Evelyn's house. While he tended to his dog, she headed for the kitchen. Working quickly, she filled the coffee basket with grounds and poured water into the canister. The rich brew would help her see things more clearly, and the caffeine would ease her fatigue.

The scent of coffee soon filled the kitchen. She pulled mugs from the cabinet and placed them on the counter. Frank entered the house and wiped his feet on the rug by the door before heading down the hallway.

Just as she expected, his gaze was filled with questions when he stepped into the kitchen.

"The coffee will be ready in a minute," she said, hoping to deflect his initial frustration.

"Are you and Vivian dealing drugs?" he asked without preamble.

"Of course not."

"A woman was shot and fell into your car. Your rear window took a hit, which means you could have been a target, yet you didn't know who the assailant was or why he was after Vivian. You didn't even claim to know her name until you inadvertently shared that information when she was fighting for her life."

Colleen bit her lip, not knowing what she should tell him and where she should start.

Frank continued to stare at her. "You know a lot more than you let on, Colleen. The video shows Vivian dealing drugs. She was injured in your car. Looks to me like you're involved. The CID will investigate, as will the local police. It's time to start talking."

Trembling internally, Colleen struggled to appear calm and in control. Thankfully, her hand didn't shake when she poured coffee and handed the filled mug to the man who had followed Frank into the kitchen.

He wore a CID windbreaker and had watched the exchange with a raised brow. The guy was shorter than Frank but carried an additional ten to twenty pounds—all muscle.

"I'm Colleen Brennan," she stated matter-of-factly. "And you are?"

"Colby Voss. Special agent, Criminal Investigation Division."

"From Fort Rickman?"

He nodded.

"Then you work with Frank," she added, following the logical progression.

"Not yet. He's on convalescent leave and will be assigned to the post CID when he goes back on active duty."

She turned to Frank. "So you're not officially on duty."

"My leave status doesn't change the fact that I'm a CID agent. We still need to talk." His gaze was chilling. He wanted answers, not random chatter.

"It's time for you to come clean, Colleen."

She nodded. After filling a cup for Frank and one for herself, she carried both of them to the kitchen table. "I'm sure you're as tired as I am. Let's sit while we talk."

He groaned with frustration, but pulled out a chair across from her and lowered himself into the seat. Grabbing the coffee mug, he took a sip.

Colby sat at the end of the table and retrieved a small tablet and pen from his pocket. "I'll make note of anything you want to share, ma'am."

"Thank you." She tried to smile. "You're investigating Vivian's shooting?"

The agent tapped his pen and then raised his gaze to meet Frank's. "Special Agent in Charge Wilson will make that call. Right now, I'm here with Frank to help with the local recovery effort."

She nodded and then hesitated, trying to determine where to begin. "At seventeen, my sister, Briana, ran away from home to marry a shiftless bum named Larry Kelsey. He promised her a lot of things, including an acting career in Hollywood. The marriage didn't last long. She got rid of Larry, but kept her dream of fame and fortune."

Colleen tried to smile. "In spite of Briana's skewed sense of what was important in life and her naïveté, she was beautiful and poised and articulate."

Everything Colleen wasn't.

"About a year after her divorce, she took up with an Atlanta photographer. Although somewhat successful, the photography business was a front for his drug-trafficking operation. He got Briana hooked and then used her as a mule to bring in drugs from Colombia. Four months ago, she overdosed from drugs he'd given her and died."

Colby shifted in his seat as he took down the information. Frank steeled his jaw and continued to stare at Colleen as she continued.

"One day, I… I ran into Trey in the grocery store." She played her finger around the rim of her mug. She wanted to laugh at the irony, but everything caught in her throat. "Our shopping carts collided, which he thought was accidental. He didn't realize I'd been watching him and had planned our meeting. Trey was apologetic and a perfect gentleman, or so he tried to seem. Because of Briana's married name, he never realized I was her sister."

"Trey's last name?" Colby asked.

"Trey Howard," she replied. "I let him take me out a few times. Nice places. Upscale eateries. Plays at the Fox, art shows at the High Museum. He said we liked the same things. At least that's what he thought." Again she hesitated.

"So you had a relationship," Frank pressed, his tone as hard as his gaze.

She held up her hand in protest. "If you're implying that we were involved or that anything happened between us, you've got it all wrong. As I kept telling Trey, we were friends, enjoying time together."

When she took a sip of coffee, Colby added, "But things changed."

"I'm a flight attendant with some seniority. I fly to Colombia two or three times a month. Trey mentioned having worked there on a resort property. He took photos for a brochure and pamphlets for vacationers looking for a new place to visit. The photos he showed me were lovely. He told me he'd arrange for me to enjoy an all-expenses-paid stay there on my next layover. The resort liked airline personnel and would be happy to have me as their guest at no expense to me."

"You took him up on the offer?" Frank asked.

"I made an excuse, but the next time I was scheduled to fly, he mentioned it again. He thought I didn't want to be beholden to anyone. He needed a package brought back into the US and suggested I do him the favor in return for the resort accommodations."

Frank leaned in closer. "Did you ask what was in the package?"

"No, but I didn't need a degree in law enforcement to know the package probably contained something the government might not want brought into this country."

"You notified the authorities?"

She pulled in a deep breath. "Trey was well connected. I needed evidence before I accused him of anything illegal."

"Go on," Frank encouraged.

"One night I surprised him at his condo. He was working in his office, but said he needed to take a break and was glad I had stopped by. We were in the living area when he got a phone call. He apologized for taking the call and said he'd be tied up for ten to fifteen minutes. I excused myself to use the restroom. His office was across the hall, but he didn't go there to talk. Instead, he went outside on the deck, which gave me the opportunity I'd been hoping for."

"You searched his office?" Frank seemed surprised.

"I had questions that needed answers and wanted to be sure I was right about who Trey really was."

"You put yourself in danger, Colleen."

"Maybe, but Trey trusted me at that point. Besides—" she raised her brow "—I'm sure you've been in harm's way a time or two."

"It's my job. You're a civilian and not law enforcement."

"That's correct, but if the authorities weren't interested in bringing down a known drug trafficker, I had to get involved."

At the time, she hadn't thought about the danger to herself. She'd thought only of gathering the evidence she needed.

"Give me all the information you have about Trey," Colby interjected.

She provided his address and phone number. "He's got a studio in College Park, not far from the airport, and another one in Midtown."

"What did you find that night?" Frank asked.

"A list of names that included two young women I'd read about in the *Atlanta Journal-Constitution* some weeks earlier. Jackie Leonard and Patty Owens."

Colby wrote the names in his notebook.

"Both women had disappeared months earlier. They worked in the King's Club downtown. Jackie's body was found stuffed in the locked trunk of an automobile in long-term parking at the airport. The car had been stolen. Patty's body was recovered in a shallow grave in Union City, south of the airport."

"Had you known the women?" Frank asked.

She shook her head. "I told you, I read about them in the *AJC*, but their stories aren't much different from Briana's. I'm sure Trey promised them payment in drugs if they brought a few packages into the country for him."

"Finding their names on a list doesn't establish the photographer's guilt."

"Maybe not, but it does increase the cloud of suspicion hanging over his head."

Frank pursed his lips. "Let's go back to when you were in Trey's office. You saw a list of names and recognized the two women in question."

"That's right." She nodded.

"Did you find anything else?"

"Trey said he'd been working, so I clicked on his computer. A photo appeared on the screen."

Colby glanced up.

"Go on," Frank prompted.

"The picture showed a table near a huge window that looked down on a swimming pool and lush gardens with the ocean in the distance. Bricks wrapped in plastic were on the table."

"Shrink-wrapped in plastic?"

She nodded.

Frank's tone hardened. "Just like the package Vivian handed off in the video."

Colleen raked her hand through her hair and sighed. "Yes."

Colby sniffed. "Seems I missed something."

Frank pulled the iPhone from his pocket and hit the home button, then the play arrow. He held it up for Colleen to see. "Who's the guy in the footage?"

She leaned across the table. "Trey Howard."

"That's what I thought." Frank handed the cell to Colby. "As I mentioned earlier, Vivian had the near-field communication function turned on."

"Because she planned to copy the video to someone else's phone." Colby made a notation in his tablet.

Frank turned back to Colleen. "How'd you hook up with Vivian?"

"Her name was on the list, along with a phone number. I recognized the Georgia area code, and did a search on the internet."

She glanced at Colby. "Vivian likes social media. I learned her husband was deployed to Afghanistan, and she was interested in modeling so she'd had photographs taken for her portfolio."

"Trey did the photography?" Frank asked.

"That's right. He can be charming when he wants something. I'm sure he told Vivian she'd be a successful cover model."

"But he wasn't interested in her career."

"Hardly." She pulled in a breath. "Trey needed another mule to transport drugs into the country."

"How can you be certain?"

"I called her. She was scared. Her husband had redeployed home, and she wanted to cut off all contact with Trey."

Frank shook his head and narrowed his gaze. His tone was laced with skepticism. "She admitted to bringing a package into the US from Colombia?"

"Not in so many words, but I understood what she was trying to tell me."

"Why would she reveal anything over the phone?"

"I knew enough about Trey and how he operated to convince her. Plus, she'd met Briana at Trey's photo studio the day she was having her portfolio done."

"Wasn't Trey afraid the girls he used would rat him out to the cops?"

"I don't know how Trey's mind functions, but he's despicable and conniving, and he kept close tabs on anyone who worked for him. If they talked about leaving his operation, he got rid of them."

"Do you know that for sure?"

She sighed. "I don't have proof. I do have what you'd call circumstantial evidence that points to him."

"You think Trey killed Jackie Leonard and Patty Owens?"

"Maybe not personally, but he could have ordered one of the thugs who are part of his operation to do his dirty work."

"Could have?" Frank repeated the phrase she had used. "Did Trey kill your sister?"

"She overdosed on drugs he provided."

"You notified the authorities?"

"I did, but they had other, more pressing cases to investigate. Or so it seemed."

"Did Briana tell you about Trey?"

"She…she was slipping into a coma and died soon after I got to the ER. The only thing she said was to stop Trey Howard."

Which Colleen had vowed to do.

Had she made a mistake by taking on so much by herself? She rubbed her forehead and swallowed the lump that clogged her throat. She wanted to cry, but she couldn't appear weak. Not with Frank sitting across the table.

He scooted out of his chair and reached for the coffee carafe. He refilled her cup and his.

Colby held up his hand. "No more for me."

"Let's go back to Vivian," Frank said when he returned to the table. "You two decided to meet?"

"That's right. At the roadside park, but Trey was hiding in the woods."

"Why risk meeting her?"

"Vivian said she had something that would prove his guilt. I wanted that evidence."

"Evidence or drugs?"

Colleen didn't know whether to burst into tears or pound her fist on the table at his pigheadedness. She did neither. Instead she willed her expression to remain neutral and her voice controlled.

"I planned to mail whatever evidence Vivian provided, along with the list of names and the photo I found on Trey's computer, to the DEA."

"You have the photo?"

"I used the camera on my phone and took a snapshot of his computer screen. It's not the best quality, but I thought it was enough to get the police interested."

"If it's still on your phone, send the photo to my email," Frank requested.

"I'll need a copy," Colby added. Both men provided their online addresses. Colleen plugged the information into her phone and sent the photo as an attachment.

Frank left the kitchen and returned with his laptop in hand. He placed it on the table, hit the power button and quickly accessed his inbox. After opening the attachment Colleen had sent, he enhanced the screen.

"There's some type of case on the edge of the table with an identity tag, although it's too blurred to read."

She nodded. "The tag says Howard. It's Trey's camera case. That's why I thought the cop would be interested."

"But he wasn't?"

"He said I could have pulled the photo off the internet."

Colby glanced at the computer screen over Frank's shoulder. "Any idea where the picture was taken?"

"In La Porta Verde, the Colombian resort Trey wanted me to visit. As I mentioned, Trey had done the photo layout for their brochures and website when the resort was first built."

Frank tapped in the name of the resort. The home page appeared. He hit Additional Photos and clicked through a series of still shots. "Here it is. The same pool and gardens with the ocean as a backdrop."

Although still not satisfied with the direction of the questioning, Colleen felt somewhat relieved that Frank and Colby recognized the connection between the photo from Trey's laptop and the resort website.

"I sent the website URL to the Atlanta police," she continued, "along with the photo. The officer who talked to me didn't see the tie-in and said neither seemed relevant to him."

"Who'd you deal with?"

"An officer named Anderson."

Colby returned to the table and made note of the name. "Did he want to talk to you in person?"

She shook her head.

"So your only dealing with the police was over the phone to a cop named Anderson?" Frank asked.

"I dealt with two different officers at two different times. After Briana died, I contacted a cop named Sutherland. He worked close to where she lived." Colleen glanced down at her partially filled mug, remembering the less than desirable area. "He was a tough guy who didn't seem interested in the fact that she'd OD'd. He kept asking pointed questions about my relationship with my sister and insinuated I had something to do with her death."

Frank shook his head. "That doesn't make sense."

Colleen bristled. "Maybe not, but I'm just telling you what happened."

Seeing the frustration plainly written on Frank's face, she glanced down and rubbed her hand over the table. "The cop talked about the free flow of drugs to the inner city often brought in by dealers who lived in the nicer neighborhoods."

"Did you mention the photographer's name?"

She shook her head. "Sutherland made it perfectly clear that he wasn't interested in the accusations of a dying addict."

"What about Anderson? Did you have any more contact with him?"

"Not face-to-face, but someone came to my apartment."

Frank glanced at Colby then back at her. "Go on."

"I had a short overnight flight. The gal who lives in the apartment across the hall called to tell me someone had been looking for me."

"Anderson?"

"I'm not sure. He wasn't in uniform, but Trey had boasted of having connections with the Atlanta PD. I was afraid Anderson might be on the take."

"Why would you jump to that conclusion?"

She shrugged. "Call it woman's intuition, but a warning bell went off. I had my carry-on bag so I checked into a motel instead of going home."

"That's when you contacted Vivian."

"A few days later. I needed more evidence, which I planned to mail to the DEA."

"Calling them on the phone would be a whole lot easier."

"Vivian didn't want her name used, and I didn't want the call traced back to me."

"Because?" Frank asked.

"I didn't know if they'd believe me."

She stared across the table at Frank, who seemed like the other cops with whom she'd dealt. "You don't believe me either."

He hesitated for a long moment. "I'm not sure what I believe."

His words cut her to the quick.

She glanced at Colby. "What about you?"

"I'm just making note of your statement, ma'am. More information will be needed before I can satisfactorily evaluate your response."

"Lots of words to say you're not on my side." She shoved her chair away from the table. "Neither of you are."

Standing, she glared at Frank. "If you'll excuse me. I'll answer any additional questions you might have in the morning."

She turned on her heel and walked with determined steps to the guest room. Closing the door behind her, she dropped her head in her hands and cried.

Frank let her go. She was worn-out and on the brink of shattering. He felt as frustrated as she looked and needed time to process what she had already revealed. Parts of her story seemed valid, although her attempt to bring down a drug dealer single-handedly was hard to accept. Yet surely she could have made up a more plausible story—and one that was less convoluted—if she was trying to cover up her own involvement.

He turned back to his laptop. "Let's check out those newspaper articles about Jackie Leonard and Patty Owens."

Searching through the *AJC* archives, Frank located

information on both women. Just as Colleen had said, the girls had worked at the King's Club in Atlanta. Frank checked the address and mentioned the location to Colby.

He nodded. "The heart of the inner city. Crime is rampant in that area. Those girls were flirting with trouble."

"Looks like they found it." Frank read the news stories about their bodies being found. "Know anyone in the Atlanta PD?"

"There used to be a guy. Former military. George Ulster. I could see if he's still there."

"Find out if he knows Sutherland or Anderson. Get his take on both guys. See if anyone suspects either of them is dirty. Then see what Ulster knows about the two women and whether the PD has any leads. Mention Colleen's sister, just in case there's a tie-in. Seems all three women were on a downward spiral." Frank shook his head with regret. "And hit bottom."

The front door opened, and Evelyn's laughter filtered down the hallway. Stepping into the kitchen, her face sobered. She glanced first at Frank, who quickly logged out of the archives, and then nodded to Colby.

Ron walked up behind her. "Evening, folks."

To her credit, Evelyn seemed to realize this wasn't the time for late-night chatter. She patted his arm. "It's late, Ron. We need to say good-night."

She hurried him toward the door. After a hasty few words, he left the house, and Evelyn headed to her room.

Frank closed his laptop and stood. The energy had drained from him. He grabbed the mugs off the table and placed them in the dishwasher.

Colby glanced at his watch. "It's late. I need to get back to post. I'll take the iPhone with me and stop by headquarters in the morning. Hopefully, I'll be able to talk to Wilson about getting a warrant to access her call list."

"The Freemont police need to be in the loop, but I want Wilson's approval before I do anything."

Colby headed for the hallway and then turned back. "Try to get some sleep, Frank. She's not going anywhere. At least not tonight. Besides, we all might think a bit more clearly in the morning."

Frank watched his friend leave the house. He planned to lock the doors and let Duke have the run of the house. If anyone tried to get in or out, the dog would sound a warning. Frank needed to be careful and cautious. He didn't want anything to happen to Colleen, whether she was telling the truth or not.

Chapter Six

Colleen woke the next morning with a pounding head-ache. She touched the lump on her forehead and groaned, thinking back over everything that had happened.

Vivian! God, help her. Heal her.

If only she could get an update on the army wife's con-dition. As soon as Vivian was able to talk, the police and military authorities would question her. The video proved she had been working for Trey. Even if she claimed inno-cence, Vivian had brought drugs into the United States from Colombia and would, no doubt, be tried and pros-ecuted.

Would her guilt rub off on Colleen?

Throwing her legs over the side of the bed, she sat up and groaned again. How had her once orderly, controlled life gotten so out of hand? She longed to flee Freemont and Georgia and wipe everything she knew about Trey and his trafficking from her memory. As if she could.

Thinking back over Frank's barrage of questions last night, she sighed. She had kept some information from Frank, not wanting to fuel the flame of his disbelief. Still, she should have mentioned seeing Trey at the triage area right after the twister hit.

How could she have been so forgetful? Actually more like stupid. Probably because of her own nervousness and because Frank's penetrating gaze had left her frazzled and totally undone.

She specifically hadn't mentioned the memory card because of the digital photo she feared Frank might see. A photo taken of her with Trey's so-called friends, who were probably involved in his drug operation.

Frank didn't believe her now, and she refused to give him any more reason to doubt her. His cryptic and caustic tone had been hard enough to deal with last night. As much as she didn't want to face him in the light of day, he needed to know Trey could still be in the area.

Leaving the comfort of the bed, she walked to the window and opened the shades. Her mood plummeted as low as the gray cloud cover that blocked the sun and put a heavy pall on the day. At least it wasn't raining.

Needing something to hold on to, she once again reviewed the steps she needed to take to get out of Freemont. Once she retrieved her identification and the memory card, she would head back to Atlanta. Catching a flight to the West Coast seemed her best option. As Frank had suggested last night, she could notify the Atlanta DEA by phone—an untraceable cell—or even by email, all the while staying out of the agency's radar and away from Trey Howard and the men who worked for him.

A safer escape plan might be to drive to Birmingham, two hours west in Alabama, and fly out of that airport. If Trey's men or the Atlanta PD were checking Hartsfield, she didn't want to walk into a trap after all her hard work trying to prove Trey's guilt.

Had he already returned to Atlanta?

Or was he still in Freemont?

If so, it was because he was looking for her. Knowing how effective Trey was in getting what he wanted, she couldn't successfully hide out for long.

With a shudder, she yanked the curtain closed again and hastily slipped into jeans and a lightweight sweater from her carry-on bag.

Colleen looked at her reflection in the mirror after she'd brushed her teeth and scrubbed her face in the adjoining bathroom. Her cheeks were flushed from the abrasive washcloth she'd scrubbed with and the cold water she'd splashed on her face.

Running a comb through her hair, she hoped to untangle the mess of curls that swirled around her face. She usually relied on the products she'd forgotten to pack to tame her unruly mane.

All she could do was roll her eyes at the halo of locks that circled her face. She'd never liked her red hair, and this morning's frizz made her look like Little Orphan Annie, only older and in no way cute or endearing.

For a fleeting moment, Colleen wondered what type of woman Frank liked. Blondes, perhaps, with rosy cheeks and finely arched brows. Maybe jet-black hair and ivory skin turned his fancy. Or women with big eyes and tiny, bow-shaped mouths.

She scoffed at her foolishness. Why would she even consider such thoughts? As far as she'd seen, the CID agent was all business with no pleasure allowed.

Colleen made the bed and tidied the room. After ensuring the colorful quilt and lace pillow shams were in place, she let out a deep breath and opened the door to the hallway.

The smell of fried eggs and bacon, mixed with the rich aroma of fresh-brewed coffee, led her to the kitchen. Usually Colleen skipped breakfast, but this morning her stomach growled with hunger, and her mouth watered for whatever Evelyn was cooking.

Stepping into the airy room, she was greeted with a wide smile from her hostess. Standing at the counter, Evelyn was arranging biscuits, still warm from the oven, in a cloth-lined basket.

"Tell me all the food I smell isn't just for you and Frank," Colleen said with a laugh.

"Help yourself. I've got four egg-and-bacon casseroles in the oven for the rescue workers. Ron's coming over at nine-thirty to take them to the triage area. You're welcome to join us if you feel able, but first, you need breakfast."

"Coffee sounds good. Mind if I pour a cup?"

"Mugs are in the cabinet closest to the stove."

Colleen selected a sturdy mug with a blue design. "Polish pottery, isn't it?"

Evelyn nodded. "Frank gave me the set for my birthday two years ago. They're popular with the military."

Colleen enjoyed the weight of the pottery as she filled it with coffee.

"Cream's in the refrigerator. There's sugar on the counter."

"Black works for me."

"You're like Frank. He claims sugar spoils the taste."

Colleen tried to seem nonchalant as she took a sip of the hot brew and then asked, "Is Frank helping with the relief effort?"

"He's in his room getting ready. I tried to convince him to sleep in this morning. I heard him pacing until the wee hours. In case you haven't noticed, my brother has a mind of his own, which sometimes causes him problems. He thinks he can do the things he used to do before his surgery."

"I heard mention of convalescent leave last night. Was Frank wounded during a deployment?"

Evelyn nodded. "He entered a building while on patrol in Afghanistan. An IED exploded and trapped him in the rubble. Duke found him and alerted the rescuers who pulled him to safety the next day."

"No wonder dog and master are so close."

"Inseparable is more like it."

"They make a good team."

"Speaking of teams, Ron needs help with the breakfast line this morning. Are you interested?"

"Count me in."

A bedroom door closed, and footsteps sounded in the hallway. Colleen tightened her grip on the mug, unsure how to react when she saw Frank.

He nodded as he entered the kitchen, looking rested and self-assured. "Morning, ladies."

"Do you have time for breakfast?" Evelyn seemed unaware of the tension Colleen felt.

"Not today." He glanced at his watch, equally oblivious to her unease. "When do you expect Ron?"

"Soon."

"Tell him folks have been notified that food will be available in the triage area. The volunteers will arrive first, followed by Amish families."

"I'll let him know."

Frank glanced at Colleen. "Can you lend a hand?"

"Of course, if Ron needs help."

"I'm sure he will." Frank stared at her a moment longer than necessary, causing her heart to flutter, but not in a good way.

She kept remembering his pointed questions from the night before.

"Then I'll see you shortly." With another nod, he hurried outside along with Duke.

He had backed his truck out the driveway before Colleen could shake off the nervous edge that hit as soon as Frank had stepped into the kitchen. If only she could react to his nearness in a less unsettling way. He seemed like a good man, but Frank was a CID agent first, and he was convinced she had some part in the drug operation.

"What would you like for breakfast?" Evelyn asked, interrupting her thoughts.

Colleen smiled. "I'd love a slice of the homemade bread you served with the soup last night."

"That's easy enough. Toasted with butter and jelly?"

"You're spoiling me."

A knock at the door had Evelyn tugging her hair into place and glancing at her reflection as she passed the mirror in the hallway.

"You look lovely," Colleen assured her and was rewarded with a backward wave of hand as Evelyn hurried to open the door.

Ron stepped inside and followed her into the kitchen, where he greeted Colleen and then began carrying the casseroles out to his car.

Colleen downed her coffee, forsaking the toast she didn't have time to fix or eat, and then grabbed the bowl of fresh fruit from the counter and hastened outside.

She stopped short on the front porch. Her heart skipped a beat as she stared at the SUV parked in the driveway.

A gold SUV.

Ron started down the sidewalk toward her.

She'd had a sense of déjà vu when Evelyn introduced them last night. No wonder.

Ron was the driver who had transported Trey to the triage area.

The temperature had risen slightly, but the day was overcast and about as gloomy as Frank's mood. The military had erected a flagpole near the triage area, and the American flag flapped in the breeze that blew from the west.

Allen Quincy was spearheading the Freemont rescue effort. Midfifties with silver hair and bushy brows, the mayor quickly briefed Frank about the rescue operation.

The engineer from Fort Rickman had checked the houses that had remained standing. A handful of the structures needed to be shored up before they'd be safe enough for the families to occupy. The army was offering manpower and supplies to any of the Amish willing to accept the help.

Earlier this morning, Colby had met with Bishop Zimmerman and eased the Amish leader's concerns about accepting the outreach. Once he realized the aid was freely given and in no way meant that his community was beholden to the military, he willingly accepted the help.

With civilian and military personnel working together, the rescue and reconstruction was progressing, but people were still without homes and many had been hospitalized.

Colby pulled to a stop in front of the tent where medical triage and evaluations were being done and waited until Frank finished talking to the mayor.

"How 'bout some coffee?" Colby called from his car, holding up two paper cups.

Frank smiled and reached through the open window to accept Colby's offer. "You must have read my mind."

"My body needed caffeine. I thought you might feel the same, especially after the late night."

"Thanks for listening to Colleen and passing the information on to the chief."

Colby held up his hand. "I didn't get Wilson. He was tied up with the general, but he sent a message through Sergeant Raynard Otis. Wilson wants to see you. Ray will call and set up an appointment."

"When?"

"Probably when post gets back to normal."

"A couple days or so?"

"That sounds about right." Colby sipped the coffee.

"I'm sure Wilson wants to know when I plan to return to duty."

"Do you have an answer for him?"

Frank shrugged. "I'm ready now, if he can use me."

"My guess, he'd tell you to stay here in the area until the relief effort is behind us. You've done a lot already."

Frank shook his head. "This is basic military operations."

"I hear you, but even the bishop mentioned your name this morning."

"He's a good man."

"So are you, Frank."

As much as he appreciated Colby's comment, Frank wasn't sure where he stood with the chief. Wilson was a competent investigator, but tight-lipped, especially with subordinates, and always faint on praise.

"I called Atlanta PD and left a message for Ulster to call me when he reports to work."

"Has anyone talked to Vivian?"

"Negative. The docs have her in an induced coma. I alerted security at the hospital on post and asked the military police to station a man outside her room."

"In case Trey returns?"

"Exactly. If he tried to kill her once, he may try again."

Would he come after Colleen, as well?

Frank let out a stiff breath. "Did anyone look at the call log on Vivian's phone?"

"We're waiting for a warrant, but I ran the plates on the blue Honda this morning."

"Colleen's car?"

Colby shrugged. "A long shot but you never know."

"You think she's lying."

"Look, Frank, we both know things aren't always as they seem. Her story's confusing enough that it just might be true, but as I mentioned last night, facts need to be verified. I wanted to ensure the car was registered to Colleen Brennan. I should hear something shortly."

"Keep me posted."

"Will do."

The coffee tasted bitter. Frank poured the remainder on the ground as Colby drove away. He crushed the recycled cardboard in his hand and tossed it in a nearby trash receptacle.

Duke had lost the keen sense of smell that had made him a valuable military working dog in the IED explosion in Afghanistan. Evidently, Frank had lost his investigative edge and ability to see things clearly, as well.

He hadn't even thought to run the plates.

In spite of what he had told Colleen last night, he wanted to believe her. The tale she had told—as Colby mentioned—seemed a bit disjointed, yet if all the pieces had been sewed too neatly together, he might have been even more suspicious.

The old Frank went on gut feelings, and his gut was telling him that Colleen was not involved in any criminal activity. He shook his head, knowing all too well that a sound investigation was based on facts, not feelings.

He couldn't let any personal feelings for Colleen get in the way of uncovering the truth. She was pretty and seemed legit, but as Colby said, looks could be deceiving. He thought of Audrey, which only drove home the fact that he wasn't a good judge of women.

Was Colleen to be trusted?

He hoped so, but he couldn't be sure.

Not with a supposed drug dealer turned killer like Trey Howard on the loose.

"What's wrong?" Evelyn asked, returning to the kitchen, where Colleen had fled, the fruit bowl still in hand, after seeing Ron's gold SUV. "I thought you were going with us. The food's in the car. Ron's ready to drive us down the hill."

"To the triage area?"

Evelyn nodded. "By the Amish Craft Shoppe."

As Frank had mentioned and where Colleen needed to go to find her purse.

Ron entered the kitchen and looked expectantly at Evelyn. "Are you ready?"

"I was just checking to ensure we got everything." After grabbing two additional serving utensils, she nodded. "I'm ready."

Evelyn pointed to the door and motioned Colleen forward. "Let's get the fruit in the car, and we'll be able to leave. People are hungry. We should hurry."

Ron and Evelyn were both staring at Colleen. She had to make a decision. Was Ron in any way involved with Trey? Or was it pure coincidence that the seemingly compassionate churchgoer had transported an injured man, who turned out to be a drug trafficker determined to cause her harm?

Colleen wasn't sure about Ron, but she trusted Evelyn, and she had to get back to her car. She'd go with them, but she'd keep her eyes open and watch for any signs that he wasn't who he seemed. For Evelyn's sake, she hoped Ron was a good man. For her own sake, as well.

Chapter Seven

Frank recognized Ron's gold SUV heading down the hill from Evelyn's house. The retired teacher was a nice guy who had been hanging around his sister recently.

Evelyn had been in love once, but she never talked about the guy or what had happened to break them up. Frank had been stationed at Fort Lewis, in Washington State.

About that same time, Evelyn had been involved in a car accident on a wet, slippery road that left her with a noticeable limp. Frank came home to help her recuperate. When he broached the subject about the former boyfriend, she had shrugged off his questions and indicated she didn't want to revisit the past. Frank had abided by her wishes. Now she seemed enamored with Ron, which made Frank happy for her sake.

Ron pulled onto the gravel path and braked to a stop. He waved as he stepped from his vehicle. "Hey there, Frank. We brought breakfast. Where do you want us?"

Frank looked past Evelyn and saw Colleen in the backseat. Her face appeared even more strained than when he'd seen her earlier in Evelyn's kitchen. They'd parted last night on an angry note, and he wanted to reassure her.

Colleen had nothing to worry about if she was telling the truth, but that was what hung heavy between them. The uncertainty of whether she was being truthful about her involvement in Trey Howard's drug operation.

Frustrated that everything seemed so complicated, even in the light of day, he turned back to Ron and pointed him toward the clearing. "You can set up your serving line in front of the tent."

The teacher helped Evelyn from the car. Frank hurried to assist Colleen, but she opened her door before he could reach for the handle.

She stepped from the backseat, looking almost hesitant, and glanced at the barn, where one wall still hung precariously over her car.

Ron pulled out the first of four folding tables from the back of the SUV. Frank helped with the setup. Once the tables were upright, Evelyn wiped them with a damp cloth, and Colleen dried them with paper towels.

"You were up early this morning," Frank told his sister.

"I was saying my morning prayers and giving thanks to the Lord for saving us in the storm. Knowing people needed food, I wanted to get a head start on the breakfast casseroles. As it was, Ron arrived soon after you left and just as I was ready to pull them from the oven."

"Perfect timing." Frank's gaze flicked to Colleen, who had yet to say anything. Her cheeks had more color, but lines of fatigue were noticeable around her eyes.

She wore an emerald-green sweater, and her hair was pulled into a bun at the base of her neck. He followed her to the SUV and took a large bowl of fresh fruit from her hands.

"How's that lump on your forehead?" he asked.

"It's fine, but I'm worried about Vivian. Do you have any news about her condition?"

"The hospital wouldn't tell me much when I called this morning. Only that she's still in ICU, and her condition's critical."

"Has anyone talked to her husband?"

Frank shook his head. "I'm not sure. CID may have."

"He didn't know about the trip to Colombia."

"That will have to be determined."

Colleen bristled.

"It's the way law enforcement operates, Colleen. Anecdotal information needs to be checked. We can't operate on hearsay."

Her eyes were guarded as she glanced up at him. "You think I'm covering up the truth?"

"I didn't say that."

"You didn't have to. You keep demanding answers to your questions, then when I provide information, you instantly discount it as not being factual."

She slipped on insulated mitts and grabbed one of the piping-hot casseroles. "I'd be better off not telling you anything, Frank. Then you could learn everything on your own, which you seem to need to do no matter what I say."

She huffed as she walked past him.

Anyone else and he wouldn't have been affected, but Colleen's sharp reproach made him flinch internally. She was right about his need to verify everything she said, but that was what investigators did, even when they believed a witness was being truthful.

He glanced at his sister, who didn't have a clue about what was going on. Ron was equally in the dark. Both of them smiled and chatted amicably as they transported the food from the SUV to the tables.

Two more carloads of volunteers parked near the Amish Craft Shoppe. They hustled forward carrying casseroles that, coupled with what Ron and Evelyn had brought, would provide an abundance of food for the workers and those displaced.

The military planned to set up a second tent this afternoon that would serve as a makeshift chow hall. Hot food in marmite containers was scheduled to arrive later in the day.

Ron would probably still be here helping out any way he could. Evelyn couldn't stand that long and would need a break. Colleen had to be tired, too.

Frank hadn't slept much last night, and he doubted she had either. He'd encourage her to rest, although he doubted she would want his advice.

A line of hungry rescue workers formed even before all the food had been placed on the tables. Ron raised his hands to get everyone's attention and offered a blessing over the food.

Colleen clasped her hands and lowered her eyes. A breeze played with a strand of hair that had come free from her neck. She pulled it behind her ear, her gaze still downward.

As Ron concluded the prayer, three flatbed trucks hauling bulldozers and backhoes came into view. American Construction was stenciled on the side of the earth-moving machinery.

Frank double-timed to the edge of the road and signaled where the vehicles should park. A man climbed down from the first truck. He wore a gray T-shirt with the construction company's logo of a bulldozer superimposed over a stenciled outline of the world.

Frank stretched out his hand and introduced himself. "You're the owner of American Construction?"

The big guy nodded. "Steve Nelson. I saw the report on the Atlanta news and called city hall in Freemont. They connected me to the mayor who's running the rescue effort. I told him we had some equipment and wanted to help."

The guy was built, at least six-two with huge biceps and a lot of definition under his shirt.

Steve wasn't a stranger to the gym. His strong grip and powerful forearm were evident when he shook Frank's hand.

"We appreciate the help."

The guy looked as Frank had at one time when weight lifting and training had been part of his daily routine.

"Frank Gallagher, Army CID. Nice to have you join us, Steve."

Two of his men approached, both big guys wearing the same company T-shirt and packing plenty of muscle. "Paul Yates and Kyle Ingram."

They shook hands. "Thanks so much," Frank said.

He filled them in on the stretch of homes that needed to be cleared along the road.

"There's food, if you want to grab some chow before you get started."

Steve held up his hand. "We ate before we left Atlanta."

Assessing the situation quickly, he sent one of the trucks farther south to connect with the effort closer to post.

"Paul and I'll get started here." Steve eyed the homes

across the road still buried in debris. "You've completed the search for injured?"

"We have. Any structure that has a large X on its door has been cleared and is ready for your men."

He nodded. "We've done this a number of times over the twelve years our company's been in operation. Just tell me where you want me to start."

Frank pointed to the Craft Shoppe. Damage to the building was minimal, but fallen trees and debris littered the entranceway. "Having the Amish store open for business would lift everyone's spirits."

Steve nodded. "We'll start there. Then head across the street and work south."

"Sounds like a plan."

Frank hustled back to the breakfast line. Colleen stood next to Evelyn, and both of them offered smiles of encouragement along with the food they dished up to the hungry workers.

Colleen chatted amicably with one of the men in line. More of her hair had pulled from the bun and blew free. For an instant, Frank had a vision of who Colleen really was. She seemed relaxed and embraced life. An inner beauty that she tried to mask was evident in the attention she showered on each person in line.

In that same moment, Frank wished he could be one of the people with whom she was interacting. Each time he and Colleen were together, she closed down, as if burdened by the weight she carried. He wanted to see her smile and hear her laughter.

Duke nuzzled close to Frank's leg as if sensing his master's confusion about the woman from Atlanta. Colleen may have told him the truth last night, but she was still embroiled in a shooting. The video found in her car only compounded the situation.

Frank needed to tread carefully. She could be hiding something behind her guarded gaze and cautious nature. He couldn't make a mistake and allow an attractive woman to throw him off course. He may be physically compromised, but he needed to think clearly.

She was someone of interest. The problem was, a part of him was interested in a way that didn't mesh with his CID background. He needed to hold his feelings in check and use his brain instead of his heart when he was dealing with Colleen.

"Do you need anything?"

Colleen startled at the sound of Frank's voice. She turned to find him behind her, standing much too close. Needing space, she took a step back, but her leg hit the table.

Wanting to maintain her self-control, she raised her chin and stared up at his angular face. For one long moment, the hustle and bustle around her melted into the background. Her breath caught in her throat, and she forgot about his questions and the doubt she had heard in his voice the night before.

Just that quickly, reason returned. "I have everything I need, but thanks for checking."

Seemingly satisfied by her response, he moved on to Evelyn and asked her the same question.

Colleen turned back to the hungry people in line. Serving food to the workers lifted her spirits. She was grateful for the continuing assortment of breakfast casseroles, baked goods and fresh fruit that poured in from people in Freemont who wanted to help. The long line of hungry rescue personnel included firefighters and emergency personnel as well as military from Fort Rickman who appreciated the home-cooked meal.

The clip-clop of horses' hooves signaled the approach of Amish families in their buggies. Frank greeted the men with a handshake and offered words of welcome to the women and children. Duke frolicked with the youngsters, and they giggled as he licked their hands and wagged his tail.

As the families approached, the workers backed up to let those who had lost much move to the front of the line.

One of the men—evidently a spokesman for the Amish group—held up his hand. "We will wait our turn. We do not want to inconvenience you who are so willing to help us in our need."

"Please," a rescue worker insisted, speaking for the others in line. "You and your family need to eat. You've lost much."

"God provides," the man said with a nod. "We appreciate your generosity."

He motioned his family forward. Others followed. The eager faces of the children, when they held out their plates, hinted at their hunger.

Colleen was impressed by the children's politeness and the way they deferred to their parents. The mothers remained close and pointed to the various foods each child could take.

One little boy with blond hair and blue eyes took two bananas and then glanced at his mother, who shook her head ever so slightly.

The child quickly returned the extra piece of fruit and looked up at Colleen. "I must only take what I can eat and leave the rest for others."

He couldn't have been more than six or seven, but his demeanor and the apology he offered were that of a much older child.

During a lull in the line, she felt something rub against her leg and looked down to find Duke at her feet. She laughed at the sweet dog and watched him scamper off when Frank called his name.

He bent to pat the dog's neck, then glancing up, he stared at Colleen. Her heart skittered in her chest, and longing for some normalcy in her life swelled within her. If only she had met Frank under different circumstances.

A man in uniform tapped his shoulder, and Frank turned away. Suddenly, she felt alone in the midst of so many.

"I'm looking for a job to fill," a middle-aged woman said some minutes later as she approached Colleen. "Ron told me you need a break."

Although she was capable of working longer, Colleen knew the woman was eager to get involved.

"A break sounds good."

She looked for Frank and saw him in the distance. He was working with other military men setting up tables and chairs where people could sit while eating their meals. A large generator was humming, and fifty-cup coffeepots had been plugged into the electrical outlets. The smell of fresh-perked coffee wafted past her in the gentle breeze, and many people were enjoying the hot brew.

A ramp extended from the end of a flatbed truck. A man in a gray T-shirt drove a bulldozer down the incline and off the truck.

With a grateful nod, Colleen handed her serving utensil to the newcomer. The woman instantly began chatting with the people in line.

Retreating to the side of the military tent, Colleen grabbed a bottle of water from an ice chest. The cold liquid tasted good and refreshed her.

Everyone was busy, and no one seemed to miss her. After downing the last of the water, she dropped the bottle in one of the temporary trash receptacles and wiped her hands on her jeans. She glanced at the barn, where the back end of her car was visible under the wreckage.

Rubbing her forehead, Colleen mentally retraced her movements yesterday. Usually she kept her purse in the passenger seat, but as she pulled into the rest stop, she'd tossed it into the rear to make room for Vivian.

Again, she checked to ensure no one needed her. Evelyn was chatting with one of the Amish ladies. The other servers seemed content doing their jobs and were focused on feeding the workers and Amish who continued to arrive by buggy.

Seeing that Frank was still tied up with the military, she hurried to the barn area, gingerly picked her way through the downed timber and ducked under the crime scene tape. She peered through the back window into her car but saw nothing except broken glass.

Rounding to the passenger side, she leaned over the front seat, shoved her fingers between the rear seat cushions and sighed with frustration when she came up empty-handed.

In the distance, the bulldozer gathered downed tree branches. The driver piled them to the edge of the road, where they could easily be picked up and carted off later in the day.

Colleen rounded the Honda, only this time, she grabbed

the beams that blocked the driver's door and shoved them aside. The wood was heavy, and her energy was quickly sapped, but she continued to work, intent on having access into the rear of her car, behind the driver's seat. Without doubt, she'd wake up sore tomorrow, but finding her purse would be worth the effort.

Her neck was damp, and her hands ached, but she smiled with success when she cleared away the last of the rubble. Opening the driver's door, she saw what she was looking for—a small leather handbag wedged under the driver's seat. The clasp had come open, and the purse was empty.

She stretched her hand under the seat and patted the floorboard, searching for the spilled contents. She found a lipstick and a comb and placed both items in her bag. Once again, she used her hand to search along the floorboard.

Please, Lord.

A sense of relief spread over her when her fingers curled around her wallet. Pulling it free, she ensured her credit cards, driver's license and airline identification were still inside.

The roar of the bulldozer grew louder.

She glanced at the food line, which had started to thin. Time was of the essence. Ron and Evelyn would begin cleaning the area once all the people had been fed.

But she still needed the memory card.

An Amish teen appeared from the rear of the barn. He stared at her for a long moment and then walked quickly to where the others were eating.

A nervous flutter rumbled through her stomach at the young man and the pensive look he had given her.

Someone screamed. Colleen turned at the sound and

saw Evelyn staring at the barn with her hands over her mouth. Ron was standing next to the young Amish boy. In the distance, she saw Frank running toward her, as if in slow motion.

For the briefest second, Colleen wondered what had caused them concern. Then she heard the *whoosh* of air and the *creak* and *groan* of wood. Glancing up, she saw the lone portion of wall still standing. Only now it was crashing down around her.

She ducked and raised her hands to protect her head. The purse dropped to her feet, its contents spilling onto the ground.

The last thing she heard was Frank's voice. He was screaming her name.

Chapter Eight

Heart in his throat, Frank followed the ambulance to the Freemont hospital. He'd been the first to get to Colleen. Medical personnel were close by to respond to the emergency. They'd started an IV line, taken her vitals and then hastened to get her into the ambulance that was currently racing along River Road to Freemont.

Frank's phone rang. Relieved the cell tower was back in operation, he glanced at Colby's name on the monitor and pushed Talk. "What'd you find out?"

"The guy driving the bulldozer was Paul Yates. He claimed he'd checked the barn and hadn't seen anyone in the area before he picked up the first load of fallen timbers. According to him, he didn't get near the wall. Steve Nelson, the construction team boss, told me Paul was a conscientious worker and doubted that his man, even inadvertently, would have knocked the load he was carrying against the edge of the barn wall."

Frank sighed, frustrated at his own mistake. "If he did cause the wall to topple, I have to take some of the blame. I told Steve his men could clear the area around the Craft Shoppe. The store's structure was in good shape. I thought the sooner we start getting some of the businesses and homes restored, the better."

"Which was sound reasoning. You're not at fault, Frank. Yates probably thought he'd clean up around the barn, although—as I mentioned—he said he never saw anyone in the area."

"Colleen was standing in plain sight by the car."

"That's what Ron Malone told me. He verified she was clearly visible when the wall came down, but she could have been hunkered down and peering into her car when Paul checked. If he checked."

Frank glanced at the purse he'd pulled from under the fallen timber, which she must have found. Colleen had wanted to retrieve her identification and credit cards, yet nothing was worth putting her life in danger.

"Your sister said to let her know when you hear from the doctor," Colby added.

"Will do. Make sure Ron takes her home so she can rest. She not only looked upset but also exhausted. She worked late last night and was back at it this morning."

"They plan to leave soon."

"Have you heard anything from Atlanta PD?"

"Negative."

"What about the check on the Honda's plates?"

"I'm not sure what the holdup is. I'll give them another call."

"Let me know."

"Will do."

"Thanks, Colby." Frank hesitated for a long moment, choosing his words. "For being there, for helping."

"You mean calming you down? It wasn't your fault she was injured."

"She's staying at my sister's house. I feel responsible. I should have posted a guard at the barn."

"That's not CID's jurisdiction. The Freemont police needed to get involved, although everyone's overworked at this point. I don't know if you heard the news. The governor called in the National Guard, but he sent them farther east to Macon, where a second tornado touched down. According to the radio report I heard, he's satisfied Freemont is well taken care of with Fort Rickman's help."

"Only Rickman has their own damage to repair." The hospital appeared in the distance. "We're approaching the medical facility. I'll call you once the doctor makes his diagnosis."

Frank kept his focus on the ambulance ahead of him. The siren wailed as the EMT at the wheel entered the intersection leading to the medical complex. Frank followed close behind.

He kept seeing the wall crash down on Colleen. He hadn't been able to get there fast enough and had frantically clawed at the fallen timbers to save her. He'd found her dazed and bleeding from a head wound that was all too close to the blow she'd taken yesterday, which made him even more concerned.

The EMTs had been concerned, as well. They'd used a backboard and neck brace to stabilize her spine and had hurried her into an ambulance.

He hoped she wouldn't have any permanent injury or hadn't suffered internal wounds that would need further medical care.

The ambulance braked to a stop in front of the ER. The automatic doors opened, and medical personnel wearing pale green scrubs raced to meet their patient.

The EMTs lowered the gurney to the pavement and

pushed her into the hospital. Nurses hovered close by, assessing her injuries as they rushed Colleen into a trauma room.

Frank found a nearby parking space and hurried inside. A nurse pointed him to a room where even more medical staff surrounded the gurney where she lay.

"Can you hear me?" a doctor questioned.

A nurse grabbed the telephone. "We've got an injury in trauma room two. I need a CBC and chemistry panel. Protime and PTT. Type and cross for two units." She nodded. "I'll place the order now."

After returning the phone to its cradle, she typed the lab orders on a nearby computer.

"BP's 130 over 70," a voice called out. "Pulse 65."

The doctor checked her pupils and had Colleen follow his finger with her eyes. All the while her head was immobilized on the backboard.

He glanced at Frank, hovering near the doorway. "Family?"

"Ah, no. I'm with the CID."

"Is she a victim of a crime?"

"Negative. Her injury was accidental."

"Then I need you to leave the room and give the patient privacy."

Frank understood the doctor's request, but he didn't want to leave Colleen. He knew how fast things could go south if an internal injury was involved.

When the medics had taken him to the field hospital in Afghanistan, he'd been in good shape. Or so everyone had thought. Too quickly his blood pressure had bottomed out. He'd gone into shock and had been rushed into surgery—the first of many.

As Colleen was being lifted into the ambulance, Evelyn had grabbed his hand. The concern in her eyes had made him aware of how much she understood the emotions that were playing havoc with his control.

"I'm praying for Colleen," she'd assured him.

Knowing his sister's deep faith and her belief in prayer had brought a bit of calm in the midst of his turmoil. Evelyn would storm heaven, of that Frank could be sure.

He wanted to stand in the hallway outside the trauma room, but a nurse escorted him to a waiting area. She promised to notify him if there was any change in Colleen's condition. Not that he could sit idly by. He paced from the door to the bay of windows on the far wall and back again, feeling trapped and confined, like a caged animal.

He looked down, expecting to find Duke at his feet and needing his calm support, but Evelyn had kept the dog with her.

Every time the door opened, Frank hoped to see one of Colleen's nurses.

No one appeared whom he recognized. He glanced at his watch. The ambulance had arrived more than thirty minutes ago. How long would the medical team take before he would receive word of her injuries?

He pulled out his phone and checked his emails, searching especially for a message from Special Agent in Charge Wilson. Frank was ready to get back on active duty. Surely Wilson could use him.

Of course, the chief might not be willing to take a chance on him. Especially after the witness Frank needed to keep safe had been injured.

The door opened, and the nurse from Colleen's room motioned him forward.

"An aide is transporting Colleen Brennan to X-ray.

They should return in a few minutes. The doctor will review the X-rays and test results once they're back from the lab. If you want to wait in her room, you can."

Relieved, Frank headed for the trauma room. His stomach tightened when he saw droplets of blood on the floor.

His mind went wild with concern. "You mentioned X-rays. Does that mean internal injuries?"

"The X-rays will tell us a lot. The doctor may order a CT scan."

Bile rose in Frank's throat. He glanced at the vinyl chair shoved in the corner and knew he couldn't sit. Backtracking to the doorway, he peered into the hall, hoping to catch sight of Colleen.

Where was she? What was her condition? What was the doctor keeping from him?

The sound of a gurney rolling over the tile floor flooded him with relief. She was alert, and her color was good. The backboard had been removed, which was another positive sign.

"Did you find the Amish boy?"

Frank didn't understand what she was saying.

"You saw him, didn't you?" she insisted. "He came out from behind the barn just before the wall toppled."

"What'd he look like?"

"Straw hat, blue shirt, suspenders."

The same as every other Amish kid. "You think he caused the wall to fall?"

"I don't know. Ask Ron. He talked to him."

"Will do, but what about you?"

"I'm okay." She grimaced. "Except for my head."

"Another concussion?"

"They haven't told me yet. The patient's the last to know."

He followed the gurney into the room. The nurse's aide held up her hand. "Give us a minute, sir, until I get Ms. Brennan settled."

"Oh, sure. Sorry." He returned to the hallway. The door closed behind him.

Colleen needed her privacy. Shame on him for barging into her room.

He started to call Colby about the Amish boy, then disconnected when the door to Colleen's room opened. The aide scurried down the hall.

Frank waited a long moment, wondering if she would return.

He hesitated too long.

Another health-care worker, wearing a white lab coat, entered the trauma room and closed the door.

Frank shook his head with frustration. At this rate, he might never see Colleen. Patience had never been his strong suit, except when he pulled surveillance. Today's wait seemed especially trying.

The main thing was to ensure Colleen was okay.

His cell rang. Colby's number.

Frank raised the mobile device to his ear. "Did you find out anything?"

"Can you talk?"

Frank's gut tightened. Needing to speak freely, he headed for the empty waiting room. Colby had information to share, but from the negative overtones in his voice, the news wasn't good.

Did it involve Colleen?

Colleen hadn't expected Frank to follow her to the hospital and then wait while the various tests were being run. She thought he had stayed behind. Spotting him in the hallway when she came back from X-ray had been a surprise that added a hint of brightness to a very bleak day.

Although from what she knew about Frank, he probably wanted to question her about breaking through the crime scene tape. Was it against the law to search for her own missing purse?

She closed her eyes and tried to relax. Knowing Frank was in the hallway made her doubly anxious.

The door opened, and someone—no doubt, Frank—entered the room. Unwilling to face the confrontation she expected to see in his eyes, she pretended to be asleep.

His footsteps were heavy as he neared the gurney.

She sensed him staring down at her.

Unnerved, she opened her eyes.

She didn't see Frank.

She saw Trey.

Chapter Nine

Colleen screamed. Trey hovered over her. He raised his hand and pressed it across her nose and mouth, cutting off her air supply and blocking any additional sound she tried to make.

She writhed and scratched his face, then grabbed his nose and twisted.

He growled and clamped his hand down even harder.

Unable to breathe, she thrashed at him, kicked her feet and shifted her weight. The gurney was narrow, and the sheet covering the vinyl pad shifted with her.

With one massive thrust, she threw her legs up and over the narrow edge. Gravity helped.

She fell to the floor, along with the sheet.

Trey lost his hold.

Gasping for air, she crawled away from him like a crab.

He reached for her again.

She kicked and screamed.

Where was Frank?

Why wouldn't he come to her rescue?

* * *

"I got a call from Ulster," Colby said.

The cop in Atlanta. Frank shoved the cell closer to his ear.

"The two women Colleen mentioned who were murdered worked at the King's Club. Guess who else worked there up until four months ago?"

"You tell me."

"Briana Doyle."

"Colleen's sister."

"Roger that."

An interesting twist. "Anything else?"

"He also said Sutherland—that Atlanta cop who gave Colleen a hard time—suffered a nervous breakdown and had to retire."

"What about the plates on the Honda?"

"The car's registered to a Ms. C. A. Brennan."

Frank couldn't help but smile. "Do me a favor, Colby. See if anyone remembers an Amish teen hanging around the barn today."

"Do you have a name?"

"Negative, but Colleen saw him talking to Ron Malone."

"Evelyn's friend?"

A sound filtered into the waiting room, like a muffled cry.

Frank tensed. "Hold for a minute."

Lowering the phone, he retraced his steps into the hallway and listened.

A woman screamed.

Colleen!

Someone ran down the corridor.

Six foot. Stocky. White lab coat.

Frank's heart stopped. He crashed into her room. Colleen was on the floor, back to the wall.

She shook her head and pointed to the hall. "I'm not hurt. Go after him."

Frank raced into the corridor.

The man rounded the corner at the end of the hallway. Frank followed.

A nurse blocked his path.

He shoved past her.

A lab technician carrying a tray with tubes of blood appeared.

"Get back," Frank yelled. He sailed around her and turned left. The hall was empty.

Glancing back, he spotted a stairwell.

Frank shoved open the heavy fire door. A short stairway led to an emergency exit, leading out of the hospital.

He bounded down the steps.

Movement behind him.

Frank turned. A fire extinguisher sailed through the air, aimed straight for him. He lifted his hands to block the hit.

The canister crashed against his chest, knocked air from his lungs and forced him off balance. He fell down the steps. His head scraped against the wall.

The stairwell door opened, and the man in the lab coat walked back into the hospital.

Frank's ears rang. Pain screamed through his body. Fighting to remain conscious, he groped for his cell and heard Colby's voice.

"What's going on, Frank?"

He'd never disconnected.

"Someone attacked Colleen." Frank struggled to his

feet. "A guy wearing a white lab coat. Six foot. Stocky. Call hospital security. Tell them to lock down the facility."

Frank grabbed the banister and pulled himself up the stairs. "Notify Freemont PD. The attack happened in trauma room two in the ER. He was last seen in the rear stairwell."

"Where'd he go from there?"

Back to Colleen!

Ice froze Frank's veins.

He jerked open the fire door and stumbled into the hallway.

"Colleen," he screamed, racing back to her.

Hurling himself into the trauma room, he expected the worst.

She sat crumpled on the floor, her face twisted with fear.

"Frank." She gasped with relief. Tears sprang from her eyes.

He was on his knees at her side, reaching for her. She collapsed into his arms. He pulled her trembling body close, feeling her warmth. Hot tears dampened his neck.

She was alive. Relief swept over him. A lump of gratitude filled his throat. He hadn't lost her. Not this time, but he hadn't reacted fast enough. She'd almost died because of his inability to protect her.

He rubbed his hand over her slender shoulders. "Shh. I've got you. You're safe."

For now. But someone wanted to kill her. Whether she had been working with Trey or against him, he was determined to end her life.

Trey would come back. No doubt about it. Would Frank be able to save her the next time?

Chapter Ten

"He must have headed down the east corridor and left from that side of the hospital," Frank had told the hospital security earlier and now repeated the details to the Freemont police officer who had answered the call.

The cop was pushing fifty with a full face and tired eyes. His name tag read Talbot. He had pulled a tablet and pen from his pocket and was making note of the information Frank provided.

As Talbot wrote, Frank rubbed his side that had taken the hit. The fire extinguisher had bruised a couple of ribs and the area around one of his incisions. The dull ache was aggravating but not serious.

Colleen was resting in the ER room across the hall, awaiting the doctor's decision about whether she would be released or admitted for observation. Frank had wanted to stay with her, but Talbot insisted on questioning Frank in private. The only way he would leave Colleen was if the door to her room and the door to the room across the hall where Frank now sat both remained opened.

The cop looked up from his notebook. "Did you see his face?"

"Only in profile, but Ms. Brennan gave you a description."

"That's correct. I just wanted verification."

Law enforcement's need to confirm anecdotal information was what Frank had tried to explain to Colleen. Now, as his own irritation began to mount, he understood her frustration.

"The man was approximately six feet tall, wearing a white lab coat. I can't be sure about his build. He appeared stocky. Muscular might be a better description."

"Ms. Brennan thought you were in the hallway. She screamed, but you failed to respond." The cop paused and pursed his lips. "Did she imagine raising her voice?"

"As I mentioned earlier, I went into the waiting room to take a call. Hearing a sound, I retraced my steps and realized Ms. Brennan was in distress."

"The person who phoned you was—"

Colby was busy dealing with the Amish. Frank didn't want him tied up, answering Talbot's questions, especially when Frank was at fault for letting Trey escape.

He scrubbed his hands over his face. What was wrong with him these days?

"The name?" the cop pressed.

"Special Agent Voss."

"First name?"

More irritation bubbled up within Frank. "Special Agent Colby Voss."

"Spelled?"

How else would Voss be spelled? "V.O.S.S." The cop was a jerk. Either that or he had a bone to pick with the military.

Needing to reassure himself that Colleen was all right, Frank glanced through the two open doorways to where she was resting in the room across the hall. Her eyes were closed and her hands folded at her waist.

He pulled his gaze back to Talbot. Dark circles rimmed his eyes.

Frank's temper subsided ever so slightly.

"Have you been involved with the search and rescue?"

The cop nodded. "When I'm not cleaning up my own property. My wife and I live on the west side of town. The twister tore the roof off our house. The wife was inside." He shook his head and looked as dejected as Frank had felt when he realized Trey had escaped. "We're living with our daughter and son-in-law. They don't have room for us."

"I'm sorry."

"It's not your fault. My wife blames God, but it's not His fault either."

Frank's opinion of the cop did a one-eighty. Although hard to admit, deep down Frank had blamed God after the IED explosion and Audrey's rejection. It was easier to claim the Lord was at fault instead of his own poor judgment.

The doctor entered Colleen's room.

"If there's anything else you need from me, call my cell." Frank gave the cop his number as well as the one for Evelyn's landline.

"I'll alert local law enforcement to be on the lookout for Trey Howard. As you're probably aware, the department's working long shifts trying to keep the peace in the areas hardest hit by the storm. Doubt we'll be back to normal operations for a few more days, so I wouldn't hold your breath about tracking him down anytime soon."

The doctor stepped into the hallway and motioned to

the nurse. "Once pharmacy fills the pain prescription for Ms. Brennan, she's free to go."

The nurse nodded. "I'll get her meds and discharge papers."

Frank climbed from the table and shook hands with the cop. "I appreciate your help today. Let me know if you find out anything about Trey Howard."

"I've got your phone number, sir. I'll contact you first thing."

Frank left the room with a better attitude. He hated that he hadn't nabbed Trey, but he'd changed his opinion of the cop. The guy was carrying a lot on his shoulders.

He knocked on Colleen's open door. His heart softened when she looked up and smiled. She was carrying a lot, too. Her sister had died because of a drug dealer who seemed to escape apprehension. Frank had to find Trey before he hurt Colleen again.

Frank's head was scraped and he looked tired, but Colleen smiled when he stepped into her room. "Did you finish answering Talbot's questions?"

"The guy's thorough."

"Don't all of you law enforcement types follow the same playbook?"

He laughed. She liked the sound.

"How's the head?" he asked.

She shrugged. "Pain is relative. I'll survive."

"And the shoulder?"

"You mean where I hit the floor after I slipped off the gurney?"

Frank nodded.

"It's probably not as painful as that scrape on your forehead."

"You need to rest."

"That's what the doctor told me. Rest and protect my head. Two cranial blows in a short span of time aren't recommended for good health. The doc doesn't want me to end up like some old prizefighter. Research claims concussions don't lead to good quality of life."

"It's not something to joke about."

"I know, but if I don't laugh, I just might cry. That wouldn't be good."

"Sometimes shedding a few tears helps."

The nurse returned to the room and dropped a plastic medicine bottle in Colleen's hand. "Take every six hours as needed for pain. They'll make you sleepy. Don't operate motor vehicles when taking them."

"My car was totaled in the storm," Colleen said.

"Tough break, huh?" The nurse sorted through the papers she carried. "Have someone check on you in the night."

She handed Colleen the release instructions. "This covers most of the questions you might have. The doctor warned you to guard your head, and don't take any more hits."

Colleen smiled. "He mentioned that might be a problem."

"He's right. Be extra careful."

"I don't plan to get into any more dangerous situations."

"Could I get that in writing?" Frank asked.

The nurse pointed to the scrape on his forehead as she left the room. "As if you should talk."

Colleen turned to Frank when they were alone. "Thank you for going after Trey. I wouldn't be here if it weren't for you." She held out her hand and gripped his in a half shake, half high-five motion.

"I didn't react fast enough," he countered.

The nurse knocked and pushed the wheelchair through the door.

"I'll drive the car to the front of the hospital." Frank hurried to the parking lot.

"He seems like a nice guy." The nurse helped Colleen off the gurney and into the wheelchair.

"He's not sure what he wants in life."

"I can relate. I still don't know what I want to do when I grow up."

Colleen raised her brow. "But you've got a great profession."

"Sometimes I want more in life. Money, fame."

"Really? I just want to be safe."

The nurse patted her hand. "Looks like you've got a special guy who's all about protection."

Colleen was taken aback. Surely she wasn't talking about Frank?

"His face softens when he looks at you," the nurse added. "I'd say he's interested."

Colleen shrugged off the statements about Frank because they weren't true. The nurse was wrong, although Colleen would like having someone to protect her. Especially if that someone was Frank Gallagher.

Chapter Eleven

Frank called Evelyn and filled her in on what had happened after he and Colleen left the hospital. She was understandably upset about the attack and concerned about Colleen's well-being.

"Is Ron there?" he asked.

"He left a short while ago, why?"

"Just wondering." He didn't mention the Amish boy Colleen had seen earlier. Evelyn didn't need anything more to add to her concern.

"Be careful," she warned before they disconnected.

Lowering his cell, he glanced at Colleen. "Evelyn's worried about you."

"And I'm worried about putting both of you in danger."

"Hey, remember—" he pointed a finger back at himself "—I'm with law enforcement and used to dealing with criminals."

"Yes, but Evelyn doesn't need to get involved."

"She's not in danger, and with the BOLO out on Trey, he'll be in custody before long."

Colleen tugged at a strand of her hair. "I'm not as optimistic as you are. Trey's cunning. He tells a lonely woman lies she wants to hear and gets her to smuggle drugs into this country. If she balks, he overdoses her or shoots her at a roadside park. He doesn't think of anyone but himself."

She glanced out the window and sighed. "Maybe I should hole up in a motel someplace. You don't need trouble underfoot."

"And prevent Evelyn from extending her gracious Southern hospitality?"

"I don't want anyone else to get hurt."

He reached for her hand. "You're not going to a motel. Evelyn wouldn't think of it, and neither would I. Plus—" he smiled "—Duke's a good watchdog."

She smiled back, and relief swept over him. He squeezed her hand to reassure her and almost groaned when his cell rang. The last thing he wanted was to pull his hand away from hers.

He glanced at the screen and hit Talk. "Yeah, Colby."

"I tried to contact Ron Malone, but I couldn't reach him. Seems there were a number of teenage Amish boys getting a free breakfast this morning. I need a name or something to distinguish the kid in question from every other Amish youth."

"Ron was at my sister's house for most of the afternoon. Colleen and I are headed there now. I'll call him." Frank paused, wondering if Colby had anything additional to add.

"Stay safe," was all he said before disconnecting.

Seems everyone was worried about their well-being. Frank punched in Ron's home number.

"Good evening. Ron Malone speaking."

The guy was definitely old-school. "Ron, this is Frank Gallagher."

"How's Colleen? Evelyn phoned and filled me in."

"She's okay. I'm calling about the accident at the barn today. Do you remember talking to an Amish boy just before it collapsed? He's probably sixteen or seventeen years old. Straw hat. Suspenders."

"That would be Isaac Fisher. He and his sister, Martha, work at the Amish Craft Shoppe."

Frank glanced at Colleen and gave her a reassuring nod as Ron continued.

"Isaac's math skills need help so I've been tutoring him. We were trying to schedule our next session around the relief effort. Why do you ask?"

"He was hanging around the barn today."

"And probably had his eye on the Craft Shoppe. He wants to go back to work. Money's tight for most of the Amish, especially for a young guy who's planning for his future."

"Any reason to think he might have done something to cause the wall to topple?"

"You're saying it wasn't an accident?"

"I'm just asking for your opinion, Ron."

"Isaac Fisher is a fine young man who would never bring dishonor to himself or his family."

"That's what I wanted to hear. Thanks."

Lowering his cell, he smiled at Colleen. "Ron vouched for the teen. Isaac Fisher. Ron called him a fine young man."

"But—"

"You don't believe Ron?"

"I'm not sure." She wrapped her arms around her waist and stared out the window.

Frank watched her out of the corner of his eye. "Take one of those pain pills when we get to Evelyn's."

"I'm fine."

But, of course, she wasn't. Frank still had a lot of questions about the photo she'd sent to the Atlanta police, about her sister knowing the two women who had been killed and about why she was suspicious of an Amish boy who sounded like a good kid.

As fragile as Colleen seemed, this wasn't the time to delve into anything that would increase her anxiety. The doctor had ordered her to rest, which was what she needed.

Frank's questions could wait until morning. Everything would seem more clear then. At least, that was his hope.

Colleen couldn't pull her thoughts together. She kept feeling Trey's hand covering her mouth and nose. Shaking her head ever so slightly, she tried to scatter the memory and focus instead on being with Frank.

"Are you sure you're okay?" he asked, concern so evident in his voice.

"I'm trying *not* to think about what happened."

He nodded as if he understood, but how could he know what she was thinking? So many questions swirled through her mind. About the man in Atlanta who had been snooping around her apartment, about whether Ron Malone could be trusted and whether a young Amish boy could somehow be involved in Trey's drug operation.

She fingered her handbag, grateful that Frank had pulled it from the debris today. At least she had her identification, but what about the memory card?

Would she ever feel confident enough to tell Frank?

He didn't need to see the photo of her with men who worked for Trey. She'd been foolish to allow Trey to take the picture. Too late, she'd realized that he wanted the picture to blackmail her, in case she decided to go to the police.

She'd outsmarted Trey, but not for long. Now he was after her. No matter what Frank thought, Trey was dangerous, and he wouldn't stop until he found her. Knowing he had been with Ron after the storm troubled her even more.

Pulling in a deep breath, she had to tell Frank.

"There's something I haven't mentioned."

He raised his brow but kept his gaze on the road.

"That first night, when the tornado touched down and then you found me—"

Frank nodded.

"I saw Trey with Ron Malone."

"Evelyn's Ron?"

"He drove Trey to the triage area."

"Ron transported a lot of folks that night." Frank glanced at her. "You took a bad hit to your head, Colleen. You couldn't remember a number of things. Are you sure you saw Trey?"

"I thought I did."

"You were frightened. Sometimes our minds play tricks on us."

"Maybe." Or maybe not. Colleen needed to find out the truth about Ron Malone and his relationship with Trey. Even if it put her in danger.

Colleen was quiet for the rest of the ride home. Frank helped her from the car, but she insisted on walking on her own.

Audrey had always sought his help and made him feel

as if he was in charge. Looking back, she'd played him and fed his ego. Had he really been in love with her?

"Oh, Colleen, we were so worried." Evelyn gave her a warm hug when they got inside. She pointed to the scrape on Frank's forehead. "Looks like you and the doc came to fisticuffs."

Colleen tried to smile, then grimaced.

"You've got two choices." Frank ushered her into the kitchen and pulled out a chair at the table. "Sit down or head straight to bed."

"I'm fine."

Colleen had grit and determination, almost to a fault. She needed to let down that strong wall of independence at times. Like now, when she was shaky and her strength compromised.

The nurse had given them instructions. Colleen needed to be checked in the night. Nausea or a severe headache could signal life-threatening complications. She'd had one brush with death already. She didn't need any more problems tonight.

Frank pointed to the chair.

"If you insist." She sat, and he pushed her closer to the table.

"Can I fix you something to eat?" Evelyn asked.

"Is there any soup left?" Colleen asked.

"Of course." She glanced at Frank. "How about you? I doubt you've eaten today."

"Soup sounds good." Once his sister thought he needed nourishment, she wouldn't let up until he agreed to eat. He'd learned that early on after he moved in following his infection.

Of course, at that point, the MRSA had taken a toll on his body and nearly done him in. The highly contagious deadly organism he'd picked up in the hospital had been hard to overcome.

"Anything I can do to help?" he asked.

"Grab a couple placemats and some silverware. You know where the napkins are."

"You're not joining us?"

"I've already eaten." Evelyn glanced at the clock. "Ron's coming over. There's a new sitcom on television. We were planning to watch it together, although I can tell him tonight might not be a good idea."

Colleen held up her hand. "Don't change your plans on account of me. I don't need to eat."

"Nonsense. I'll heat the soup and let Frank take over while I freshen up."

"Ron's visiting quite often these days." Frank set the table and winked at Colleen.

Fatigue rimmed her eyes and her face was even more pale than usual.

The doorbell rang.

"He's early." Evelyn's voice held a note of flustered alarm.

"Go. Put on your lipstick." Frank pointed to her bedroom. "I'll take care of the door and the soup." He smiled as his sister scurried from the kitchen.

Frank lowered the heat under the pan and then hurried to open the door.

"Good to see you," Ron said as soon as he stepped inside. He glanced into the kitchen, where Colleen sat. "We were all concerned about you today."

"I'm fine. Just a bit worn-out."

"Evelyn and I prayed for you." He pointed his thumb at Frank. "We've been praying for this guy for a long time."

"No wonder I'm doing so well." Frank smiled. "Colleen's tired but pretending to be stronger than she looks."

"That last part sounds like Evelyn."

"She'll join you in a minute, Ron. Can I get you some coffee or a cola?"

"Thanks, but I'll make myself at home in the den."

"I need to ask you something, Ron." Colleen sat up straighter in the chair. She glanced at Frank and then back at the former teacher. "The night of the storm, do you remember transporting a man in a black hooded sweatshirt to the triage area?"

"Sure do. He was the first of many who needed help. I found him walking along Amish Road. He was shook up and didn't have much to say except that the twister had picked up his car. No telling where it landed. I left him with the EMTs, who said they'd take care of him. Do you know the guy?"

Frank nodded. "We think he's the man who came after Colleen today."

Ron gasped. "I had no idea. Is he from around here?"

"Atlanta."

"What brought him to Freemont?"

"It's a long story."

Evelyn's footsteps sounded in the hallway. Ron turned his full attention to her when she entered the kitchen. Her cheeks glowed pink, and her eyes were bright and focused on Ron.

"The show's almost ready to start," she said, motioning him into the den.

"Enjoy the program." Frank turned back to the stove. Steam was rising from the pan. He stirred the soup and dished up two bowls, placing them on the table.

Settling into the chair across from Colleen, he smiled. "Are you okay with Ron?"

"I'm sorry about all the questions I asked."

"Evelyn's a good judge of character."

"She met him at church?"

"That's right. He's started to come over more often since I moved in." Frank hesitated. "I don't think he's involved with Trey."

"I'm sure you're right. It's nice that he's been praying for you."

Frank nodded. "I knew Evie prayed, but I didn't think other folks in her church were praying for me, as well."

"It may sound like a strange question, but how's that make you feel?" Colleen's gaze was intense.

"Humbled. At one point, the docs weren't sure I'd pull through. My sister must have spread the word that I needed prayer."

"Your injury was severe."

He nodded. "I walked into a building before Duke cleared it of explosives. Broke my pelvis and a few other bones."

Frank smiled down at the trusty dog at his feet. "Duke was scraped up pretty badly, but he stayed with me and alerted the guys who came looking for me the next day. I went to Lanstuhl in Germany for my first operation. Then Walter Reed. My final surgery was at Augusta, about five hours from here."

"Then you came here to recover?"

"Eventually. Somewhere along the line I was exposed to MRSA. My immune system was compromised, and I had a hard time fighting the infection."

He tried to smile. "You know how Evie likes to cook,

which worked to my advantage since I'd lost so much weight and strength."

"Your sister's generous with her love." Colleen peered at Duke under the table. "How'd you end up with your sweet pup?"

As if knowing Colleen was talking about him, Duke pranced to her side of the table and sat at her feet.

"The explosion did something to his nose," Frank continued. "When a military working dog can't track a scent, he's forced to retire. I heard he was at Fort Rickman and asked if I could adopt him."

He smiled, watching as Colleen rubbed Duke's neck. "We've been through a lot together."

"Duke's probably enjoying retirement, but it sounds like you're ready to go back to work."

"That's my hope." Or was it?

Not wanting to open that door tonight, he pointed to the bowls of soup. "Dinner's getting cold."

"You're right." Colleen lowered her head.

"If you want to pray out loud, I'll join you."

She glanced up at him, seemingly startled.

"We both have a lot for which to be thankful."

Her face softened, and she smiled. Warmth spread through him.

Her hand was still on the table. He reached out and grasped it before his internal voice of reason could tell him to be cautious. After everything that had happened, he wanted to join Colleen in prayer, even if he didn't know what words to say. He'd let her lead this time. Maybe he'd be able to say his own prayers, in time.

After they finished the soup, Frank walked Colleen to the guest room and said good-night at the door.

"Is there anything you need?" he asked.

She shook her head, grateful for the concern she heard in his voice and the sincerity in his expression. Something had changed since the run-in with Trey at the hospital. Maybe Frank finally believed her.

"Thanks."

He raised his brow. "For saying good-night?"

She laughed. "For saving my life. If…if you hadn't been there—"

"I almost didn't make it in time."

"You scared Trey off."

"But he escaped."

"At that moment, all I cared about was staying alive."

The thought of what could have happened made her shiver.

Frank reached for her. She stepped closer, and his arms circled her shoulders. She laid her head on his shoulder.

Frank had to be as tired as she was, yet she could feel his strength and determination. He had saved her from Trey. She thought she could bring the drug dealer to justice on her own, but she needed help. She needed Frank.

At the moment, she didn't think of Frank as a cop. She thought of him as a man. He was tall and strong, even though he still wore some of the ravages of the infection he had battled.

Colleen had been so wrong about who he really was. Now she saw him in a better light, and she liked what she saw.

She allowed herself to rest in his embrace for a long moment before she pulled back. "Thanks again for today." She flipped on the overhead light in the bedroom. "If you'll excuse me, I'm tired and need to sleep."

Stepping into the room, she closed the door and sighed.

Frank hadn't believed her last night. Did he now? She didn't know for sure.

Until she knew his true feelings, she had to be careful and guard her heart.

Chapter Twelve

Colleen inhaled the clean smell of the outdoors as she snuggled between the crisp sheets—no doubt dried on the line—and pulled the quilt up to her shoulders. Feeling pampered by the fresh linens, she fell asleep quickly and woke with a start some hours later from a dream that seemed too real.

She saw Trey in the woods, rifle raised, and heard Vivian's cry for help, along with the deafening roar of the twister.

Throwing back the covers, Colleen grabbed the robe Evelyn had provided and shrugged into the soft cotton. Reaching to turn on the bedside lamp, she hesitated, her hand in midair.

A sound upset the stillness.

With every nerve on high alert, she turned her ear toward the double French doors leading to the porch and strained to decipher the sound that came again.

Metal on metal?

Ever so quietly, she slipped from the bed and tiptoed to the window. With her back to the wall, she lifted the edge of the curtain.

Darkness.

Staring into the black night, she willed her eyes to focus. Slowly, they adjusted.

Movement.

Snip. Then another.

Her pulse raced and fear clawed at her throat.

The sound repeated over and over again.

She strained to make out some faint outline that could identify who was trying to gain access.

There. A hand thrust through the porch screen.

A portion of the wire mesh pulled free.

She dropped the curtain and turned to flee.

Tired though he was, Frank couldn't sleep. He kept seeing Colleen buried in the rubble, first when the twister hit and then later when the barn wall had collapsed on top of her. He'd screamed and raced forward, but he couldn't get to Colleen in time.

Thankfully, the roof of the Honda had stopped the momentum of the wall's downward collapse. Colleen had been hit by broken boards, but not with the full force of the larger section.

He'd asked Evie to check on Colleen during the night. No doubt, his sister was also giving thanks to the Lord about the right resolution to a very dangerous situation today. Frank wasn't used to turning to God, yet a swell of gratitude rose within him.

Dropping his legs over the side of the bed, he sat up and stared into the darkness. "I don't know what to say except thank you, Lord."

Satisfied with his first significant attempt in years to communicate directly with the Almighty, Frank lay back down, hoping to grab some shut-eye.

Duke stirred at the foot of the bed.

"Easy, boy. What is it?"

The dog whined and trotted to the door.

"You hear something?"

He pranced and whined again.

Frank stood, slipped into a pair of jeans and grabbed his service weapon.

Opening the door ever so carefully, he glanced at the door to Evelyn's bedroom and stepped into the hallway. Duke trotted toward the kitchen and turned into the rear hallway leading to the sewing room, where Colleen now slept.

Frank followed and stopped outside Colleen's room. All he heard was the beat of his heart and the dog's even breaths at his feet.

Had he imagined something?

Duke had seemed a bit skittish since the tornado. Both of them were having problems settling back into a routine ever since Colleen had blown into their lives.

Convinced they'd overreacted, Frank started to turn away.

A sound made him pause.

A scurry of footsteps inside the room.

Before he could raise his hand to knock, Colleen's door opened.

Eyes wide. Hair in disarray. Lips still swollen with sleep.

"Someone's—" She gasped and pointed to the French doors. "Someone's on the back porch."

"Evie's bedroom is down the hall on the left. Stay with her. Lock the door. Don't let anyone in unless I tell you it's clear. Call 911 and notify the police."

She scurried past him.

"Come on, boy."

Duke followed him through the kitchen. Frank grabbed his Maglite and slipped outside, the dog at his side.

A breeze blew through the trees, the sound of rustling leaves covering their footfalls. Frank's heart pounded. Trey wouldn't escape this time.

Gripping the Maglite in his left hand and his weapon in the right, Frank inched around the corner. A dark shadow, big and bulky, peered through the French doors into the room where Colleen had slept moments earlier.

At the same instant, sirens sounded in the distance.

The dark shadow turned and ran.

"Stop. Law enforcement."

The guy fled into the woods. Frank gave the command. Duke ran after him. Frank followed.

Shots fired.

Fearing Duke had been hit, Frank increased his pace and pushed harder.

The sound of a car engine filled the night. Tires screeched.

Frank whistled. The dog bounded from the wooded area.

Relieved to see his trusty friend unharmed, Frank slapped his leg. "Come on, boy."

They hurried back to the house. A police squad car pulled into the driveway.

"I didn't expect you to respond so quickly," Frank said to the cop who climbed from the car.

His name tag read Stoddard. He was tall and lean, midtwenties and blond. "I was in the area, sir."

Frank quickly filled him in on what he'd seen and heard.

Using the radio, Stoddard alerted other patrol cars. "The man is armed and dangerous."

While the officer examined the cut screen, Frank stepped inside and headed to Evelyn's room. He tapped on the door.

"It's Frank. You can come out. The guy ran off."

Evelyn threw open the door and gasped with relief when she saw Frank. "Colleen and I thought something had happened to you. We heard the shots and—"

He patted her shoulder. "The shots were aimed at Duke."

Colleen looked alarmed. "Is he okay?"

"Seems to be fine."

"Did you see the guy?" she asked.

"Only from the rear. He was wearing dark slacks and a hooded sweatshirt."

"It was Trey."

"We don't know that for sure."

The cop called from the front of the house. Evelyn tied her robe more tightly around her. "I'll brew coffee."

She hurried to the kitchen.

Colleen stepped closer. "Something woke me. I couldn't recognize the sound at first. Looking out the window, I saw him cut through the screen."

"Frank." Evelyn's voice. "The officer needs to ask you some questions."

"He'll want to talk to me, too," Colleen said.

"I'll stay with you."

She nodded. "It's okay. I don't have anything to hide."

The officer accepted a cup of coffee from Evelyn and took down the information that Frank and Colleen provided.

"Ma'am, did you recognize the prowler?" he eventually asked.

"I... I couldn't tell who he was. It was dark. I don't know if it was Trey Howard or someone else."

"I'll check with Officer Talbot, whom you spoke with at the hospital, and see if he's uncovered anything new."

"The officer said he'd issue a Bee Low," she added.

Frank smiled. "That's BOLO. A Be On the Lookout order was sent to all law enforcement in the area."

The blond officer scratched his head. "Which I never received. I'll check that with Talbot, as well."

He glanced at Evelyn as he scooted back from the table and stood. "Thanks for the coffee, ma'am."

"I wish you'd take a slice of coffee cake for later."

He nodded his appreciation. "I'm training for a marathon next month and keeping my sugar to a minimum. But the coffee hit the spot."

Frank walked Stoddard to the front door and offered his hand. "Ms. Brennan's car is at the barn. See if your crime scene folks can get to it in the morning."

"I'll make that happen, sir."

The cop was young and seemed competent. Colleen had answered all the questions, but Frank wondered if she was holding something back.

Why did Trey keep coming after Colleen? Was it because of what she knew? Or did it involve more than a list of names and a photo?

There had to be something else that Trey wanted.

But what?

Just before Stoddard left the house, a car pulled into the driveway. While Colleen helped Evelyn tidy the kitchen, Frank opened the door, surprised to find Mayor Allen Quincy standing on the porch.

"Evening, Frank. Officer Stoddard." Tall, balding and wearing his fatigue, the mayor stepped into the foyer. He dropped his keys on a nearby table and shook both men's hands.

"Actually, sir," Stoddard said, "evening has long since passed. Everything okay?"

"Just doing a last-minute check in the Amish area." Pulling a handkerchief from his pocket, the mayor wiped his forehead and smiled. "Age seems to be catching up with me."

"I doubt that, sir," Stoddard was quick to reply.

The mayor smiled. "I saw your squad car when I drove by. The dispatcher said there was a break-in."

"An attempted break-in," Frank explained. "The guy got as far as the screened-in porch."

The mayor shook his head with regret, his shoulders sagging ever so slightly. "We've had vandalism in the trailer park that was hit by the tornado. I had hoped the Amish area wouldn't have that problem."

Evelyn wiped her hands on a towel and joined the men in the foyer. "Care for a cup of coffee, Allen?"

"Thanks, Evelyn, but I'll take a rain check."

Another knock. "Seems everyone's stopping by tonight." Frank opened the door.

A second police officer stood on the porch with his hand on the shoulder of a young Amish boy.

"Evening, Mayor. Ma'am. Sir." He peered through the crowd at Colleen and nodded to her, as well.

"I hate to bother you folks this late," the officer said, "but I found this young man walking through your property. I wanted to see if you could identify him as your prowler."

Colleen stared at the Amish lad. "You were behind the barn when the wall came down."

The boy tensed. "I did nothing wrong."

"What about tonight, son?" Frank asked. "What were you doing this far from home, especially so late?"

Evelyn reached for the boy's hand. "Isaac, it's good to see you. Was Mr. Malone tutoring you? Did you have a night session?"

The boy shook his head. "I... I was talking to Lucy Wyatt."

"Marsha and Carter Wyatt's daughter?"

"*Jah*. They are her parents."

Evelyn looked at the two officers and the mayor. "I can vouch for Isaac. He works at the Craft Shoppe and selects the best produce and baked goods for me. He's a fine young man."

Recalling the bulk of the guy on the porch, Frank had to agree with his sister. "The intruder was taller and more filled out."

He turned to Isaac. "Did you see anyone in the woods when you were with Lucy?"

The Amish boy shook his head. "No one."

The mayor checked his watch. "I'm headed back your way, Isaac. I'll take you home."

He hung his head. "My *dat* does not know I left the house."

The mayor thought for a moment and then patted the boy's shoulder. "Then we won't tell him. I'll drop you at the end of your driveway. He won't hear my car."

Turning to the officer still standing on the porch, the mayor asked, "Does that meet with your approval?"

"Yes, sir. No need for me to file a report as long as you're taking the boy home."

"Thanks for your hospitality, Evelyn."

"Anytime, Mayor."

As he turned to leave, Colleen pointed to the keys on the foyer table. A plastic picture frame was attached to the chain.

Frank followed her gaze and stared at the photo of a young woman in a wedding dress.

The mayor patted his pocket and then laughed as he reached for the forgotten keys. "Isaac and I wouldn't have gotten far without these."

"The photo?" Colleen asked.

"That's my daughter." The mayor beamed with pride. "She got married in Atlanta last summer and gave the key chain with the attached picture to me for Christmas."

"She used an Atlanta photographer?"

"That's right. He seemed like a nice guy. My daughter was happy with the photos, so that's all that matters."

Once everyone left, Frank closed and locked the door. "A busy place tonight."

Evelyn shook her head with regret. "I fear Isaac's heart is going to be broken."

"Oh?"

"Lucy Wyatt is not Amish."

Evelyn returned to the kitchen.

Colleen's eyes were wide. She grabbed Frank's hand. "The bride's picture had the name of the photographer written in the corner."

Frank knew before she told him.

"The photographer was Trey Howard."

Chapter Thirteen

Colleen woke the next morning and stretched out her hand to pet Duke. Frank had insisted the dog stay in her room throughout the night. She had slept soundly knowing the German shepherd was standing guard.

"You're such a good dog." Duke lifted his ears and tilted his head, letting her rub behind his ears and pat his neck. "Thanks for taking care of me last night."

She glanced at the clock and groaned—9:00 a.m. She'd slept later than she wanted. At first, she'd tossed and turned while reviewing the questions the police officer had asked. True to his word, Frank had sat next to her and filled in any blanks when she got stuck on an answer. Evelyn had stayed up and encouraged them to eat the cake and cookies she served, never appearing fazed by Frank's explanation about Trey and his drug operation.

The arrival of the Amish boy and the mayor added to her concern, especially when she'd seen Trey's name on the key-chain photo. Surely the mayor wasn't involved in a drug operation, yet the coincidence added to her unease.

Crawling from bed, Colleen quickly showered and changed into jeans and a pullover top. The memory card was weighing heavily on her mind.

Hurrying into the kitchen, her enthusiasm plummeted when she found a note from Evelyn on the counter. "I have to work at the library for a few hours. I'll be home in time for lunch."

Knowing Frank was probably at the triage site, Colleen glanced out the kitchen window, searching for a glimpse of him in the valley below. Hopefully Evelyn wouldn't be gone too long. Feeling a bit skittish at being alone, she rubbed her hands over her arms and tried to still her growing anxiety.

Duke stood at the front door and barked. Of course, she wasn't alone. She had a wonderful guard dog.

"Sorry, boy, I wasn't thinking of you."

She let him out and returned to the kitchen to brew coffee. Evelyn had left coffee cake on the counter with a second note. "Help yourself. Eggs and bacon are in the fridge. Homemade bread is next to the stove."

She smiled, grateful for Evelyn's hospitality.

As the coffee dripped, Colleen hurried back to check on Duke.

Footsteps sounded on the front porch.

She stopped short. Her stomach tightened. She hadn't completely closed the door. Through the cracked opening, she saw a man, wearing jeans and a black sweater.

Heart in her throat, she backed into the kitchen and grabbed a knife from the wooden butcher block by the stove. Holding it close to her side, she mentally outlined her options.

How much protection would the knife provide?

Not enough.

She needed help.

She needed Frank.

"Colleen?"

Frank's voice. She gasped with relief and felt foolish for thinking Frank could possibly be Trey. She dropped the knife on the table and tried to blink back tears, but she couldn't stop the rush of emotion that swept over her.

Frank's face was twisted with concern. He opened his arms, and she fell into his embrace.

Her control broke. She sobbed, unable to stop the onslaught. She had been so strong for so long. She'd stood by her dying sister and promised she'd bring Trey to justice, but she hadn't been able to gather enough evidence or convince law enforcement of his guilt.

No one believed her. Not even Frank.

Until now.

Much as she didn't want to admit the truth, Colleen felt responsible for her sister's death. She'd been so determined to show Briana tough love that she'd failed to respond to her plea for help.

Why hadn't she been more sensitive, more caring, more who Christ wanted her to be? Maybe because she'd been burned by Briana so many times in the past. Still, that wasn't reason to forsake her sister in a time of need.

Frank pulled her closer. His hand rubbed over her shoulders. Lips close to her ear, he whispered soothing words that were like a lifeline to a drowning woman.

"Shh, Colleen, I've got you. I won't let anyone hurt you."

"I... I thought you were—"

"I'm sorry for scaring you. I went out to get the morning paper. When I saw Duke, I wanted to make sure you were okay."

She nodded and wiped her cheeks, concentrating on Frank's strength and the understanding so evident in his voice.

"I… I closed my heart to Briana." The words came unbidden. She had to admit her mistake.

"It's okay, honey."

"She had nowhere else to turn except to Trey."

"Even with your help, she probably would have gone back to him. The statistics aren't good for anyone hooked on drugs. Without rehab, without the will to make a change—"

"Without God," Colleen added, her lips trembling.

"That's it exactly. As much as you wanted Briana to walk away from her addiction, she couldn't, and you couldn't do it for her. She went to Trey, not because of you, but because of her need for drugs."

"If only she hadn't gotten involved with him."

"Where'd they meet?"

"I'm not sure. She worked at the King's Club for almost two years. It's in the heart of the city and known to have the wrong type of clientele. Trey may have been a regular. I told her it was a bad place. I don't know if she quit the job because of me or if she got tired of what she saw."

"Did she know the two women who died?"

"She never mentioned them. The last time she phoned wanting money, I said no. She overdosed a few days later."

Colleen looked into Frank's dark eyes, which reflected the pain she was carrying.

"I have to stop Trey. That's the promise I made to Briana."

He nodded. "I'm in this with you. We'll get him. He won't hurt anyone again."

"There's...there's something else I have to tell you."

Frank tensed ever so slightly.

She felt the change, but she couldn't stop now. Everything needed to be revealed.

"When I entered Trey's office, I was searching for evidence that would convince the police. I told you about the picture on his screen."

Frank nodded. "Go on."

"That night, Trey was using an external card reader to view his digital photographs from a memory card. I needed more evidence, so I took the card, although I never had time to look at the pictures."

"He must have realized the memory card was gone. Didn't he come after you?"

"He sent one of his men to my apartment later that night. I was scheduled on a flight early the next morning. My carry-on was packed so I left through a back door, made my flight the next day and then checked into a motel when I got back to Atlanta. That's when the gal who lived across the hall called me. She said someone else had been snooping around."

"You thought that was Anderson, the cop from Atlanta."

"I'm not sure. Anderson or one of Trey's men. Soon after that, I called Vivian. She had evidence that would prove Trey's involvement. At least that's what she told me."

"The video."

"She didn't tell me what she had, but she did ask what type of phone I used."

"Why didn't you tell me before about the memory card?"

"Trey took my photograph with a couple of the men who worked for him. I didn't want to be in the picture, but he insisted. If I made too much of it, I knew he'd get suspicious."

"What's that have to do with not telling me?"

"I... I wasn't sure how you'd react if you saw me with the men. You didn't believe me earlier. The photo wouldn't have improved my credibility, especially if they were known drug traffickers. Plus, I worried Trey might have doctored the photo to incriminate me even more. Guilt by association, they call it, but I'm innocent of any wrongdoing."

She glanced up, and her breath hitched. "Do you believe me, Frank?"

"Why wouldn't I?" His voice was flat and his eyes had lost their spark of interest. He was trying to cover up his true feelings.

"Where's the memory card now?" He took a step back, distancing himself from her.

She shook her head, struggling to control a second wave of tears that threatened. Frank didn't believe her.

"It was in my purse. The contents were strewn under the seat in the storm. I'm sure it's still in the car."

"I'll check it out."

He started to turn away from her. She grabbed his arm.

"I'm going with you."

She'd ride to the triage area with Frank. Hopefully they'd find the memory card, but then she'd leave Freemont and go someplace safe.

She never wanted Trey or his men to find her.

She didn't want Frank to find her either.

A stiff breeze blew as Frank pulled out of Evelyn's driveway. He'd left Duke behind, but Colleen sat next to him, her arms crossed and her shoulders straight.

Frank had been attracted to Colleen and ready to go the distance for her. Then she mentioned the memory card, which was another bit of evidence she had kept from him.

He didn't understand her or her actions.

She wanted Trey stopped, yet she refused to share crucial information with him. Didn't she trust him to be an effective investigator?

After his injury, he hadn't been enough of a man for Audrey. Evidently he wasn't enough of an investigator for Colleen.

He remembered the way she had felt in his arms. Truth be told, he hadn't wanted to let her go. Instead, he wanted to protect her and do whatever he could to stop her tears and bring joy to her life.

He hadn't felt that way with Audrey. Their relationship had been surface, which Audrey had made blatantly clear when she'd walked away. Too late he realized the truth. Frank had being drawn to Audrey by her outward looks, not by an inner beauty.

Colleen was beautiful inside and out, but it wasn't her looks that attracted him to her. It was her focus, her strength and her need to right the wrong that drugs had caused her sister. Frank knew that drive. It's why he had joined the military and eventually transferred to the CID. He wanted to right wrongs and help those in need.

If only he could explain his feelings to Colleen, but she

was centered on finding the memory card and bringing Trey to justice. No reason to mix personal relationships with an investigation. He knew better, even if Colleen had pulled him off course.

He drove down the hill faster than he should have and braked to a stop beside the barn.

"Where's my car?" Colleen demanded, the first comment she'd made since climbing into his truck at his sister's house.

"Stay here."

"I will not." She threw open the door and jumped down. "What did you do with my Honda?"

"Nothing."

"Did the local cops impound the car?"

"I'll find out."

Frank pulled his cell from his pocket and called the Freemont PD. He asked to speak with Officer Stoddard.

"I told you about the car buried in debris in the barn," Frank said when Stoddard came on the line.

"Yes, sir."

"Did your crime scene team check it out?"

"Ah, I'm not sure. Give me a minute."

Frank waited, his frustration rising.

"Sir." Stoddard returned. "Our crime scene team scheduled the Honda for late afternoon."

"That would work except the car is gone."

"Gone?"

"Exactly. Someone's taken the car, and I want it found."

"Yes, sir."

Frank disconnected. "The cops don't know what happened," he told Colleen.

"Someone does."

A horse and buggy clip-clopped along the road. Frank flagged down the bearded farmer. He wore a light blue shirt and a straw hat that nearly covered his eyes. A teen-age boy, clean-shaven and similarly dressed, sat next to him.

"Mr. Fisher?"

"Whoa, there. Whoa." He pulled his horse to a stop.

Frank pointed to the barn. "There was a car in that barn. Do you know where it's been taken?"

The Amish man shook his head.

Frank turned to the teen. "What about you, Isaac? Did you do anything to the car?"

The bearded man bristled. "Why do you ask this of my son?"

Holding up his hand, Frank said, "Sir, let him answer the question."

"A bulldozer was in the area." The teen pointed across the street to the construction worker clearing debris around the farmhouse. "Ask that man."

Frank nodded his thanks and waited until the buggy had passed before he hurried across the street.

Spotting his approach, the driver shoved the gear in Neutral and allowed the bulldozer to idle in place.

"Paul, isn't it?" The guy who had worked around the barn yesterday.

He nodded. "That's right. Paul Yates."

"What happened to the car that was in the barn?" Frank pointed back to where Colleen stood staring at the ground.

"Someone loaded it on a flatbed." Paul rubbed his chin. "Junkyard Jack? Junkyard Jason? Seems it started with the letter *J*."

"Junkyard Joe's."

The guy nodded. "That's it."

"Who authorized the pickup?" Probably a long shot to think the Atlanta construction worker would know, but no harm asking.

"No clue about authorization, but the guy in charge of the whole cleanup was talking to the driver of the flatbed. Someone said he was the mayor."

"Allen Quincy. Did you see anyone else?"

"Just the two guys from the junkyard."

Frank nodded his thanks and hustled back to Colleen, who was picking through the hay and debris.

"I'm checking the ground in case the memory card ended up outside the car," she explained as he neared. "When the twister hit, my only thought was staying alive."

"Find anything?"

"Lots of stuff. No memory card. Any luck on your end?"

"Seems the mayor may have gotten carried away with his cleanup campaign and had your car hauled off to the local junkyard."

"That's our next stop?"

He nodded. "But first, let's give this area a thorough search so we don't have to backtrack."

Frank worked back and forth, in a grid-like pattern, just as he had been trained to do with crime scene investigations. Colleen walked beside him, and both of them seemed satisfied when they left in Frank's pickup forty-five minutes later.

"Junkyard Joe's sits on the other side of town," Frank said. "I'll give you a tour of Freemont on the way."

He turned off Amish Road and headed due east, first through a residential area that had escaped damage and then along a country lane.

"Such a beautiful area." She took in the rolling hills and sprawling farms that stretched on each side of the roadway.

A newer home with an expansive back deck was visible in the distance, situated on a road that ran parallel of the one they traveled.

"Dawson Timmons, a former CID agent, lives there." Frank pointed to the house and surrounding farmland. "He got out of the army, married a local girl, bought land and started farming. They're nice folks who go to Evelyn's church."

"But you don't?"

Frank glanced at her. "Don't go to church?"

She nodded.

"I haven't yet. Maybe one of these days."

Silent for a long moment, Colleen finally spoke. "I didn't think much about religion until my sister died. Since then I've tried to do better, but I haven't joined a church."

"You were busy tracking down Trey."

"Looking back, I realize trying to take him down by myself was probably a mistake."

"It's fairly obvious you don't trust law enforcement."

There, he'd stated the major obstacle that stood between them. She didn't trust anyone with a badge, yet she couldn't achieve her goal without law enforcement's help.

"Not all of us are on the take, Colleen."

"As I recall, you have trust issues, too." Her voice was tight, her focus still on the road.

"Because I question information that can't be substantiated?"

"Because you don't believe me."

He pulled in a ragged breath. He wanted to believe

Colleen. When he looked into her eyes, he saw a good woman who was trying to do what was right, but he had this fear of not making the right decision or seeing things the way they really were.

Was that holding him back?

"It's not personal."

She harrumphed. "You've talked yourself into thinking you're doing what's right, yet you can't see the truth."

"The truth about—"

"The truth about me. I'm trying to gather enough evidence to put Trey Howard in jail for life. You and I are actually on the same side of the law. The problem is you're always questioning your own ability and your compromised strength and your weakened condition."

Did he appear weak to her?

"You think your injury and infection affected your investigative skills," she continued, hardly pausing long enough to take a breath. "You're still the man you were before, Frank. You're still a CID agent able to track down evidence and bring the guilty to justice. You just lack confidence. You're looking back at what happened in Afghanistan and during your long hospitalization. It must have been difficult, but you've healed. You're ready to get back to work, to embrace life fully."

She sighed. "You're the same man, only maybe a bit more cautious and more aware of your own mortality. That's not a bad thing. Sometimes when we think we can do it all ourselves, we forget about God. But we can't do anything without Him. Allow Him into your brokenness, and you'll be able to heal."

He hesitated for a long moment. Then pulling in a deep breath, he asked, "What about you, Colleen? Have you healed?"

She shook her head. "I still can't get over losing Briana. Much as I want to believe the tough love was for her own good, I keep wondering if it led to her death. If only I'd opened my heart and brought her back into my life, I could have taken care of her. I could have loved her. I could have helped her battle her addiction."

"She needed rehab."

Colleen shook her head. "She'd been to rehab. It hadn't stopped her from finding drugs."

"Chances are she wouldn't have done anything different the second time. Drug addiction is like quicksand. She couldn't free herself even if she wanted to, and you couldn't have pulled her out. It's not easy to realize drugs have such control over someone we love, but it's the truth. She loved drugs more than she loved herself."

"More than she loved me," Colleen whispered.

Frank didn't know anything else he could say that would ease Colleen's guilt or assuage her grief. If Trey had been guilty of drug trafficking, he needed to be stopped so that no other woman was sucked into the downward spiral of addiction. The addict wasn't the only one affected. The entire family was, as well.

Colleen was proof of that.

She deserved more than heartbreak over a sister's dependence on cocaine. Colleen deserved to be loved and accepted. If only she would lower the wall she had raised around her heart.

Frank didn't know how to change her opinion of law enforcement, but he wanted her future to be bright. He was beginning to think being part of her future might be good for him, as well.

Chapter Fourteen

A musty smell wafted past Colleen and mixed with the haze of dust and the cloying scent of rusted metal when they drove into the junkyard. Stepping out of the pickup, she tried to hold her breath but quickly ran out of air.

"Are you okay?" Frank asked.

"I'm fine." Which she wasn't. Her head ached, and she was tired of arguing about trust and the lack thereof.

A man left the ramshackle shack that served as an office and headed to a Ford 4x4 parked nearby. The truck looked new.

"Joe?" Frank waved to the guy as he opened the door and started to climb behind the wheel.

Evidently the owner. Joe looked as scruffy as his junkyard, although his truck was pristine. Untrimmed beard, long hair pulled into a ponytail topped with a baseball hat. His name was embroidered on the front chest pocket of his work shirt.

"You need something?" he called back to them.

"A blue Honda injured in the tornado. You or a couple of your workers picked it up this morning." Frank held up his CID badge.

"They unloaded in the west end." Joe pointed them in the right direction. "Head along the path around the mound of old parts. You'll see the Honda."

Frank reached for Colleen's hand. She hadn't expected his grip to be so strong.

"Let's go."

She hurried after him.

Passing the pile of car parts and twisted metal, she groaned when the expansive west end, as Joe had called it, came into view. The junkyard extended for acres. "This might take some time."

Two paths wove through a graveyard of discarded cars. Doors hung open. The hoods on many of the vehicles were raised, allowing engines to rust from the elements. Trunks were cocked at odd angles. Birds perched on the bottom rims pecked at bugs that lived in the shaded interior.

Colleen glanced at the ground, expecting to see vermin underfoot.

Frank squeezed her hand.

"I'm imagining rats and other creatures," she admitted.

"We'll make noise to scare away anything on four legs."

"What about the two-legged vermin?"

"I'll watch for them, as well."

Trey would do anything to save himself and his profitable drug operation. Colleen stood in his way.

He'd tried to kill her before. He'd try again.

She glanced at Frank's hand that still held hers.

He didn't believe her, yet Frank was helping her find the memory card. Probably because he needed the evidence that would end Trey's hateful abuse of the women he trafficked and the men and women—many young kids who didn't make good decisions—who used the drugs he brought illegally into the United States.

He had to be stopped.

Frank would help her bring Trey to justice. He'd also work to keep her safe, but once he had the digital memory card, he'd no longer need Colleen.

She dropped his hand and started down one of two paths winding through the rows of cars.

Colleen had to rely on her own ability, her own strength. She'd made a mistake letting her guard down around Frank. A mistake she already regretted. At least she hadn't made an even bigger mistake by giving him her heart.

Frank didn't know why he had taken Colleen's hand, especially after the tension that had sparked between them earlier.

He blamed it on his protective nature when he was around her. An inner voice kept warning him to be alert to danger.

Joe was a typical redneck who ran a fairly profitable business despite his scrubby beard and ponytail. The junkyard was a fixture in Freemont, and even Evelyn gave her stamp of approval when Frank had called her and mentioned Joe's name.

Still, something niggled within Frank, a nervous anxiety that had him looking over his shoulder and wanting to keep Colleen close by his side.

She, on the other hand, had charged off in one direction to cover more area, while he followed on the neighboring path.

He cupped his hands around his mouth. "See anything?"

She shook her head. "A lot of junk but no blue Honda."

Frank spotted an old woody station wagon, a Studebaker and other makes and models that had to be classics by now. Some of them could be refurbished into a decent ride, for the right price.

That was the point. No one would spend hard-earned cash for a rusty car that had been exposed to the elements. Joe made money by selling parts, which left the cars picked over like roadkill.

His eyes scanned rows of automobiles, trucks, even a couple of buses and an RV that had all seen better days. Some had been plucked clean. Others sat seemingly untouched in the afternoon sun.

The two paths came together up ahead. In the distance, Frank noted movement on a small hill that formed a natural end to Joe's acreage.

He squinted, trying to determine what he'd seen. A gust of wind stirred trees on the gentle slope. Surely that's what had diverted his attention.

He glanced over his shoulder, ensuring they weren't being followed.

Turning back to the hill, he focused on a narrow dirt path, barely wide enough for a compact car.

"Something wrong?" Colleen asked.

"Just checking the area."

"I see a blue car just beyond the fork where the two paths meet."

Frank followed her gaze. "Looks like your Honda."

He hurried to meet up with her.

The Honda sat behind a wall of vehicles.

"How do we crawl through all that wreckage?" she asked.

"We'll go around some of the cars and over others." He glanced at her feet, glad to see she was wearing shoes with rubber soles.

"Let me check it out. You stay on the path."

She shook her head, just as he'd known she would. "We go together."

"You could twist an ankle or get cut on a piece of metal."

She nodded. "That's a risk I'll take. Plus, I could offer the same warning to you."

"Shall I lead then?"

"Be my guest."

Frank climbed onto the hood of a four-door sedan and offered Colleen his hand. She put her foot on the front bumper, and he helped her up to where he stood. The hood buckled. "Watch your step."

He leaped to the next car and reached for her as she followed. "Two more cars to go."

They crawled across the front seat of a third car and inched their way around a fourth to reach the Honda.

Frank jerked open the driver's door. Colleen looked under the front seat. "The memory card was in my purse."

"Did anything else fall out?"

She nodded. "Everything, including my wallet and lipstick." She patted the floorboard and shook her head when she came up empty-handed. "Maybe it's in the backseat."

"Watch out for broken glass," Frank cautioned.

She searched the rear, but found nothing.

With a sigh, she extracted herself. "It's not there."

"Let me try."

She stepped back to give him room. Bending down, he tugged at the carpet. Two sections were attached by Velcro. Pulling the rug away from the floorboard, he smiled, seeing a small square card.

Grabbing it, he started to stand.

"Look what—"

A shot pinged against the car.

Colleen screamed.

He grasped her shoulders and shoved her down, protecting her body with his own.

Reaching for the Glock on his hip, he glared at the hill and the narrow path where he'd seen movement.

Another ping. Glass exploded as the shot hit the window of the car behind them.

"It's Trey, isn't it?" Colleen cried.

"At this point it doesn't matter who's shooting at us. We need to get out of here."

Frank pulled his cell phone free. He called 911 and relayed the information to the operator. "Tell the police to get here now."

A narrow path led toward a rusted school bus that offered better protection.

"Keep low."

More shots followed them.

"Are you hurt?" Frank asked, once they were behind the bus.

Fear flashed from her eyes, but she shook her head. "I'm okay."

He peered around the corner of the bus and studied the hillside.

Movement. A man aimed a rifle.

Frank raised his Glock and fired three shots.

The guy ducked into the underbrush.

Glancing behind him, Frank searched for another exit. Leaving the protection of the bus would put them in the shooter's sights.

Another volley of fire. A bus window shattered. Frank threw himself over Colleen to shield her from the falling shards.

"Stay down," he warned again.

Frank stared at the hillside. The breeze blew the trees, but a bush moved in the opposite direction. The guy was trying to escape.

Frank took aim and squeezed the trigger.

Sirens sounded in the distance.

He fired again.

The police cars rolled into the junkyard. Four cops jumped from their sedans, weapons drawn, and raced to the bus.

Frank quickly filled them in and pointed to the hill.

Another police car circled around the perimeter of the junkyard and raced up the slope. The cop screeched to a stop and took cover as he climbed from his vehicle. After a quick search, he raised his hand and shook his head.

Behind Frank, an officer spoke into his radio. "The area's clear?"

Static squawked.

"Roger that. Looks like our shooter left before we arrived."

He stepped to where Frank helped Colleen to her feet.

"The shooter took off, sir. We'll set up roadblocks. You were looking for something in the blue Honda?"

"That's correct. He must have followed us."

"We've got a BOLO out on Trey Howard. I'll notify you if we spot the suspect."

Frank took Colleen's hand and helped her back to his truck.

She looked exhausted and scared. He put his arm around her shoulders.

"We'll get him," he kept saying, although he didn't think she believed him.

"He wants to kill me," she whispered, her voice thick.

"You saw him shoot Vivian. He doesn't want you to testify against him. He may plan to escape to that Colombian resort he told you about."

"You can't let him leave the country." She grabbed Frank's hand.

"I'll have CID contact the airlines in Atlanta and the surrounding areas, Birmingham, Jacksonville, Nashville. He won't leave by air. At least not if we can help it."

She rested her head against his shoulder and sighed. "If only we'd found the memory chip, then we'd have proof. All I wanted was enough evidence to see him behind bars."

"I found it, Colleen."

"The memory card?"

He nodded.

She grabbed his hand, pried it open and found it empty. She stared up at him, perplexed and almost angry. "I'm not laughing if you think teasing me is funny."

"Trust me," he said as he dug into his pants pocket and pulled out the memory card.

"Oh, Frank, you found it. Now you can arrest Trey and try him for drug trafficking."

Frank looked at the hill where two additional police cars now searched for any clue that would lead them to the shooter.

To Colleen it all seemed so simple. They had the evidence. The photos along with Vivian's testimony would be enough to try him and hopefully find him guilty in a court of law.

But finding Trey was the challenge.

Even with the mounting police effort, he could elude the roadblocks. If he left the country, they'd never bring him to justice.

The old Frank wouldn't have felt discouraged, but the injured Frank—the one who was still out of shape—didn't know who would win in the end.

Chapter Fifteen

"Go on, Frank," Colleen said once they were back at Evelyn's house. "You need to take the memory card to CID Headquarters. Show it to Colby. I'm sure Special Agent in Charge Wilson will be interested, as well."

"We could look at the photos here on my computer, and then email them to Wilson," he suggested.

"Doesn't he need the evidence in hand?"

Frank nodded but still hesitated.

"Your sister and I both insist you get going," Colleen continued. "We'll be fine. Duke will protect us if anyone unsavory comes around."

"Trey's on the loose. He knows you're here."

"And didn't police notify you that the highway patrol apprehended a man who fit his description?" Evelyn interjected.

"His identify hasn't been verified yet."

"Maybe not," Colleen said with a sigh, "but he was stopped on the interstate, heading to Atlanta, soon after the shooting at Junkyard Joe's. The rifle in his car had recently been shot. It all adds up, Frank."

"Except he claims to have been hunting earlier today."

"You two can keep arguing." Evelyn picked up the telephone. "I'm calling Ron and asking him to stay with us while you're gone."

She raised her brow at her brother. "Will that convince you that we'll be safe?"

"Does Ron know how to use a gun?"

"He served in the military and goes hunting with his uncle. The awards hanging in his office attest to his marksmanship."

Frank nodded. "Tell him I'll leave a weapon in the top drawer of my dresser. It'll be loaded, just in case."

Evelyn passed on the information to Ron after he accepted the invitation to visit.

She hung up with a smile. "He considers it an honor to defend two lovely women."

Colleen ignored the niggling concern she still had about Ron, and instead smiled at the twinkle in Evelyn's eyes. She was lucky to have someone who cared for her.

Feeling a tug at her heart, Colleen glanced at Frank, wishing things could be different between them. He was a good and caring man and a good investigator even after the medical problems he'd undergone.

The way he talked about the military and the CID, he was ready to return to active duty. Maybe Special Agent in Charge Wilson would say he was needed now.

Peering out the kitchen window, Colleen stared at the cleanup and reconstruction going on along Amish Road. The collapsed structures and downed trees had been cleared and either piled at the edge of the road or already transported to the town landfill and dump.

Frank came up behind her and touched her arm. "You're okay with me going?"

"Of course." She wouldn't tell him about the tingle

of concern that had her rubbing her arms and asking for the Lord's protection.

Trey was probably already in custody.

Pulling in a cleansing breath, she smiled. Frank had a newfound energy and enthusiasm in his step. Going back to work would be just what the doctor ordered.

"Don't worry," she insisted. "We'll be fine."

"I won't be long."

He looked at Duke, lying in the corner. "Stay. Take care of Colleen and Evelyn."

Duke tilted his head as if he understood.

"Frank," Colleen called after him, "be safe."

But he'd already left the house.

Frank headed toward town and River Road, which would take him to post. Colleen was right. He and Colby needed to go over the photos on the memory card. The authorities in Atlanta would have to be notified. DEA would also be interested in what they uncovered.

His cell rang. "Special Agent Gallagher."

"Sir, this is Officer Stoddard, Freemont PD. I notified you that Georgia Highway Patrol pulled over a white male wearing a red plaid shirt."

"That's right. Trey Howard. Is he in custody?"

"Not yet, sir. They need someone to ID him."

Frank had seen him in the hospital and on the video. "Give me directions."

Five miles north of Freemont on the interstate. The detour wouldn't take long. "I'm headed there now."

Frank disconnected and increased his speed. Knowing Trey would soon be in custody gave Frank a sense of satisfaction. Working on the case felt good. Knowing

Trey wouldn't be able to draw others into his drug world was even better.

Frank would like to tell the guy a thing or two, in a professional way, of course. Then he'd drive to post and drop off the memory chip. Colby could do the initial review of the pictures while he hurried back to be with Colleen.

Was he crazy to be attracted to a woman who didn't trust law enforcement? Probably, but he'd never taken the easy route in life, and right now, he wanted to tell her how she made him feel.

After Frank left the house, Colleen tried to convince herself that everything was working out just the way she had wanted. Trey had been apprehended, but she was unsettled by a sense of concern she couldn't shake. She wandered back to the kitchen, where Evelyn was washing dishes.

Reaching for a dish towel, Colleen stepped toward the sink. "Mind if I dry?"

"No need, unless you want something to do."

Evelyn had a knack for knowing what was on Colleen's mind. "Frank's ready to get back to work."

"He's been ready for some time, although his strength needed to improve." Evelyn sighed. "The explosion in Afghanistan was traumatic enough, but he had to face the surgeries in Landstuhl and then more at Walter Reed and in Augusta. He wanted to move on with his life."

She ran more hot water in the sink. "Did he tell you about Audrey?"

Colleen shook her head. "We haven't discussed personal matters. Usually we're talking about Trey." And struggling with trust issues, which she didn't mention.

"Frank doesn't talk about the past to me either. It's as if he wants to bury the memories with the rubble that buried him in Afghanistan."

Colleen dried a glass and placed it in the cabinet, waiting for Evelyn to continue.

"He dated Audrey before his unit deployed. Frank thought she'd wait for him."

"They were good together?" Colleen asked.

"Frank thought so."

"But you didn't agree?"

"What do sisters know?" Evelyn shrugged. "I didn't tell Frank, but Audrey seemed more interested in having a handsome guy on her arm than being with Frank."

Colleen nodded, thinking of Briana's attraction for wealth and power and surface attractions.

"When Audrey left him, Frank tried to shrug off the hurt, then the infection set in. At one point, I feared he'd lose the will to live."

"That doesn't sound like Frank."

"He lost so much weight. He was on a ventilator. His kidneys started to shut down. The doctors didn't give me much hope."

"I'm sure you kept praying."

Evelyn nodded. "I prayed. Ron prayed. The whole church community prayed. His recovery was slow and hard, but Frank turned the corner, although he's still testing his own ability as if he's not quite sure of himself."

"He's stronger than he realizes. He'll be fine."

"Maybe, but he needs a good woman to encourage him."

"I doubt Frank thinks he needs anyone's help."

"Maybe not, but he does. I see the way he looks at you."

Colleen's breath hitched. "What do you mean?"

"You touch a spot in him. Someplace he's kept hidden. You've been a good influence."

She shook her head. "The only thing I've done is cause problems."

"That's not true. You've made him interested in life again."

Taken aback by Evelyn's comment, Colleen searched for a way to change the subject. "Ron seems like a great guy."

She nodded. "I'm very thankful he came into my life. He's everything Dan wasn't."

Colleen reached for another glass. "Is there something you want to talk about?"

Evelyn nodded. "How to tell Ron. He needs to know the truth about a guy I dated and thought was Mr. Right. I believed all his sweet talk and was naive to think our relationship would lead to marriage."

"Dan didn't feel the same way?"

"He invited me to meet him at a nearby state park for a late-afternoon picnic lunch. Of course, I expected something special. Storm clouds hovered overhead, but I didn't let that dampen my enthusiasm. Only Dan didn't plan to propose. He wanted to soothe his conscience and tell me about his wife and three children."

"Oh, Evelyn, I'm so sorry."

"I had no idea. He'd been so good at keeping everything secret, and I hadn't seen through his duplicity."

"What happened?"

"I railed at him. Told him he was despicable for what he'd done to his family as well as me. I told him I never wanted to see him again."

Evelyn sighed, and the weight of her upset was still

evident. "The storm hit as I left the park. The road was slick. Visibility was bad. I was driving much too fast and didn't make one of the curves."

"The accident that hurt your leg. Frank told me he came home to help you."

"I was too embarrassed to tell him about Dan or the reason for the accident. Growing up, Frank never struggled with relationships. He had lots of girlfriends over the years. He was tall and strong and handsome. I was always the sister no one noticed."

Colleen knew the feeling. "That's a hard place to be."

"I love Frank. He's got a heart of gold, but he needs to find God and learn what's important in life. As much as I hated to see him suffer through all those operations and the infection, they've opened his eyes. He realizes he can't take care of everything. If only he would start relying on God."

"You're a good influence on him, Evelyn."

"Which is what I said about you." She laughed. "Maybe we both have a positive effect on him."

"And Ron?"

"I want to tell him about Dan, but I'm not sure how he'll react."

"Ron cares deeply for you, Evelyn. He'll understand."

"I hope so." Evelyn checked her watch. "Wonder what's keeping him. He was ready to leave the house when I called. The drive only takes a few minutes."

"He's probably on the way."

"I'm going to phone just to be safe."

Safe. That's what Colleen wanted. She wanted Trey behind bars so she wouldn't have to worry anymore or look over her shoulder to see if she was being followed.

"Ron?" Evelyn held the phone close to her ear. Her

voice held more than a note of concern. "You don't sound well. Tell me what happened."

So there had been a problem.

Colleen finished drying the dishes. She didn't want to eavesdrop, but the tremble in Evelyn's voice was worrisome.

"I'm coming over." Evelyn's face was pale and her hand shook as she disconnected.

She grabbed the keys to her car and her purse. "I have to hurry. Ron blacked out earlier. He came to feeling queasy and weak. You'll be okay?"

"Of course. Don't worry about me."

"Pray for Ron," Evelyn said as she left the house.

Lord, help Ron. Don't let anything happen to him.

Colleen locked the door and called Duke.

No reason for her to be worried about her own safety. She wasn't alone. Duke would protect her. At least, she hoped he would.

Frank drove hurriedly through town and headed for I-75, the interstate that stretched from Florida to Atlanta and then farther north into Tennessee.

Two miles outside Freemont, he spied a gathering of highway patrol cars parked on the side of the interstate. Their lights flashed, warning motorists to move to the far lane and give them a wide berth.

Frank braked to a stop and parked behind a Freemont police cruiser. Before exiting his car, he called Colleen.

"You're okay?" he asked when she answered. With a growing concern for her well-being, he feared leaving had been a mistake.

"I'm fine. Where are you?"

"Parked on the side of the interstate with the highway patrol. They want me to ID Trey."

Frank had planned to visit CID Headquarters next, but he felt a sudden need to change his plans. "I'll stop by the house on my way to Fort Rickman."

"You don't have to worry."

"I want to ensure you're safe," he said before he disconnected.

Crawling from his truck, he flashed his badge to the closest officer and introduced himself. "Freemont police called. You've apprehended a possible suspect in a shooting?"

The cop nodded. "His rifle's been fired recently. We received the BOLO. The latest update said he could be wearing a red plaid shirt."

Frank nodded. "Take me to him."

The officer led the way through a swarm of uniforms. Twenty feet from the road, a man sat on the ground, hands cuffed behind his back.

"Who's in charge?" Frank asked.

The officer pointed to a big guy wearing a highway patrol uniform and a Smokey Bear hat. Again Frank showed his badge and provided his name.

"Trey Howard shot a military wife at a roadside park near Freemont. Army CID is working the investigation," he quickly filled in.

"Can you ID the guy?" the patrolman asked. "His driver's license says he's Vince Lawson."

The memory of the man in the white lab coat who threw the fire extinguisher appeared in his mind's eye.

Frank nodded. "I can identify Trey Howard."

"Come with me."

Frank followed the patrolman to the suspect.

The guy turned and glared up at Frank. Brown hair. Dark eyes.

Frank shook his head. "That's not Howard."

"Then who is he?" the cop asked.

"I guess he's who he said he was."

Frustrated by the wild-goose chase, Frank walked back to his car and stared into the distance.

Where was Trey?

Chapter Sixteen

Duke whined at the door.

"Didn't Frank take you for a walk earlier this morning? He'll be home soon, but I know you want to go out now."

The dog barked.

"You need another romp, right?" She laughed at Duke's attempt to win her heart, which he'd already accomplished.

She unlocked and opened the door. Duke lunged onto the porch and bounded down the steps. He picked up a stick and returned to the open doorway where she stood.

Feeling her mood lighten, she took it from his mouth and threw it into the woods. He scurried off to retrieve the impromptu toy.

Colleen closed her eyes, inhaling the fresh air. The warm breeze brought thoughts of summer vacation when she and Briana were young. Life seemed full of promise then. Now Briana was gone and Colleen was stranded in Freemont.

As a youth, her younger sister had often complained that life wasn't fair. Colleen had known that as soon as

Briana had been born. Even at a young age, she'd struggled to accept her curly red hair and had been awed by her sister's beauty right from the start.

Maybe it wasn't fair, but it was also life. Some were given more, some less.

God loves all his children. Words from her Sunday school class played in her mind.

Duke barked.

"Fetch the stick." She opened her eyes.

He barked again.

"Come, Duke."

He refused to obey and stared at something in the woods. A skunk or raccoon? Neither of which she wanted to confront.

"Come on, boy." She slapped her leg as she'd seen Frank do.

Duke growled at the underbrush and held his ground.

The afternoon turned ominously quiet. Birds stopped chirping. Even the cicadas went silent.

Feeling exposed and vulnerable, Colleen stepped back into the house. A sense of relief washed over her as she closed and locked the door. Duke would let her know when he wanted in.

Foolish of her to be so nervous. Trey had been apprehended, and Frank would return soon. She hadn't told him about her being alone when he phoned. He had enough worries.

Once Trey was behind bars, her anxiety would ease, and she'd see everything in a new light.

Then she'd no longer be stranded in Freemont. She would testify when Trey stood trial, but that wouldn't take more than a day or two. He'd trafficked drugs in Atlanta. The trial might be held there. Either way, she would take the stand and tell the truth so that Trey would be stopped forever.

The house phone rang. Maybe it was Frank with news of Trey's arrest.

Evelyn's voice was tight with concern when she greeted Colleen. "Ron's clammy and doesn't remember everything that happened to him. I'm afraid it's his heart. I called an ambulance. Tell Frank when he gets home. Are you sure you're okay?"

"I'm fine. Take care of Ron."

Duke barked.

Colleen returned the phone to the cradle and opened the door to get Duke. She stopped short. A man stood at the foot of the steps, dressed in a red plaid shirt, with a gun in his hand.

Trey.

Taking a step back, Colleen tried to close the door. Trey raced up the steps. His hand reached for her.

She screamed, anticipating his grasp.

Duke snarled, running toward Trey.

"What the—"

He stopped.

Seeing it unfold as if in slow motion, her heart broke. Trey raised his gun, aimed at Duke and fired.

The dog yelped. His head flew back, his body twisted in the air before he fell to the ground.

"No!"

Trey fired again. The shot went wide and hit the side of the porch. Wood splintered.

She pushed on the door that wouldn't close. His foot was wedged across the threshold. She ground her heel into his toes. He growled and lunged.

The door flew open. The force threw her against the table in the foyer. A lamp overturned and crashed to the floor. She ran for the hallway, skidded around the corner.

Frank's room.

His words played through her mind. *Loaded gun... dresser drawer.*

She slammed his bedroom door and turned the lock. Would it hold?

Heart pounding, she pulled open the top drawer on the closest dresser. Socks and underwear neatly arranged. She threw them aside, searching for the gun she couldn't find.

Frantic, she opened a second drawer. T-shirts and running shorts. No weapon.

Crossing the room, she grabbed the phone off the nightstand and yanked on the top drawer of the second dresser.

An army beret. Boxes of military medals. Searching, her hand connected with cold, hard metal.

Relief swept over her. Her fingers wrapped around the grip.

Trey's footsteps sounded in the hallway. He jiggled the knob, pounded on the door.

"I know you're in there, Colleen."

She backed into the bathroom.

He threw himself against the bedroom door. Once, twice.

The wood buckled.

Colleen screamed. Trey crashed into the room.

She slammed the bathroom door. Mouth dry. Heart in her throat. Her hands shook. She could barely turn the lock.

Hitting 9-1-1, she raised the phone and her voice when

the operator answered. "This is Colleen Brennan. I'm at Evelyn Gallagher's house just off Amish Road. An intruder with a gun is after me. Send the police. His name is Trey Howard. I'm armed, and I'll shoot if he comes near me."

"Stay on the line—"

Trey threw his weight. The bathroom door flew open.

He stood in the doorway, hair disheveled, eyes wild with fury.

"I'll kill you. Then I'll go to the hospital and finish off Vivian. You can't get away from me. I have too much power. The cops will never believe you. They didn't believe the others."

Like Briana.

He lunged for her.

No time to think. She squeezed the trigger.

Bam!

A deafening explosion. The gun kicked. She flinched. Her ears roared.

Blood darkened Trey's shirt, but he kept coming.

Bam! A second round.

More blood. He grabbed his thigh.

"Why you—" Foul words spewed from his mouth.

Before she could fire again, he turned and hobbled from the bedroom and into the hallway.

Trembling, she stood in the bathroom, unable to breathe, unable to hear anything except for the ringing in her ears.

She slid to the floor, the gun still raised and aimed in case Trey returned. At her feet, she saw spatters of his blood.

Chapter Seventeen

Frank saw the police cars as he pulled off the main road and headed back to Evelyn's house. Heart in his throat, he floored the accelerator and screeched into the driveway, where a group of police officers stood. A body lay at their feet.

Colleen? He jumped from the car, pushed through the uniforms and almost cried out when he saw Trey.

"Where is she?"

"Your sister's at the hospital."

His worst fear. "What's her condition?"

"She's fine. Ron Malone may have suffered a heart attack."

"Was he shot?"

"Negative."

"What about Colleen Brennan?"

"She's inside."

Dead or alive? Frank was afraid to ask.

He pushed past two officers in the kitchen, wild to find her.

"Where is she?"

One of the men pointed to the hallway.

Frank tore around the corner. The door to his bedroom lay in pieces. His dresser drawers hung open. Stepping over the clothing scattered on the floor, he saw her.

She was alive.

He ran to where she sat on the bed, her eyes dull, her face pale.

"He hurt you?"

She shook her head and pointed to the bathroom, where two patrolmen were photographing the broken door and blood-covered tiles where his gun lay.

"You shot Trey?"

"He came after me. I called 911. I told them I'd shoot."

"Having the gun saved her life," one of the cops said from the bathroom. "She wounded him in his right arm and left thigh. He stumbled outside just as we pulled into the driveway."

"We warned him to drop his gun," a second officer volunteered. "Instead he opened fire."

The police had taken Trey down, but only after Colleen had tried to protect herself.

"I remembered your gun, Frank."

"Oh, honey, you did the right thing." He pulled her into his arms, feeling the rapid beat of her heart.

Frank hadn't been here to protect her. He should have waited until the cops determined if the guy on the highway was Trey. His impetuousness had almost cost Colleen her life.

He pulled her closer and whispered words of comfort, all the while chastising himself for failing her once again.

Colleen didn't need him. She and the police had taken Trey down. She'd return to Atlanta and her life. What would Frank do?

He inhaled the sweet smell of her hair and pulled her

even closer, knowing he had already lost Colleen before he'd even told her how he felt. Her life would go on. Frank would put in his papers to get out of the army and make a new life for himself.

He'd survived without Audrey, but he didn't know if he could survive when Colleen walked out of his life.

"He tried to protect me," Colleen told Frank as he knelt next to Duke.

"Good boy." He rubbed Duke's neck. "You're going to be okay."

Colleen wasn't so sure. The bullet had grazed his hip, leaving him dazed and subdued.

One of the officers had wrapped the wound and placed him on a mat in the kitchen. "It's a makeshift fix, but it'll stop the bleeding until you can get him to the vet."

Footsteps sounded in the hallway. Evelyn rushed into the room. "The police told me."

Her eyes were wide, her face drawn. She reached for Colleen and pulled her close. "Are you okay?"

The embrace, so nurturing, so comforting, brought tears to her eyes. She struggled to blink them back, needing to be strong.

"Duke was hit," she said, her voice heavy with emotion.

"He's a good watchdog." Evelyn squeezed Colleen's arm and stepped toward Frank. She rubbed her hand over his shoulder. "How is he?"

"Probably frustrated that he couldn't take Trey down."

Frank was transferring his own feelings to the dog. Colleen didn't understand his need to be the hero. Trey was dead. Did it matter who had fired the fatal round?

"You'd better get him to the vet," Evelyn suggested.

"The police will be here for some time. I'll fix coffee. Colleen can rest."

"Probably a good idea," the cop standing nearby said. "The wound needs to be cleaned. The vet might put him on an antibiotic. You don't want to mess around with a gunshot wound."

Frank glanced at Colleen. "You'll be okay if I leave?"

No, but Duke needed treatment. She didn't want anything to happen to that faithful dog who had tried to protect her. As much as she wanted to go with Frank, she knew there wouldn't be room with Duke stretched out on the passenger seat. Plus, the police would probably have more questions for her to answer.

"Your sister's right. Take Duke to the vet. The danger's passed. Trey can't hurt me now."

Frank loaded Duke in his pickup and drove to the veterinary clinic on post.

"It looks worse than it is," the doc said once he completed his examination. "I'll keep Duke overnight for observation. He should be able to go home tomorrow with a slight limp that will improve with time."

Frank knew about limps and walkers and reprogramming his mind to guard the weakened portion of his body. When Frank had finally walked without relying on a cane, he thought he was ready to go back to work. Then the raging fever and infection had landed him back in the hospital.

"One overnight seems doable." He scratched the scruff on Duke's neck. "You need to stay with the doc tonight."

He licked Frank's hand and laid his head on his paws as if to show he understood.

"See you in the morning, boy." Frank had full confidence in the vet and was grateful Duke was in good hands.

Frank drove across post and parked in front of the CID Headquarters building.

Colby glanced up when Frank entered his cubicle. He looked tired and irritable.

"I take it your wife isn't home yet."

"Becca's temporary duty was extended a few more days."

"Tough break."

Colby nodded. "I wander around the house not knowing what to do when she's not there."

Frank thought of how empty Evelyn's house would seem today without Duke and, even more so, when Colleen returned to Atlanta. It was time for him to find his own place. A small condo that wouldn't bring Colleen to mind.

"I wanted to talk to Wilson. Someone's in his office. I told Sergeant Otis to let me know when he's available."

"Can I help?"

Frank shrugged. "I need to iron out my options."

"You mean when you should come back to work?"

"More or less."

Colby stared at him for a long moment. "I heard what happened. Are you okay?"

"Because Duke was hurt?"

"That and because Trey came after Colleen. I heard she found one of your guns and wounded him."

"All true. He stumbled out of the house and into the sights of the Freemont cops, only he made a fatal mistake and opened fire."

Frank tossed the memory card on Colby's desk. "This

is what she took from Trey's office. I thought we needed to take a look."

"She never mentioned a memory card the night we questioned her."

"Colleen wasn't sure she could trust me."

Colby raised his brow and shrugged. "If that's the way you see it."

"You don't?"

"Let's check the photos on the card. We might learn more about why she withheld information."

"A lot had happened. I'm sure she wasn't thinking clearly."

Colby pursed his lips. He didn't appear to accept Frank's explanation.

Sergeant Otis peered into the cubicle. "Sir, the chief can see you now."

"Thanks, Ray."

"While you're talking to Wilson," Colby said, "I'll go over the memory card."

Frank hurried to the chief's office. Wilson was at his desk and glanced up when Frank knocked.

He entered and saluted. "Sir, we need to talk."

Wilson pointed to a chair. "Colby updated me about Colleen Brennan. Sounds like the Freemont police got our man."

Without Frank's help. "Yes, sir. Trey Howard appears to have trafficked drugs into the US. Vivian Davis acted as his mule."

"We haven't been able to question her. The doctor said her condition has improved, but she's still intubated and unable to talk."

"Has her husband provided evidence?"

"Negative. He was completely in the dark. Tough place

to be. Redeployed back to Fort Rickman and eager to move to his next duty station at Fort Hood, then his wife is shot and he learns she's been involved in criminal activity." Wilson sniffed. "That's a hard homecoming."

Frank thought of his own medical evacuation back to the States and his eagerness to see Audrey. "Life isn't always fair."

"Roger that." The chief leaned back in his chair. "Thanks for all your help on the relief effort. Says a lot about you, Frank, that you rolled up your sleeves even though you were still on convalescent leave."

"That's what I want to discuss, sir."

"What's on your mind?"

"Whether I should continue on active duty."

Too much had happened too fast, and Colleen had a hard time trying to come to terms with Trey's death.

She hadn't wanted that for him. She'd wanted him stopped and put behind bars. Now he wouldn't stand trial, and the truth wouldn't come out about his drug-trafficking operation.

The police would consider the case closed and not pursue the other people involved. The whole operation had to be far-reaching, stretching to Colombia and the resort where Trey had invited her to stay.

The memory of Briana played and replayed in her mind. Trey had introduced her to drugs and enticed her to do his bidding, but other folks had worked with him.

Colleen crossed her arms and looked out the French doors beyond the screen porch. Police cars were still parked in the drive, and the crime scene team was finishing up its work.

Evelyn had called a local carpenter who was replacing the doors Trey had broken.

Thinking back to when he'd crashed into the bathroom made her shiver. It all seemed surreal, almost like a dream.

Then she'd been in Frank's arms, feeling his strength and support, which she'd needed. She hadn't wanted to leave his embrace, but he had to take care of Duke. That sweet, faithful dog had done his best to save her from Trey. If Duke took a turn for the worse, she'd never forgive herself.

Tears burned her eyes. Frank had mumbled something about not being there for her. Then he'd left with Duke.

Evelyn had hovered nearby, no doubt sensing Colleen's unease. Although she appreciated Evie's support, Colleen longed to have Frank standing at her side.

Not wanting to answer any more questions, she had retreated to the guest room, claiming she needed rest.

She couldn't relax. All she could do was think back to what had happened and glance at her watch.

What was taking Frank so long?

Chapter Eighteen

Frank left the chief's office still unsure of his future. Wilson had listened to the concerns Frank had about his compromised condition. An extended PT program would build him up physically, but a bigger problem was whether he was still an effective investigator. Although Frank hated to admit his limitations, after everything that had happened with Colleen, he was convinced he'd lost his edge.

The chief wasn't known for empathy, but he'd offered advice. "Give yourself more time. Return to active duty, but not to full-blown investigative work at first." Wilson suggested a desk job that wouldn't be as taxing, either physically or mentally.

The thought of pushing papers left a bad taste in Frank's mouth.

He exited the chief's office still unsure of what he should do. The decision didn't get any easier when he faced Colby again.

The other agent was at his desk and pointed to his computer screen. "I've been going over the photos on the memory card."

"What'd you find?"

"It's more like whom." Colby hesitated. "I found Colleen."

Frank nodded. "With a couple guys who work for Trey. She told me all about it. Trey insisted on taking the snapshot. Her refusal would have raised suspicion."

"Not one photo, Frank. Many photos with known drug dealers."

Colby scrolled through the digital pictures and stopped at one that showed Colleen on a couch flanked by two men, neither of whom looked like salt-of-the-earth types.

"Do you recognize those guys?" Colby asked.

"Negative."

Colby provided names. "Atlanta's Narcotics Enforcement Unit said they're bad dudes."

"You called them?"

"And emailed a copy of the photo."

Frank sighed with exasperation. "I told you, Colleen needed to be careful and not raise Trey's suspicion."

Colby shook his head. "I not only question Colleen's judgment but also the other dealers'. Why would they expose themselves to the camera and allow Trey to take their pictures? It doesn't make sense unless they didn't know they were being photographed. Maybe Trey wanted to have the goods on them in case they turned on him. He keeps the photos on the memory card. If the dealers give him a hard time, he's got a way to blackmail them. He could control Colleen that way, too." Colby sniffed. "Isn't that what you thought Vivian and Colleen might be doing with that phone video?"

"Blackmailing Trey?"

"Exactly."

"Vivian could have been, but Colleen just wanted more evidence to prove Trey's guilt."

"If that were the case, she took the wrong memory card. Trey's not in any of these photos."

"What are you trying to say, Colby?"

"I'm saying be careful. Colleen isn't who you think she is."

Frank clamped down on his jaw. The two men had known each other since their early days in the military, but Colby was walking close to the edge of their friendship.

"I'm heading back to Evelyn's."

"I may have it wrong, Frank. Colleen may be innocent, but—" Colby turned back to the monitor and tapped the screen. "In this photo everyone's having fun. Laughing, eating, drinking. Some of them are smoking what looks like weed. The bowls of white powder on the table could be cocaine."

Frank stared at the screen, unable to make sense of what he saw. "Colleen doesn't do drugs. Her sister died of an overdose."

"Which doesn't mean she's not involved. When Briana died, the Atlanta PD thought Colleen might have been her supplier."

"How'd you find that out?"

"Ulster called again. He talked to Anderson."

"Anderson's got it wrong." Frank mumbled a terse goodbye and headed back to his truck, frustrated with Colby.

He thought of the picture he'd seen of Colleen surrounded by a roomful of known criminals.

She was innocent of any involvement with drugs.

Frank was sure of it. Or would Colleen prove him wrong?

* * *

Colleen checked the time and then berated herself for being so concerned about Frank. The investigation was winding down, and Frank's attention was back on his job. Trey was dead, and the CID had the memory chip. She was no longer needed.

Grabbing a tissue from the box near the bed, she wiped her eyes and pulled in a cleansing breath before she opened the door.

Evelyn was in the kitchen, making sandwiches that she offered to the police officers who stood nearby.

"May I help?" Colleen wanted to feel useful.

"I thought you were resting."

She looked down at her hands. "I cleaned up a bit, but I couldn't rest. I kept reliving what happened. It's better if I have something to do."

"There's a pitcher of iced tea in the refrigerator. Fill some glasses and see who wants to take a break. The police have been working nonstop."

Pounding came from the hallway.

"That's Zack Barber. He's a retired carpenter from my church. He was nearby, helping to restore one of the Amish farmhouses. He had some spare doors in the back of his truck that hadn't fit the house he was helping to refurbish. He assured me the repairs wouldn't take long."

Colleen poured the tea and kept glancing down, expecting to see Duke. Not having him close by was unsettling. Remembering the reason troubled her even more.

She grabbed a tray from a cabinet and loaded it with the filled glasses.

"I'll be outside."

The officers thanked her profusely as they reached for the refreshing tea. A few followed her back into the kitchen. Evelyn was talking to Ron on the phone and smiled as they helped themselves to the sandwiches she had prepared.

"We'll be finished shortly, ma'am," one of them told Colleen, his voice low so he wouldn't interfere with Evelyn's phone call.

Colleen had struggled with law enforcement in Atlanta, but these men had come to her rescue when the 911 operator had notified them about the break-in. Their rapid response had stopped Trey and potentially saved her life.

Yesterday, Officer Stoddard, the blond marathon runner, had been considerate when he questioned her. His voice had been filled with compassion, and he made note of everything she told him without raising his brow or shaking his head in disapproval.

Frank had been right. Not all cops were on the take.

As soon as he returned, she'd tell him she'd been wrong. She'd also thank him for inviting her to stay at his sister's house and for helping her track down the memory card. He had protected her at the hospital and again the night Trey had broken into the screen porch as well as at the junkyard.

All Frank focused on was his bad timing, but he'd left Duke to guard the house and had counted on Ron and the loaded gun to ensure her safety. His foresight had allowed her to survive.

She steeled her spine. She could take care of herself. She'd done so in the past and she could again, but when Frank walked into the kitchen, she realized her mistake. She didn't want to go back to Atlanta and be alone again. She wanted what Evelyn and Ron had.

Colleen wanted to smile and laugh and flirt whenever she saw Frank. She wanted to let her eyes twinkle with merriment and joy, which was the same look she'd seen in Evelyn's eyes when Ron was nearby.

Stepping closer to Frank, she asked, "Is Duke okay?"

"The vet said he'll be fine, but he needs to stay overnight for observation."

"I know it was hard for you to leave him." She pointed to the sandwiches. "Evelyn prepared food for the workers. I could pour you a glass of iced tea."

He shook his head. "Don't trouble yourself."

The sharpness in his tone cut her to the core. Why was Frank acting so aloof?

The carpenter lumbered into the kitchen and nodded to Frank. "Tell Evelyn I finished working on those doors. I'll come back in a few days in case she has any other repairs."

When Evelyn got off the phone, she had a lightness to her step, which was a good sign.

After greeting Frank, she shared the news. "The doctor thinks Ron's problem was a lack of potassium. He's been working out recently and probably overdid it being in the sun so long with the relief effort. The doctor ordered more tests for tomorrow, but he's optimistic and so is Ron."

The good news lifted Colleen's spirits. "Are you going back to the hospital?"

"Ron assured me he'll be fine. I'll visit him in the morning."

She stepped closer to her brother. "He wanted to apologize for not coming over while you were gone. I told him he was silly to even give it a thought."

Frank steeled his jaw. "I'm glad Ron's doing better. He doesn't need to worry. Colleen was able to handle the situation."

She stared at him, unable to determine what he meant or what was bothering him.

"I need to talk to the police before they leave." Frank left the kitchen.

Evelyn patted Colleen's hand. "He's struggling because he wasn't here to rescue you."

She shook her head. "There's more to it. It's not about Frank. It's about me."

"Give him a little time. He's still trying to find himself."

Colleen was running out of time. She needed to leave Freemont. Evidently she needed to leave Frank, as well.

Chapter Nineteen

Frank had gotten a full summary of the crime scene investigation from Stoddard before he and the other officers left the area. They had bagged Frank's weapon and had taken blood specimens from the bathroom floor. They'd lifted prints that were probably Trey's and had photographed the entire house.

Once satisfied they'd gotten everything they needed, the police caravan pulled out of the driveway, and Frank headed back inside. Colleen was still in the kitchen, rinsing dishes and placing them in the dishwasher.

"Evelyn's in her room. She looked tired. I told her to get some rest."

"You should, as well."

"As soon as I finish here." She placed a glass in the upper rack. "I… I'm sorry about Duke."

"He'll be fine, I told you."

"Still. I know how close you are."

Frank nodded. "He's a good dog, and he's been a faithful companion. I can trust him."

From the expression on her face, Frank knew his

words had hit hard. He wasn't talking about Duke, and she knew it.

More than anything, Frank wanted to believe Colleen. Colby was convinced of her involvement with the drug operation. The pictures proved it. At least that's what Colby thought.

Frank wanted to defend her, which he had tried to do at CID Headquarters. Unfortunately, Colby had already made up his mind. Frank needed information that would prove her innocence without a shadow of a doubt. Information he could shove in Colby's face and take to Special Agent in Charge Wilson.

"Are we back to trust issues again?" she asked.

"Colby found photos of you with a number of known drug dealers." Frank wouldn't mince words. He wanted everything out in the open.

She bristled, immediately on guard. "Haven't we been over this before? I told you about the photo and why I agreed to have my picture taken."

"There were more photos, Colleen. Lots of them showing you fraternizing with drug dealers."

"I wasn't fraternizing."

"What were you doing?"

"Gathering evidence. Just as you do with your investigations."

"I'm trained. You're not. Why didn't you let law enforcement handle it?"

"Because I don't trust cops."

He let out a lungful of hot air. "What about the joints everyone was smoking? The cocaine on the table?"

She shook her head. "I don't know what you're talking about."

"I'm surprised the dealers would let Trey take their photo."

"They might not have known."

"What?"

"One night, I saw him hide a camera behind books on a shelf by his fireplace and program the shots to snap at a certain time."

"You knew about the secret photos?"

Coleen was digging a bigger hole. One Frank didn't want her to step into because the water in the hole wasn't clear. It had turned a murky brown.

"He didn't see me spying on him. I feigned a headache and went home early that night. I thought that was the only time he'd taken photos on the sly. Evidently I was wrong."

"Did he plan to blackmail the others?"

"I'm not sure. He didn't like people questioning his authority."

"Did he suspect you?"

"Not until I took the memory card."

"Vivian admitted to working for Trey."

Colleen nodded.

"Was she blackmailing him? Is that why you arranged to meet at the roadside park?"

He waited for her to prove him wrong, but she just stared at him. Her cheeks were flushed and her eyes filled with sorrow because she couldn't deny what she knew to be the truth.

Had Colby been right all along?

Frank wanted to hit his hand into his other palm and feel pain for what he'd done to Colleen. He had wanted to prove her innocence. Instead her reticence was telling. His gut twisted. How had he been so wrong?

Colleen turned and hurried down the hall to the guest bedroom. The door slammed, slamming the door to his heart, as well.

Frank was back to when he'd first stumbled upon Colleen in the barn.

He didn't know what to believe.

Tears burned Colleen's eyes. She couldn't stand there and listen to his accusations any longer. Nothing had changed. Frank didn't see things clearly anymore. Maybe he'd suffered some traumatic brain injury when he'd been caught in the rubble. He couldn't get past thinking she was guilty.

What a fool she'd been to trust him with the memory card and with her heart.

She wouldn't make that mistake again.

Throwing herself on the bed, she cried for all she'd lost. Her sister and now Frank's trust that she'd never had. Tomorrow she'd leave Freemont and head back to Atlanta.

She didn't want to see Frank again. The pain of his betrayal was too deep and too raw. Just as planned, she'd catch a flight to California and never return to Georgia again.

Frank picked up one of the sandwiches on the counter. His stomach was empty, and he needed food, but when he took a bite, it lodged in his throat. How could he have been so mistaken about Colleen?

He checked the doors to ensure they were secure out of habit. Trey would never hurt her again.

Turning off the overhead light, Frank headed to his room, but the thought of what had happened there kept playing in his head.

If he hadn't left a loaded gun—just in case—the night would have had a completely different ending.

At least Colleen hadn't been hurt.

He sat on the edge of his bed and dropped his head in his hands. If Duke were here, the trusty dog would have licked Frank's hand and offered support. His nearness and the understanding in his brown eyes would have brought comfort.

But Duke wasn't here, and Frank had nowhere to turn.

Come back to me.

Words from scripture he'd heard after the storm repeated again in his mind.

He rubbed his forehead. The reconstruction was going well, and the Amish were getting their lives back together while his was falling apart. They were a faithful people who put their hope in God.

He'd stopped relying on the Lord years ago. In those days, the old Frank could take care of himself. He made good decisions and was quickly earning a name for himself in investigation channels. Then he'd made a fateful mistake that nearly cost him his life.

Lord, forgive me for being too haughty, too proud to realize I needed you. The injury and illness opened my eyes to what's important in life, and it isn't good looks or brains and brawn. It's you, Lord. I need you.

His heavy heart weighed him down. He needed Colleen, but not if she was mixed up with drug dealers and trafficking.

Help me see clearly, Lord.

All through the night, Frank sat on his bed and prayed for strength. He'd give himself more time to heal, but he needed clear vision about Colleen.

Was she holding on to things in the past with her sister? Frank realized he was doing the same thing. Audrey was then. Colleen was now.

Opening the drawer on his nightstand, he pulled out a photograph and looked down at the woman with blond hair and blue eyes he had once thought he loved.

He'd been wrong.

True love wasn't about good looks and good times, and it wasn't easy. It could hurt and get twisted and tied up with other events and other people.

Love was painful. It was now.

He dropped Audrey's photo on his dresser and left the house before Colleen got up. He wanted Duke back at his side, and he wanted to stop by CID Headquarters and review the photos again.

He wouldn't lose Colleen without a fight. Colby had his opinion, but Frank didn't buy it. He believed in Colleen, even if she didn't think he did.

Chapter Twenty

Colleen woke with a pounding headache probably brought on by all the tears she'd shed. After getting dressed, she tidied the room and packed her carry-on bag.

She met Evelyn in the kitchen. "I'm heading to the hospital early. Ron thinks he might be released by noon. I want to talk to the doctors when they make their rounds."

Colleen poured a mug of coffee. "Thanks for all you've done for me. I can't tell you how much I appreciate your kindness."

Evelyn tilted her head. "If I didn't know better, I'd think you were saying goodbye."

"I need to get back to Atlanta. I'd taken a leave of absence from my job. I have to tell them to put me back on the schedule."

"I'm sure Frank will drive you to Atlanta." She smiled. "Something tells me he'll be making quite a few trips into the city in the days ahead."

For all her thoughtfulness, Evelyn didn't realize what had happened last night. Colleen wouldn't tell her.

"I doubt he'll have any spare time once he returns to work. You mentioned a bus station in Freemont."

"The number's in the phone book." She pointed. "First drawer next to the fridge, but I'm sure Frank will find a way to take you himself. You're welcome to stay as long as you like, Colleen. You know Frank and I both enjoy having you here with us."

Evelyn's sincerity touched Colleen. Tears welled up in her eyes. To hide her emotions that seemed so raw this morning, she peered from the window and looked down into the valley.

"The Amish have rebuilt so much, so quickly."

"I'm glad to see it. They help one another and come together as a community."

"The whole town did. It's been encouraging to see."

"I guess you weren't raised in a small town."

Colleen shook her head. "We lived in Savannah and moved to Atlanta soon after my sister was born."

"Small towns take care of their own. From what Frank says, the military is the same way. Maybe even more so since they're often far from family and home."

Family. The word brought another lump to Colleen's throat.

"You've made me feel part of your family, Evelyn. Thank you."

"Why wouldn't we?" She wrapped her arms around Colleen and gave her a hug. "All this talk has me upset, thinking about you leaving."

She pulled back and laughed as she reached for her purse. "I'll expect to see you this evening. I'll bake chicken and have some fresh vegetables. Ron might join us if he feels up to it."

Colleen stood at the door and waved when Evelyn backed out of the drive. Once the car disappeared from sight, Colleen returned to the kitchen and pulled the phone book from the drawer. After finding the number for the bus station, she called and got an automated recording that listed the arrivals and departures. A bus left for Atlanta at ten this morning.

Unsure how long it would take to get to the station, Colleen called for a cab. Returning to her room, she grabbed her carry-on and placed it by the door so she'd be ready when the ride arrived.

Turning, she glanced over the house. So much had happened here. She needed to accept the good along with the bad.

She wanted to retrace the steps she'd taken yesterday so broken doors and blood spatters wouldn't be her last memories of the home. Entering Frank's room, she inhaled the lingering scent of his aftershave and had to close her eyes to keep the tears at bay when she thought of being in his arms.

Peering into the bathroom, she appreciated Zack's workmanship and all that had been done to remove any trace of the tragedy that had unfolded here.

Now Colleen could move on and remember the room as it should be remembered. Leaving the bathroom, she noticed a photo on the dresser.

The picture was of a beautiful blonde with big eyes and an engaging smile that was sure to melt the hardest heart. Curious, Colleen turned the photo over.

To my wonderful Frank. I'll always love you, Audrey.

Colleen dropped the photo and hurried from the room. Frank still loved Audrey. Colleen had been so wrong about everything. He had never wanted anything from her except information.

She hoped he and Audrey could get together again.

That would make Frank happy, which is what Colleen wanted for him.

A knock sounded at the front door.

She glanced at her watch. The cab was twenty minutes early. At least she'd get to the bus station ahead of schedule.

She hurried to the foyer and opened the door.

A man. T-shirt. Baseball cap. Not the cabbie.

"Excuse me, ma'am. I'm Steve Nelson."

Frank had mentioned his name. "You're with the construction company here to help with the relief effort."

"That's right." He smiled. "I'm having problems with my cell phone and need to call the mayor's office downtown. We're scheduled to do some demolition today. I was driving by your house when I realized my problem and thought you might be able to help."

"Of course, come in. But it's not my house. I'm just visiting."

He wiped his feet on the doormat and pointed to her carry-on bag as he followed her to the kitchen. "Looks like you're going someplace."

She nodded. "The bus station."

"I'm headed downtown. Let me give you a lift."

"I've already called a cab."

"Easy enough to cancel."

He motioned her to the phone.

She waved him off. "No, you go ahead. Call the mayor."

Grabbing her cell, she checked the coverage. "I'm not having any trouble with my cell reception." Which didn't make sense.

"Really?" He stepped closer. Too close.

Colleen tried to move aside.

He grabbed her arm. "Where's the memory card? Trey said you have it."

"Let me go." She struggled to free herself.

"Trey said you sent a picture to the cops, only it wasn't his operation. It was mine. I need to destroy the memory card."

"You'll never find it."

His grip tightened on her arm. She clawed at his cheek and screamed for help.

The guy pulled a gun. She tried to back away.

"Tell me or you'll die."

"You'll go to jail." Colleen had never seen the photos on the memory card, but she needed something to hold over his head. "Trey took pictures of you that prove your guilt."

Rage twisted his face. "I don't want to hear anything about Trey."

"He outsmarted you," she pressed.

"Shut up." He raised the gun and slammed it against her head.

She gasped with pain.

Darkness settled over her.

Colleen's last thought was of Frank.

Chapter Twenty-One

"He had a good night," the vet said when Frank arrived at the clinic.

Duke licked his hand. "I missed you, boy. How's the leg?"

"The wound's healing." The vet handed Frank ointment. "Change the dressing daily and apply more ointment. If it starts to bleed or looks infected, bring him back. Otherwise Duke should be feeling like his old self in seven to ten days."

Frank still didn't feel like his old self, but he appreciated the vet's help, and having Duke by his side made the overcast day seem less gray.

Opening the passenger door, he smiled as the dog hopped into the truck seemingly without effort. "You're going to be chasing squirrels again before long. I'll have to hold you back."

Duke barked. Frank laughed and rounded the car.

"If you don't mind, I want to stop at CID Headquarters and look at some pictures."

The drive across post took fewer than ten minutes. Colby's car was in the parking lot.

"I need to see those photos," Frank said as he entered Colby's cubicle.

"Hey there, Duke." Colby scratched the dog's scruff. Then he stood and motioned Frank to take his place at the computer.

"Have at it. I'm getting a refill of coffee. Can I get a cup for you?"

"Sounds good. Black."

Frank started scrolling through the photos and stopped when he saw the one Colleen had sent to the police. He enhanced the picture until he could read the name tag on the camera case sitting next to the shrink-wrapped bricks. *Howard.*

Colby came back, carrying two cups. He handed one to Frank.

"Colleen was right about the camera case." He pointed to the monitor. "Looks like it may have belonged to Trey."

"Lots of people are named Howard."

Colby's outlook hadn't improved.

"Has anyone questioned Vivian?" Frank took a slug of the coffee.

"Not yet. The doctor wants to wait another day or two before he weans her off the ventilator."

"And her husband?"

"Faithfully sitting at her bedside."

Frank continued to scroll through the photos, searching for anything that would incriminate the dealers and shed more light on Colleen's innocence.

Colby leaned over his shoulder and sipped his coffee. The process was slow and monotonous.

Many of the shots showed the Colombian resort after its completion. Trey had taken pictures for the travel brochures and advertisements that drew tourists from all over the world. The property was top of the line.

An army wife like Vivian with a deployed husband could easily be swayed by Trey's talk of a modeling career, especially when he included an all-expenses-paid vacation to such a plush resort.

A number of photos showed parties in full swing. Groups of people mixed and mingled, many sipping cocktails. The men were a diverse group. Some wore sport coats; others were in polo shirts and slacks. Attractive women mingled with them, serving drinks and hanging on their arms. Colleen stood to the side, looking very much alone.

Frank's heart went out to her. She hadn't been part of the drug operation. Colleen was an outsider trying to fit in—and failing, in Frank's opinion. It was a wonder Trey hadn't seen through her charade. Determined to bring down the man who had hooked her sister on drugs, Colleen had put herself in danger. Just as she'd told Frank from the beginning, she needed evidence and she found it by infiltrating a large and corrupt drug-trafficking operation.

Frank had to apologize to her for the way he'd acted. She deserved a medal instead of chastisement.

Colby looked at his watch and patted Frank's shoulder. "You keep searching. I've got to be at Post Headquarters in fifteen minutes for a meeting with the chief of staff about the reconstruction. The Freemont mayor will be there to talk about their efforts. The last project is the warehouse demolition by the river."

Frank waved his hand in farewell and glanced down at Duke once Colby had left the room. "Time for us to get going, boy. I need to talk to Colleen and apologize for my actions."

Even with Trey dead, Colleen still needed to be careful, especially if the photos ever got out. Just as she had said, the pictures had served as protection for Trey in case anyone tried to do him harm, but Colleen was front and center. Not a safe place to be.

Frank needed to warn her.

Duke lay his head on Frank's knee, blocking the chair. "What is it, boy? Not ready to leave yet? You like being back at work?"

He chuckled and reached for the mouse. "A few more minutes here won't hurt."

The next section of photos showed the beginning construction effort for the resort. A large sign announced the groundbreaking for La Porta Verde.

Three men stood in front of the sign. A short man with dark skin appeared to be the local contact. Another man, dressed in a flowery Hawaiian shirt, held a stack of papers and must have been part of the initial building project.

A third man shook the Colombian's hand. He was standing to the side, his face in profile. In the distance, a backhoe was poised, ready to break ground.

Frank zoomed in. His gut tightened.

The man in profile was Steve Nelson, the head of the company helping with Freemont's reconstruction.

Frank grabbed his cell and called Evelyn's house.

His sister answered.

"I thought you'd be at the hospital."

"I just got home. Ron's tests came back. The doctor said it was an electrolyte imbalance and released him.

I dropped him off at his place and came home to check on Colleen."

"Let me speak to her."

"That's the strange thing, Frank."

He jammed the phone closer to his ear.

"A cab was waiting out front when I pulled up. He said someone needed a ride to the bus station in town."

Colleen was leaving?

"I have to talk to her."

"She's not here."

Frank pushed back from the desk, raced from the cubicle and out the rear door that led to the parking lot. Duke ran beside him.

"I'm on my way to the bus station. If Colleen calls, convince her not to leave town, and tell her she's still in danger."

"You're scaring me, Frank. What's going on?"

"I'll tell you once I find Colleen. What time does the bus leave for Atlanta?"

"Give me a minute to check."

Frank didn't have a minute. He was at his truck. Duke hopped in through the driver's side.

"The bus departs in twenty minutes, but there's something else you need to know."

Climbing behind the wheel, Frank started the ignition. "What is it, Evelyn?"

"Colleen left her carry-on bag by the front door. Her things are strewn all over the floor."

Pain!

Colleen thrashed, trying to escape the burning fire that seared through her head. She moaned, then blinked her eyes open and stared into the damp dimness.

A small room. Table.

She struggled to sit up, realizing too late her hands and feet were bound. A wave of nausea washed over her and sent her crashing back to the musty mattress and pile of rags.

The faint light filtering through the open doorway caused another jolt of pain. She shut her eyes and groaned.

"Coming around?"

A deep voice.

Frank?

She blinked again. Not Frank.

The construction boss. What was his name? Steve. Steve Nelson. Bile rose in her throat as she remembered his attack. "Where...where am I?"

"Someplace safe. At least for now. Where's the memory card?"

"Gone...in the storm."

He bent down, his face inches from hers. His sour sweat and stale breath made her want to gag.

"You only have a few minutes to tell me the truth."

"What...what happens then?"

"Poof!" He threw his hands in the air. "An explosion brings down the building. Tell me about the memory card or you'll die in the blast."

"You're worried. Trey took incriminating photos of you, along with the other dealers." At least she presumed he had.

Steve's eyes widened with fury. "I brought Trey into the operation, but he got greedy and started running his own girls. If the cops hadn't killed him, I would have. They saved me the trouble."

"You're despicable. Trey hooked my sister, Briana,

on drugs that caused her to overdose. You're responsible, too."

His lips twisted into a maniacal smile. "Briana wanted out. She went to the cops and told them about Trey. Only one of the cops needed money and passed the information on to me."

Colleen gasped. "You killed my sister."

"She forced my hand. I had to kill her. Just like I have to kill you because you know too much."

"The police have the memory card from Trey's camera. They'll find you and everyone else in your operation. You're finished, Steve."

He shook his head. "I can move to Colombia."

"They'll extradite you back to the States, where you'll spend the rest of your life in jail."

He stepped to the table, leaned over a small gym bag and fiddled with the contents. Nodding to himself as if satisfied with what he'd done, he wiped his hands on his pants and then turned back to her.

"You've got ten minutes. Tell me now or tell me never."

"I'll never tell you anything. The cops will find you and bring you to justice."

"Cops?" He raised his brow. "Or your boyfriend, Frank?"

Her heart lodged in her throat. "He doesn't know anything."

"Of course he does. You gave him the digital card. After I leave the building, I'll go back to his sister's house and wait for him there."

"No." She struggled to free herself.

He turned for the door. All she heard were his footfalls on the old oak floor and his laughter.

Lord, save me. Save Frank.

Chapter Twenty-Two

Frank left Fort Rickman and increased his speed. River Road wove along the water and led to the older section of downtown Freemont, where the bus station was located. Hopefully Evelyn had phoned Colleen to warn her.

He tried again. All he got was her voice mail.

"Call me, Colleen. Don't leave Freemont. You're in danger."

Which she had been all along. Frank hadn't been able to protect her. He hadn't been there when she'd confronted Trey. Now someone else was after her.

"Steve Nelson is part of the operation in Atlanta," he relayed to her voice mail. "Watch out. I'll be at the bus station in less than five minutes. Stay safe."

After disconnecting, he called Freemont police.

"Head to the old part of Freemont around the bus station. Apprehend anyone wearing an American Construction Company T-shirt or driving one of their vehicles."

He threw the phone on the dashboard and gripped the steering wheel. Pushing down on the accelerator, he willed his truck to go faster. The stretch of road had never seemed so long and so winding.

Frank had been wrong about Colleen. How could he ever prove himself to her?

Lord, forgive me. Lead me to Colleen.

The outskirts of Freemont appeared in the distance.

Although traffic was light, Frank didn't want to stop at intersections in the downtown area. Instead, he remained on River Road. A side street, farther north, would lead to the bus station.

He passed the first of a row of warehouses on his left. The tornado had damaged a portion of the old brick facades on the formidable structures with historic charm.

In days past, boats would unload their wares, and the goods would be stored in the warehouses until wagons transported them to local markets. He didn't have time to bemoan the destruction of a treasure from the past. He needed to find Colleen.

Passing the second building, something caught his eye. He glanced left.

A utility truck sat parked next to a side door.

He stared for half a heartbeat at the company name painted on the van's side panel.

American Construction.

Frank turned the wheel and screeched into the narrow alleyway. He braked to a stop and hit the pavement running.

The big burly guy sat at the wheel. Frank threw open the door. He grabbed Steve's arm and yanked him to the pavement.

The guy reached for the gun tucked in his waistband.

Frank kicked it out of his hand.

"Where is she?"

"You'll never get to her in time." The big guy lunged. His fist jammed into Frank's side, close to his incision.

Air whooshed from his lungs. He doubled over.

Steve stumbled back and grabbed his own gun.

He took aim. "Your girlfriend dies in five minutes, but you die now."

Duke leaped, and his teeth sank into Steve's arm. He screamed with pain. The gun fell from his hand and slid under the van.

The dog didn't let go. Steve toppled backward. His head crashed against the pavement. Gasping in pain, he backpedaled. "Get...the dog...off me."

Sirens sounded nearby.

"Duke, guard." The dog bared his teeth and hovered over Steve. Once big and strong, the construction worker looked like a blubbering baby as he covered his face with his hands and cried.

Frank ran into the warehouse. Shadows played over the expansive area inside. Cobwebs tangled around central support beams and wove their way to the ceiling rafters.

"Colleen!" Her name echoed across the scarred oak floors and bounced off windows fogged with decades of dirt.

Where was she?

Please, God.

He checked his watch. How much time did he have? Five minutes max.

"Colleen?"

He raced forward. An enclosed office sat in the middle of the giant empty space.

He shoved the door open. A library table, overturned chairs. Two bookcases.

A sound.

Another door.

He turned the knob. The door creaked as it opened. An antique safe stood against the far wall. The room was so dark and so confined that he almost missed the pile of bedding in the corner.

A rustle of movement. Another moan.

He pulled back the blanket and gasped in relief.

Colleen.

Blood matted her beautiful hair and stained the mattress on which she lay. She'd suffered another blow in the same spot. Three strikes.

"I'm here, honey. I'll get you free."

"Explosives...detonate..."

"I know. We don't have much time." Using his pocketknife, he cut through the plastic ties that secured her hands and feet.

He wrapped his arm around her shoulders and helped her to her feet. She faltered.

Half supporting her, half carrying her, he ushered her through the office.

"We have to hurry," he warned.

Sirens sounded outside. Pulsating lights flashed through the filthy windows.

The side door opened. A cop started inside.

"Stay back," Frank shouted. "It's ready to blow."

His side screamed with pain, but he had to save Colleen. She staggered beside him.

Glancing at his watch, his heart lurched. No more time.

"Run." He pushed her toward the open door. She had to get to safety.

The cop grabbed her hand and tugged her through the doorway.

"Take cover," Frank screamed.

He followed her to the threshold of the door. The police had backed off. The cop was ushering Colleen away from the building. She turned, searching for Frank.

Her scream was lost in the blast.

Duke ran toward him.

Frank put up his hand to stop his faithful dog just as an avalanche of bricks started to fall.

Afghanistan. The IED.

Duke wouldn't be able to rescue him this time.

But Frank had saved Colleen.

She was alive.

Nothing else mattered.

"Frank," Colleen screamed.

She fought her way free from the cop who had pulled her from the building. He'd held her back and kept her from Frank.

Duke bounded onto the fallen bricks, the dust thick.

He barked, then sniffed the pile of debris that covered the doorway where Frank had stood seconds earlier.

Now he lay buried beneath the rubble.

She raced forward and clawed at the bricks. Duke dug with his paws, neither of them making progress.

Frank had to be alive. She wouldn't give up hope.

Please God, save him.

Policemen swarmed around them. They shoved aside pieces of brick and piles of dirt that came down with the building.

"Frank, hold on. We'll get you out."

Only she didn't know if he could hear her.

Duke barked. If anything, Frank would hear his trusty dog.

A large beam stretched across the fallen rubble, forming a protective pocket.

If only—

Colleen peered into the opening and glimpsed a hand. She reached to touch him. Cold. Lifeless.

"Don't leave me, Frank."

His fingers moved.

"He's alive," she shouted. "Hurry."

In a matter of seconds, the cops removed the remaining bricks covering the opening.

Frank's face. Swollen, battered, scraped and bleeding. His eyes shut.

"Watch his neck."

A backboard. They hoisted him carefully onto the wooden brace.

The cops hustled him toward the ambulance.

An EMT approached Colleen and pointed to her forehead. "Ma'am, you need to be examined."

He helped her into the ambulance where two EMTS worked on Frank. She sat opposite them and took his hand. She wouldn't let go.

Duke climbed in beside her.

The doors closed, and the ambulance took off, siren screaming.

Colleen couldn't stop watching the rise and fall of Frank's chest. He was breathing. He was alive, but just barely.

Chapter Twenty-Three

Although his prognosis wasn't good, Colleen was so grateful Frank was still alive. His condition was critical when he was raced into the Fort Rickman Hospital emergency room yesterday.

An entire medical team had worked on him in the trauma room until a bed opened in the ICU. Since then, he'd been hooked to wires that monitored his pulse, oxygen level, heart rate and blood pressure.

The occasional beep and the thrust and pull of the medical machinery made Colleen even more anxious about his condition.

She'd sat by his side throughout the night. Evelyn said she would stay, but fatigue had increased her limp and her eyes lacked their usual sparkle. She had been worried about Ron. Now her concern was for her brother.

"Go home, Evelyn. Sleep. You can spell me in the morning," Colleen had told her.

Civilians weren't usually treated at military hospitals, but one of the emergency room docs had checked Colleen over. Another slight concussion. Her third. The doc laughed as he said that she'd struck out. At least he didn't seem overly concerned, especially since she planned to stay the night at Frank's bedside.

The RN on duty had provided blankets and showed her how the vinyl chair extended into a semiflat position. Colleen had tried to sleep, but with the constant flow of medical caregivers who checked on Frank, she'd dozed off only a few times and then not for long.

The morning-shift nurse had provided a sealed plastic container of toiletries that included a toothbrush and comb. Colleen had given up trying to bring order to her matted hair and had used a rubber band to pull her unruly locks into a makeshift bun that at least got the curly strands out of her face.

Since first light, she'd hovered close to Frank's bedside, watching in case his eyes opened. She'd prayed throughout the night that God, who heard all, would answer her request and restore Frank to health.

"If he does respond," the doctors cautioned, "a full recovery will take time."

She sighed as the weight of that one comment sank in. If he recovered? A full recovery will take time? How long?

It didn't matter. She'd wait forever, if Frank wanted her to stay. That was the problem. She didn't know what he wanted.

She glanced at the floor, wishing Duke were with her. The military doctors hadn't been as welcoming as the EMTs in the ambulance had been. As soon as Ron and Evelyn arrived at the hospital, they'd been instructed to take the dog home.

A knock sounded. The door to Frank's room opened, and a man in uniform entered. He was tall with a full face and gentle smile.

"I'm Major Hughes, one of the chaplains on post."

"Thank you for coming."

He glanced at Frank. "Mind if I say a prayer?"

She rose from the chair. "Of course not. Yours might bring better results than mine."

"You've had a long night. The nurse told me you've been at his bedside."

"Praying." She tried to smile, but tears filled her eyes. She didn't want to cry in front of the chaplain.

He reached for her hand. "God knows our hearts. He responds. Although sometimes he's not as timely as we'd want."

"That's what worries me."

"We need to trust."

She nodded. Her weak suit, especially when it came to Frank. "He's a good man. Compassionate, caring, but he's been through so much."

"I was told a war injury and multiple surgeries followed by a life-threatening infection."

Colleen nodded. How much could someone endure? "He ignored his own condition to help me. I... I made a mistake and wasn't completely forthright."

She turned her head and bit her lip.

The chaplain patted her shoulder. "Our limitations are always easier to see in hindsight. When we're in the middle of a stressful situation, our vision is often cloudy. The Lord is a God of forgiveness. You can trust him." He glanced at Frank. "I have a feeling you can trust Special Agent Gallagher, as well."

Buoyed by the chaplain's words, she folded her hands and bowed her head as he prayed, knowing God was in charge. He was the Divine Physician who would return Frank to health.

That was her hope.

That was her prayer.

Someone patted Frank's arm. He heard voices and tried to comprehend what they were saying.

"I think he's coming around."

Evelyn?

He sensed someone else bending over his bedside. "Agent Gallagher? Frank? Can you hear me?"

He fought his way from the darkness.

"Open your eyes?"

He tried. They remained shut.

"My name's Molly. I'm the nurse who's taking care of you today. You're in the hospital at Fort Rickman. Do you remember what happened?"

He turned his head.

"Open your eyes, Frank." Evelyn's voice. She patted his hand.

Still so tired, but he wanted to see—

Light. Too bright.

"That was great. Try opening your eyes again."

He blinked. Twice.

"Even better. Keep working. I bet your eyes are blue."

Brown. He licked his lips, but the word wouldn't form.

"Eyes opened wide. That's what I want to see."

Again, he blinked against the light. The nurse smiled down at him.

He turned his head ever so slightly. Evelyn came into view.

"Oh, Frank," she gushed. A tear ran down her cheek. "I've been so worried."

She squeezed his hand. He squeezed back.

"Wh...where—"

Slowly, his gaze swept the room. A knife stabbed his heart. He had expected to see Colleen.

Audrey had left him. Now Colleen.

He didn't want to keep struggling any longer. He was worn-out and unwilling to fight back from the brink of despair again.

He had almost died last time. He wasn't willing to bear the hurt again.

"Keep your eyes open, Frank."

He ignored the nurse and slipped back into the darkness, where he couldn't feel pain. Why should he open his eyes? He didn't want to see anything if he couldn't see Colleen.

"You need to go back to my place and get some sleep," Evelyn suggested.

Colleen shook her head. "The last time I stepped out for coffee, Frank opened his eyes. I want to be here next time."

"If there is a next time," Evelyn said. Her voice contained all the fear Colleen felt.

She shook her head. "Don't say that."

"The doctors warned us. We need to realize what could happen."

"God won't take him from me. I've lost Briana. I can't lose Frank."

Evelyn rubbed her shoulder. "Life isn't always fair."

Colleen nodded. How well she knew that to be true.

She thought of Evelyn's first love and the pain she'd experienced when he revealed the truth about his marriage.

"You've had your share of suffering."

"But now I have Ron."

"Did you tell him about Dan?"

Evelyn nodded. "Just as you mentioned, he was loving and caring. Although like a typical male, Ron wanted to punch Dan. Even if he hadn't been married, what he and I had wasn't true love. It was something that fell far short. Looking back, I know God saved me for Ron."

Colleen squeezed Evelyn's hand. "I wasn't sure about Ron because of seeing him with Trey the night of the tornado, but I was wrong, too. He's got a big heart and a lot of love to shower on you, Evelyn."

She glanced at her brother. "Frank does, too. He just needs to wake up and accept your love."

The phone rang. Evelyn reached for the receiver. "Yes?"

She smiled. "You're downstairs? I'll be right there." She hung up and patted Colleen's hand.

"Ron's in the lobby. I'm going to meet him for coffee in the cafeteria. Can I bring you anything?"

"Bring your brother back, and I'll be happy."

"Ron and I are praying. The whole church community is, as well."

Would it be enough? Colleen wasn't sure.

Colleen heard Frank's voice in her dream. She smiled and squeezed his hand.

"Ouch."

Her eyes popped open. Sitting in the chair at Frank's bedside, she had rested her head on the edge of his mattress and dozed off.

His eyes were still closed. Her dream had been so real. Had she imagined his voice?

Maybe the three strikes were finally catching up to her.

She rubbed her hand over his. His fingers moved.

Her heart skittered in her chest.

"Frank?"

One eye blinked open.

The IV solution was providing fluids, but that didn't keep his lips from being cracked and chapped.

"C...ol...leen?"

Surely he didn't think she was Audrey.

His smile widened. His fingers wrapped through hers. "You...you...didn't leave me."

"Oh, Frank, I'll never leave you."

Tears filled her eyes and spilled down her cheeks.

She moved closer to him. His other eye opened. "Now... I...see you."

"I haven't even combed my hair."

"You...you're beautiful."

"Do you remember what happened?"

He nodded ever so slightly. "I...saved...you."

She smiled. "That's exactly right. You saved my life."

His brow wrinkled. "D... Duke?"

"He's fine. Evelyn claims his sense of smell returned, since he was able to find you in the rubble. I'm sure you heard him barking."

Frank wrinkled his forehead. "I... I heard...your voice. You...gave...me...will to live."

"Oh, Frank, I was so wrong about you and about law enforcement. You were trying to find the truth, and I kept holding back information."

The words gushed out. Colleen couldn't stop them. "Briana's death had taken me to the depths of despair. I'd turned my grief into a need to bring all those involved with drug trafficking to justice."

She shook her head, frustrated at her own actions. "Only I was headstrong and foolish to take on Trey and his operation. You kept trying to protect me, but I wasn't sure of where I stood with you. I'd been so determined to bring Trey down that I almost got myself killed and you killed, as well."

Frank rubbed her hand. "Before…thought I was invincible…didn't need God…didn't need anyone. Dated a girl. She…must have known. Only person… I… I… loved was my…self."

"You're not that man any longer. You're not self-serving or self-centered. You're a wonderful man who has a bright future ahead in law enforcement. You check every detail and make sure hearsay isn't taken as fact. I thought Trey had caused Briana's death, but Steve Nelson was to blame. I went after the wrong man."

"Trey…led you to Steve."

"You're right. Colby stopped by after work last night. He said the photos on the memory card revealed even more drug dealers involved in Steve Nelson's far-reaching operations. The resort is being cleaned out in Colombia, and the DEA is going after traffickers throughout the Southeast. Colby called it a good day for law enforcement."

"Be…cause of you."

"Because you helped me find the memory card."

Frank smiled.

"Colby said Anderson, the cop I contacted in Atlanta, was tied in with Trey. He's been arrested."

"Vi…vian?"

"She confessed to smuggling drugs into the US and provided information about others involved. Colby said the judge will take that into consideration."

"I'm…sorry… I…"

She smiled. "Didn't believe me?"

He nodded.

"You were being that wonderful investigator who I'm beginning to think I love."

His eyes opened a bit wider, and the smile that filled his face made her heart soar with joy.

"I…love…you, Colleen."

Her grip tightened on his hand, and she bent over his bedside. His condition was still fragile, and he had a long recuperation ahead, but Colleen wanted him to know the way she felt. She had waited too long to tell him the truth.

"I love you, Frank."

She gently lowered her lips to his, and for one long moment the earth stood still.

Pulling back ever so slightly, she added, "And I'll never leave you." She smiled. "Cross my heart."

His eyes closed, and he fell back to sleep. Resting her cheek against his hand, she gave thanks to God for bringing this wonderful, strong man into her life.

Chapter Twenty-Four

Frank sat on Evelyn's front porch and listened for the sound of tires on the driveway. Seeing Colleen's new red Mustang convertible, he hurried down the steps and opened her door as she pulled to a stop.

Before either of them spoke, he reached for her and pulled her into his arms. Their lips met, and the lingering kiss did more for him than all the physical therapy he'd been having over the past five weeks.

Evelyn stood in the open doorway and waved. Duke bounded around her and barked with glee, causing Colleen to push away from Frank and laugh.

"Are you jealous of Frank?" she asked as the dog danced at her feet. She patted his sleek coat and scratched behind his ears.

"How was your flight?" Evelyn asked from the porch.

"Easy. I'm enjoying working short domestic flights again."

"And we like having you spend time between trips with us."

Frank grabbed her carry-on from the backseat. "The Mustang suits you."

"Oh? Is it the color?"

"You mean because it matches your hair?"

She laughed. "I didn't think you noticed."

"I notice everything about you."

"Be still my heart. I like having a man who's observant."

"And I like your hair loose around your face. It suits you just like the car."

He ran his hand through the curls that fell free around her shoulders. Leaning close, he inhaled the flowery scent of her shampoo, which made him want to kiss her again.

She giggled. "Looks like you're feeling better. Did you talk to Wilson?"

"He wants me back doing CID investigations as soon as I'm ready."

Colleen narrowed her gaze. "What'd you tell him?"

"Next Monday. I'm ready."

She nodded. "I know you are."

"What smells so good?" Colleen asked as they followed Evelyn into the kitchen.

"I've got a rib roast in the oven, and Isaac selected fresh corn from the Amish Craft Shoppe for us, along with homegrown lettuce and an apple pie for dessert."

"You always spoil me, Evelyn."

"Ron's joining us for dinner."

"How's he feeling?"

"Strong as an ox."

Colleen laughed. "Is he still working out?"

Evelyn nodded. "He has to keep in shape to keep up with me." She winked at Colleen, who laughed again.

Her joy was infectious, and Frank's heart soared. "Let's go for a drive."

She looked confused. "I… I just got here."

"I know, but there's something I want to show you."

She glanced at Evelyn, who smiled knowingly but didn't say anything.

He took her hand and hurried her to his truck. He held the passenger door for her, and lowered the back for Duke. They were soon heading along the country road they'd traveled weeks before.

They passed Dawson Timmons's house. Frank turned at the next intersection and headed north for a little over three miles.

"This area is so beautiful." Colleen's smile said as much as her comment.

He stopped at the top of a small rise and helped her out. Duke jumped from the rear and immediately chased after a gray squirrel that scurried up a sturdy oak.

Frank pointed to a small pond and the gentle rise where more hardwoods grew.

"I thought a house overlooking the pond might be nice. The trees would provide shade in summer."

Her eyes widened with surprise. "You're buying the land?"

"I went to the bank, but I haven't signed the papers yet."

"Does that mean you're getting out of the army?"

"Not now. I've got ten years on active duty already. I'll stay in for at least ten more before I retire from military service. I thought farming the land, raising a few head of cattle, might be something for the future. I'll live here for the next three years while I complete my assignment at Fort Rickman. When I'm transferred, I'll still need a place to come back to for vacations and to visit Evelyn."

Colleen turned to look at the expanse of land. "It's lovely. A good place to call home."

"How would you feel about living here?"

She took a step back. "I'm not sure what you're saying."

He laughed, realizing his mistake. "Looks like I got ahead of myself."

Digging into his pocket, his fingers touched a small box. He pulled it out. "I'm not overly romantic, and I may not have the right words, but I love you, Colleen. You're my everything, and I never want to spend a day without you. Will you—"

He opened the box. "Will you marry me?"

Colleen's heart stopped for a long moment as Frank removed the solitaire diamond and held it out ready to put on her finger.

"Will you marry me?" he asked again when she failed to respond.

Tears filled her eyes. She brushed them away, knowing her cheeks would blotch and her mascara would run, but she didn't care. All she cared about was Frank.

"Yes," she almost screamed, holding out her hand. He slipped the ring over her finger, then he pulled her into his arms.

"I love you."

"Oh, Frank, I love you, too."

They kissed under the shade of the oak tree. Duke fetched a twig and raced back to where they stood, wrapped in each other's arms. He danced at their feet, trying to get their attention until another squirrel caught his eye. Then he bounded off in pursuit, while Frank pulled Colleen even closer, and she nestled in his arms.

His kisses were as sweet as the wildflowers blooming on the hillside and as warm as the sunshine overhead.

This land, their home, would be the perfect place to seal their love and raise a family.

Colleen glanced at the ring and then raised her lips again to the wonderful man, the strong and determined man with whom she planned to spend the rest of her life.

God had answered her prayers. Every one of them.

* * * * *

WE HOPE YOU ENJOYED THESE
LOVE INSPIRED®
AND
LOVE INSPIRED®
SUSPENSE
BOOKS.

Whether you prefer heartwarming contemporary romance or heart-pounding suspense, Love Inspired® books has it all!

Look for 6 new titles available every month from both Love Inspired® and Love Inspired® Suspense.

Love Inspired®

Love Inspired®

Save $1.00

on the purchase of any
Love Inspired®,
Love Inspired® Suspense or
Love Inspired® Historical book.

Available wherever books are sold, including
most bookstores, supermarkets, drugstores
and discount stores.

Save $1.00

on the purchase of any Love Inspired®, Love Inspired® Suspense
or Love Inspired® Historical book.

Coupon valid until November 30, 2016. Redeemable at participating retail outlets
in the U.S. and Canada only. Limit one coupon per customer.

52614200

5 65373 00076 2   (8100)0 12211

When a handsome Amish mill owner breaks his leg, a feisty young Amish woman agrees to be his housekeeper. But will two weeks together lead to romance or heartbreak?

Read on for a sneak preview of
A BEAU FOR KATIE,
the third book in Emma Miller's miniseries
***THE AMISH MATCHMAKER**.*

"Here's Katie," Sara the matchmaker announced. "She'll lend a hand with the housework until you're back on your feet." She motioned Katie to approach the bed. "I think you two already know each other."

"*Ya*," Freeman admitted gruffly. "We do."

Katie removed her black bonnet. Freeman Kemp wasn't hard on the eyes. Even lying flat in a bed, one leg in a cast, he was still a striking figure of a man. The pain lines at the corners of his mouth couldn't hide his masculine jaw. His wavy brown hair badly needed a haircut, and he had at least a week's growth of dark beard, but the cotton undershirt revealed broad, muscular shoulders and arms.

Freeman's compelling gaze met hers. His eyes were brown, almost amber, with darker swirls of color. Unnerved, she uttered in a hushed tone, "Good morning, Freeman."

Then Katie turned away to inspect the kitchen that would be her domain for the next two weeks. She'd never been inside the house before, but from the outside, she'd thought it was beautiful. Now, standing in the spacious kitchen, she liked it even more. The only thing that looked out of place was the bed containing the frowning Freeman.

"You must be in a lot of pain," Sara remarked, gently patting Freeman's cast.

"*Ne*. Nothing to speak of."

Katie nodded. "Well, rest and proper food for an invalid will do you the most good."

Freeman glanced away. "I'm *not* an invalid."

Katie sighed. If your leg encased in a cast didn't make you an invalid, she didn't know what did. But Freeman, as she recalled, had a stubborn nature.

For an eligible bachelor who owned a house, a mill and two hundred acres of prime land to remain single into his midthirties was almost unheard of among the Amish. Add to that, Freeman's rugged good looks. It made him the catch of the county. They could have him. She was not a giggling teenager who could be swept off her feet by a pretty face. Working in his house for two whole weeks wasn't going to be easy, but he didn't intimidate her. She'd told Sara she'd take the job and she was a woman of her word.

Don't miss
A BEAU FOR KATIE by Emma Miller,
available August 2016 wherever
Love Inspired® books and ebooks are sold.

www.LoveInspired.com

*When a pregnant widow becomes the target of a killer,
a rookie K-9 unit officer and his loyal dog must step up
to protect her.*

*Read on for an excerpt from
SECRETS AND LIES,
the next book in the exciting K-9 cop miniseries
ROOKIE K-9 UNIT.*

Glass shattering.

Rookie K-9 officer Tristan McKeller heard it as he hooked his K-9 partner to a lead. The yellow Lab cocked his head to the side, growling softly.

"What is it, boy?" Tristan asked, scanning the school parking lot. Only one other vehicle was parked there—a shiny black minivan that he knew belonged to Ariel Martin, the teacher he was supposed be meeting with. He was late. Of course. That seemed to be the story of his life this summer. Work was crazy, and his sister was crazier, and finding time to meet with her summer-school teacher? He'd already canceled two previous meetings. He couldn't cancel this one. Not if Mia had any hope of getting through summer school.

He was going to be even later than he'd anticipated, though, because Jesse was still growling, alerted to something that must have to do with the shattering glass.

"Find!" he commanded, and Jesse took off, pulling against the leash in his haste to get to the corner of the building and around it. Trained in arson detection, the dog had an unerring nose for almost anything. Right now, he was on a scent, and Tristan trusted him enough to let him have his head.

Glass glittered on the pavement twenty feet away, and Jesse beelined for it, barking raucously, his tail stiff and high.

A woman appeared in the window. Dark hair. Pale skin. Freckles. Very pregnant belly that wasn't cooperating as she struggled to crawl through the opening. Ariel Martin. The newest teacher at Desert Valley High School. Smart. Enthusiastic. Patient. He'd heard that from more than one parent. He'd even heard it from Mia.

"You okay?" he asked, running to her side.

She shook her head, dark gray eyes wide with shock, a smear of blood on her right hand. She'd cut herself. It looked deep, but she didn't seem to notice. "He's got a gun. He tried to shoot me."

Don't miss SECRETS AND LIES
by Shirlee McCoy, available wherever
Love Inspired® Suspense books and ebooks are sold.

www.LoveInspired.com

LISEXP0716